Penguin Books
A Far-Off Place

Laurens van der Post was born in Africa in 1906. Most of his adult life has been spent with one foot there and one in England. His professions of writer and farmer were interrupted by ten years of soldiering – behind enemy lines in Abyssinia, and also in the Western Desert and the Far East, where he was taken prisoner by the Japanese while commanding a small guerrilla unit. He went straight from prison back to active service in Java, served on Lord Mountbatten's staff, and, when the British forces withdrew from Java, remained behind as Military Attaché to the British Minister. Since 1949 he has undertaken several official missions exploring little-known parts of Africa. His independent expedition to the Kalahari Desert in search of the Bushmen was the subject of his famous documentary film. Besides the original Kalahari series, his other TV films include 'The Story of Carl Gustav Jung', 'A Region of Shadow' and 'All Africa Within Us'. His other books include *Venture to the Interior* (1952), *The Face Beside the Fire* (1953), *Flamingo Feather* (1955), *The Dark Eye in Africa* (1955), *The Heart of the Hunter*, (1961), *The Seed and the Sower* (1963), *Journey into Russia* (1964), *The Hunter and the Whale* (1967), *A Portrait of Japan* (1968), *A Story like the Wind* (1972), *A Mantis Carol* (1975), *Jung and the Story of Our Time* (1976), *First Catch Your Eland: a Taste of Africa* (1977), *Yet Being Someone Other* (1982) (with Jane Taylor), *Testament to the Bushman* (1984) and (with Jean-Marc Pottiez), *A Walk with a White Bushman* (1986). Many of these are published in Penguin.

Colonel van der Post, who is married to Ingaret Giffard, was awarded the C.B.E. for his services in the field, and was knighted in 1981.

Laurens van der Post

A Far-Off Place

'The story is like the wind,' a
Bushman called Xhabbo said.
*'It comes from a far-off place
and we feel it.'*

Penguin Books

PENGUIN BOOKS

Published by the Penguin Group
27 Wrights Lane, London W8 5TZ, England
Viking Penguin Inc., 40 West 23rd Street, New York, New York 10010, USA
Penguin Books Australia Ltd, Ringwood, Victoria, Australia
Penguin Books Canada Ltd, 2801 John Street, Markham, Ontario, Canada L3R 1B4
Penguin Books (NZ) Ltd, 182–190 Wairau Road, Auckland 10, New Zealand

Penguin Books Ltd, Registered Offices: Harmondsworth, Middlesex, England

First published by the Hogarth Press 1974
Published in Penguin Books 1976
10 9 8 7

Printed and bound in Great Britain by
Cox & Wyman Ltd, Reading
Set in Intertype Times

Contents

Prelude

'*A Far-Off Place*' is a continuation of *A Story Like the Wind*. Yet
it is self-contained, so that it can be read on its own provided
this much of its predecessor is remembered.

A Story Like the Wind is an account of the life of a boy
about to become a man. His name is François Joubert, and he
is born in the remote interior of southern Africa. He is the son
of Pierre-Paul Joubert, a distinguished educationalist who had
been totally ostracized by the European community, because of
his emancipated attitude to his black and coloured countrymen.
As a result a career to which he is utterly dedicated comes
abruptly to an end.

He goes to one of the most inaccessible parts of the country,
deep in the north-western bush. There he establishes a vast
farming enterprise and tries to make it a model of a larger
world to come without discrimination on grounds of race, creed
or colour. He deliberately chooses this remote country on the
banks of a great river, the Amanzim-tetse, because it is close to
the lands of a branch of the great Matabele people, as yet comparatively uncontaminated by contact with European colonial
society and still integrated in an authentic primitive pattern of
Africa.

The farm is called Hunter's Drift* because it is close to where
one of the oldest roads in Africa, the Punda-Ma-Tenka, or
Hunter's Road, crosses the river. On this road, even at this late,
twentieth-century hour, there is still a constant and colourful
flow of human traffic between the settled, increasingly metropolitan Africa of the south and the vast and comparatively
untouched interior to the north. The homestead itself is a contemporary version of the home built by the first Jouberts who
fled from the Huguenot persecution in France after the Re-

* Ford

vocation of the Edict of Nantes in 1685. They had established themselves in 1688 in the then remote uplands of the Cape of Good Hope.

Pierre-Paul persuades an off-shoot of a distinguished Matabele clan living nearby at Osebeni, the Sindabele word meaning a place by the river, to join him in his enterprise, and develop the farm not as paid servants but honoured partners. Hunter's Drift prospers and expands rapidly, because from a railway siding close by it, it supplies a great mining city with most of its meat, fruit, milk and vegetables. His Matabele partners call him 'the great white bird' because his unexpected appearance among them was almost like that of the descent of a rare new bird out of the sky. But in his own household he is known as Ouwa – meaning an old wagon for, as one of the coloured people tells François, his father carries so many people with him through life.

Pierre-Paul is married to a beautiful, highly educated, sensitive, intelligent woman of marked character who fully shares his aspirations. She is never called anything but Lammie, the little lamb, by everyone involved in the Hunter's Drift experiment. The relationship between Lammie and Ouwa is unusually complete. It is almost impossible to imagine an enlargement of the love which it exemplifies. When, many years after their marriage, François is conceived, however surprising it sounds, it is yet understandable why Lammie, in her announcement of the event, refers to it as the 'coming of another little person' into their lives.

The consequences of such an approach to their one and only child are as profound as they are subtle in the evolution of François's character. Although Lammie's love of her son is never in doubt, it is hard to know whether the dignity implicit in such a concept is not conferred on François too soon, and that he might not have welcomed a little less honour and somewhat more immediate and less conceptualized love. As a result, he turns for more spontaneous manifestations of human feelings to the coloured and black people around him.

First of all there is his old nurse, Koba. Koba is a survivor of the cruelly persecuted and almost vanished first people of Africa, the Bushmen. Koba not only brings him up with a passionate, instinctive love but also opens wide his imagination to perhaps the oldest pattern of life to be found in the world today. Indeed he becomes so committed to it that he acquires the difficult clicking Bushman tongue as if it were his own.

Another great source of primitive love in his life is their cook and housekeeper, a large, formidable African lady known to François and his parents as Ousie – little old mother – Johanna, but to the Matabele she is 'The Princess of the Pots'. She is a superb cook, warm-hearted, beloved by all, and makes her kitchen, pantry, larder and quarters in the household a kingdom of her own.

Then there is the hereditary head of the clan who have joined Ouwa at Hunter's Drift. He is a natural Matabele aristocrat called 'Bamuthi, and becomes in the male sense to François what his old nurse Koba was to him in the female. His influence on François is wide and deep and the love between them as great as it is immediate. There is no corner of the spirit of the emerging man in François where 'Bamuthi's presence, voice and being is not present, and no shadow in his spirit which is not illuminated by 'Bamuthi's tender concern for what is unafraid and self-reliant in men.

It is 'Bamuthi who names François 'Little Feather', and Little Feather he is to everyone at Hunter's Drift, except his parents, to whom in moments of intimacy he becomes Coiske (pronounced Swaske) and in more authoritarian intervals, just François.

Since both François's parents are fully qualified teachers, he is never sent to school but educated entirely in the European sense of the word by his father and mother. In other and equally important underlying levels, however, he is educated in the primitive sense first by Bushman induction of old Koba, then by the example and exhortation of 'Bamuthi and the African children with whom he plays.

This has the result that he moves through the story as a character standing in relation to Africa and its bewildering context of peoples and cultures rather as Kipling's Kim stood to the India of Kipling's day.

As dear and of as great a consequence to François is his relationship with the closest friend of his parents, an almost legendary white hunter turned conservationist, officially styled Colonel H. H. Théron but known far and wide by his African name, Mopani.

The son of a hunter himself, he has had little formal schooling. Almost the only books in his life have been, first the Bible and then books inspired by the Bible, like *Pilgrim's Progress*. His university has really been the bush and veld of Africa. A world war in which he fought as a famous scout has sickened him of killing. He is a frequent visitor to François's home. It is difficult to say who matters most to him, the Ouwa with whom he fought in the war, or Lammie, for whom one suspects he has feelings deeper than he cares to acknowledge, despite some intangible reservations about her concept of François as 'another little person'.

About his relationship with François, however, there is no doubt. He loves his 'little cousin' as he calls François, as if the boy were his heir and successor. From an early age he takes François on long and dangerous patrols against the armed poachers who are always raiding his immense game reserve. He becomes accordingly in European pioneering terms to François what the noble 'Bamuthi is to him in a primitive sense.

He is, moreover, as Ouwa often stresses to Lammie, a poet both in heart and deed, as well as a natural philosopher. As a result, therefore, he has the imagination to transform a highly dangerous confrontation with a rogue elephant of legendary proportions, Uprooter of Great Trees, into a natural ritual of initiation to manhood for François.

Mopani has a habit of arriving at Hunter's Drift on a horse called Noble, always accompanied by two ridge-backs of illustrious pedigree, a great hunting dog called Dingiswayo, or 'Swayo for short, and a bitch called Nandi. This tawny couple are the parents of a puppy which Ouwa brings to François on a cold winter's day, so small that it is hidden for warmth in the pocket of his great-coat. François calls him Hintza, after a great Amaxosa chief, but for good Bushman reasons he is compelled to call him Hin to his face.

The arrival of Hintza in François's life is a turning point in more ways than one. It marks the moment when he becomes conscious of himself as a person in his own right, and it coincides with the general realization that Ouwa, his father, is far from well.

Through François's loving, detailed absorption in the education of Hintza he has more and more a life of his own. Yet he cannot ignore a profound dismay as Ouwa's condition grows rapidly worse. It increases when all the doctors and specialists who are consulted can find nothing physically wrong with Ouwa.

Ousie-Johanna, their African cook, is convinced that Ouwa has been bewitched by his European countrymen. So is 'Bamuthi. They both urge François to consult a great African seer and healer who lives some two days' march away through the bush. The seer's name is uLangalibalela, the Right Hon. Sun-is-Hot. François only does so when Lammie, in desperation, takes Ouwa away to the Cape of Good Hope to consult another round of specialists.

On this hazardous journey to uLangalibalela, François and 'Bamuthi come across the first direct evidence that great and terrible changes in the life of the bush might be imminent. They narrowly escape confrontation with a group of men who are travelling by a little known and obscure route, under command of a Chinese officer, apparently to join African insurgents in the hinterland of Angola. From then on François feels guilty for not telling Mopani about these men. He keeps it secret because he feels that his visit to uLangalibalela might not meet with Mopani's approval.

uLangalibalela immediately diagnoses Ouwa's illness as a curse inflicted on him by 'the turning of the backs' of his European countrymen. This 'turning of the backs' as the smallest Matabele boy knows, is pronouncement of an infallible sentence of death unless speedily suspended by exercise of great magic. uLangalibalela promises to do all he can to cure Ouwa, in spite of grave misgivings that he has been consulted too late. However, despite all uLangalibalela's efforts, soon after François's return to Hunter's Drift, Mopani arrives with the news that Ouwa has died at the Cape, from no ascertainable cause.

Meanwhile, François has acquired another, even greater secret. Hintza, nearly full-grown, wakes François early one morning and compels him to follow him out in the bush along a narrow track, where every night huge steel lion traps are laid, baited with meat, for the many carnivorous animals who persist in raiding the livestock at Hunter's Drift. They arrive at the lion trap at first light to find caught in it not a lion but a young Bushman, who might have walked out of the dream of the ideal Bushman implanted in François's imagination by his old nurse.

François rescues the Bushman from the trap and has no difficulty, since Koba has taught him the language, in reassuring the badly injured and naturally apprehensive Bushman. He discovers that his name is Xhabbo (the Bushman word for dream). He learns that Xhabbo has just come on a long and dangerous journey from his people in the heart of the great desert, stretching for some fifteen hundred miles to the west of Hunter's Drift right up to the edge of the Atlantic. He has done so in order to visit a vast cave deep in a hill overlooking the Amanzim-tetse river. The cave, which neither the Matabele nor even François had discovered for themselves, was once both a home to the Bushmen and a kind of temple to their god, the Praying Mantis, before the Matabele invasion of the country compelled them to seek refuge in the desert. Despite generations of exile in the desert, Xhabbo informs François that one or more representatives of his people are compelled to visit the cave from time to time to inform it of important changes in the fortunes of the Bushmen. He himself was on his way to announce to Mantis and all that the cave represents, that his own father had just died and that he, Xhabbo, had now taken over the leadership of his people.

François manages to get Xhabbo into the cave unseen. In the days that follow he succeeds in smuggling sedatives, sleeping draughts, antibiotics and food and drink into the cave and to nurse Xhabbo tenderly until his terrible wound is healed. Since François rescued Xhabbo at first light, when the morning star was high and bright, Xhabbo gives François, who already feels he is somewhat overburdened with names, a Bushman one which is his own special salute for the planet, 'Foot of the Day'. He adds a great deal to the knowledge François acquired from Koba, above all a phenomenon the Bushmen refer to as 'tapping within themselves'. This 'tapping' appears to be a physical manifestation of a profound gift for intuitive apprehension of the future.

When at last the time comes for Xhabbo to leave he has become such a close and unique friend that François is heartbroken. Xhabbo is equally distressed. As a result, they form a pact that as soon as possible Xhabbo will return to visit François and that he will announce his coming by an unusual combination of the call of the night-plover and the bark of a jackal. He cannot return openly, of course, because his people still live in peril of all other men.

After Xhabbo has gone, François, out of a devastating sense of bereavement, has an instinct to continue equipping the cave with provisions, food and water, medicines, guns and ammunitions, so that it is always in a state of readiness for Xhabbo's return. He does all this, of course, in great secrecy and this secret, like that regarding the 'insurgents', keeps his Huguenot conscience in a state of unease. Yet he sees no way of sharing either of these secrets, even with Mopani.

At the same time both François and 'Bamuthi are increasingly perturbed by strange new traffic along the Punda-Ma-Tenka road, across the ford at Hunter's Drift and on into the even more remote interior to the north and north-west. There are several ominous encounters with aggressive African truck drivers, and one occasion on which François catches a glimpse of what he believed to be the face of a Chinese 'officer'. They are also perturbed by visits of strange European priests whom Ousie-Johanna calls 'the crows of God' and who purport to be representatives of the World Council of Christian Churches, on their way to help the struggle of repressed African peoples against their European oppressors.

Mopani adds to their general disquiet by pointing out to François how even the birds in the bush have 'changed their tune' and how this only happened when great destructive elements appeared to threaten the natural life of the bush.

At this strange, uneasy moment another and more welcome change occurs. A new neighbour arrives, a distinguished colonial governor, Sir James Archibald Sinclair Monckton, K.C.M.G., D.S.C., B.A.(Cantab.). As a young district commissioner, he had fallen in love with the country of the Amanzim-tetse river and bought a concession of land next to Hunter's Drift. Now retired, he has decided to develop his concession and to build there a new home for himself and his young daughter. He is a widower. His wife, a young Portuguese woman, the daughter of a colonial governor, was killed a few years before in northern Angola where an 'army of liberation' poured out of the bush one morning and massacred some thirty-four thousand people, of whom only a few thousand were Portuguese. François, who encounters the Moncktons in th. bush on his way from Mopani's reserve to Hunter's Drift, finds the daughter Luciana the most attractive and lovely person he has ever seen, but tends to be incapable of understanding or knowing precisely how to respond to her, because she is the first European girl he has ever met.

Luciana, barely adolescent, is in the charge of a formidable sort of Portuguese Ousie-Johanna, a governess called Amelia. François spends some of his happiest days introducing Luciana to the life of the bush, sharing some of the things he and Hintza treasure most. He shows her a 'baboon finishing school' and animals so familiar and dear that they are almost personified and carry human names like the great male lions, Chaliapin and Caruso, and a lioness with a passion for being left alone, called Garbo. One bird, in particular, an African partridge called a francolin, is held up to her as the bravest of the brave, as he discovers her barely visible in the hissing grass, defending her clutch of eggs with the transparent armour of utter silence, immobility and stillness, an example of courage and total acceptance of danger and fear that never leaves the two of them.

Overjoyed that Luciana and her father are going to be permanent neighbours on land which her father calls Silverton Hill, François and Mopani are amazed by the sense of order and speed with which Sir James sets about building his new home. He is helped in this by seven ox-wagon loads of Cape-coloured builders and artisans and their vivid gypsy families. He feels desperately bereaved when Sir James is suddenly recalled to Britain to serve on a Royal Commission and takes Luciana out of his life so soon after she had entered it.

16

Although François is not aware of it, he has had as great an impact on Luciana as she on him. She writes to François constantly, sends Hintza a metal-studded collar for his protection and François a painting of the patron saint of hunters, St Hubert. Despite his Huguenot prejudices, François takes the painting to Xhabbo's cave and installs it there. Just above the painting there is a red cross painted on the rock long ago by a Bushman artist.

From then on the indefinable feeling of menace in the life of the bush builds up. The tension caused in François by Luciana's absence, and above all by the failure of Xhabbo to return, becomes almost unbearable. It is all the more acute because Lammie, now in sole command of Hunter's Drift, threatens to send him away for his education. Secretly he is determined that he will not leave until he has seen Xhabbo at least once more.

This tension, both in the bush and in François is at its highest when Sir James, Amelia and Luciana return unexpectedly after the absence of more than a year. Everyone at Hunter's Drift is overjoyed. Both Luciana and François, too, are excited to see Lammie and Sir James, who had not met before, taking a great liking to each other.

Luciana, by this time, had ceased to be 'Luciana' to François. He had given her a name of his own – Nonnie – which literally means 'little mistress'. The day of reunion ends with one of Ousie-Johanna's best dinners, complete with the finest wine and brandy from the great cellar under the house. The meal goes on for so long that Nonnie is peremptorily ordered to bed. But not before she and François have reaffirmed their secret pact to meet at dawn for their first excursion into the bush.

François, however, is woken well before dawn by Hintza. Even half-asleep François recognizes Xhabbo's pre-arranged call sign of night-plover and then jackal. He jumps out of bed immediately and is dressing as fast as he can when the call comes again in a way which suggests that it is of imperative, even desperate import. As he dashes out of his room, gun in hand, a torch flashes in his face and he finds Nonnie, fully dressed, waiting for him. The excitement at the prospect of accompanying François into the bush has woken her earlier than arranged. He has no option but to tell her to follow. As he speaks, the call sign breaks again on the silence.

Soon they are all three outside, and Hintza leads them in the direction from which the call had come, so fast that they have to run to keep up with him. Hintza leads them parallel to the river towards the hill of Xhabbo's cave. On the way, François thinks he sees an ominous mass of something moving by the river half behind them, but has no time to stop and observe it closer, because at that moment the call is repeated more urgently than ever.

Almost at once he finds himself in the presence of Xhabbo, who wastes no time in formal greetings, but commands them to follow him. He leads them fast and straight up the hill and into shelter just behind the great boulder which hides the entrance to the cave. There François and Nonnie meet Xhabbo's Nuin-Tara, 'daughter of a star', who Xhabbo describes as his 'utterly woman'. He then tells François how he and Nuin-Tara have travelled for many, many days, marching by night and hiding by day, to come and warn him that thousands of armed Africans were coming from the north-west to attack Hunter's Drift and invade the country beyond.

At that moment they hear the great voice of 'Bamuthi calling out pure and unafraid, the Matabele equivalent of the medieval knight's 'To me!' and hard on that, an outburst of automatic rifle fire. This is followed immediately by a piercing blast on military whistles all round the homestead, and then the full discharge of sustained rifle and automatic fire from hundreds of infantrymen.

Xhabbo wants them all to withdraw into the cáve at once, but François refuses. He announces that whatever happens he at least must answer 'Bamuthi's call. Nuin-Tara and Nonnie are therefore made to go into the cave and Xhabbo and François carefully make their way into the bush where they find several African soldiers in uniform lying dead in the track, and not far away the body of 'Bamuthi. They are prevented from retreating to the cave itself immediately, both because the bush itself is now swarming with soldiers, and because they find the body of a mortally wounded Matabele kinsman of 'Bamuthi's, a man called Mtunywa (Messenger), also one of François's beloved companions. They manage to hide the wounded Mtunywa in a ledge under the rocks where François had once given Xhabbo a provisional shelter.

Mtunywa tells François that he believes that every man, woman and child at Hunter's Drift, whether European or Matabele, has been killed and that Sir James himself has been shot down in the doorway of François's home. Mtunywa dies late in the day with his hand in François's, and it is only towards sunset that Xhabbo and François manage to make their way safely up the hill again to the cave, where they find Nuin-Tara and Nonnie, beside herself with fear, shock and anxiety.

For a moment they all stand there as the last light of a red, mythological sunset dies away and they see the stars appear, and as the stars appear an extraordinary display of meteors flashing out of the sky, so that Xhabbo is moved to say to François,

'Xhabbo knew that the stars who hide in light as do other things hide in darkness were there to see all today. For the stars do fall in this manner when our hearts fall down ... and that they must, falling, go to tell other people that a bad thing has happened at another place. Tell this utterly your woman, Foot of the Day, that the stars are acting thus on account of us and that we are not alone.'

Xhabbo pauses until François has told Nonnie and, in the telling, notices how the tension goes out of the hand in his. Hintza, too, is still, his head on one side, listening. Then they see Xhabbo pointing high, and hear him say, 'Look, Foot of the Day, how those stars which have not fallen over are full of a tapping as I, Xhabbo, am full of a tapping. And their tapping is joined to Xhabbo's tapping, seeking to tell me of the way we must go. I must go into the cave and sit apart, listening utterly to this tapping, in order to learn of this way we must go.'

So *A Story Like the Wind* ends with Xhabbo, Nuin-Tara, Nonnie and Hintza crawling into the cave and François going last, as the book says, like someone turning for help to the last temple left on earth. *A Far-Off Place* takes up the story at this point.

CHAPTER ONE

The Owl and the Cave

So great and deep a cave, of course, had to be dark. But it was even darker than François had expected when he crawled through the narrow entrance. Then he could tell from the feel of the sand underneath his hands that he was inside it in depth. He looked carefully all round him but could see nothing to indicate the presence of Xhabbo, Nuin-Tara and Nonnie. Were it not for Hintza, who as always, unless ordered away, was close to him, he could easily have thought himself to be alone. The darkness, indeed, was so dense that it was almost tangible and as he stood up, silently and slowly, his left hand brushed the air in front of his face as if to clear the black matter from his eyes. It was a most unpleasant feeling, as if this profound darkness round him had found an ally in the darkness within inflicted on them all by the tragic events of the day. The whole was not just a sensation conveyed by the senses but a powerful emotion arguing with the voice of despair that the last light was about to be extracted from life on earth.

Fortunately François, who so often before had had to find his way through the dark in the bush, knew that the glimpse of a distant fire, or the striking of a match, was enough to blind one's eyes for a moment to such light as there always was even in the blackest of the cloud-covered nights. In remembering this, the alliance of darkness without and darkness within was broken, and he realized, with relief, that the cave appeared so impenetrably and solidly black because for the moment he was star-blind. More, it was almost as if he were star-deaf as well.

The intense and varied sounds which had accompanied the quick, piercing, dancing, starlight as it assailed their eyes from above when the five of them had been standing outside, had made, as it were, a single orchestra of cosmic proportions. First there had been the abiding background noise of the sea of darkness, breaking like a Pacific swell over a great barrier reef to produce the star spume and foam of light which men call the Milky Way. There, on what might be the beach of the universe, the horses of the seas of night perpetually pound with their lacquered hooves. All around were the millions of stars and satellites that produce the quick 'tapping sound' to which Xhabbo had referred. There were some stars that naturally arranged themselves in triangles and sent out a kind of rhythmic tinkling to synchronize with the many that in one vast, wheeling movement let the blackness rushing by use them as wind instruments. The greatest, like Sirius, Aldebaran and the Santauries, stretched their wings of light taut between Heaven and earth to give each according to its nature, the violins, harps and 'cellos of this orchestra. There were star voices, too, to swell the volume like those of children lost in some deep valley in the mountains of the night, singing to keep up their courage. Then came the reassuring responses from the great stars such as the Three Kings, the Seven Sisters, Heavenly Twins and the vortex of Andromeda. Yet there in the cave, all this sound which had accompanied the light outside was suddenly and totally extinguished and this made the silence as solid and opaque as the darkness.

François listened in vain for some whisper or whisk of movement to tell him where his companions were. Then instinctively, he put his hands in his pockets, took out the matches he always carried and struck one.

Even then he did not see at once any of the others. Perhaps because he was intent on lighting the candles which had stood there so long by the altar of pebbles below the painting of St Hubert and the sign of the cross on the walls of the cave. Quickly, before the fragile light of the match could go out (for already some new awareness in him was warning him that even trifles like matches could no longer be wasted), he hastened to the candles and managed to light them just before the match faded. To him, the light growing from the two black wicks until their flames stood clear-cut and straight, was beautiful.

Turning away from the candles he saw, over the back of Hintza, first of all Nonnie, her eyes darker and wider than ever, and fixed on the candles as if not certain she could believe they were real. Beyond her, Xhabbo and Nuin-Tara, squatting side by side on the floor of the cave, turning their faces, alive with wonder and delight at what was to them (since they had never seen candles before), such magic of light. However it was Nonnie who caught François's attention. Her whole attitude as she stood there looked so slight, forlorn, so very much too young for the tragedy inflicted on her that day. The shock of the disaster held her like someone in a profound trance and left her poised exactly on the frontier where candle-light ended and line of ink of the cave began. Indeed, he was so moved by the eloquence of her plight that he forgot his own and was about to go to her when her whole expression suddenly changed.

For the first time since morning her spirit seemed capable of detaching itself from the horror of the day and to come alive. At the same time she must have noticed the red cross on the wall above the candles for slowly she herself made a sign of the cross, as if she were unconsciously imitating the movement of the hand which many thousands of years before had painted it on those ancient honey-coloured walls of stone.

Clasping her hands together in front of her, she said as if speaking to herself: 'Oh, how wonderful! How could I have spent a whole day in this place and not noticed it before?'

It was an indication perhaps of how death, the sudden crumbling of a world and a way of life which all had seemed so real that one could be pardoned for having been deluded into thinking they would endure for ever, could abolish with unbelievable swiftness any desire in the human spirit to maintain appearances. For then Nonnie did something which she would never have done before except in the privacy of her room or in the protective context of a church. She went up to François's home-made little shrine and knelt down in front of it to pray. She did not speak but merely stayed on her knees, her hands clasped in her lap, while she looked deeply and long into the copy of the painting which she had chosen for François a year ago on one bright summer day in a Europe which, at that moment, must have seemed to her more like something experienced in a dream than in measurable reality.

François did not know precisely what was happening but the meaning of the act was plain enough and too important to be interrupted. He turned to look at Xhabbo and Nuin-Tara. Their glances met his and told him that, although they might not know what was happening to Nonnie, they realized it was something which should be respected with silence. All the same, to make it quite certain, François moved silently over to join them where they sat against the far wall directly behind Nonnie, motioning to Hintza to come to him as he did so. Putting his head close to Xhabbo's, he whispered so low that the sound could not possibly have carried any further: 'I think she is listening in to a tapping of her own.' He put it like that because he knew it to be the only way in which Xhabbo would understand an act of prayer.

Xhabbo immediately leaned sideways and repeated softly to Nuin-Tara what François had whispered to him. Both turned as one to François. Their eyes were like old Koba's, his Bushman nurse, full and overflowing with the first light of human life on earth, but still now brighter with understanding and approval.

Xhabbo spoke almost inaudibly for them both: 'She has gone utterly to the place for such a listening. For look, Foot of the Day, the sign on the wall!'

Xhabbo was not only pointing at the cross above picture and candles, but going on to describe with his right hand stretched out, first a long horizontal movement from left to right, and then another with the palm vertical moving from high above, downwards, to make what seemed to François a perfectly symmetrical cross. 'That sign is the sign we Bushmen, since the days of the People of the Early Race, have always made at the place where asking and tapping meet. Xhabbo too is going presently to sit by himself listening utterly for the tapping to tell of the way we shall have to go.'

As if knowing how in those cataclysmic moments no words are as eloquent as physical contact, he hooked the little finger of his right hand in François little finger, as the finger of his left was already hooked in Nuin-Tara's. François instinctively put his other hand lightly on Hintza's head, and the four of them went on sitting there with their eyes on Nonnie, as if she were leading them in some profound ritual of communion. So totally excluded was the world of appearance and illusion that not only was François not at all embarrassed, but felt as if this were the only possible preliminary to finding a way out of the terrible peril and unknowingness which now held them far more inexorably than that terrible lion trap in the track without had once held Xhabbo.

How long they sat there it was impossible to tell because in the manner of all meaningful things the moment vanished like the shadow of a dream. It seemed to him that time was only a flash of lightning between the moment when Nonnie had sat down on her knees and began to get up. Then suddenly from the main opening in the ceiling of the cave, there came the loud, prolonged and whistling, night-sea call of an owl.

It was a sound François knew well but familiarity could not deprive it of its aboriginal freshness. Always it seemed to carry some new tone, some fresh meaning for him. Of all the calls of the many species of owls of the bush, this one, however uncomfortable and unendingly evocative, was his favourite. Quick, therefore, to identify the call, he had barely done so when the call was repeated more loudly and urgently, as if the owl had its head in the opening above them and were calling directly down at them.

Nonnie, who had obviously never heard the sound before, was on her feet at once and turned round quickly looking strangely startled. However as the call was repeated a third time, François was happy to notice that it was only the suddenness of the sound which had startled her, and not its nature.

She asked, more in wonder than dismay: 'What's that? What can it possibly be, calling to us like that?'

The sound of her voice released Xhabbo and Nuin-Tara from their self-imposed vow of silence. They too jumped to their feet and rushed up to Nonnie doing what François knew was a little dance of gladness in front of her. This puzzled her even more than the sound of the owl, for she looked bewildered and turned her eyes to François for help.

François did not know how to explain because he feared any explanation could only reawaken her sadness. For what Xhabbo and Nuin-Tara were calling out to Nonnie while doing their gay little dance of joy in front of her, was: 'They have arrived! The owl says, "they have arrived"!'

The 'they' referred to, of course, were not only Sir James and Amelia, but Lammie, Ousie-Johanna, 'Bamuthi and all the many others who had been massacred that day. Both words and dance were Xhabbo's and Nuin-Tara's way of informing Nonnie that this particular owl, in its role of messenger of the dead which is given to it by the Bushmen, had come specially to tell her that the journey of all those killed to the day beyond death had been safely accomplished. They clearly believed the news would comfort her as it had gladdened them. But François had a special reason of his own to be overawed by the intrusion of the owl in their lives at that moment. For the owl possessed the onomatopoeic African name of 'Sephookoo-koo', but his own people called it the 'Nonnietjie-owl' – in other words, the 'Little Nonnie owl', so that even the name seemed to support the Bushman interpretation that the owl was there as a private and personal messenger from the dead.

The coincidence was too overwhelming to be kept secret. So François went to Nonnie, took her gently by the arm and led her to the side of the cave where they had all been sitting, made her sit beside him and explained as best he could. Xhabbo and Nuin-Tara joined them to listen intently as if they understood every word of his English.

To his relief, Nonnie listened with increasing interest so that he was encouraged into giving her not only the Bushman interpretation but told her all he knew about the owl, how in the far south for instance, it preferred to make its home in church steeples or tombs. Here in the bush where steeples and grave-yards were lacking, it sought out hermit-like holes or caves in the cliffs. Significantly, if those were lacking, it would take over the abandoned nests of that strange water bird, the hammerhead. François explained that he used the word 'significant' because the hammerhead, according to the Bushmen, was chief reporter of the supernatural. Always it was to be seen on its way from its nest to the water at the first glimmer of light, and then on its way back again at dusk and so was ideally cast for its role as an observer of all that passed between night and day.

At that moment, Xhabbo, who already seemed to know from their expression and tone the meaning of the exchange between them, interrupted. He was obviously concerned that François and Nonnie should not underrate the message the owl had brought them. He explained that while they had all been standing outside the cave, he had noticed that when the first great shooting star 'fell over on its side', a big hammerhead rose up from the river below and made its way ponderously to the cliffs where the kind of owl they had just heard nested. The hammerhead (Xhabbo's tone and earnestness of manner were begging François to believe him) did this because, looking deep into the water as it did all day long, it saw things which human eyes could not see. Above all, in the gathering darkness when water was the only sheen of light left on earth, it would note any reflections of things that lived only between night and day. No star could shine or 'fall over on its side' at that brief hour without the bird seeing it, and seeing it, it would know too that somewhere someone who also had been upright, had fallen over utterly on his side. The moment it saw that, it would hasten to tell the owls because they were the only birds who had eyes big enough to see right through the night. The appointed owl then would watch and watch until the 'fallen-over thing' emerged upright again from night into day and then would fly to the right place where people listening in to the 'tapping' could be told of the news. Having been told now, Xhabbo pleaded, it would be wrong for François and Nonnie not to be glad.

François translated all this, told in much greater detail than recorded here, and it was extraordinary how in the telling what the civilized world would have dismissed as superstition consoled the two of them. For the first time, they both seemed able to externalize the tragic day.

Nonnie, who had not been content merely to hold on to François's little finger but had put her arm through his to move as close as possible against him for reassurance, exclaimed bravely, 'Oh, how wonderful, I would never have thought that anything like this could make any sense at all. But you know, François, what your friend has just told us, the call of the owl, that picture I bought for you in Paris, the candles, the altar and that cross you painted above them, all seem suddenly to fall into place and belong to one another and force one to accept everything your friend has just said. And it was very sweet of you, considering you are such a desperate old Huguenot, to have put that idolatrous cross on the wall.'

For the first time there was just the faintest suggestion of teasing in Nonnie's voice, as if her spirit which, as Xhabbo would have put it, 'had so utterly fallen over', had not only picked itself up but was beginning, newly born like a child, to make its first tentative essay into walking upright again. It seemed indeed so brave that François was moved almost to tears. He pressed her arm closer against him and it was some little while before the respect for truth and nothing but the truth, which suffering and disaster bring to the human spirit and which is perhaps one of the main reasons why life calls upon both so often in so complex a measure, compelled him to say: 'But I'm sorry, Nonnie. I didn't paint that cross. I would like to think I might have done it if it hadn't been there, but I doubt it. No, I put your picture and the candles there as you asked because the cross was already there.'

Nonnie's eyes widened with a surprise close to unbelief as she remarked, 'It was already there? I didn't know that any Christian missionaries had ever come as far as this. How amazing! Please tell me more.'

François shook his head. 'No, Nonnie, no Christian missionaries did it. In fact, no Europeans except you and I have ever been in this cave. That sign of the cross was painted by one of the artists who painted these paintings all round you. And do you know, there's something even stranger. That cross was painted long, long before the crucifixion. I know that, because my father told me that there are other places in Africa with the same sign painted on stone thousands of years before the coming of Christ. Xhabbo only just told me that ever since the days of the people of the early race, Bushmen have painted that sign of the cross to mark places where their asking, in moments of despair, and what they call the answer and the asking-in-tapping meet.'

'The tapping?' Nonnie looked so bewildered that François hastened to explain.

'It's their way of saying that they have sounds within,' he said, 'that tell them of things the eye cannot see, even things before they happen, so that they can know what to do about them, much in the same way as your Joan of Arc heard voices within her telling her what to do.'

This helped Nonnie so much that she wanted him to go on, and he would have done so, because he too was beginning to feel less abandoned in the process. He was finding what other civilized human beings have found in moments of disaster, in the thunder of avalanches and voice of storms at sea, that when all the many subtle, complex and impressive devices they have contrived for their security and intelligence against unpredictable forces of nature have all broken down, there is organic in the natural world around them another system to which their long-rejected instincts compel them to turn for guidance. The great trouble then is that this natural system is encoded in symbols on which the world has long since turned its back, as it did on Ouwa, and, in the turning, lost the key to the cypher. Yet, thanks to 'Bamuthi and the pagan world of his childhood, thanks above all to Koba, François had his own access to the system. Above all in Xhabbo he had perhaps the greatest expert alive in this radar of meaning, built into every living being, navigating on courses of fire through the life of the dark bush around him, achieving its most comprehensive telegraphic intelligence in what Xhabbo called 'tapping'.

Some realization of all this produced an inrush of warmth to François which must have communicated itself to Nonnie, for why otherwise should she then have pressed closer to him and said in a very small voice, 'I may not know precisely what your friend means by his tapping, but whatever it means, tapping, shooting stars, cross, your hammerhead, owl and all, I thank them and believe they'll help.'

Perhaps the clearest indication of how much they were already helping was that for the first time then François realized that none of them had had anything to eat or drink that day. One must not create the impression that he was as hungry and thirsty as he would have normally felt after so long a period of abstinence. The most that can be said for certain is that he was aware of the need for them all to make some effort now to eat and drink. Accordingly he started to extract his arm gently from Nonnie's as a preliminary to getting up and going to his secret store of food. The movement sent a shudder of alarm through Nonnie. Something akin to bewilderment possessed her that François should be so insensitive as not to realize how necessary such nearness was to her at that moment: indeed so precious that the thought of doing without it even for a brief moment, in the face of a future in which she would now be deprived of all other living contacts, on which she had depended from childhood, was unendurable. Her grip on François's arm tightened. It was all she could do to hold back a cry of protest close to hysteria. Luckily François seemed to understand what was happening to her, very largely because he himself did not want to be separate and alone just then, and was acting purely under a compulsion of will.

'I shan't be a minute,' he told Nonnie, as he once used to tell Hintza on such occasions when he was still an anxious little puppy, 'but I think it's time we thought about food and drink.'

He paused because the explanation of his action was so remote from anything Nonnie had anticipated, and in any case she had never felt less like eating in her life. However, she made a face at him which made him smile before he added: 'Yes, I know. I don't feel like food either although I could do with a drink. I have never felt so thirsty, ever. But I promise you, we have just got to make an effort to eat. We'll need all the strength we've got. Besides, we'll feel the better for it. You know, Mopani has often told me that always in the war, just before going into action, when he and his men felt that food was the last thing on earth they wanted, he would force them all to eat because eating helped even more than prayer would have done. And for somebody as religious as Mopani, Nonnie, I promise, that was some admission.'

Nonnie repressed an inner exclamation: 'But oh God, how like a man to think like that and leave one when one needs them to hold on most! How is one ever to make him understand?'

She did not notice that her imagination in one startled upward flight had promoted François to manhood. She let him go as if some intuition were compelling her not to fail to match any step of his towards maturity and she watched him intently, almost as if seeing him for the first time, while he explained to Xhabbo and Nuin-Tara what he was about. Listening to that quick electric sound of Bushman, clicking and crackling so easily and lightly on their lips, she felt like a child having her first lesson in some kindergarten for schooling the Ruth that is always in woman alone in an alien world. That too was of some astringent help and she was almost sorry when Xhabbo put an end to the conversation by vigorously nodding his head, getting up and going with François to vanish into the darkness at the far end of the cave. Soon they were back, each carrying a haversack full of things that they started unpacking on to the floor of the cave, half-way between where she was sitting and the candles against the wall.

François was feeling so much the better for having something concrete to do that he thought it would do Nonnie good too. He tried to make his invitation to help as light as possible. Important as were these slight and subtle improvements in their mood, the weight of what had happened and the awareness of the acute peril of their own plight was still great and precariously poised within.

'Perhaps you would be good enough,' he said with an exaggerated bow in her direction, impatiently imitated in an exaggerated curtsy by Hintza, who knew precisely what was about to happen and whose hunger was so great that he was watering at the mouth, 'to come and tell us what you would like for your dinner.'

Nonnie made a show of eagerness she was far from feeling. She jumped to her feet and joined them, to see for the first time a sample of the stores François had accumulated in secret over the long months. He had extracted only the tins of delicacies because already he knew that when they left the cave as they would have to before long, they would not be able to carry tins, and would have to rely on the lighter substances, like the biltong and rusks. Even he who had been responsible for building up the store was now amazed at the quality and variety of the food, and marvelled at the strange, prophetic impulse which had compelled him so blindly, despite the affront it was to his reason at the time.

Nonnie, totally unprepared, was almost as astonished as Nuin-Tara. Sinking on to her knees, she examined the tins with a look on her face of someone from a remote country place, bewildered by the variety and range of choice in her first super-market of some great city.

'Heavens, François.' She looked up amazed. 'You must have been at it for years. How . . .?' François was never to know her intended question, because suddenly something else far more important had come to her mind. She gasped and put her hand to her mouth. 'Your secret! This must be your famous secret! Isn't that so?'

François just nodded, with some slight relief, because that part of his burden was shed at last, while Nonnie went on, pointing at Xhabbo, 'And he must be the friend you mentioned and had to ask before you could tell me.'

Again François just nodded, not at all unhappy to be a witness at last in such a court.

'Well then, what did I tell you?' Nonnie went on, pleased to discover that she had known better all along. 'That ought to teach you that secrets are not the bad things you imagined. What would have become of us now if it hadn't been for this secret between you and him? How did it start?'

'I'll have to tell you that later,' François replied. 'The thing is, the sooner we eat, the sooner we can try to get to sleep. We've just got to try to eat and to rest, because I suspect we've a lot of hard days in front of us now.'

'I expect you're right,' Nonnie answered without any great enthusiasm. It only took the slightest thing, like François's reference to the 'hard days' ahead, to get through the wafer-thin new skin they were both trying so desperately to grow over the wound of the day. Nonetheless she dutifully chose some soup, tinned meat and vegetables, and put them in a gleaming pile on one side before asking, 'Do you think that will be enough for us all?'

François knew that there would have been enough for normal appetites like his and Nonnie's but was certain that Xhabbo and Nuin-Tara needed far more. The strains of their long and dangerous march to come and warn François were only too obvious in their appearance. Their eyes were sunk deep into their heads and their cheeks, under the high and wide Mongolian bone, were hollow, showing not only how long and hard they had travelled but also how little they must have had to eat on the way. So he doubled the amount Nonnie had chosen. Then he went back to his store to fetch a large tin of chocolate and two of condensed milk, as well as a bundle of dried wood to lay a fire for cooking.

The moment Xhabbo saw the wood he protested vehemently. He warned François that the smell of smoke and fire would linger for days, and could be picked up clinging to the bush round the openings above to betray their hiding place. No matter how hard François searched the cave, he pointed out, he would find no trace of any previous fire. It had been an absolute law of Bushman survival that no fires were allowed there because quite apart from the question of smoke and smell, there was also the danger that the light of a fire might show in the darkness above.

This made immediate sense to François – to such an extent that he became anxious even over their candles. He asked Xhabbo at once if candle-light could be dangerous as well. Xhabbo answered that he had asked himself the question many times but those 'burning things' as he put it, 'were only small and feeling themselves to be utterly small, burned only making the littlest of smells that not even a jackal outside smelling would feel the smell.'

'But the light?' François insisted.

Xhabbo shook his head, saying it was an 'altogether other thing.' He had no experience of the 'burning things' and had been asking himself whether someone passing by in the night might not see some glow in the shades of the bushes above where no glow had been before, though he doubted it.

His answer made François feel culpably ashamed for not having thought of any of these aspects before. He immediately picked up his rifle and told Xhabbo that he would go outside at once to see what effect the light of the candles might have among the bushes above.

For a moment it looked as if Xhabbo was going to accompany François, but something which had long been troubling him, reasserted itself and he changed his mind, saying: 'Yes, Foot of the Day, you go, going utterly carefully and going, looking all round. Xhabbo would come with you but the time is now when he must go and sit by that mark on the wall and sitting listen to the tapping inside him. Only a fool would go on ignoring this tapping as he has been ignoring it because if Xhabbo does not go soon, to sit and listen to the tapping, it could utterly leave him.'

With that he turned his back on them and went to sit close by the cross on the wall, arms resting on his knees and head on his arms, his body still, and as if alone in the world. And yet his attitude emanated such an atmosphere of significance that all the others moved around on tip-toe and when one had to speak, did so in whispers.

Meanwhile François had quickly and deftly checked his gun and in doing so, noticed a look of intense alarm on Nonnie's face. So he whispered to her, 'I'm just going outside to make quite certain the light from the candles isn't giving us away. I shan't be long. Could you please start opening the tins and putting the food in those dixies?'

The announcement brought back all Nonnie's terror of being left alone and it was all she could do not to cry out, 'Please don't leave me, don't leave me!' She knew this was impossible, yet she felt she had to say something, so she compromised by converting the 'Don't leave me' into a determined: 'Then I am coming with you.'

'You'll do nothing of the sort!' François told her, rather fiercely, because he did not know how he would stop her if she insisted on coming, and also because he was convinced that it was work better and more safely done by one than two, particularly when the second was someone like Nonnie, who did not know the nature of the ground outside as he did. 'It would be much more helpful if you did as I ask, and got Nuin-Tara to give you a hand with the food.'

Pretending he took her consent for granted, he turned sideways to tell Nuin-Tara in turn what he had just said. The look on her face told him that the incredible gift which primitive people of Africa possess for reading European meaning, sometimes even more accurately from manner, tone, expression or behaviour than the Europeans themselves can do from the words they use for the same purpose, had enabled her to know precisely what had just occurred between Nonnie and himself. Not only had she understood but had become acutely critical of

34

Nonnie. She herself would no more have imposed her own opinions or emotions on Xhabbo at a time like that than she would have allowed Xhabbo to interfere in matters such as child-bearing. Life for her was an entity of two equal and complementary halves: one masculine and one feminine. All her instincts prompted her that to confuse one half with the other only made the problems of life more difficult and showed an elementary lack of dignity and respect for the character of the other. She had of course no means of telling that Nonnie had never been confronted as she herself had so often been, with so terrible a situation. Terrible as it all was to Nonnie, for Nuin-Tara, tragedy and disaster were great constantly recurring realities of Bushman life. Man and woman could only help one another by trusting each other to bear their half of the burden with all their mind and soul.

Luckily, François's decisive response to Nonnie's relapse into fear was the best thing he could have done. In despair, almost any decision is better than none, and his authoritative tone brought alive some of the Nuin-Tara in Nonnie. He would have liked to explain and excuse her, because from the way that Nuin-Tara had picked up one of the heavier tins and held it out to Nonnie, shaking it at her as if to say, 'Now take this and get on with your business and leave him alone to get on with his,' he knew how disapproving of Nonnie she was just then. But feeling somehow that all that would sort itself out in time and Nuin-Tara would soon know for herself the person of spirit he himself knew Nonnie to be, he merely remarked more gently, 'You see, I'm not even taking Hin. Please keep him by you and I promise not to be long.'

Before Nonnie could even call out, 'Oh, please be careful,' he was down on all fours at the exit and crawling forward into the night.

CHAPTER TWO

Another Kind of Music

The night was black and brilliant as ever but the sound of the
concert of stars now had been suppressed by another kind of
music. Standing up slowly, carefully, leaning against the dark
rock screened by the black bushes at the entrance, so that his
eyes could become accustomed to the night, he heard men singing down at Hunter's Drift. They were singing as only the men
of Africa can sing, from somewhere far down, not just in the
physical body of themselves but at the source of the well of
what is perhaps the deepest racial memory in existence. Although the song was only another in the series of sloganized
music to be heard everywhere in a world dedicated to changing human societies by force and bloodshed, and as such
obvious and trivial enough, yet those voices transformed it into
a chorale of great portent and beauty.

In fact it was all so unexpected that François, who had
never heard anything like it before, was profoundly shocked
and angered, that men who had done what those men had done
that day, could be down there in his violated home, feasting at
ease by the light of lamps and warmed by fire, uttering such
beauty in song as if they had never been party to ugliness or
wrong. His anger indeed was so great that it almost went out to
that superb spread of stars above. There seemed something
grossly unfair about such assertion of beauty and he felt like
abusing them for continuing in their normal courses as if
nothing black had been done on earth that day. Then he remembered how Xhabbo would have reproved him and reminded him of those shooting stars they had witnessed earlier
on, begging him to accept them as evidence that the universe
had taken note of the cruelty of the day behind them.

But the singing was another matter. He just could not make
his peace with it. Embittered by that sound, his eyes accustomed

to the dark at last, he set out on a wide, meticulous patrol of the area all round the roof of the cave. He was immensely re-assured to find that no trace of light or candle smell rose into that gentle, impressionable and innocent air of the early night. He crawled through the bushes to look down into the biggest opening in the roof of the cave itself. The bush hat he always wore at night to hide his tell-tale white face which, tanned as it was, might otherwise have given him away, was nearly knocked from his head by the wings of the great old Nonnietjie owl. It was a tribute to the skill with which he did his work that he nearly walked into it before it flew out of his way with a wild, long, 'Sephoo-koo-koo.'

Looking down the hole as if into a deep well, he could just see like a faint flake of amber water, a suggestion of reflected candle-glow. It convinced him that even if they lit a dozen more candles, their light would not be strong enough to penetrate the dark where he crouched, and even should any soldiers come prowling near the cave they would have to find the hole first and look down into it before they would detect any light. He was certain that no strangers, like those men singing down there so ardently, were going to stumble around among the rocks and bushes of the steep cliff in which the cave was concealed, on so dark a night.

He turned back to the entrance of the cave but once there, found himself strangely reluctant to go inside. There was some unknown thought trying the door of his imagination as Nonnie had once tried the door of his room in the homestead below. He could not return to the others until he let it in and knew what it was. He suspected that it was his version of what Xhabbo would have called 'tapping', and at that the answer came. Mtunwya (Messenger) had told him that everyone at Hunter's Drift had been killed, but François now knew that he would never for-give himself unless he went down there to make absolutely cer-tain that none of the many people who had been so good to him and whom he had loved so dearly were not still alive.

It was extraordinary how well-armed this realization sprang to his head for it brought also the exact knowledge of how he would have to set about it. He would have to wait until those singing men were asleep. Somehow he assumed that with all the good food and wine they would have found they would sleep early and sleep well after their own long day. Of course, he was aware that such well-trained men in uniform would post sentries for the night as a matter of routine. But he did not imagine that the sentries would be over-watchful, for knowing themselves to be in one of the remotest parts of the bush, the danger of intrusion by night was negligible.

If he waited another three or four hours, he was certain he would have a chance of getting close to the homestead or even within it undetected. If there were any of his own left alive, although he had to admit to himself it was unlikely, he would have to consult with Xhabbo how best to rescue them. Their only hope then perhaps might be for one of them to make for Mopani's main camp. It was unlikely that if anybody were still alive with the men down below they would be killed suddenly, but even should there be no one, François realized with a start, there still would be the problem of Mopani.

Mopani had been due back a week before from an international convention abroad. One of his first plans would be to visit Hunter's Drift; indeed he could even be on his way, totally unaware of the peril awaiting him. Somehow Mopani had to be warned. And those poor coloured people of Silverton Hill, what of them?

He was overwhelmed by the impossible amount of things that needed doing, the odds against doing them and the lack of time. He was certain of only one dominant priority. He had to find out what had happened and what was happening below. It was something he knew would have to be done alone. Not even Xhabbo could help, for all his supreme hunter's eye and skill so infinitely greater than François's own, because his Bushman friend did not know the land below as it would have to be known. Only François, who knew it out of love and experience as the one and only patch of earth in his life, could have any chance of success. And that was doubtful.

Even Hintza would have to be left behind. For once there was only danger and no safety left in numbers. And here he realized that Nonnie would be an added problem for him, not because she would not accept his decision to go when he explained it all to her, but because he feared that another anxiety, added to all she had already suffered, would be unfair, if not too much for her. He would have to go without her knowing.

In all this he was sure somehow that Xhabbo and Nuin-Tara would understand. They would help, and from there he came to the answer. He had already concluded that Nonnie could not be expected to sleep as she should sleep that night unless he gave her some of those old tranquillizers and sleeping draughts of Ouwa's which he had left in the cave and which he had once used on Xhabbo. He would make her eat as good a meal as possible, make her drink a couple of mugs of the best of his hot chocolate and sweet condensed milk which he thought he made as well, if not better, than dear old Ousie-Johanna herself (the thought of her nearly sent him on a course of tears of his own), followed by the kind of sedatives Ouwa took in an extremity. He knew the appropriate measure and felt that drugs which had worked so well on persons so much bigger as Ouwa and Xhabbo, would be doubly effective on someone so slight and young as Nonnie. Only when these preliminaries were determined, did he turn his back on the night and that insufferable beauty of the singing below, and crawl back into the cave.

Nonnie, warned of his return by Hintza who had left her and was standing with his tail wagging enthusiastically at the entrance when François crawled through it, neither looked nor spoke to him. She could not trust herself to do so in case the relief at his reappearance showed through the tears which it had brought to her eyes. She felt she had had enough of crying that day and was angry and humiliated within herself for having done it so often and long. She thought it high time that the practice should cease. If it couldn't cease, then at best it must be continued as discreetly as possible.

Xhabbo was still visible like a shape in one of those fantasies that Goya painted by candle-light, sitting bowed over his knees, his head now slightly turned on one side as if listening to some far-off sound from the frontiers of the night. Nuin-Tara, however, was a totally different person. She was obviously excited and full of a lively interest in the things Nonnie had extracted from the tins, watching her opening the biggest of them with its tiny metal key, like someone in a play in a theatre. These commonplaces of existence to Nonnie were acts of the greatest magic for Nuin-Tara which united to restore Nonnie fully to her grace.

François warmed to the sight of the two of them there, heads close together, engaged in that antique ritual of women preparing food for their men at the end of the day. He only wished that Nonnie could understand the words of wonder pouring out of Nuin-Tara, although he felt Nonnie must have had some idea from the manner and tone in which they were uttered.

As he joined them Nonnie, without looking up, whispered in as matter-of-fact a tone as she could manage, 'I expect we'd better eat this stuff cold, as your friend there just now seemed to be against us lighting fires.'

'Not at all,' François hastened to reply, happy because for once he had something positive to announce. 'I've been all over the roof outside and we're quite safe in here as long as we use only candles. Now I'll show you exactly how we are going to set about preparing a three-course dinner for you.'

He went to his store and brought back six long candles. He took out his knife, cut the candles in half and tapered each of the six bottom halves until the wicks were exposed. He arranged the halves in two separate groups of six, each set in the sand in two rows of three close together. That done, he went back to the far end of the cave to collect some stones, banked the stones on either side of the candles, to make two rudimentary fire-places. He then lit the candles, told Nonnie to pour the cans of soup into both halves of each dixie and arranged them in pairs over each fire-place.

Nuin-Tara watched the congealed soup melt, uttering sounds of astonishment as it became liquid and gradually filled the air above the candle fires with a new smell of food strange to her. Indeed, judging by their expressions, she and Hintza were running a kind of race to see whose appetite for food could grow fastest as the smell of cooking increased. Hintza was lying as close to the candles as possible, flat on his tummy in the way which only he could lie, his legs stretched out straight behind him and his paws in front, with his head and chin out resting on the sand between them, as if he himself were listening in to some kind of dog's equivalent of tapping. But any impression that his concentration was the result of an exercise in profound inner contemplation was belied by the fact that he was unashamedly dribbling at the corners of his long mouth and that his silk black nose was constantly wrinkling and unwrinkling with each new onslaught of smell.

Consoling Hintza with the remark that he would not have long to wait, François realized, somewhat stricken with conscience, that there was something more he could do to help. Accustomed as he was to going without anything to drink between sunrise and sunset, he was suddenly amazed at how thirsty he was and realized how the others, particularly Nonnie, must be suffering. So he immediately went to his store and brought a bottle of Ousie-Johanna's famous concentrate of lemons. He had two mugs in the cave which he filled with cool water, added some of the concentrate to each. He gave one to Nuin-Tara and the other to Nonnie, saying: 'I'm sorry, you must be dying of thirst, but could you wait for a second because there's something I want you to take with it.'

He quickly fetched his little Red Cross store, took out a yellow tranquillizer and held it out to Nonnie, saying, 'Please swallow this with your lemonade.'

'What is it?' she asked, suspicious of the tablet.

Before he could explain, Xhabbo, who, unnoticed by them all, had apparently at last done with his tapping, came to squat beside them and instantly recognized the tablet. A wide smile broke over his emaciated features and immediately he began to tell Nuin-Tara that it was the very thing about which he had so often spoken. Small as it was, it killed the greatest of pains. He personified the little tablet and the pain as if they were some Bushman David and Goliath, challenged to battle before them.

Obviously every detail of what had happened between him and François had been told over and over again by many Bushman fires in the remote desert. Nuin-Tara became almost excited as Xhabbo was. She herself had just swallowed the last of her drink and could not yet believe that any liquid could be as sweet as what she had just tasted. Xhabbo recognized the

41

bottle too. It was another great figure in the epic of his first encounter with François eighteen months ago, and its magical properties had to be recounted at great dramatic length.

In all this excitement and chatter, Nonnie's question was almost forgotten, even by herself, so curious had she become. He had to explain to her how these tablets had come to help Xhabbo and added that Nonnie could do now with a tablet herself.

For a moment it looked as if she were going to refuse. She had in any case a powerful instinct against anything which might isolate her from reality, even so painful and dangerous a reality as the present. But one look at the pleading expression on François's face as well as the realization that if she refused she might not only cause him to lose face with his friends but re-antagonize Nuin-Tara herself, made her change her mind. She took the tablet with her first sip of lemonade. The sharp, sweet taste of the lemon woke the giant thirst which the anguish of the day had repressed. She found herself emptying the mug in a way she had not done since she had left her nursery.

'Merveilloso, que merveilloso!' she exclaimed instinctively drawing on the schoolgirl Portuguese she had always used on Amelia and added, 'That was super.'

She handed the mug back to François, begging, 'It was so good, I'd love some more if you don't mind.'

'I know,' François observed, nearly adding that it was one of Ousie-Johanna's own inventions and to him by far her best, but his wounded self cancelled it and he merely added, 'I think it would be wise to wait for a bit before I give you any more. I'd love to but I know from experience that it's stupid to drink too much when you've gone so long without water.'

'I expect you're right, but I can hardly bear to wait,' Nonnie answered, resigned, and with no inkling of how encouraged François was by this first indication of a re-awakening of some awareness of her natural needs.

Meanwhile, he had Xhabbo and Hintza and Nuin-Tara to think of as well. He filled Nuin-Tara's empty mug for Xhabbo. Then he filled his bush hat to the brim with water and put it in front of Hintza. Fondly he watched him lapping it up as if it were a dog's dream champagne.

The soup, meat and vegetables that followed, after being heated in the dixies, were still more successful. Even though François gave himself and Nonnie half the amount he gave Xhabbo and Nuin-Tara, the Bushman couple finished long before they did. Finally François fetched the largest piece of biltong from his store while the meat was cooking and squatted, 'Bamuthi-wise, and cut it into chunks. He fed it to Hintza, listening as he did so to Xhabbo telling Nuin-Tara how he had experienced this sort of food before, and so could foretell what other delights were still to come.

Both François and Nonnie were content to leave the talking to them, not only because it made all sound so normal and happy, but also because it helped their spirit to contain the storm of thought and feeling silently raging within them. It was accordingly, using the word in the most relative sense, the best moment as yet of their tragic day, so good that François could not resist, despite a guilty feeling of dangerous extravagance, if not sheer waste, an impulse to make the most of it by taking two enormous tins of peaches from his store. He quietened his conscience with the thought that they could not be carried with them when they left the cave.

Since their dixies were contaminated by the previous courses and he knew they could not yet spare any water for washing them, he pinned on the point of his knife the great halved St Helena peaches and handed one half at a time to each one there, including Hintza, who had the most un-doglike passion for canned peaches.

The first went to Xhabbo, since Bushman manners demanded that the man be served first. François was amused at the astonishment on his face because this was an eventuality which had not yet been thought of in his philosophy of food. His joyful reaction to the fresh, cool taste was to declare it 'food of utterly honey' before he looked intently at Nuin-Tara so as not to miss what expression the new substance would bring to her face when she tasted it. When she had swallowed her first peach and looked at him as if she could not believe what she had tasted, a glitter of delighted laughter fell from him and they started hugging each other repeatedly until they stopped to turn to François and Nonnie for more.

François emptied the tins in the proportion of two halves to Nuin-Tara and Xhabbo each for his, Nonnie's and Hintza's one. As a climax to the feast he gave the couple a tin each to drink the remainder of the rich juice. That perhaps, as far as they were concerned, was the ultimate delight of the evening, for when the last drop of juice had been eagerly and loudly sucked out of the tins, they improvised a little chant in low, murmuring voices for the magic of the food which they had just eaten. The chant had an odd prayer of thanks quality about it. Even Nonnie, though she could not understand a word, and so had no definite guide for its meaning, somehow knew why they were doing it.

She turned to François, remarking in a voice much more her own; 'I don't think I've ever known a nicer way of ending a meal.'

'And I,' François turned to her, putting his hand on hers, said, 'have never been to a braver meal. Thank you, Nonnie, for eating your food. I do know you felt even less like eating than I did.'

She turned her head away, because more emotion, even so good and positive as those words of praise from François, was too much for one so charged with feelings as she was. She heard François ask, 'Would you like me to translate what they're chanting? I think you'd like it.'

She nodded, in case the effort to speak broke her self-control.

'I can only do it badly,' François replied. 'As always when anything is connected with their god, Mantis, they're using very old words. Sometimes they themselves don't even know the meaning of them. They are just starting it again for the third time. It's strange how on these occasions they always do things at least three times. It goes something like this:

> And so on our feet upright walking,
> After many days, we came at last
> To the place of our father Mantis,
> The snatcher of fire.
> And on our heels sitting
> Among those rocks of many colours,
> Marked by men of the early race
> In order to marking show

The place was utterly his.
We drank water of honey,
And ate the food so that the hunger
With which walking we came dying,
Died instead, on account of it.
Yes, here! Oh yes! Here,
In the place of our father,
Hunger died, on account of it.

Nonnie, lifted out of herself by this rendering of the chant, had the same look as she had had when she had been told that the cross on the walls of the cave was the work of Bushman. She said, 'You know, when they first started chanting, it sounded a bit like a sort of prayer of thanks to me; but it's almost like a psalm, don't you think?'

François could not have been more pleased at her response. It seemed to be a sign that despite the enormous gap between Nonnie's own culture and that of the Bushmen, she could bridge it to become as devoted to them as he was. But he left it at that and all he said was, 'I'm so glad you feel as I do about it.'

They listened in silence until the chanting was over. Then François thought that with all they had to do, the sooner they went to sleep the better, and he asked Nonnie: 'I wonder if you wouldn't mind please taking the two empty tins, filling them with water and putting them on to boil, because I want to make some hot chocolate and milk for us as soon as possible, so that we can all try and sleep. We'll need all the sleep we can get tonight and the sooner we have a go at it, the better. While you are doing that, forgive me if I don't speak to you, because there are some things I have to talk over with Xhabbo.'

Despite the effect of François's tranquillizer, sleep for Nonnie was the one thing of which she thought herself incapable. She would of course do her best, but knowing how often she had been kept awake by the anticipation even of pleasant things: how for instance she had not slept at all out of excitement the night before she and her father had flown out to Africa last, she thought sleep after such a day would be utterly out of the question. Nonetheless as a sign of her willingness to do all she could to help, she went immediately without a word to fill the large tins to the brim with water and placed them on their candle fires. She then tried to relax by lying sideways on the sand, leaning on her right elbow, close to Hintza where she could not only feel the ample warmth of his urgent body but could stroke his head and back, as much for her own comfort as for his. In that position she could keep her eye on the tins as well as watch the changes of expression on the faces of Xhabbo, Nuin-Tara and François as they came and went quickly in the ebb and flow of the long tidal swell of their talk, and which were her only guides to what they were saying.

Xhabbo's account of his communion with his tapping can be summed up in a few sentences though it was long and elaborate in the telling. It amounted to this: the tapping had told him that their enemies down there in François's place had not done with their search for François yet. They were determined to find him. Moreover they were not only in and around François's home. It would be a fatal mistake to think that. They were in thousands everywhere, spread over the country, many, many days' marching to the north and to the west, and coming in many thousands more from far away to spread out south and west into the world of the Europeans beyond.

That the tapping was true, Xhabbo could tell from his own experience on their long march to warn François, because the days were almost without number in which the two of them had not been hiding from dawn to sunset, and walking only by night in order to remain unseen by the hundreds of black men marching on Hunter's Drift. Hence the tapping had warned Xhabbo that they must stay in the cave for many days, not coming out of it until the tapping told them it was time to stir again.

This was sombre news to François, not only because the tapping seemed to pronounce against what he was resolved to do that very night, but seemed to rule out the possibility of turning for help, such as trying to reach Mopani and his body of well-armed rangers, or stopping a train at Hunter's Drift Siding or, if that were not possible, making their way on foot through the bush to the great mining city which Hunter's Drift had supplied with fresh meat and vegetables for so long. There was also the matter of warning the coloured people at Silverton Hill, but all these things now seemed forbidden by Xhabbo's tapping. He knew how difficult, if not impossible and even immoral, it might be to get Xhabbo to go against his tapping.

So many indeed were his misgivings over what Xhabbo had just told him, that he had to struggle to keep them out of his voice, as he tried to answer Xhabbo in the only way he felt he could understand. He began by asking Nuin-Tara and Xhabbo to avoid any inflection of tone or expression which would tell Nonnie, who was watching them closely, that they were at all perturbed, by what he was going to say to them.

Of course he believed in Xhabbo's tapping, he told them, but he had a tapping of his own which he could not disregard. This tapping was for him alone and it told him to go from the cave to do something of the greatest importance to him. Asking them not even to glance in her direction, he explained that as soon as Nonnie was asleep, he would have to go down to Hunter's Drift to find out if his mother, Nonnie's father or any other people, were still alive.

Xhabbo and Nuin-Tara did not immediately protest. They just sat there in silence, looking hard and long at him with the utmost commiseration before they both shook their heads and in voices low under the weight of natural compassion, exclaimed, 'But surely you must know, Foot of the Day, that all your people have been killed?'

François admitted that he feared they were right, but he could not accept it until he had proved it to be a fact. He put the question to them with that primitive gravity he had so often seen in 'Bamuthi when his people doubted him. Would they, he asked them, if they were in his position and their people had been attacked that day, have gone away without making certain that there were no survivors held prisoner by such terrible enemies?

François wisely then left unanswered a question so full of meaning for them that it became almost tangible, like a dark presence there in the candle shadows peering over their shoulders, determined not to be denied. It did so because the question had been asked so many times among themselves in the course of their long history of persecution and was all the graver because it was combined with the tragic fore-knowledge induced in them by the experience of their race, that for all the necessity of asking the question, the exercise of proving his answer was invariably in vain.

Finally Xhabbo said, with fatalistic determination, 'If you go, Foot of the Day, Xhabbo goes too.'

'No Xhabbo, no,' François replied immediately, struggling to keep down the emotion which Xhabbo's loyal acceptance aroused in him. He knew how difficult it must be for Xhabbo to disobey when all his instincts were telling him it was wrong and disobedient to offer to come with him. 'No, Xhabbo. I can't let you do something which is against your own tapping. Besides, I think it is work that one can do more safely than two. And that one must be me. Only I know the ground down there below and the way of getting among those people without being seen. But I can't tell you how my heart utterly thanks you for wanting to go with me.'

He stretched out his hand, put it on Xhabbo's and pressed it. He would have said more had not Nonnie, who fortunately had not thought any more of the conversation than that they were reviewing the events of the day, called out just then in a voice as light and gay as she could make it, 'Kettles all a-boiling sir!'

'I'll be with you in a second,' François called back over his shoulder and hastened to ask Xhabbo and Nuin-Tara's help, taking their agreement for granted, 'I don't want her to know what I'm going to do tonight. You must please help me. As soon as we have drunk the liquid I'm going to prepare for us, we must put out the fires and go to sleep as if we are going to do nothing but sleep all night. I will not go until I am certain she is fast asleep.'

Nuin-Tara gave him a look, as if to say it was just like a man to assume that a woman could just lie down and calmly go to sleep after what Nonnie had been through. But she did François an injustice because he had already realized this difficulty and thought of a way of solving it. However she merely looked meaningfully at him and did not speak.

François then joined Nonnie and together they poured large amounts of the best Hunter's Drift chocolate into the two mugs and added boiling water, stirring each with his knife. He added a fistful of sugar to each. With the boiling water left he repeated the process in the two old peach tins, finally adding to mugs and tins the contents of a tin of sweet condensed milk. He gave the mugs to Nonnie and Nuin-Tara, and the tins to Xhabbo and himself, but before drinking the fragrant, steaming brew, he took two sleeping draughts from his store and held them out to Nonnie, saying, 'Please take these with your chocolate.'

It was perhaps a sign of the new Nonnie that was being painfully born that although everything in her clamoured to reject the capsules, she paused only briefly before taking them from him and swallowing them.

Patting her chest lightly with the flat of her hand, as if to help down the capsules, she made a face at François before exclaiming, not with a certain air of triumph, 'There, I think I did rather well, don't you?'

François did not get a chance to say how grateful he was because the sight of the capsules produced the greatest surge of excitement in Xhabbo yet. He was nudging Nuin-Tara, exhorting her, unusually imperative, to look quickly, because there were the most magic things of all about which he had told her; the things which, all the time he was lying in the cave so full of pain that even his tapping could not get through to him, would send him to sleep. More, they would give him unfailingly what he called 'the sleep of honey with dreams of honey.'

Nonnie compelled François to translate all this though he would obviously rather not have done so. In the process, he confirmed her fears that she was being further drugged, though they were somewhat calmed by François's declaration, 'I myself won't hesitate to take some of these if I find I can't sleep. My father took them for years without them doing him any harm.'

François's version of hot chocolate seemed to raise the spirits of Xhabbo and Nuin-Tara to a new height of delight, and their many gestures and expressions of astonishment were so novel and vivid that Nonnie, watching them, forgot the capsules. They would without a doubt have celebrated the end of the chocolate with another chant but François prevented them by getting up and giving them a meaning look. He said it was time they all went to bed.

Going to bed for Nuin-Tara and Xhabbo was a simple

process. Nuin-Tara just stretched herself out on the sand, lying on her left side with her head on her arm, her legs slightly drawn up. Xhabbo lay close up against her, with his head on one hand and his right arm round her. So at home and belonging to the ground did they appear, that the earth which itself was asleep under the great blanket of an African night and dreaming of infinite summers of increase communicated its own heavy need for slumber to them, so that they were hardly in position before they were both instantly asleep. One aspect of their capacity for instant sleep which must not be overlooked for all its prosaic nature, was the far, hard walk behind them.

Nonnie's bed, which François prepared on the sand near the picture of St Hubert, was only a slightly more elaborate affair. He emptied the largest haversack, half-filled it with fresh, clean sand, fastened the buckles of the flap and placed it firmly on the softest, level sand.

Calling Hintza to him he said firmly, 'Now, Hin, you lie there and sleep, and do not move until I call you.' He pointed to a place at right angles to the haversack but slightly to the side.

Turning to Nonnie, he said: 'There, Nonnie, is your pillow and Hin is your hot-water-bottle. I'm sorry I haven't got an eiderdown for you as well, but please try it. It might not be so hard and cold as it looks, with Hin to warm you.'

'But what about you?' Nonnie asked. 'Where are you going to sleep?'

François's answer was oblique if not evasive: 'I'm afraid I can't go to sleep just yet. I have something to write before I can go to sleep.' Seeing her astonishment, he explained, without really explaining, 'It's some writing we may need in the morning. When I have done that, any old place will do for me. I have slept out on the ground so much, you know!'

'But can't the writing wait until morning?' Nonnie protested, strangely dismayed by François's reply for many reasons she herself did not understand at the time, but fastening on this one aspect to express all her disappointment.

'No, I'm afraid it can't,' François answered with that unexpected firmness she was now beginning to realize had to be accepted. 'We'll have a lot of other things to do in the morning. It has got to be now.'

Nonnie wanted to ask more about this mysterious writing, not just out of curiosity but also to protract the moment. The last thing she wanted was to be left alone during what she was convinced would be a sleepless night. Yet, despite all the wretchedness of the day behind taking her by the throat again, her proud, young spirit felt she had no dignified option but to turn her back on François, go over to Hintza, lie down and curl up beside him. Doing so, she put her arm round him as Xhabbo had his round Nuin-Tara. She was rewarded by a whimper of welcome from Hintza who, in his expert manner, would not sacrifice the least bit of anything so useful to an exhausted dog as sleep in order to be aware of what was happening in the world around him. She lay there, eyes wide open, smarting with hurt, staring to where St Hubert was lost in candle shadow.

Meanwhile François took his candle and stood it in the sand against a far wall of the cave where its light would least trouble the sleepers. He took out the dispatch note-book which he always carried. From the moment he had learned to write, Mopani had insisted that no hunter of any worth went into the bush without paper and pencil in case of emergency. Mopani had told him many stories of Europeans in Africa who had got into trouble because they had ignored this simple and obvious precaution and so could not summon any help, because they spoke neither the language of the people among whom they found themselves, nor possessed material for a written message. Mopani had delivered his lesson so graphically and so often that François had never yet gone out into the bush without a note-book and pencil in a side pocket of his bush shirt.

Perhaps Nonnie's forlorn attempt to out-stare the darkness round her would have been less forlorn, had she known how much she was in his heart and mind as he sat there now with the note-book on his knees, writing a long letter to her.

It was a letter which he knew was vital in case he did not come back from his excursion. Long as it was however it had no room for personal emotion of any kind. It had to concern itself entirely with essential and immediate realities. Beyond a brief explanation of why he had gone, why he had not told her before and why he would not be there instead of the letter, it went on to ask her to put herself entirely in the hands of Xhabbo. He was certain that sooner or later Xhabbo would take her somewhere safe. Apart from begging her not to despair, he told her some of the things necessary for her survival. He wrote a detailed list of all the stores in the cave, what should be taken when they left and what should be eaten first while they remained hidden. He gave her detailed instructions of how and when she should drink, eat and generally behave on the march. Most important of all, was his catalogue of medicine: a full description of what they were all for and how they should be used, not excluding the spare snake-bite kit which he stressed Nonnie was to have on her whenever she left the cave. He ended his letter with just a brief, final good night that showed, perhaps, for the first time a trace of the emotion which was full as a sea within him. 'Forgive me for leaving you in the dark, darling Nonnie. I could not help it. Please look after yourself and my beloved Hin, please. And God and Mantis, bless you always and always. Your François.'

He folded the pages carefully together, printed Nonnie's name in large capital letters on the outside and put the letter white and upright in the sand close by their candle fire-place so she could not fail to see it when she woke in the morning, looking in her direction as he did so to make certain she was not awake and watching him. In that dim light, it looked to him reassuringly as if she were already asleep. He was about to go back to his place by the candles against the wall when Nuin-Tara, to his amazement, appeared at his side.

Considering how exhausted she was and how fast asleep she must have been, it was extraordinary how wide awake and how militantly she stood up to him. In that uninhibited Bushman way of hers, the Bushman way which holds it far more culpable to be dishonest about feelings than false in words, she upbraided him in whispers; 'You can't be so cruel, Foot of the Day. You cannot leave that utterly-young woman of yours alone, lying there in the dark after what she has suffered this day. You cannot do it, Foot of the Day. Nuin-Tara will not allow it!'

Before François really knew what was happening to him, he

52

was pulled along noiselessly over the sand and forced to lie down beside Nonniè while she urged in the most authoritative Bushman whisper: 'You stay there just like that until you have to do what you have got to do, and do not move a moment before.'

François wanted to protest that he had to put out the candle first, but Nuin-Tara made a silent sign at him as if to indicate that, after seeing him put out those 'burning things' all evening, she was not so stupid as to be incapable of putting one small one out by herself.

With that she left him without another word or sound. In a second the candle was out and the cave black. In the darkness François found himself quite naturally forced to put his arm round Nonnie as Xhabbo had his round Nuin-Tara and Nonnie round Hintza. Doing so, he felt a great shudder go through Nonnie as if all the terrible tensions in her were ending.

Nuin-Tara, with deliberate forethought, had done her work so skilfully that Nonnie was oblivious of her part in bringing François there. Happy in the thought that he had come out of his own volition, she said in a whisper: 'Oh thank you, François. Thank you for coming. I was so terrified here, all alone, and so wanted you to be with me. It's been such a terrible, terrible day. Thank you and bless you, and good night.'

'Good night, Nonnie,' he answered, realizing perhaps for the first time how her presence gave meaning and hope to all he was attempting, for he added full and overflowing with gratitude in turn, 'It's I who have to thank you. Good night, and please sleep well.'

Nonnie's response was to snuggle backwards closer against him. Again François was possessed by that extraordinary feeling which the contact first with Xhabbo, then with Nuin-Tara and now again with Nonnie and which both death and danger in their abolition of illusion and appearance, had made accessible to him. It was exactly as if they were not two but one person under one skin. Only this feeling of oneness now was grown so great that it obliterated all the pain of the day behind them, as well as all thought of what was ended. Time became so recharged and winged with meaning that it seemed in François's

own especial measure of these things that he had only just come
to lie down beside Nonnie and put his arm round her, before
she was as deeply asleep as Hintza, Xhabbo and Nuin-Tara, and
he the only person left awake in the cave.

CHAPTER THREE

Footpath in the Night

The moment François realized that he was the only person left awake, he knew the time had come to go. But that, he now found, was more easily thought of than done. He was confronted with a difficulty completely outside his experience. As far as he could recollect, he had never shared a bed, even so bare a bed of sand, with anyone else. There may have been a moment in the remote past when his mother, still Lammie in his memory, moved by his helplessness and those unpredictable and inexplicable storms of distress that shake an infant world, and expose how often growing older, however lovingly, is a process of increasing forgetfulness of the mystery of belonging in the beginning, might have taken him for his comfort to her bed. But if so it was long before he was capable of remembering.

As far as he recollected, the role of that 'other little person' was imposed upon him so early in his life that he had no other coherent memory than of always sleeping alone, until the coming of Hintza.

Indeed this dignified state of a person in his own right, ascribed to him even before he was born, was taken so for granted that it had never even occurred to him that he could all the time have been longing in some underworld of himself not to be so utterly 'other' and needed some form of physical companionship to equal the lively mental companionship and thoughtful concern which he received from his parents.

He had no natural preparation therefore for the effect of this first experience of lying in the dark so closely snuggled up to another person as he was to Nonnie. Indeed one is tempted to say that he had no natural immunity to protect him against being overwhelmed by the many feelings released in him by so simple and natural an event. He had neither mind nor that space of spirit we call time, to analyse what was happening to him. He had just perhaps a fragment of a second to recognize that this act of his present togetherness revealed, as does one blinding flash of lightning a whole world drowned in a sea of darkness, how alone he had been all his life. He marvelled at his blindness in not perceiving before even a new-moon sliver of some longing not to be alone that must have been secretly at work within his being during all those charged years of growing up at Hunter's Drift. That brittle fragment of time in which he acknowledged the inadequacy of the status of that 'other little person', for all the ostensible honours and advantages of dignity and self-responsibility it had heaped on him, was overwhelmed almost at once by another emotion for which there is only that one travel-stained word of 'sweetness'. It was as if, without knowing it, the taste of his being before had been bitter and now instantly was sweet. So great, so real, so tangible was the feeling that it almost caused him to panic. This sweetness assumed so precious and transcendental an importance from the split-second moment of its invasion, that he feared he would never summon up the resolve to abandon it of his own free will. Worse still, he feared that even if he refound his will to go on with his purpose, will alone would not enable him to break out from the power which this sweetness had so swiftly acquired over him.

He knew that the sooner he went, the better, because already the enemy down below could be expected to be asleep as were his companions. If he left at once, the greater would be his chances of returning before Nonnie woke, for in the next three or four hours the power of the tranquillizers and sleeping draughts he had given her would be at their most effective. Then they would begin to wane and, after what she had suffered, she could wake up unusually early. Yet obvious as all this was, it seemed to him that he lay there for hours struggling with himself, without being able to give up this sweet and living partnership in sleep which held him there in the dark beside Nonnie, and to become alone and 'bitter' again in his own savour of himself. For not the least of the casualties to be listed in this roll-call in François's spirit at the end of that terrible day, was the authority of the concept of 'the other person' proclaimed by Lammie before he was even born.

He had only one ally to help swing his spirit back on to its predetermined course, pedestrian it is true, but experienced enough to overcome this untried new emotion, powerful as it was. He had that Calvinist upbringing of his, that habit of conscience inspired by Ouwa's loyal example, and habit forced him at last to go.

He began to withdraw the arm he had round Nonnie very gently but gently as he did so, it was enough to alarm Hintza. He felt more than saw Hintza raise his head beside his hand and immediately François put it on Hintza's neck, pressing the soft warm skin in the way Hintza had been taught was the signal at the climax of a critical stalk, to keep quiet and in position until ordered not to. Obediently the head went down to resume its sleeping position between his paws, but François knew that both eyes and ears would be alert and following his movements until he left the cave and that until his return Hintza would be awake and on watch in his stead. Only when he was certain that Hintza had understood, did he detach his arm completely, and very slowly rose to his feet without a sound. It was more like an amputation of his arm than the gentlest and most sensitive of separations. Yet, lest he changed his mind, he paused only to check his person carefully to make certain he had nothing on him that could possibly rattle, pick up his gun and bush hat and then crawl quietly out of the cave.

It was extraordinary, after the blackness of the cave, how the night lit only by stars dazzled and glittered. Indeed the stars were so full and dripping with light that he reminded himself not to look at them, in case they deprived him of the vital capacity of seeing through the blackness when he might need to most. So vital was this that after his first quick scanning of the sky, he stood back against rocks and bushes with his eyes on the ground, not only for his vision to recover but also to listen in to what the sound could tell him of the night.

The first and most obvious change since he had last stood there was the fact that no longer was any singing coming from his home. The men down there, as far as he could tell, must be asleep, because even voices talking normally would have been audible from where he stood.

Yet he waited long after his eyes were readjusted to the dark hoping that a challenge or two from sentries he was certain so well-trained an enemy could not have failed to post, would reach him to tell him where they stood. But for all he heard, the whole of the invading force might have assumed intruders in so remote a place to be so unlikely that it had not even bothered to mount guards at all.

Luckily François was not deceived. He had of course no direct experience of such a situation but he had heard enough from Mopani and Ouwa who had both served through a world war, to know that there must be sentries on watch down there below, and their silence did not indicate neglect but, on the contrary, could be proof of an extra degree of cunning and foresight of those in command. No watch in that still night air of the bush, through which the slightest sound tends to travel the greatest distance, could ever be more effective than a silent and invisible one.

His reading of the absence of human sound was confirmed when almost exactly where he knew his home to be, François's eyes became aware of a sort of amber glow on the dark beyond the vast shadow of the great gardens and orchards, blacker even than that of night. Since the glow was without a flicker, he knew it was not reflection of any open fire. It could only come from the great oil lamps in his home and he wondered that such a careful enemy had not bothered to draw the shutters. It struck him as a touch of indiscretion in their cunning and, slight as it was, it gave François hope that his desperate plan might, after all, succeed. For if those men were fallible in that one small regard, surely they could be fallible in other and perhaps more important ones as well? It did not occur to him as it might have done if he had continued speculating on that amber glow, so deceptively naïve and confiding in appearance, that the reason why the light was not screened might have been due to the destruction of the shutters during the attack. But his attention was diverted by another sound troubling the silence of the night.

It was the noise the cattle, particularly cows and their calves, were making down by the old Matabele kraals. The noise amazed him, for it showed that the invaders, despite all their urgent military business, had gathered the cattle and driven them into their kraals for the night. But they had either not been milked properly or, as seemed far more likely to François, were so troubled by the sudden disappearance of the familiar hands and voices which had tended them from birth and so disturbed by the presence of strangers, that they could not sleep as they normally did, and their repeated lowing expressed a profound unease. François knew how deep that unease would be out of his intense experience of the active participation of Matabele herdsmen and their cattle in one another's states of being. Yet there was another aspect of the mournful sound, the thought of which made the hair on the back of his head go as magnetic and erect as those on the ridge of Hintza's back in times of apprehension. He remembered the Matabele belief that the great spirits and those of the immediate dead spoke through the voices of their beloved cattle gathered at night in the safety of their kraals. Judging by the pitiful calling of the cows to their calves, the pathetic answers that came back and occasionally the more definite wailing of a bull, both spirits and newly dead were urging the cattle to proclaim repeatedly their misgivings and to warn the life of the bush far and wide of the great new danger that had come to imperil it.

This interpretation was strengthened by the absence of any of the normal sounds François would have expected at that hour. In between the lowing of cattle he listened in vain for the bush-buck barking, as it came to feed at the edge of the bush on the fringe of the clearing and the great old hippopotamus bulls, coming from the Amanzim-tetse to graze along its banks and snort with delight in between mouthfuls of their favourite salad of grass with a dressing of dew. And what had happened to the owls and night-jars and the cough of the leopard warning a jackal to keep its distance? François only heard the cry of carrion. Never in all his years at Hunter's Drift, had he heard jackals and hyenas in such numbers so close to the homestead, so bold and insistent in their claim to be fed.

A day of and for carrion, he thought bitterly, would have to be followed by a night for carrion. As he thought this, he heard the sound of the great river flowing steadily on, straight down below him, and it was as if this sound were directed specially at him, to remind him that all things, no matter how great and powerful they might appear, did not last. They had to move on and in their time pass into darkness, as that river flowed on, into and through the night. With his night vision as good as it was ever going to be, with nothing more to learn from listening where he stood, François knew that he had better follow the example of the river and move on as well.

He had no preconceived plan as to how to get into his home except for the preliminary approach. All his training in stalking warned him against pre-judgement and declared that the only safe way was to use the utmost vigilance, and be wide open to all possibilities. His first approach could follow only straight down the side of the hill, the shortest way through bushes and boulders to the shelter of the reeds on the river bank. Once in the reeds, he could make his way unseen to an old hippotamus track – a track far older than any footpath of man in the bush – made by generations of hippopotamuses to their choice grazing grounds in the great clearing in which his home stood and where the wide gardens and great orchards had been planted. From time to time, the hippopotamuses, with memories almost as long as those of the elephant, would still try the track, impelled by a vision of paradisical grazing beyond, only to find the way denied to them and their sortie vain, except that it kept the track in being for a day when the intruders might vanish as swiftly as they had come. This track would give him cover right up to the main irrigation ditch along which the water, diverted from the river, flowed to the head of the gardens.

The ditch not only avoided the Matabele kraals but ended half-way between them and the homestead by a deep reservoir which supplied minor furrows branching out in many directions for watering all parts of the spread-out garden. Once in this ditch, protected by its high walls, François was hopeful that he could reach the ample cover of the orchard without detection. But beyond that he avoided all plans and preconceptions. All would depend on what he heard and saw once in the orchard, close to the homestead. He had not worked himself at irrigating the gardens for so many years, nor played hide-and-seek in it with his Matabele friends so often, without knowing many hidden and cunning approaches to the house, to feel certain of finding an approach to take him in closer unobserved.

Much as he missed Hintza, since this was the first time

François had ever ventured out on anything so important without him, he was glad he had come alone. Hintza could not possibly have managed the furrow. The water there was too deep for a dog to stay on his feet and he would have been carried along swimming for his life into the night and ultimately forced to scramble for safety up and over the walls, with every chance of betraying them against the star sheen on the skyline of the furrow.

The first part of the approach went quickly and according to plan, except when he stopped by the river, where a new thought struck him. Remembering his tell-tale white face and knowing he was near an ample source of black potter's clay, he made his way to it, crouching low among the reeds. Removing his bush hat, he rubbed his face, nose, forehead, neck, all over with a layer of the black clay, put on his bush hat again, pulling the strap firmly underneath his chin so that there would be no danger of it being dislodged. From there he made his way swiftly but carefully to the furrow. He reached it with immense relief, yet he was so close to the great stream that he could not hear any sound except that of the infinitely objective onflowing water, and was deprived of one of his most valuable sources of intelligence in the dark. However, the further he moved from the river, the less insistent became its sound, and at the point where the old hippopotamus track ended against the furrow, he heard again the pitiful lowing of the cattle mixed with that strange upstart barking and howling of hungry jackals and always complaining hyenas.

Still he was afraid that once in the furrow the noise of rapidly flowing water might suppress all other sounds again. To his delight however the water there went by him so quietly and smoothly that he could hear it rippling only faintly around his legs as he went down it slowly, bent double so that no part of him could show above the walls, taking care also that he himself did no splashing. All again went well until he arrived at a point exactly opposite the Matabele kraals, half-way between them and the house. There suddenly he heard a murmur of human voices. Afraid that they might come from men on patrol, and perhaps on a beat that would take them right across his protective furrow, he paused at once to investigate.

All the while he had kept his eyes averted from stars and starlight, even their reflection in the water, focusing mostly on the darkness ahead, so that as he now crawled up the wall in order to peer over the top he found that he not only heard the voices but could see the kraals themselves, clearly outlined against the star sheen lying like water on the dark of the clearing between river and bush. He could not, of course, make out any detail in the kraals themselves but was startled to notice that they were not destroyed. Somehow he had assumed that they would have been.

There was nothing, in fact, to show any observant eye that they were not still what they had been the day before, the homes of scores of innocent Matabele people, looking as if their owners might still be asleep inside them, despite the unusual volume of noise coming from the cattle hard by in their enclosures. In the intervals between the cattle noises, François lying tensely alert, distinctly heard men talking to each other in low, fluent voices. By looking hard and long in the direction of the sound, he was able to make out the shapes of two men, facing each other, from their perches on the walls on either side of the wide gate to the main kraal. He could not gather what they were saying or even what language they used, but they sounded for all the world innocent enough, until his eyes made out at last the full silhouettes. Then he saw, high above the shoulders of each, the sharp pointed bracket made by bayonets fixed to service rifles.

His sense of the dangers of his undertaking heightened immeasurably. If there were men on guard so far away from the homestead, he could expect a far more highly organized and alert concentration of sentries closer in. He had done well to presume the worst, but even his worst now seemed inadequate in the face of what he had just discovered. Yet there was some relief in the fact that the sentries appeared utterly unsuspecting and at their ease. Above all they were stationary and not on patrol. With a heightened sense of danger, he slid slowly back into the water of the furrow and more deliberately and carefully than ever, resumed his way towards the garden, praying that however much greater the numbers of men on watch around the homestead were, they too would be stationary, at their ease and engaged in casual conversation.

Soon the voices vanished, the lowing of the cattle grew fainter and with this fading of sound, the ripple of the water round his legs began to sound ominously loud. Afraid that even so slight a sound might make him impervious to more significant noises, he began to stop every ten yards not only to listen carefully, but to crawl slowly up the wall of the furrow, first on one side and then the other, in order to look around for any indication of movement. But he heard and saw nothing. Even the amber glow had now gone behind the shadow thrown by the trees in the garden, particularly by the thick lines of fig trees round its perimeter. The fig trees and the orchards they sheltered were high, wide and dense. They obliterated the star sheen which had been so helpful, and stifled the cries of jackals and hyenas which he knew were massed on the edge of the clearing on the far side of his home. This absence of light and sound was a complication he would have given anything to avoid as the most critical moment of his advance approached. Had he been pushed to such a terrible alternative, he would have preferred a temporary blindness of vision to such a total deprivation of sound, for in the garden he was certain the blackness would overwhelm the brightest of starlight. The great tree shadows there would double the night, and only sound could help him not to blunder into guards who might well be posted there invisible in a position which would give them a field of vision over the wide clearing between the house and bush.

Despite the temptation to hasten that the sense of imminent danger brings to the human spirit, François, thanking life many times over in his heart for the lessons and examples of 'Bamuthi and Mopani, managed to accomplish with the utmost patience and vigilance the last fifty yards to the reservoir. At moments it was almost as if 'Bamuthi were stalking the enemy with him, and every now and then from close behind him came a voice full of concern to whisper: 'Careful, Little Feather, careful. He whose eye reaches the end of the spoor before his feet falls into the pit dug for game, and great heights have never been subdued by haste.'

All this helped to make François restrain himself and pause for a thorough examination of the night on either side of the furrow when he at last reached the edge of the reservoir itself.

Normally at the end of the day the reservoir would be empty as a result of the irrigation of the garden and the water from the furrow would flow into it, making a noise like a small waterfall, as it plunged over the high wide concrete walls of the basin, carved out of the slope from the hill which ended there on the level clearing. But obviously no irrigation had been done that day. The reservoir was full and close to overflowing, for the water entered without a murmur. It was as well because for François one of the most vulnerable moments of his venture had come. Before he could make the shelter of the wide row of fig trees and bushes which impinged here on either side of the reservoir, he would have to crawl with no cover at all for some ten yards. However flat he pressed himself down, however slowly and carefully he went, a really observant pair of eyes would have every chance of seeing him move over the bare concrete wall.

So he took his time to first look and listen into the night north of the furrow, the side farthest away from the homestead. He saw and heard nothing except the sound of water seeping as it always aid from the base of furrow and reservoir. He then did the same from the rim of the southern wall which overlooked the area between him and the house, where danger was likely to be the greatest. He was on the point of withdrawing, when some thirty yards away he saw a sort of fire-fly flicker among the leaves of the base of the trees. He stared unbelievingly because if fire-flies were causing the flickering, they must be of a giant species he had not met before, and he was convinced that he could not leave until he knew precisely what were those stitches of red flashing in and out of the black cloth distance. The explanation came almost immediately. Both the movement of the red light, still at one moment and then travelling upward to be held still and expand, before contracting and moving down again, told him that there were men smoking nearby, and judging by the way the fire moved in and out of the dark on a limited orbit, the smokers, like the men at the Matabele kraals too, were stationary, relaxed and not on patrol.

This, added to other instances of negligence he fancied he had already encountered, began to look as if the fallibility of his enemy might be greater than he had dared hope. Indeed he had to reprimand himself not to build too much of these instances in case they made him careless. The reprimand was vindicated at once for the glow of cigarettes suddenly vanished, and François was startled to find that he was so close to the smokers that he distinctly heard what he assumed was the sound of their bodies brushing against the leaves of the trees against which they must have been sitting before they jumped up.

Hard on this he heard the undisguised crunch of boots coming down the main path from the homestead to the reservoir, from somewhere not fifty yards beyond the smokers. He had a hunch that the men must have been smoking against orders, and would therefore have their attention entirely focused on re-establishing an appearance of innocence before the boots reached them. The conviction that this was perhaps the perfect moment, sent him as by reflex down the side of the furrow, to move quickly forward and crawl over the northern edge of the reservoir and lower himself down the far wall. All this was done at such a speed that the grip of his hands on the edge of the smooth concrete top nearly failed him. He only just saved himself from falling backwards into the fig trees and heavy bushes round their base and making a noise which those men could not have failed to hear. As it was the butt of his rifle, which he had slung horizontally across his shoulders from a sling shortened round his neck, tapped against the wall as he went down it, far too loudly for his comfort. Luckily it was only a single tap against the wall farthest away from the enemy, assuming of course that the enemy was only between him and his home. Nonetheless he was so alarmed by his carelessness and fearful of its consequences, that he crawled immediately on into some dense wild raisin bushes which had often hidden him during his games with his friends, to lie there with a quickened pulse, listening in case he had given himself away.

The men coming from the house with no effort at concealment, however, were making so much noise with their heavy tread on the ground, that the sound had gone unnoticed. They came on with an ominous deliberation and with no slackening to suggest that they were aware of anything abnormal.

Reassured, François used the shadow and cover of bushes, trees and the high wall to crawl farther to the eastern corner of the reservoir and take up a position, heavily camouflaged with shadow and leaves, to survey the comparatively open vegetable garden, its many paths and water furrows, right up to where it ended against the walls of the courtyard between his home, stables and outhouses.

The first thing he noticed was that the door leading into the courtyard must be open because in its frame stood a clear rectangle of amber upright in the dark, coming no doubt from the glow of lamps he had noticed from afar. He could only assume that the door was left open because the men approaching the smokers would be going back. He thought he would only have to lie there watching until the amber glow vanished again in order to know when the men left the garden and he could be on his way again in relative safety. He reached the comforting conclusion just as the newcomers and smokers met and a series of loud peremptory questions and answers, broke the silence. They were the sort of sounds he expected between officers and warrant officers and pickets on a round of inspection.

François assumed that the men doing the tour of inspection would return to the house once they had done with that particular picket, but he was dismayed when questions and answers ended, and the heavy tread recommenced, this time making for the reservoir. He promptly wriggled backwards deeper into the wild raisin bushes. He was hardly under their thickest cover when the boots arrived at the reservoir.

Convinced as he was that if the smokers had reported anything unusual, the boots would not have crunched their way so frankly, François's sense of danger compelled him to consider whether this frank approach could not be the best possible disguise for a more sinister design. Indeed this aspect appeared so serious, that he automatically disengaged the sling of his rifle from his neck and laid his gun in the crook of his right arm ready beside him. The heavy boots came to within five yards of where he lay, did not stop but went on parallel to the rows of great trees for some fifty yards in the direction of the far corner of the garden. There they halted and the same sort of question which had introduced the series of questions and answers broke the silence abruptly. That truly frightened François. He had observed the garden as closely as the area on the side of the house and had noticed nothing. It could only mean that men there had been more disciplined and kept a far better watch on the night than the others.

The conclusion became more pointed and agonizing when the question which he assumed must have drawn a reply, was answered so quietly that he could not hear it. Worse, the answer was not followed as before by any audible questions. For all he could tell, the night now was as silent as if no one were about and that slow, peaceful seeping of reassuring water from the walls near him was so faint that every now and then a remote echo of the complaining jackals and hyenas on the far side of his home reached him.

Whatever the reasons for this highly disquieting silence, François could do nothing except lie where he was. His only chance of avoiding detection should the patrol, made suspicious by the picket, as he now believed it had been, come back to the reservoir, was to keep as still as that francolin which he had shown Nonnie one bright summer's day more than a year ago, sitting without a shiver of down on her eggs, deep in the grass on that hillside overlooking Hunter's Drift, terrified and yet brave as a racing little pulse would allow it to be. It was extraordinary how apprehension sharpened his hearing because, within seconds, he knew that the men, doing their utmost not to make a sound, were coming towards him. Fortunately the men were not dressed for such an exercise. Their boots were too rigid and heavy, the bayonet scabbards on their hips as well as their water flasks, were not tied back and all emitting a faint rattle which François detected when they were still only half-way towards him.

As they came nearer, the more obvious became the line of their approach. Although they did not speak, François knew when the main body halted by the head of the reservoir and sent one man on his toes down the side of the track, since François could hear the grass and leaves distinctly swish back into position as his boots and legs brushed them aside.

Plainer still was the sound of the men presumably joined by the smokers, returning to the others by the reservoir. There were so many of them so close that he only needed to raise his head to see as well as hear them. Yet as long as he could hear there was no point but only danger in looking. He must not risk the movement of head and readjustment of body that looking would demand in case he rustled the bush which was packed close and thick with leaves all round him.

The two lots of men had hardly become one when a slight bustle of bodies and feet through the bush and grass round the reservoir and the far side of the rows of fig trees, told him that the area was being surrounded. For all its circumspection, the operation did not take long to complete and soon François was startled by the volume of sound that assailed him from all directions as the men, with no effort at secrecy began to close in on the reservoir, beating the grass and bushes with the butts of their rifles and calling quite audibly to one another to keep contact. Within seconds it sounded as if one pair of boots was going to walk straight into his own bush.

The temptation to prepare for this became almost overwhelming. Everything within him seemed to urge him to be ready both with his rifle and hunting knife to meet his enemy, quickly to do away with him and try to escape as fast as he could back into the night. But it was extraordinary how the vivid image of the francolin shone in his imagination at that moment and restrained him. The explanation he had once given to Nonnie that he needed the example of the birds and animals for sanity as well as for controlling his fears, impulsiveness and predilection for quick and spectacular answers to problems, was totally vindicated, in the severest test to which it could possibly be submitted. For francolin-wise, if he moved then it was only to press himself more closely to the gravel. Just when it seemed as if the boots would crash down on the bush and trample it flat, they stopped. Instead the butt of the rifle started to beat at the branches and leaves vigorously. Fortunately the elastic bush stood where its own wide shadow increased the blackness of the night and both were reinforced by the shadows of fig trees and their broad leaves which François had always admired so ardently and now loved all the more for their help, as well as the broad band of ink of the high wall of the reservoir itself. The owner of the boots could have seen nothing in the bush for after a brief period of frantic beating, the boots once more trod on, passing the bush to continue searching and beating the grass all along the wall of the reservoir, until a voice of command farther away stopped it, to François's amazement, in English.

It was not English English. The officer, because François somehow assumed that the owner of the voice had to be an officer, spoke with what he recognized as a very pronounced Scottish accent and turn of phrase. Scots had played a conspicuous role in pioneering the interior of Africa and many had visited Hunter's Drift over the years. François knew their inflection and idiom well. Moreover, he almost preferred it to other ways of speaking English, particularly the affected kind of superior officials in Government service, whom even Ousie-Johanna had condemned for making sounds as if with 'sweet potatoes in their mouths'. He also remembered Ouwa remarking to him once after a visit from a Scottish inspector of schools: 'You know, Coiske, there's something rather unfair about the Scottish way of speaking English. There is always a ring about it which predisposes one to accept implicitly that the owner of such a voice must always and inevitably be sincere and dependable. If I had to pass off a lie as a truth I could think of no better way than of doing it with a Scottish voice.'

It was indeed amazing how free of evil that voice sounded, as it called out, 'That will do, lads. Just gather round and I'll read you the book for the night.'

The voice rolled the r's and lengthened the o's in the Scots manner, particularly in the currency common in the slums of Glasgow.

The thrashing and beating stopped. The men rallied loudly to their officer. Almost immediately another voice, also in English but with heavy African inflections, excused itself, 'Sorry sah! I swear I saw something crawl along the wall of the dam and drop over the side, but I expect it was some wild animal. Sorry sah!'

'Ach, dinna fash yourself, mon,' the officer replied. 'You did the right thing, forbye. That lad and his doggie have still not been found. Until he is I want every man-jack of you to keep his eyes as wide open as you have done. That lad, you must remember, has lived here all his life and we know he is uncommonly experienced for his years, and knows the bush as few of us here do. We know he was here last night just before sundown. He and his doggie just could not have vanished into thin air. We've just got to find him or he'll give our show away. I warn you one and all, it's so important that if we don't, Chairman Mao back there in the house will have more than one of his pregnant thoughts to give us. Now back to your posts, lads, and keep a sharper look out than before. And you lot there, any old tabby would have told you it's easier to put out cigarettes than get rid of the smell of tobacco. If there's any more smoking on this caper tonight, I'll have you up in front of the Chairman.'

The discomfiture of the guards who had been smoking must have been obvious to the rest of the men because the reprimand was followed by a prolonged giggle, before the pickets made their way back to their posts and what sounded like two other men marched on towards the house. François had just time enough to crawl out into a place from which he could once more see the amber of the open door before it was darkened by the shapes of men passing through, and the glow vanished as the door shut behind them.

François trembled all over with relief. He had to force himself to lose precious minutes so as to calm down and find the heart to go on. One stresses the preciousness of time because, careful and deliberate as his progress had been up to now, it would look like racing compared to the rate his circumstances were about to impose upon him. He now had to crawl out of his shelter into the vegetable garden, unseen and without noise. For the men reprimanded by an officer who, judging by the responses they absolutely respected, were certain to be more watchful than ever. Once his way out was chosen, he would be compelled to go forward to the house not in feet but in inches.

He had a number of routes from which he could choose. He knew them all well enough to find and follow them blindfold, for he had used them and observed them so many times in the past that it was almost as if his memory of them was tangible, stretched out like his hand upwards in the dark before his eyes, and they lay there distinct like the lines in his palm waiting to be read by an expert palmist. He considered them all closely before finally deciding on the deepest and most direct one; the way, significantly enough, that was the lifeline among them because it was the main irrigation ditch leading from the reservoir right to the heart of the garden. It had the advantage of starting immediately among the shadows against the reservoir sluice, had walls on either side, not as high as those of the great furrow leading from the river, but substantial enough, and a floor which he was certain, despite the fact that no irrigating had been done that day, would be sufficiently wet to prevent its surface from grating or scraping underneath him as he crawled along it.

That decided, he acted at once, before delay could add to the loss of courage from which he was suffering and endanger his resolution. Using the cover close to the reservoir in order to test out precisely what kind of crawling and at what rate made the least noise, François went out along the ditch on his stomach until he was well clear of the protective shadow of trees, bushes and walls. He was deeply disturbed at how clear and transparent the night appeared to be after the darkness which had sheltered him so effectively. It was so clear indeed that some two hundred yards beyond the place where he was crawling, he could see at the far end of the garden the 'phantom' glimmer of the white of the walls and gables of his home and knew that if anything ever forced him to leave the furrow, the eyes of the sentries protected by the shadows of their posts could hardly fail to spot him. For a moment, it seemed as if his resolution would be crushed between two great irresistibles: on one hand a paralysis of fear and presentiment of the impossibility of his effort, and the urge to hasten through that dangerous zone of comparative light as fast as he could, even if he were somewhat noisy in the process.

Fortunately he had been schooled by men who believed that all creative training is meant to provide human beings with reflexes of behaviour which will rescue them in moments of crisis when reason and courage tend to desert them. He found himself guided not so much by a rational self as by all the experience and love 'Bamuthi and Mopani had put into his upbringing. This was so great that he ceased being afraid when he came to the heart of the garden. There he paused at a great crossway of lesser irrigation furrows leading away to all quarters of the garden, right up against the first of the many large beds of tomatoes. He realized how well and how far he had come without a sound and found the power to reason with himself again, while recovering his breath, because crawling in that way, however slowly, is one of the most exhausting exercises of which a human being is capable.

That done, he rose on his elbows to look about him. The white of the walls of his home was far more pronounced, the gables and the clear-cut line of the long thatched roof were black and distinct against the star sheen. Below and to the side of them, the door leading into the garden was still firmly shut, for no glow or flicker of light was visible there.

He looked back behind him. He searched the garden on both sides of him and saw clearly that it was empty of human beings. He noticed that in front of him the tomato beds had been trampled all over, presumably in the course of the attack, and that even the ditch ahead of him was heaped over with crushed and tangled tomato bushes. It was a complication, he felt bitterly, he might have been spared because if he were going to get on and underneath them as he had to, he would have to go even more slowly than before to avoid noise. He would have liked a longer rest, but this gratuitous complication decided him to move on at once. His one consolation was that once he edged his way underneath the broken tomato bushes, no one who came to inspect the garden would have much chance of discovering him in the shadow there.

It seemed many long hours, though it could hardly have been more than a quarter of one, before he painfully came to the end of the ditch up against a smaller sluice gate. Here he looked over into another empty water furrow which ran parallel to the walls of the courtyard and stables as well as the side of his house. He was within knocking distance of his home.

Very slowly he slid the gate without noise out of its frame, laid it softly in the bottom of the ditch behind him, and crawled forward into the furrow. There in the shadow of the high wide walls he paused once more to listen with an ear against their base for any murmur or vibration of sound that might be behind them. He heard nothing at all. He looked up and along the walls in case any light showed but the night there was as deprived of light as it was of sound. Again he was faced with several choices of action all of which appeared extremely hazardous.

For instance, he felt it would be fatal to try going through the door of the garden. He neither knew what might be waiting on the far side nor could ignore the fact that once he opened the door, his shadow would be as visible in the amber glow as those of his enemies had been. His dismissed climbing over the wall as he knew he could do from a half a dozen points in the garden where trees provided him convenient perches. None of those would do because he had to remember the greater glow of amber which he had seen from afar, also all the many eyes that might be awake and wide open within its circumference, and the fact that nothing could loom so great and so distinct against it as the silhouette of the human body meeting it on a skyline. There was another gate in the wall far to the east but he rejected that as well because it would bring him out into the gravelled drive passing by and round the flank of the house to come out by the front door.

There were other possibilities as well which were dismissed, and helped to prove that he really had only a single choice: that was to try a wooden half-door, half-window, level with the surface of the garden and used in summer to air the deep, vast cellar that ran the whole length of the basement of the house. The cellar was not only a cellar but a kind of store room for all sorts of supplies that had to be kept in the cool and were used directly in the house. Because of this, the cellar had one set of stone steps leading up to a door giving on to the big pantry, between the kitchen and the dining-room. But the main entrance, where the supplies could be carried from the trucks straight into the cellar, was at the end farthest away from him.

From where he lay, the half-door appeared tightly pressed against the smooth white wall. That did not perturb him; it had been firmly shut against him on countless occasions and over the years he had perfected a technique of opening it. This had been inspired by the fact that among the supplies in the cool were many bags of raisins and other dried fruits which came in vast quantities every year from his cousins in the far south. In a world without sweets, those dehydrated and crystallized fruits were the most tempting delicacies to François and his Matabele companions. Even the generous Ousie-Johanna was found guilty of distributing them in a miserly manner. Besides, there was always the incentive of getting the better of authority, however beloved, which had made François ultimately an expert at entry of this kind. Crawling up to the door now with his hunting knife in his hand, he could feel how ironic it was that as a child he had thought it dangerous, for if dangerous were the word for it then, what was he to call it now?

Though it was years since he had last forced this particular cellar entrance, he had forgotten none of the art. Deftly he worked his knife under the edge of the door, until it was under the loose, upright bolt in its shallow socket, and lifted it gently clear of the sill. Gently as he did it, the bolt groaned slightly in a way François thought a watchful person could not fail to hear. So he waited until he was quite certain that the sound had not travelled any distance, before he pulled the door slowly towards him, far more slowly than even he had expected to be necessary, because the hinges were somewhat rusty and on the verge of complaining too.

Careful to swing the door not an inch wider than necessary, he held it there while he looked all round him to make certain he had not been seen. In that clear star-sheen, trembling like distilled water in the dark over the garden, nothing moved at all. Quickly he slid over the sill, until he was resting his hands on the huge keg of brandy which, as the result of a visit to the cellar only the night before to fetch some wine and brandy for Sir James's return, he knew was standing there. He was then able to pull the rest of his body after him, keeping one foot on the sill so the door could not slam, turn over and seat himself on top of the keg. He bent over towards the door, put a hand on the bolt, brought it back into position and pushed the bolt home.

CHAPTER FOUR

An Amen of Annihilation

The physical darkness around him was as great as in the cave. It could only mean that all the other exits and entrances into the cellar were firmly shut. His problem now would be not to stumble over anything in the cellar and raise a clatter on his way to the steps leading up into the pantry. So convinced was he that the cellar was perfectly screened against the outside world and that if there were any human beings within it his entrance would have already compelled them to give themselves away, that he had no hesitation in striking a match and looking around him as he held the flame cupped in his hands.

The light was of the briefest but long enough to show him that a number of the wine racks which when he last saw them had been full of bottles of choice wine and brandy, were now empty. The enemy obviously had celebrated their victory liberally and should be sleeping soundly. As the match died out, he struck another and quickly made his way to the steps leading up into the pantry, noticing that the door was not shut but drawn to from without, for he not only saw a glint of light on the metal against the lintels but heard a faint murmur of voices beyond.

Reaching the bottom step, he sat down, laid his rifle carefully against it in a position in which if necessary, he was certain to find it quickly, took off his soft ankle boots, placed them next to the rifle, and then, hunting knife between his teeth, went catwise up the steps to the pantry door.

He was right. The door was not shut. Without hesitating he drew it towards him, because unlike the one which gave on to the garden, it was in constant use, well-oiled and not given to complaint. He had it barely a foot open and was getting ready to crawl round the edge into the shadow of the great flour-bins and cupboards, with shelves piled high above them, full of jars

75

of conserved fruit, jams, bottled vegetables, pickles and all the scores of things they used to see them through their comparatively barren winters, when he saw a distinct glow of light on the tiled floor and heard that murmur of voices more pronounced than ever. It could only mean that the door between the pantry and pantry hall which gave on to the kitchen on one side and dining-room on the other, was open as well, and that the voices were coming either from the kitchen or dining-room, if not both. His need for caution was greater than ever. Yet provided there was nobody within the long pantry itself, he should at the least get unobserved to the shelter of the cupboards which lined the walls on either side of the far door. He was about to enter the pantry when the dark was suddenly and violently illuminated by a brilliant light falling on the ceiling above him. Shocked, he pulled back into the black cellar.

Before he had time to question the cause of the light, the noise of a truck, approaching fast from the direction of Silverton Hill, told him what it was: headlights piercing the unshuttered windows of the pantry. Shaken but reassured, François got to his feet, pushed the door to so that there was only a crack wide enough for him to peer through. He saw then why the window was not shuttered. In the brilliant light playing on ceiling and walls, he looked on a tall wide window, glass shattered and frame splintered, presumably by rifle- and machine-gun fire. The shelves immediately opposite him held only shattered bottles and jars, their contents scattered over the tops of the cupboards below, and the tiled floor itself covered with fragments of broken glass.

For a moment, it looked as if he would have to abandon entering the house from that end, because he could not possibly walk in his socks over such a floor without injuring the soles of feet he needed as never before, and even if he returned for his boots, the broken glass would undoubtedly grind and crunch underfoot so much that he would certainly be heard. By this time the light from the oncoming truck had lit up the pantry so widely that he saw it as if by daylight. Thank Heaven, the damage was merely in that one corner by the window and he would have just room enough, provided he kept to his side of the room, to cross the jagged fragments of glass on a floor two inches or more thick with layers of jams and preserves. He reached this conclusion as the lights of the truck vanished and he heard it pull up abruptly in the courtyard, almost underneath the shattered window.

He heard the doors of the truck being flung open, men jumping out and then a familiar voice bantering in that maddeningly calm, deliberate and ironic tone that appeared fundamental to it, 'So there you are at last, my guid officer and gentleman of France. And not one wee bit too soon. Even our philosophic Chairman's philosophy is looking somewhat down at heel on your account.'

The answer was in fluent English, though with a marked French accent. 'Unfortunately, it was not a philosophic exercise on which I was engaged, *mon cher*.'

There was enough of an implication of a rebuke in the remark to make the Scottish voice say, rather regretfully, 'As if I dinna ken that. Aye, here too I've been wishing that we had a little more philosophy and less action. But how did you get on?'

'What is it that you would wish? We killed them all as you, I expect, did here, but it took all day. There were so many of them and they scattered and hid in so many places, that we were not done until sundown.'

'The lot?' The Scottish voice sharpened noticeably. 'What do you mean by that?'

The Frenchman was obviously finding the questioning distasteful and said curtly, 'I pray it of you to excuse. You will hear the history soon enough when I speak of it to our comrade-in-chief inside. All that is necessary to say now is that it was long and hard work and . . .'

'Work! You call it just work?' The Scottish voice lost its banter and rose on a note of mixed surprise and condemnation. 'It's the understatement of centuries. Guid God, mon . . .'

He was interrupted in his turn, rather wearily by the Frenchman. With a bleak note of deprivation in his voice that touched even François's unbearably tense and pre-determined heart, he said, 'Yes, work, *mon cher*, nothing but work. The only work I have ever known. I wish . . .' The voice paused, rejected the longing as the life and its owner must have rejected it, and resumed, 'Yes, work, and such hard work today that I have a hunger formidable and a thirst sensational to quench.'

'And so you shall. So you shall,' the Scottish voice replied more understandingly as they walked past the window, so close that François heard the man being patted on the back before the Scottish voice added, 'I tell you, mon. There's wine enough for even a French palate waiting inside. More bottles indeed to choose from than even our great Chairman has thoughts for our future.'

With that they were silent. François heard them walking quickly on to climb the steps on to the stoep outside the kitchen, he felt the vibrations of their tread on the broad boards in the kitchen floor and the sound of feet at the end of the apparently open pantry door, going straight into the dining-room, the door of which must have been left wide open too, or he would have heard the great lock being turned.

If ever François was to get properly into the pantry and above all the shelter of those cupboards, the moment was as good as it was ever going to be, for the attention of the people inside would be entirely concentrated on the French officer, and the report he brought.

Once more, François pulled the door just wide enough for him to crawl through. Although the glow from the light of the lamps in the dining-room was strong enough to gleam on the broken glass and the layers of jam on the floor in the corner, the shadows there under that dark, thick wall were solid enough, he was certain, not to show him up in the dim light.

It was one of the fastest crawls he had ever done, and well that it was so. He was hardly flat on his stomach beside the cupboards by the door opposite the dining-room entrance, when the half-open dining-room door swung wide and light fell over the sill. Someone with a heavy tread went quickly by and entered the kitchen, where he started giving orders in English, but with an African accent, to men who must be acting as cooks and kitchen hands.

At the same time a lively conversation, or perhaps cross-examination would be a better word, started up in the dining-room. With his enemies divided between the far end of the kitchen and dining-room, François thought he would risk crawling out into the entrance of the hall to try to hear, and best of all see, what was happening beyond. Knowing his home so well and having done things in his childhood not unlike what he was attempting now, he could tell to a split-second and a millimetre how long and how far he could go without being caught, particularly now that his senses and reflexes were at their most intense under the stimulation of his peril.

He wriggled round the cupboards, and half-way out of the pantry door stopped where he was certain he could withdraw instantly into the pantry if necessary, as a tortoise withdraws its head and neck into its shell. At the far end of the table where Ouwa had always sat, was a man with a face which he had seen only twice before but could never forget. It was the Chinese face first seen on the hillock in the valley of the Mist of Death on the way to uLangalibalela, and then again at the back of a truck which he and 'Bamuthi had once hauled out of the mud beyond the ford with their oxen and thereby unwittingly aided the disaster which had overtaken them that day.

It was extraordinary how, even in his tragic plight and with the horror of such an imposition in Ouwa's place, François once again remarked how superior that Chinese person, obviously the Scottish officer's 'Chairman', looked in comparison with the men sitting on either side of the table. Apart from the Scottish and French officers there were eight others, all African. Without exception their uniforms were dirty, they themselves unwashed, unshaven, uncouth and their faces embittered and unhappy. Even the Scot and the Frenchman, standing on either side of the Chinese person's chair, looked little better. It would have been easier for François, perhaps, had they not in their air of tiredness and tragedy looked more like the monsters their deeds had made them in his imagination. He had to concentrate on their obvious leader to recover an unmixed feeling of purpose. This person, the Chinese, was immaculate in his sky-blue tunic, red star over the breast pocket, and dark hair cut short, neatly parted and brushed. His face, even in that lamplight, looked as if he had just come fresh out of a bath. The whole expression was serene, the eyes steady and untroubled and the general bearing of the man so dignified and impressive as almost to be exalted and Olympian, to an extent that deprived him of human qualification as far as François was concerned.

Without looking at the two officers beside him, his head merely turning slightly towards whoever was speaking, he was listening to the French officer's reports, again given in English. Obviously, with so many nationalities and races incorporated into the forces under his command (François could tell that among the African officers alone, there were not two of the same tribe) English served as their Esperanto.

François had not to listen long to be confirmed in what he had already suspected. The French officer had been in charge of the force sent to attack the coloured families completing the building of Sir James's dream retreat at Silverton Hill. No one among that gay, light-hearted, colourful group of warm and affectionate human beings, had been allowed to live, for what else could have made the Scottish officer exclaim involuntarily, 'You didna' spare even a bairn among 'em? Ne'er a bairn? You bonnie French gentleman.'

The French officer for a moment forgot he was reporting to a superior officer. He turned fiercely defensive towards the Scot and spoke with a passion which clearly showed how distasteful he had found the business, 'Since seventeen, when I joined the Foreign Legion, it is nearly forty years now that I have made war, year in and year out, nothing but war and more war. I have seen more of war and nothing but war than anyone in this room, is it not? And I assure you, still I look for a way of making war which does not take life. If you can tell me of a way as our chefs would say, of making the omelette of war without breaking the eggs, please be so kind as to tell me of it.'

'But Guid God, lad,' the Scottish officer replied, unappeased, 'surely you need not break all the eggs in the larder to make one miserable omelette.'

'Ah, but I had my orders you see, *mon cher*, as you had yours. Did you not break all of your eggs here too today?'

The point must have gone home for the Scot did not answer for the moment and before he could think of one the Chinese at the head of the table, ignoring the Frenchman's reply, turned to look at the Scot, as if he had had trouble on this particular score before that day, and said slowly, in a sing-song voice, 'Velly funny, Mister Lauder, velly funny. Only we have no time to be funny. We have more serious things to discuss. I told you before: now we take little life so not to take much later on. When real war starts we take proper prisoners. I will not tell you again!'

There François had to retreat backwards into the shelter of the pantry. The talking in the kitchen suddenly stopped and someone started back towards the dining-room. From his shelter, convinced that flat on the floor with blackened face and in the shadows, no one would have mind or other incentive to look and discover him, he dared to peer round the corner of the cupboard out of a hunch that perhaps the most important part of what the night could tell him was still to come. Already the conversation in the dining-room had fulfilled the main part of his mission, and he could no longer doubt that in addition to the massacre at Silverton Hill, there were no survivors left from among his own people at Hunter's Drift. All of course had been foreseen and foresuffered in the course of the day behind him, so that the final confirmation did not really add to the emotional consequence of the tragedy except to swell his resolution to do what he could to hurt the people responsible and, as a preliminary to hurting, find out all he could about their plans.

In that state, he saw the silhouette of a man pass through the hall into the dining-room, making no effort to shut the door behind him, and walk up to the head of the table, where he placed a large tray laden with wine, bread, butter, cheese, jam and pink slices of biltong. That done, he stepped back to stand still somewhere out of sight in the shadows against the wall while the Chinese, a map wide open in front of him, started to explain in his slow, fastidious sing-song manner what his plan was.

He took his time, so much so indeed that François feared at one moment that he might have to leave before the end, in case the darkness ran out on him for his journey back to the cave. As he listened, he was more and more horrified at the subtlety, cunning and breadth of the scheme. His horror was made more terrible with disgust when he heard that apparently among the people planning the operation was a kinsman of 'Bamuthi from Osebeni, chosen because he knew the way of life and nature of farming at Hunter's Drift. François remembered meeting the man who had stayed with 'Bamuthi often when he was young and helped at the farm. Even Ouwa had praised the man as living proof of the great natural intelligence of African people, because even with the little schooling he received as a boy, and a little coaching too, from Ouwa, he had proved himself so gifted that the people at Osebeni, as well as Lammie and Ouwa had combined to send him to one of the rare schools and colleges for Africans in the country. There he had lived fully up to his promise and become a teacher himself. He returned as such, on annual vacation, to Osebeni, and would visit his people at Hunter's Drift as well. Gradually the visits became less frequent and then finally ceased. The man even stopped writing in the end and all that was known of him came from hearsay and rumour, of which the last and most sustained was that he had become an influential political leader and as such had been forced ultimately to leave the country.

His name cropped up early on when the Chinese explained that it was his plan to rest his forces for a week at Hunter's Drift and Silverton Hill. They had come long and far and here they had a wonderful opportunity not only to rest undiscovered but had enough food and supplies to restore their energies.

At that point the Scottish officer, Mr Lauder, as François now took his name to be, unabashed as ever, interjected, not without some sarcasm: 'And perhaps, the august chairman will condescend to tell us what the people on the railway and the great mining city are going to do when the supplies which they have been receiving without a break every day for so many years from here, have not turned up? Surely our illustrious chairman will have spared one of his great thoughts for such an eventuality?'

'Always, Mister Lauder, you so funny,' the Chinese replied, apparently unperturbed. 'But that precisely is what your chairman has done.'

François amazed heard then the first mention of 'Bamuthi's kinsman. With this man in charge, the cows that had been gathered in the kraal, would be properly milked at first light. Men expert at milking had already been detailed for the purpose, others would be set to work in the gardens which fortunately had only been partially damaged, to gather vegetables and fruit.

The cattle would be sent out to graze under men dressed more or less like Matabele herdsmen. The irrigation furrows would be filled with water again and all day long it would look from a distance as if Hunter's Drift were its full productive self. In the evening, 'Bamuthi's kinsman himself would take milk and fresh supplies, double the normal quantity, to the railway siding with many apologies and plausible explanations of why there had been an interruption.

Meanwhile the reinforcements and supplies coming down the trail behind them from the north and west could be assembled in the bush all round Hunter's Drift. When they were complete the great army would resume their advance undetected and achieve the military perfection of surprise. One small column would go due east, surround and capture the main camp in Mopani's reserve to cut the only telephone line to the world beyond. The main body would first overwhelm Hunter's Drift Siding and then push on straight for the mining city, surround it at night, attack at dawn and capture it, not quite as they had destroyed these two small outposts so successfully that day, for the Chairman added: 'Then and only then, Mister Lauder, you can take all prisoners you want.'

It was the first attempt at a lighter tone that evening, but still the critical Scottish voice wanted to know what was going to happen if any trader making his way north by truck, or any visitors (since they knew from the intelligence they had collected over the years that Hunter's Drift was a place much favoured by visitors), came closer and saw what a sham it all was. What were they going to do then?

The answer, delivered in that maddeningly meticulous Chinese way again was that, of course, first thing in the morning a patrol would be sent out all the way down Hunter's Drift Road to prevent just that as well as to leave some scouts behind to keep the main camp in Mopani's reserve under observation. Another patrol would do the same on the road running towards the railway siding and then of course the search for that boy would be widened and speeded up, because until he was found he was the greatest danger of the news leaking out to the world beyond.

'And when we find the laddie, as nae doot we shall,' the Scot interrupted, 'ye will not be thinking of taking his life as well, now, will ye? He surely is the one prisoner we can afford to keep.'

'No, Mister Lauder, no,' the Chairman, staring in front of him across the table, answered in that monotonous, unemotional sing-song voice. 'No. He is one life we must take. If we do not take now then one day he tell what happen today, and only what we say happen must be told to world.'

There followed a long silence in which François heard plainly the wine gurgling out of a bottle as glasses were being refilled, and then a series of questions were asked from all sides of the table, which François did not wait to hear. He knew all that was important to know, far more than he had ever dreamt of hearing. There was only one thing to be done, to get away as fast as he could.

So he glided backwards into the pantry, turned about, wriggled quickly to the cellar door, through it and once his hand touched the steps he came quietly to his feet, pushed the door to exactly as it had been when he had first found it, made his way to the bottom and put on his shoes. To his amazement, his hands and fingers trembled so violently, he did not know whether with fear, horror or anger, but probably with a volcanic compound of all three, that he could hardly fasten the laces properly. He took up his rifle and was about to make for the half-door into the garden when a thought, greater even than any of the other turbulent emotions within him, struck him and made him stand still, aghast. He had to stop those people from using Hunter's Drift as a camouflage for the terrible plan the Chinese had unfolded in the dining-room. Even more than the thought, what took away his breath was that he seemed to know at once exactly what to do to stop them.

There were two ways. First he could set his home on fire. 'Home?' From the moment he had seen the Chinese officer in Ouwa's place at the head of the table, all that home meant to him had died a sudden death. He had no emotion left to impede his thought of destroying it.

Among the straw and packing cases which were piled in the cellar he could start such a fire as the men above would find difficult to put out. But there was just a chance that the smoke and flame might give him away before he had escaped, and that did not make the plan as appealing as another. This was more desperate and dangerous but also more effective.

In the far corner by the great double door was a huge, old wagon chest of ironwood. This chest was always full of dynamite and the fuses used for the blasting they had to do from time to time to make new irrigation furrows through the rock as well as to quarry the gravel for their roads. The dynamite was kept in the cellar because it was the coolest and driest place with the smallest variations of temperature on the farm. François knew even as a child, for it had been impressed on him so often, that if dynamite were not kept in such conditions it could become highly unstable and dangerous. It was weeks since he had last looked into that box and found it full. No blasting had been done since and he safely assumed it would still be full.

The one trouble about this plan was that the box was extremely well made, of the hardest wood in Africa and, because of its contents, always locked. The lock was by far the most complicated and strongest of the few locks in the house. For Hunter's Drift itself was never locked, even in his parents' absence. As Ouwa had always been so fond of saying, 'Life in the bush is far safer and more honest than in any city in Africa.' In all the years they had been there, not even the over-scrupulous Ousie-Johanna had suspicions of anything important being stolen, unless it was from her supplies of dried and preserved fruit. The great-hearted old lady of the kitchen, the Princess of the Pots, always kept that kind of suspicion to herself for the tenderest of reasons.

Before deciding on a plan, he had to see whether he could get at the dynamite. If he failed, it would have to be a fire. Whatever the risks to himself, he was not going to leave the house to evil men for an evil use. (It was remarkable how quickly they lost their qualifications for humanity when he no longer had his eyes upon them.) That decided, he struck a match and picked out a way clear of obstacles. When the match died between his hands, he waited just an instant for the effect of the flare on his vision to weaken before going carefully on hands and knees in the direction in which he had aligned his body. Thank God, he managed to do so without a clatter. Far sooner than he expected, his left hand fastened on the chest.

Quickly he felt the lock, and, indeed, it was firmly shut. He had to light another match while he tried to insert the blade of his hunting knife into one of the screws which kept the hasp in place. For a moment he thought the screw was not going to budge. He was near despair when at last the screw gave and allowed itself to be turned. Then, as fast as he could, he extracted one screw after another until both hasp and lock fell into the palm of his outstretched hand.

He opened the chest and hastily extracted a carton full of dynamite sticks, found the instantaneous detonating fuse – he had so often participated in this kind of work that the preparation presented no problem – wrapped it round the dynamite and then joined it securely to the end of a roll of ordinary blasting fuse, duly capped. He reinserted the roll into its place in the chest and crawled backwards, unwinding the roll as he moved to the half-door giving on to the garden. To his immense relief, the fuse stretched three-quarters of the way so that from the time he lit it to the moment when it would ignite its detonating counterpart, to set off the charge of dynamite in the chest, he would have at the least ten minutes to a quarter of an hour for his get-away.

That was little enough, considering the slow rate at which he would have to crawl through the garden. Yet he was concerned not so much with getting out of the garden as to be far enough away from his home not to be injured, or even killed, by the explosion, which would be colossal. Once the charge went off, he felt that the panic among the men would be so great and the need for rescuing what remained of life in the shattered house so urgent that they would give no further thought for a time to him, or anything else abroad in the night.

He just had to be certain before he lit the fuse that there was nobody about in the garden to delay his escape through the half-door itself. So, placing the end of the fuse carefully on the hilt of his knife, he went to the half-door, undid the bolt again and opened the door slowly, and looked out.

Thank Heaven he had done so! There were men on the main path, already so close to the house that he quickly pulled the door towards him until only the smallest of cracks was left to peer through. Had they seen anything? Were they coming back to report some new suspicion that would send another patrol out into the night? Had he come so far and so close to accomplishing what he had set out to do and indeed so much more, and now was not going to be allowed to see it through?

It was, perhaps, the most agonizing of many agonizing moments of the long hours behind him. Although the noise of boots told him the men were walking briskly to the main door in the garden wall, they went by far too slowly for his racing heart. Luckily, when the terrible retarded moment came and the door of the garden was at last open and the men stood briefly black in the glow from the house beyond, before they vanished and the door was shut again, he was instantly calm again with hope. Yet he waited in case their mission was not mere routine and for the hundredth time thanked Heaven for Mopani and 'Bamuthi's teaching that patience was not only nature's greatest prescription of wisdom but often also the quickest possible solution of the most urgent problems.

Some five minutes later the gate opened again, and the same number of men passed through the rectangle of amber but not the same men. François could tell that from the kind of shadow they made against the glow, brief as it was. The men marched off briskly down the main path so that he felt he had every right to assume he had merely been witnessing a change of guard, and that he could not have been presented with a better moment for his exit.

Accordingly, he ducked down into the cellar, groped his way back to his knife, found the end of the fuse and quickly lit it. It started off spluttering in such a manner that to François's exaggerated sense of hearing it made a crackling that he feared must be audible outside and perhaps even in the rooms above. Near panic, he drove his knife back into his sheath and was down on his hands and knees crawling as fast as he could to the half-door. Reaching it, he opened it deftly and luckily in the act of opening, became calm enough again, because close as he was to the burning fuse, flashing in the dark like a swarm of tiny fire flies as it spluttered on its way among wine-racks, barrels, kegs, vats, packing cases and supplies of all kinds to the wagon chest invisible in the darkness beyond, he no longer heard it. Above all its train of sparks cast no reflection on the darkness and could only be visible to eyes looking directly down into the cellar floor itself.

With that consoling thought he was through the half-door, composed enough to force the bolt back into its catch and then crawling into the ditch and, for all his exhortation to the contrary, going faster than he had come to the centre of the garden. If he could only get there before the dynamite went up, he felt he had a fair chance of survival.

Had there been some Olympic record for crawling on one's stomach, François's progress along the ditch to the comparative safety of the centre of the garden would surely have broken it. Yet he himself continued to feel as if he were some sort of insect struggling through a sea of treacle. So great was this feeling of slowness as well as his sense of the vital necessity of getting as far from the house as possible before the explosion came, that he would not allow himself a pause for breath as he had done on the way in. Exhausted as he became, something from he knew not where provided him with energy to keep on crawling. The sound of his heart and his blood in his ears became so loud that he was convinced he must be deaf to all other sound. All else was utterly still and he was amazed suddenly to himself at the crossways of the various furrows and ditches on the edge of the great tomato beds at the centre of the garden with the explosion from the house still to come.

There he had reached a distance from the house at which he might be relatively safe from the effects of the explosion, yet even then he did not pause for breath. Instead of following the ditch which had brought him from the reservoir, he chose a furrow leading directly to the end of the garden and orchard on the edge of the clearing between the homelands and the bush, because that was the shortest way to the cave. It meant crossing the clearing without the comforting shelter of the walls of the main irrigation ditch and increasing the risks of being seen. But he took to these readily because he was convinced that one certain consequence of the explosion would be to draw every guard and sentry towards his shattered headquarters, and that the shortest and quickest way out therefore would also be the safest. Once the panic caused by the explosion had passed and the rescue work done, his enemies would be free to give their minds to the causes of the explosion. That could only lead to one conclusion: a conclusion pointed at him, for what other explanation could there possibly be? Then, it was certain, the most intensive of searches would immediately be mounted.

He had gone some twenty yards along his new course, sweating from exhaustion and wondering how much longer he could go on, as well as worrying increasingly that something may have gone wrong with his fuse, for why had the explosion not yet come, when he was horrified to hear a muffled sort of shouting from the direction of the house. It sounded very much as if someone were in the cellar and giving an hysterical alarm.

The shout was immediately answered by others, louder, though still somewhat muffled, suggesting that though they were still coming from within the house, they were from persons on a higher level, he assumed the level of dining-room and kitchen. Hardly had these shouts died away when, in that silence of steel of what must now be the closing hours of the night, he heard first a peremptory blast on a military whistle and a great cry in a voice which he recognized from the way it rolled its 'r's', even at that pitch and volume, to be that of a Scot. 'Guard! Stand to! Guard!'

François's heart, as 'Bamuthi would have said, turned black on him then. He could not doubt that someone had gone into the cellar, probably for more wine, and discovered his fuse, wrenched it out of its charge and rushed to warn the officers he had seen in conference in the dining-room above. The great search he had half-feared was being organized at that very moment, he was certain, and within minutes would be set in motion all round house and garden. His despair and frustration were so great then that, added to physical exhaustion, the power to crawl seemed to have left him. But the terrible conviction of failure had hardly overwhelmed him when, even there where he lay with his eyes on a black, dank irrigation furrow, he was blinded by a violent flash of light. It was followed by a blast so powerful that the walls of the furrow above him were stripped of all their covering bushes and a wave of shock tore at his tough whipcord jacket so that his belt was jerked upwards into his armpits. The jacket itself was thrown like a sack over his head, the strap of his hat was torn from its clasp and carried away into the darkness ahead.

Stunned, he felt he would never be able to see or hear again but he could indeed hear, for some long seconds later, fragments of what had once been his home spattered down like hail all round him. One half brick landed on the earth wall of the furrow beside him, shooting dirt like buckshot stinging against his cheek and head. There followed a moment of strange, awesome silence, until from the great smooth cliff face where the irrigation furrow left the river, came the echo of the explosion. Though it was only an echo from far away, the volume and slow intensity of its rumble was like an omen of annihilation. It was quickly followed by all kinds of cries and shouts of dismay and outrage and bewildered commands. What was of more immediate importance to François, there appeared from the direction of the reservoir on his left, as well as the far end of the garden ahead and the wall to his right, diminished as his senses were by the blast, the shapes of men making no effort at disguise. They were running as fast as ditches and vegetable beds would allow them, straight towards his shattered home.

François propped himself on his elbows, certain now that no one would have eyes and ears for him. He watched the shapes draw level and pass by him on all sides before turning his head, determined to make certain that they had all indeed gone back to their base. He was in time to see the first flames of fire flower proudly in the dark above the house.

Obviously there was soon going to be such a blaze that the garden would be lit as if by day. The thought sent him to his feet and doubling down a furrow he knew by heart. He paused only to pick up his hat some fifty feet from where he had lain and then hurried on, passing through the rows of fig trees, climbing over the last wall and for the first time felt he could pause purely to rest.

Even so he did not rest long. He suspected that the moment daylight came a new search for him would be started. This time, the men would not look for him in the text-book military manner as the day before, but set the best trackers among their soldiers – and most Africans from the interior were inspired

trackers – to cast about for spoor of him, and then by methodically following the signs he could not avoid leaving behind,
track him down. So, instead of preparing to go straight back to
the cave which was so temptingly near, on a direct line from
where he was, François set off in the opposite direction, to carry
him on a parallel course, past the house towards the bush, and
right away from the cave. He would have liked more rest but
from the way the fire was soaring up and lighting up the landscape, he knew he could not afford to wait.

Once more running, he took to a cattle trail which led away
from the old kraals in his chosen direction. When clear of the
garden wall, where the fire was beginning to propel waves of
light to break over the darkness above the clearing, he slowed
down to make himself as inconspicuous as possible by bending
double and carrying his rifle in his hand at the trail. The precaution seemed all the more urgent, because all the shouting
and screaming had died away. All he heard was the crackling of
flames and this somehow told him that the men there were
already organized into rescue parties and order being brought
to the situation.

The temptation to stop, and look back to see if there might
not already be men between him and the flames was great, but
he resisted it. He needed all he had of vision for the track in
order to travel as fast as possible. Besides, even more than the
enemy just then, he feared he would not have the strength, fit as
he was, to go on again fast enough to save himself if he paused
to look back. However, his desperation enabled him to cross the
clearing and reach the cover of the bush.

Only then did he allow himself to feel exhaustion, as even he
had never known it. It was almost too much for him to turn
over on to his stomach, crawl into the shelter of a bush right on
the fringe of the clearing and, gasping for breath, compel himself to look back and make certain that he had not been followed.

The fire now stood high, wide and awesome. The clearing was
lit as a stage. One quick glance was enough to show it empty.

At once his head fell back on his arms, and he lay prone until
his breathing was more or less normal again. Yet even then he
felt paralysed with a fatigue of monstrous proportions because

it was a fatigue of body joined to an immense weariness of heart and mind. He was, without knowing it, a victim of an instinctive provision in the life of man which, in moments of danger, suppresses all thoughts and emotions that might confuse the appropriate reaction to the situation and so make the human response inadequate for survival. But once the danger is overcome, all that has been irrelevant to the immediate need – the fear, the anguish, the physical pain, the fatigue and all the other subtle variations of these things that are held back to form a volcanic charge of negation, erupt as another challenge.

This was so overwhelming in François's case that it seemed to him that he lay there for hours, eyes shut, head pressed on his arm and body clinging to the earth like a frightened child against its mother. He felt as if he would never be able to separate himself from his native earth because just then it seemed the only solid and unchanging substance left in a shattered world. He was terrified that he would not have the strength of mind or body to deny himself the sense of comfort and support which he derived in the process, and he might have gone on lying there, irresolute behind the cover of the bush far too long for his safety, had it not been for the fire.

The fire had grown so great that the lids of his eyes suddenly seemed translucent and the darkness into which his fatigue had plunged him diminished. He opened his eyes wide, raised his head and looked on the greatest peak of flame he had ever seen. He knew, of course, that he had started the fire. Yet it looked now as if some other force had joined in it to make it more than a fire of thatch and wood. All feeling of his predicament and fatigue were eliminated by the wonder of the magnitude and terrible beauty of it. He found himself observing it as if it were a supernatural beacon on the marches of some strange no-man's area of life. Indeed, somewhere far back, a memory prompted him, as if he were an actor who had forgotten his lines, that there was some Biblical illustration connected with it. And at once all was plain. At that precise moment, the long, pointed blade of flame prodding the stars became a sword, the whole surround of fire sustaining it, a carving by light out of darkness, another Gothic version in flame of the archangel mounted over

92

the gate of the garden at the beginning of the day man was expelled from it for ever.

Watching the archangelic shape of fire reach still higher and the vast garden and orchards of his own beginning with its surround of his beloved fig trees allegorical with flame, the feeling that invaded François of being sentenced to irrevocable exile was too much. He knew instantly then, not as thought but as an acute physical pain, that never again could there be a return to a world of innocence where animal, bird, flower, fruit and men had been so at one as at Hunter's Drift. And, at that moment, the discharge of emotion, stress and fatigue that would have interfered with his efficiency earlier on left him without shield against this first sword-thrust of banishment.

All at once he was crying as he had never cried before. It was just as well that he was alone and unobserved then, and that this equinoctial storm of heart and mind in a bitter seasonal transition could sweep through him with no outside restraint, and that he had just enough time there in the dark to let it run its natural course.

As a result, his unconditional surrender to natural emotion, which the civilized human being would have rejected as weakness, became a source of new strength. Indeed, it had so cathartic an effect that, when it ended, his fatigue, great as it was, had been blown over the horizon of his mind and he was free to think of the urgent future. How free was clear from the fact that he suddenly seized his rifle and jumped to his feet. He took a last look across the still empty clearing and the sword of flame plunged up to its hilt into the sky. Instinctively he made a sign of the cross against the night, not in Nonnie's but in Xhabbo's way, with the whole of his hand, palm wide open and fingers together as if the 'asking' and 'tapping' in him had met in order to exorcize the last spell of negation of an enchanted past upon this new, locked-out self. And he could almost hear 'Bamuthi's voice in his ear repeating one of his favourite sayings as it had so often done in tones of gravity, heavy enough to match the seriousness he himself attached to its truth. 'The child can look back straight to the river, the man always has eyes only for the crooked footpath and the hills in front.'

Then he promptly turned his back on his home and went

along the narrow track deeper into the bush. He made no effort to go silently, or to conceal his spoor, until he came, in a roundabout way, to the place where he had once hidden Xhabbo after rescuing him from the lion trap. There, he stepped carefully on to the first outcropping of stone on to the flank of the hill leading up to the cave. Knowing the ground so well, he managed to step from one stone to the other not once putting his feet to the earth, bushes or grass in between. He had no objection to the trackers, which the enemy would have on his spoor in the morning, discovering any tracks of his in the bush below. But for obvious reasons it was more imperative than ever that he should leave no fresh mark or indication of the faintest kind to draw the enemy's attention to the hill. Once incited into examining the hill, he was convinced that his enemies would have trackers inspired enough to discover enough signs to lead them to the cave.

Somehow he had to draw them away from the hill, and convince them that, after the destruction of his home, he had left the area for good. He had heard enough to know that his enemies were exceedingly well-informed about the detail of life at Hunter's Drift. After all, they had as a source of intelligence 'Bamuthi's kinsman from Osebeni, who had joined forces with them. For instance they knew all about Hintza and the fact that the two of them were inseparable. They could not, therefore, fail to know about his relationship with Mopani, who, after all, had bred Hintza. Indeed, Mopani and his well-equipped headquarters in the vast game reserve, with its ample communications by telephone with the outside world, itself was an urgent military objective if the enemy were to secure the period of unobserved rest and regrouping which he had heard them discuss only a few hours before. They must already have planned to cut the communications between Mopani's camp and the outside world as soon as possible, and respect for detail of which he already had such terrifying evidence. François was certain that they must have reckoned with the probability that Mopani's main camp would have been the obvious place for François to turn for help.

He would, of course, have preferred to set out for Mopani's headquarters in a manner which would make it as hard as possible for his enemies to track him down. He knew various, secret approaches along which it would have been difficult for the enemy to overtake him. But, alas, if he was to draw their attention away from his hiding place that was now out of the question. He would have to take the shortest route to Mopani's camp so as to make it obvious to even the most simple-minded of African trackers that he had left the area. If he did that, he was certain that his friends in the cave had a good chance of remaining undiscovered long enough for the enemy to move on and any garrison they left behind at Hunter's Drift would become so relaxed that Xhabbo would find an opportunity of leading Nonnie and Nuin-Tara out of the cave without danger of detection.

His conviction in this regard was absolute. Nothing he had overheard on his reconnaisance showed that the enemy were aware of the existence of Xhabbo, Nuin-Tara, or even of Nonnie. Thank Heaven, Nonnie and her father had arrived at Hunter's Drift so late the previous night and, in any case, had been out of the district for so long, that even 'Bamuthi's kins-man could not have known of Nonnie's return.

What he had to do, therefore, was to return to the cave, tell Xhabbo what had happened and how they had to change their plans. Then he would have to get Hintza out of the cave as soon as possible to accompany him on his way to Mopani's camp because no set of tracks of his own, however plain, was going to convince his well-informed enemy, unless accompanied by those of his faithful dog.

Moreover, he realized that he had little time to arrange all this. He had to reckon with the fact that the explosion and fire that was still standing there, so high in the night, must have woken everybody in the cave and that he could find himself involved in argument and discussion with his companions that would take more time than he could afford. Already the stars he knew so well showed him that he had not much more than an hour or two of darkness left, and he would have to be on his way before dawn. He was convinced that the greatest search the bush had ever experienced was already being organized and would be set in motion the moment it was light enough to see the ground.

Yet, long as all this takes in the telling, the new course of action was perceived and completed in François's mind before he reached the top of the hill and came to the place where he had to go down on hands and knees to crawl along the narrow track leading to the boulders and dense bushes that concealed the entrance to the cave. He was about to close in on the boulders when a dark shape came hurtling over their top and someone landed lightly on his feet on the track in front of him. It was the darkest hour of night, too dark to see anything except the blurred silhouette against the sheen of stars of someone crouched with an arm raised above a shoulder and a glint of metal that left François with no doubt that it was someone with spear at the ready.

Fortunately, François's sense of smell was as keen as ever and his nose instantly told him that it could only be Xhabbo. The moment Xhabbo's feet found the track he called out in a whisper almost too loud for safety, 'Xhabbo, Xhabbo, it's me, Foot of the Day!'

Xhabbo must have been nearer to using his spear than even François had dreaded, because relief at the sound of François's voice broke almost like a sob from him. He fell on his knees down on the track beside François and took both his hands in his. He said, with emotion that made those electric Bushman words of his almost too indistinct for even François's expert ears: 'Foot of the Day, Foot of the Day, Xhabbo lives again.'

Straight away, Xhabbo rushed on to explain how a sound, greater than any thunder he had ever heard, had jerked both himself and Nuin-Tara out of their sleep; how the earth underneath them shook and all the rocks trembled, until pebbles and sand came down on them like hail from the roof of the cave. François, fearful of the effect on Nonnie of such a shock was about to speak but Xhabbo seemed to know his mind. There was one most extraordinary thing, he said. When the last rumble and re-echo of the explosion had died, they could detect no sign that Nonnie was awake.

The silence in the cave had been so dense that he thought the explosion had ruined his hearing. For, even if Nonnie had not stirred, why had there been no movement from Hintza? Surely no dog so 'utterly a hunter' could have slept through such an event. Perhaps the trouble was not with his hearing but something more sinister. For instance, could part of the roof have fallen in and buried both? Immediately he had crawled towards the place where Nonnie lay. To his amazement she was still fast asleep. But stranger still was the behaviour of Hintza. He was, indeed as awake as Foot of the Day would have wished him to be; head high, ears erect, nose sniffing the air, ready for any danger. Yet he had not moved from Nonnie's side, or uttered a single sound. He had just turned his head to lick Xhabbo's hand and then resumed his position of extreme watchfulness.

It is impossible to describe what effect this simple description of Hintza's behaviour had on François. If ever a dog had provocation to ignore a master's command to stay at his post, surely Hintza had had it that night. Yet that he should have rejected the temptation, struck François as such a demonstration of trust that he was almost overcome with emotion. In that microscopic vision of reality, instilled in men by disaster and danger, it was as if Hintza then became the plenipotentiary of all that was natural and instinctive in life and his behaviour a pledge that, no matter how the world of men might be ranged against François, nature was on his side and nature would see him through.

He longed to go into the cave at once, just to touch Hintza and thank him with the special Bushman sounds he used when Hintza had done something remarkable and done it well. But he had to restrain himself for Xhabbo's account had only just begun. He went on at once to describe how he had then left Hintza and Nonnie, told Nuin-Tara to sit there watching over them, seized his spear and crawled quickly outside to see if he could discover anything to show what terrible thing had shaken the earth. He had emerged to find Hunter's Drift already in flames and, amazed, he watched the fire mount high in the sky.

The fire obviously was connected with the explosion and both with Foot of the Day's mission. The thought of this connection and its consequence so filled him with fear that for once he looked in vain inside himself for any tapping that might help him to understand what had occurred. There was just no tapping that he could hear; only a black hole of a feeling that so great an explosion and so large a fire could only mean that his own Foot of the Day, like so many other people that day, 'had utterly fallen over on his side'.

This feeling was immediately converted into the horror of certainty for, as he crouched there behind those great boulders for cover, staring over their broken rims into the fire and the night beyond, suddenly a great star came falling slowly, burning, out of the sky to vanish in the dark over the desert where he had his home. Hard on that there came the sound of their enemies screaming, shouting and calling at one another down below as if they were still masters of the world. In the end, he was about to go back to see whether, in the silence of the cave, some form of tapping would return to tell him what to do, when he had heard the first faint sounds of someone coming up the hill. Faint as the sounds were, they were so loud by Bushman and, he believed, Foot of the Day's standards that he assumed that they must be made by one of their over-confident enemies.

As Xhabbo said this, François realized how tired he was and in how great a hurry, to have made so clumsy an approach over country he knew so well; all the more so when Xhabbo declared that he did not understand what had prevented him from using his spear immediately, when François's shadow rose up from the track in front of the boulder behind which he was crouching, so certain had he been that the noise was made by an enemy. What terrible thing, he asked, had made François so reckless? What horror had caused that great fire and commotion down below?

He wanted to take François back into the cave at once to answer his many questions in full and with the attention to detail which is so dear to Bushman imagination and, incidentally, makes them perhaps the finest conversationalists on earth. But François held him back, and hastened to say that it would be better if Xhabbo heard what he had to say out there in case they woke up Nonnie, and that he wanted to avoid if at all possible. Xhabbo, therefore, had to be content with a quick summary of all that had happened; what François had overheard to make him change his plans and how, if he were to draw the enemy's suspicions from the hill successfully, he had no time to lose.

Xhabbo, despite his longing to hear all, listened without interruption and with growing understanding of how even more desperate their situation had become. When François came, at last, to the point where he emphasized that the sooner he left for Mopani's camp the better, Xhabbo showed, in the most convincing manner, not only how he had come to understand but agreed. Taking François by the arm and pointing towards the clear-cut gap in the hills, where the great Amanzim-tetse river flowed like a wind to the East, he said: 'Yes, you must utterly hasten. For look, there already is the big toe of Foot of the Day.'

So clear was the night, so defined the horizon in the wide gap in hill and bush that François, for the first time in his life, saw star-rise. First, a fine spike of silver above a line of ink, followed by a faint glow until suddenly, five-pointed and darting light, needle-fine at their eyes, was the whole of the morning star, old Koba's Dawn's Heart, Xhabbo's Foot of the Day. That was sign enough to send them hurrying into the cave.

Nuin-Tara was inside the entrance, waiting, François was to find, with a wooden cudgel in hand which she dropped when she felt rather than saw François coming after Xhabbo. Relief broke also like a great sigh from her. She would have spoken too, no doubt, had not Xhabbo whispered to her that they had to be more quiet than ever, but for once the atmosphere was not under the command of only the three of them.

François's presence, which Hintza's infallible nose detected at once, was too much for him. His loyalty to François still held him on the ground beside Nonnie but, for the moment, he had lost control of his tail. François's fear of waking Nonnie barely balanced his joy at the sound of Hintza's tail, lashing the floor of the cave. It was as loud in his ears as that of those broomsticks his fastidious old Ousie-Johanna once had used daily to beat the dust out of her bedside rug which never had any dust in it to beat out. Afraid that Hintza's eager tail might do what the explosion had failed to do, and wake Nonnie, he went to him quickly, but this time with his habitual and expert silence. He knelt beside Hintza in the dark, stroked him fondly with one hand while he took him by the tail with the other before coaxing him gently away from Nonnie's side, to post

him as their sentry by the entrance to the cave. He then lit a
candle, as far away from Nonnie as possible, and asked Xhabbo
and Nuin-Tara to crouch between the candle and Nonnie so
that the light should not disturb her.

That done, he took up the letter he had written some hours
before, hardly believing that it was not all done in another age.
He would have liked to re-write it but all he could do was to
add a postscript, telling her briefly that the mission of the night
was successfully accomplished, so successfully that he was leaving immediately now to go to Mopani for help. While he was
away – he underlined the sentence – *none of them was to leave
the cave on any occount whatsoever.* He hastened to stress that
his new mission would be far less dangerous than the last. He
believed that he had every chance of success and, with luck, he
should be back with help in four or five days' time at the most.
(He deliberately exaggerated the time it would take in case of
accidents because, if all went well, he knew he could do the
journey in two days and nights.) He added that, should he not
return in a week, she must please do what he had asked her to
do had he failed to return from his excursion to his home the
previous night.

It did not take him long to write this, yet, in the process, he
must have looked in Nonnie's direction a dozen times to be
reassured that she remained asleep. The moment the postscript
was written, he went to his store of food at the far end of the
cave, helped himself to a few rusks and some biltong – just
enough to see him and Hintza on the way. Food in the future
for them all was going to be one of their greatest problems and
his instincts already warned him that it should be as sparingly
used as possible.

That done, he said good-bye to Xhabbo and Nuin-Tara.
Xhabbo wanted to come outside with him but François begged
him not to. He stressed that even so great an expert as Xhabbo,
from now on, should not leave the cave, in case he left some
fresh sign outside. Old signs would not matter but any new ones
made after dew-fall in the day to come could be fatal. Xhabbo,
for a moment, looked as if he would protest, but then exclaimed
softly that as the last thing his tapping had told him was to stay
quietly in the cave, he would do as François asked. He would

keep to the cave for seven days and seven nights without moving from it. If François had not come back on the seventh night, he would ask his tapping what to do unless the tapping, of its own account, came to him with a new summons before. But meanwhile he would have to listen to François's tapping as if it were his own, because that seemed to be the only tapping left in that dark world at the moment.

As he told François this, François thought he saw, by that very still, upright candle flame between them, a look come into both Xhabbo's and Nuin-Tara's eyes which he had never encountered before. It was a very old look, perhaps the oldest look of which the eyes of the oldest living people in the world are capable: the look on a beloved person as though for the last time. It so nearly unmanned him that he blew out the candle before he himself could take a last look at Nonnie. The sound of the blood in his ears was so loud that he hardly heard Xhabbo's and Nuin-Tara's whispered, 'Go carefully, Foot of the Day. Go carefully, and our father Mantis goes with you.'

He answered with an almost inaudible, 'And may you stay in peace.'

Rifle in hand, haversack of food slung across his shoulder, he whispered to Hintza to follow and crawled out of the cave. He stayed on hands and knees at the exit just long enough to make certain that his eyes could see through the dark. Then he slung his rifle too across his shoulder and called Hintza to him. As Hintza's head and shoulders appeared at the entrance, François held out his arms and picked him up.

It had been a long time since he had last carried Hintza and he was astonished to find him almost too heavy to manage. But carry him he had to, if Hintza was not to leave marks on dew-wet grass and bushes on the side of the hill. Somehow, François found the strength to step with Hintza carefully from stone to stone, until at last he reached the track at the bottom of the hill. With immense relief he put him down and had a quick look at the sky. Thank God! It was still dark. The morning star was high, but there was, surprisingly, no streak as yet of first light.

With Hintza now at his side, François retraced his steps to Hunter's Drift. When he arrived opposite the overhang of rock

where he, Xhabbo, Hintza and the dying Mtunywa had successfully hidden from the enemy the previous day, he stepped
out of the track. Making no effort to conceal his spoor, he
walked firmly to the ledge of rock and the fringe of bushes
concealing the cavity underneath, crawled through it and, as he
expected, found Mtunywa's body stretched out on the sand
exactly as they had left him. With great difficulty he forced
himself to crawl all round Mtunywa, roughing up the surface of
sand and pebbles, so as to remove any prints Xhabbo's naked
feet might have left on them. He knew it was all necessary work
and yet felt as if he were desecrating a tomb and was not surprised that Hintza shared his feelings, to such an extent that at
the first scent of Mtunywa a whimper of dismay escaped from
him, loud and long enough to draw a half-hearted reprimand
from François for the breach of discipline it was.

His relief when he could leave was immense and once
through the fringe of bushes, he paused only to tear a page
from his dispatch book, crumple it up in his hand and drop it in
a conspicuous place nearby, convinced that his enemies would
see it later and, seeing it, be led to discover his hiding place and
Mtunywa's body. Once that happened, he was certain, they
would be convinced that they had solved the mystery of where
he had disappeared to the previous day, and look no further.

From there he hurried to the edge of the clearing, to stand
immovable in the shadow of the bushes. Carefully he observed
the slowly dying fire of his home and the clearing in between. It
was still empty and so quiet that the pitiful sound of the cattle
lowing in their kraals once more reached him distinctly. Kneeling down beside Hintza, he told him to scout quickly in the
direction of his home to look for any sign of leopard. He knew,
of course, that there would be none after such a night of fire
and clamour and destruction, but he knew that a dog as intelligent as Hintza always needed a definite and plausible task.

Hintza, who loved nothing more than a feeling of being important to François, had the additional incentive of a night of
inactivity behind him and he vanished like a Bushman arrow
into the clearing. He was only gone some five minutes, but
even that was almost too much for he returned just as the first
light, 'Bamuthi's 'hour of the horns of the bullock', showed

red as blood against the far edge of the bush across the clearing.

Yet François was content, knowing that even five minutes would have been long enough for a dog as fast as Hintza to cover the clearing with spoor which the enemy could not fail to find and finding, conclude that Hintza had been with him all the time. That done, he turned his back on his home and started down the track leading to Mopani's camp, at a double of which even Nonnie's father would have approved, and without any attempt to conceal their spoor.

CHAPTER FIVE

The Dawn of Heitse-Eibib

Normally, of course, François would never have been so reckless as to travel through the bush at that hour, at such a pace. It was the moment when the carnivorous animals who had failed to kill the evening before or during the night, would lie in wait for some defenceless prey. They knew only too well that the relief which the end of a night, made darker and longer by danger and need for unceasing vigilance, brought to the life of the bush was always so great as the day flowered wide open around them that they would allow themselves the rare luxury of unawareness, and behave as if they had no enemies.

This was one reason why François had always loved that moment, perhaps above all others. Then one saw the baboons, apes and monkeys, the birds, insects and buck, all in their coats of many colours, washed clean in quicksilver dew, setting out on their lawful occasions with the grace of the total absence of unease, and a carriage eurhythmic with lack of haste. It was a glimpse of the sort of Paradise regained that freedom from fear briefly gives to life.

He called it the bush's moment of innocence; an innocence made all the greater and more poignant because it was vulnerable as only innocence can be to the terrible exceptions brought about by frustrated creatures who had not done their killing at the moments prescribed for it in the general law of the bush and so, made cunning by desperation, prepared to do it at this unlawful hour. He knew far too many examples for his comfort, not just of animals but of human beings who, unaware of the terrible exceptions necessary to prove the rule of life in the bush, had lost their own lives as a result. But for once he deliberately chose to discount this particular peril to which travelling so fast along the narrow, winding track exposed him. He did so without hesitation or remorse, though by doing so he was transgressing all the precepts which Mopani and 'Bamuthi had

104

impressed upon him over many years so effectively that obedience to them had almost become a reflex of his character. Even so, he did it because, great as the dangers might be ahead of him, none of them could be as great as the danger which was being organized and might already be coming up fast behind him. He allowed himself time only for one precaution. When he was deep inside the bush he stopped, called Hintza to his side, knelt by him and whispered in Bushman in his ear, his voice tender with the knowledge of the danger of the role he was about to inflict on him: 'I'm afraid, dearest Hin, you'll have to take the lead. So take care. And not only take care but go fast. Remember as always when in doubt, stop, crouch down low and wait for me to catch up. Then show me. So go, dear Hin, go! Today we must go faster than we've ever gone before.'

Hintza looked deep and straight into his eyes, as only a dog among the animals of the world can look into the human eye, and then did something he had not done since his adolescent days. He put up that cool, forever wrinkling and forever keen-scenting nose of his, which seemed to work at scenting twenty-four hours a day, perhaps harder even in sleep than in waking hours because it did the work then for all his other senses, and gave François one of the longest and wettest licks on the cheek he had ever received from him, as if it were meant to indicate that he would have done it long before if only François had given him a chance to show that he, Hintza, also knew the awfulness of what had happened and understood entirely this need for haste.

The feeling of their partnership in that second was transformed and raised to a dimension where Hintza was more than a dog and almost a precious extension of François's being, so that when he saw the burnished, lithe, magnetic shape of Hintza leap elongated with speed into the track, his eyes clouded with tears. He had to restrain himself by immediately standing up straight, adjusting the sack of provisions across his shoulder, eliminating a rattle he had detected on this first lap of his journey, checking over his rifle to make certain that the bolt was moving freely and that there was a bullet in the breech so that he would only have to flick over the safety catch to be ready to shoot, should he run into trouble. He could not recollect ever having gone through the bush with his rifle in such an advanced state of preparation before, because that too in the past had been strictly forbidden. One never carried one's gun cocked even with the safety catch on until one knew for certain that the moment to shoot was upon one.

Standing there doing all this in seconds, he noticed how the bush was as disturbingly quiet as it had been at dawn the fatal morning before. He knew, of course that the bush there was as crowded with life as it had always been everywhere else, but all the many and infinitely various voices which were normally raised in a great chorale of thanksgiving for the coming of the sacred light of day were totally silenced. And yet he knew too that poised there to move off, he was like an actor before an audience in a packed theatre not just silent but holding its breath for the climax of this terrible new drama which was having its first performance there.

All that he was feeling then about the horror and the extra dimension of tragedy and frightfulness which he himself had brought to this world of innocence and beauty by the destruction of his own home, came swiftly to a point then for François in the quick glimpse he had of the kind of dawn which had exploded in the east. It was sending the night wheeling, startled upwards like the densest ever flight of black crows, to vanish in one of the most acid blues he had ever seen. It was the particular colour of this explosion, singular in its absence of nuance and intimation of other shades of colour, that made François's senses, as it were, like the hair at the back of his neck, stand on end. The colour was that startlingly vital, vivid red to which even the well-proved comparison with blood could not do justice. It seemed redder even than immediate human or animal blood. It was in fact a red very rarely seen even in the sky and, according to the mythology on which François's imagination had been nourished by his old Bushman nurse as much as his body had been fed by her with food, it was so because it was the blood of a god.

This god was the great Heitse-Eibib of the almost vanished, copper-coloured Hottentots of southern Africa – a race not un-akin to his beloved Bushmen – and like the Bushmen cruelly persecuted and ultimately destroyed through violence or corruption by both black and white invaders of the land. François knew this god, compassionate, upright and beautiful with a spine of purest copper, by many names, like 'The one who foretells'; 'The messenger'; 'The tree of light'; 'The one with the wounded knee'; and many others. But it was 'The one with the wounded knee' which was uppermost in François's mind and heart as he noticed the still multitudinous leaves of the incarnadined sea of trees between him and the dawn, so wet and dripping with the blood of this light that their own vivid green did not show through it, but merely served as points for the red to darken and congeal until the top of the bush appeared clotted with blood. He stood there briefly, humbled before the feelings of the inevitability of just such a dawn having to come up fast in such a light on such a day, as if it too were a sign for his abandoned heart, just like the shooting stars the night before, that the universe itself, contrary to other appearances, was not disinterested in what was happening but committed to the battle itself. He felt this keenly because, according to his old nurse, this dawn only came whenever Heitse-Eibib realized that the power of darkness in the universe had grown too great again. So in the course of his own chosen night he would have gone to battle to reduce it to its proper proportions. In the course of the battle, which was always long and terrible, he would be wounded among many other places in his knee. As he came fast over the horizon back from his field of battle he walked in the manner in which the Hottentots always walked, lifting their copper legs so that their knees were raised high and well out in front. As a result, the first thing human beings on earth would see as token of their re-delivery from excess of darkness was the blood streaming from the deep gash in the knee of Heitse-Eibib.

The impact on François of all the many dear, happy and life-giving associations with the past which this mythological light evoked compelled him to respond quickly as he had been taught the Hottentots always responded on such an occasion. He knelt down in the track and in a few seconds had selected, from among the stones mixed with the earth on the footpath, some of the roundest and smoothest of pebbles to raise where he was standing a small pile of a kind of wayside shrine to the god. It was extraordinary how great a comfort so small and hurried an exercise of ritual brought him. He rose and picked up his rifle almost with zest, balanced it at the trail beside him, and set out fast down the track after the vanished Hintza.

How wise he had been to let Hintza lead was proved a mile or so further along, when he rounded a curve in the track and saw his dog standing sideways in the distance. Hintza's tail was stiff and trembling, as it was only when he wanted to convey the most portentous of warnings. His head was moving first to François and then pointing sideways upwards in the opposite direction at something invisible beyond, and then back to François again. Seeing Hintza thus, François, who had not taken any particular account of the noise he made trotting freely along the track, slowed down and carefully went forward without a sound to kneel down beside Hintza.

'What is it, Hin?' he asked in a whisper.

Asking, he put his hand on Hintza's back at the centre of his magnetic field of hair. So long and such close partners had they been in exactly this sort of experience that François could tell the answer from the intensity of the sniff which Hintza allowed himself at François's ear and the vibration of tension along his electric spine. It could only mean there were lion ahead. With the utmost care, the safety catch on his rifle released, and with Hintza by his side, he crawled slowly forward.

This deliberation exacted all the discipline of which François was capable, because all the time he was more conscious than ever of the probability that the search for the two of them must surely now have started and the need for maintaining their lead on the enemy greater than ever. He was convinced that once their trackers had clearly established that it was his and Hintza's spoor in the track and noticed, as they could not fail to notice, both how fresh it was and with what speed it had been made, they would not waste any more time in looking around for confirmatory signs but assume correctly where they were going and hasten as they themselves had hastened along the track itself.

Yet he knew also that he could not afford not to give himself time enough to deal successfully with the problem of the lion ahead. Accordingly they crawled another thirty yards forward in this fastidious manner, down the crooked, narrow track until it suddenly broadened out and François caught the glimpse of a clearing ahead. It was a clearing he knew well, not far from one of the permanent water holes in that part of the bush and so much favoured by game. He had barely seen it when Hintza nudged him with his nose and stopped wriggling forward, his head pointing slightly sideways to the left; his long lips were trembling with excitement and the strange kind of anger which lions always raised in him. It was an anger François had never been able to understand completely for it was a feeling exclusively reserved by Hintza for lions. The only explanation, if one could call a deep suspicion an explanation, which had ever occurred to François was that Hintza himself, so much the colour of a lion and with so much of the heart of the lion in himself, somewhere in his proud, mysterious and sensitive depths might be inordinately jealous of lions for being more lion-like than he could ever be. However reprehensible the emotion of jealousy or even its middle-class version of envy was held to be in his Calvinist scale of values, François himself had already suspected that in a strange way what one envied was a measure of one's own proudly hidden aristocracy of spirit. Knowing the scale of Hintza's rage as he did, he tried to appease it by gently stroking him as he looked in the direction Hintza clearly wanted him to look.

There he saw the back of a lion, moving restlessly backwards and forwards above the shining fringes of grass and brush. François crept further forward until he could see more. The back belonged to an enormous, but still young, lion. All his youth shone like silk in the hair of his coat on which the first light of the sun came down like slanted rain, smoking over the powerful back. This lion was obviously aware that something strange had been approaching, and was walking up and down like an alerted sentry on his beat in front of six other young lions of similar size and condition, all lying with eyes half shut behind him. They were each wrapped in a yellow shawl of sun, purring ecstatically and so loudly that both François and Hintza could hear them. All six had their paws stretched far out in front of them, so that the sun could dry their coats, wet and drenched with dew. The dew itself was sparkling on the grass all around them as if the window of the day itself had just been shattered there. In one place among the bushes, the tall strands of tasselled rushes and long blades of elephant and buffalo grass under an overhang of dark purple shadow, a complex of cobwebs had been spun, and had been so behung with drops of pointed dew that it appeared lit with chandeliers.

It was the sort of vision of innocence, natural delicacy and tenderness always moving in the great and the strong, that normally François would have loved to go on observing until it came to its natural end, when, their coats and paws dried out and their hedonistic hearts sweetened and warmed through with honeyed sun, the lions would stalk off into the bush to find other shade dark enough to enable them to sleep unobserved through the heat of the day.

But of course he had not such time, or for that matter any time to spare at all. And yet he could not bring himself, as he knew he was able, to compel this pride of seven young lions to give way to him by showing himself at the edge of the clearing and advancing determinedly on them with his rifle at the ready. They might pretend aggressiveness but their whole attitude betrayed the fact that they had fed too well to be inclined for any exercise. Instantly he knew why he could not, because it touched on one of the deepest axioms of his being, taught him and carefully kept alive and cultivated by Mopani.

Far back in the beginning, which linked him with this chain of terrible events, François had already mentioned it to Xhabbo, and had had its truth confirmed in Xhabbo's instant acceptance of it. He had also tried to pass something of it on to Luciana before she had become the Nonnie she was now to him. It was as if, standing there, he could hear Mopani, to whom he was even now hastening for help, beside him, and saying to him over and over again, as if it were some self-made Sermon of his own Mount:

'Remember always, Little Cousin, that no matter how awful or insignificant, how ugly or beautiful, it might look to you, everything in the bush has its own right to be there. No one can challenge this right unless compelled by some necessity of life itself. Everything has its own dignity, however absurd it might seem to you, and we are all bound to recognize and respect it as we wish our own to be recognized and respected. Life in the bush is necessity, and it understands all form of necessity. It will always forgive what is imposed upon it out of necessity, but it will never understand and accept anything less than necessity. And remember that, everywhere, it has its own watchers to see whether the law of necessity is being observed. You may often think that deep in the darkness and the density of the bush you are alone and unobserved, but that, Little Cousin, would be an illusion of the most dangerous kind. One is never alone in the bush. One is never unobserved. One is always known as people in the towns and cities of the world are no longer known. It is true there are many parts of the bush where no human eye might be able to penetrate but there is always, like some spy of God Himself, an eye upon you, even if it is only the eye of some animal, bird, reptile or little insect, recording in its own way in the book of life how you carry yourself.

'And beside the eyes – do not underrate them – there are the tendrils of the plants, the grasses, the leaves of the trees and the roots of all growing things, which lead the warmth of the sun deep down into the darkest and coldest recesses of the earth, to quicken them with new life. They too shake with the shock of our feet and vibrate to the measure of our tread and I am certain have their own ways of registering what we bring or take from the life for which they are a home. Often as I have seen how a blade of grass will suddenly shiver on a windless day at my approach or the leaves of the trees tremble, I have thought that they too must have a heart beating within them and that my coming has quickened their pulse with apprehension until I can note the alarm vibrating at their delicate wrists and their high, translucid temples. Often when I have heard a bird suddenly break off its song, some beetle or cricket cease its chanting, because of my presence, I have felt uninvited like an intruder in a concert in some inner chamber of our royal environment and stood reproved for being so rough and not more mindful of my manners.

'All of these animal, insect and vegetable senses put together add up to a magnitude of awareness, a watch so great, minute, many-sided and awesome that there is nothing small enough to escape its notice, and I have sometimes felt involuntarily exposed in the heart of the bush as I have only on some wide open plain of our blue highveld in the south when alone on a cloud-less night of stars. It is difficult to express how small, vulner-able, confessed and revealed so immense and sharp-eyed a concourse of sentinels have made me feel, even in my innermost and most secret self. It is as if even the hidden frame of bone and sinew within me was apparent to their X-ray vision. You must be mindful, therefore, of the great company that you are compelled to keep, whether you like it or not, wherever you go. Remember that whatever you do will have its effect on them and influence them for good or ill.

'I do not want to give you the impression that all in the life of the bush is pure joy and beauty if left to itself. It is also full of suffering and tragedy and things that are ugly, but if you look deeply into them all, tragic and painful as they might be, there is no horror in them. Horror is the invention of unnatural men who inflict unnecessary suffering and destruction on life. Horror indeed is unnecessary avoidable tragedy; suffering and tragedy of the life in the bush are bearable and redeemed pre-cisely because they are part of the great necessities, part I be-lieve of the tragedy and the pain that the act of creation and its unfolding impose also upon the creator. It is the charge laid upon us for the privilege of participating in creation ourselves and which outweighs any pain involved in the process. There is balance and proportion provided in all this, the proportion that is freedom from chaos and old night, and so implicit in the organization of all being, that should you exceed them, you shatter the harmony which they serve and set up a tyranny of action and reaction for which all of us, not least of all you, some time, somewhere, will be called to reckoning.

'So, François, please see that always you observe the rhythm that serves this law of the life of the bush. Never disturb it lightly or needlessly. And this rhythm, like the presence of which I read to you the other night in the Psalm of the young David that was like a mantle around him, will also be a mantle for you. No man can escape the necessities of his own being. It may well be that the necessities of your own could lead you as it did the young David through the valley of the shadow of death; but this rhythm observed will keep you inside the harmony of all the life that is, that has been and ever will be, and will shield you against all that is irrelevant and accidental to your own self. And so, Little Cousin, "Amen" to an old man's over-long sermon to you.'

So fountain-wise did all this spring in François's memory that an Amen of his own came to his parched lips. Also, long as it has taken in the telling it presented itself not in words but in one overwhelming feeling like a flash of lightning in a mind darkened with fatigue, and so became immediate as a life-giving resolution.

At once he was compelling a reluctant Hintza to turn slowly about, reluctant because the clearing was hemmed in there by a wide belt of impenetrable thorn. They had to crawl back to the point where he had first received Hintza's warning. From there he made his way with great difficulty and care, in a slow, wide circle, around the clearing until, a quarter of an hour later they were back on the edge of the track, well behind that yellow beach of light where the young lions were so abandonedly bathing in a surf of sun.

He was about to step clear of the bush on to the track when that characteristic, high-pitched warning whimper from Hintza stopped him. Hintza was not only sniffing the air to his right but also his ears were erect and pointed. François heard it too then; it was the unmistakable rumble of an elephant whose digestion had set his stomach like a great kettle on the boil. Slowly he came to his feet and there, monumental as a statue raised to promote confession of Mopani's creed, right in the centre of the track where no shadow could trouble the morning air, stood one of the largest and blackest old elephants François had ever seen. His skin shone as if just re-lacquered with dew. His long, ivory tusks were yellow and gleaming like Saracen swords drawn bare and on guard in front of him. His trunk hung from on high, limp and loose between the tusks. His eyes were so tightly shut that even the deep furrows of a century of experience that were corrugated in his broad temple, were smoothed out and drew no lines of shadow.

He was standing heavily on only three of the classical columns of his long legs. The fourth was delicately raised so that it only touched the ground with its sensitive toes, ready to correct his balance against overweight of sleep and in the

113

process demonstrating the limit of relaxation to which a wise old elephant could abandon itself, short of going to bed on the ground. So enormous was the elephant and so vast its sleep and hence so great the manifestation of the act of trust in life which sleep is within itself that François, perhaps not surprisingly considering how long it was since he himself had slept, felt as if he were about to be overpowered by that remarkable example. Even Hintza, who had come to stand beside him and now saw the glistening, granite monument of the elephant, suddenly yawned so ardently and widely that it looked to François as if his jaws were in danger of splitting apart and his long, glistening pink tongue hung so far out from its muzzle that it looked like a canna petal about to fall from its stem. For the first time since Nonnie's return, François came near to laughing.

He might have gone on standing there, enjoying the slight ease of tension which came to him from the elephant, facing him like the great god of sleep, had not his unusual respect for the special discipline each and every occasion in the bush demanded, goaded him on with the realization that as if the delay caused by the obstruction of the lions had not been bad enough, he would now have to add to it by making another silent detour around the old elephant. The consequences of disturbing the huge dream that must be unfolding itself in so great a sleep in so great an animal, surely could be ignored with even less impunity than the rest of an arrogant pride of young lions.

So once more François pulled back into the bush and made another long and painful detour through the thorns, before coming back into the track again, where he ordered Hintza off faster than ever in the direction of Mopani's camp. He followed now not at the double but at a fast trot, so heightened was his feeling of urgency. Even this new pace was one he normally could have kept up for hours, but he doubted whether he could do so now after such a day and such a night behind him. Within an hour François's doubts of his powers of keeping up the pace became first a real anxiety and finally an acute fear.

Early as it was, the day was already hot. Before long the heat would be so great that it would add to the problems already created by sheer physical fatigue and lack of sleep. He tried to focus his mind on what was positive even in this as he tended by nature to do with everything. He comforted himself with the thought that now there would be no danger from beasts of prey on his road and that it no longer mattered how loudly and even carelessly he travelled. His only reservation was that both he and Hintza would have to watch the world around their feet now as never before, because it was the sort of day which brought out the cold-blooded snakes and pythons of the bush to warm themselves in the unfiltered sun to be found only on and beside the track.

Already the heat was beginning to move in transparent rills of shining vapour over the blood red earth. He did not fear for Hintza in this particular regard. Hintza had been taught from his earliest puppy days that snakes were to be left severely alone and if to be dealt with, then by François alone. They were never any dog's business in François's order of things; he had seen too many dogs die of snake-bite to permit it even for mongrel strays, let alone Hintza. In a sense they were not even his chosen affair, because though snakes made him uneasy too and the sight of their bright coils unwinding always made him feel as if what was left of an umbilical cord behind his navel, was being unscrewed as well. He had none of the mysterious compulsion of the European to kill them on sight, perhaps because of the Matabele example which held them to be messengers of the vanished dead, if not a return in disguise of the beloved dead themselves. There were even moments at night alone in bed, when full of wonder of the strange, rich, infinitely varied natural life of his world, his wondering was pierced by intimations of the horror of what it must be to have to live the life of the snake. He knew no form of life so loathed, persecuted and capable of pronouncing a sentence of death upon itself just because of what it was and not because of what it did. Even when it was utterly innocent and merely sunning itself in the intervals of rest between earning its living, it had just to be seen to be found guilty to the point of sentence of instant death.

He knew the horror of all this, for, despite his own intimations of compassion, he realized that even he himself could never trust and accept snakes as he did all other forms of life. All other forms of life in the bush seemed to have friends of a kind among other species. But not snakes. They hardly seemed to have any friends, even among their own kind. One always saw them alone, although one knew they must meet to procreate. Even that, one imagined, would have to be the briefest and crudest of encounters, leaving them lonelier and more than ever on their own. The utmost he could get himself to do was to keep his eyes open for them, avoid them if possible and never kill them automatically, and feel sad and guilty that, though his eyes informed him of the singular beauty patterned in their skin and expressed in the rhythm of their movement, his feelings refused to join in any act of appreciation.

He had hardly thought this when he received his first warning of how careful they would have to be. Representatives of the most authoritarian snakes he knew were already beginning to reconnoitre the track. They added a strange, nightmare quality to his progress along the path because he was beginning to draw on his last reserves of energy to propel him forward at such a pace. All the energy which could come from a pure act of will was rapidly being exhausted and he was now becoming dependent on energies he had never tapped before, or even knew he had within himself. Those are the energies available only to missions of life and death and fortunately for our egotistical wilful selves are far greater than those we consciously call upon or for that matter can ever be conceived of by our fireside selves. They tend to emerge only when put to the test in a race for life itself and so come from a level so far below one's daytime knowing that François became like some transfigured somnambulist, not walking but running in his sleep.

Accordingly, all around him assumed, as his weariness increased, a more and more vivid, dream-like quality. When the sun rose and all the many singing beetles in the bush combined to form a vast choir for serenading in their devout, glittering voices the light and the heat they loved, they joined the crescendo of the singing of his own blood in his ears. The nightmare feeling acquired a kind of rhythm of hallucination whose tempo quickened when the heat of the sun finally infected the day with fever and the delirium which distorts the sun's own clarity at the climax of the African day.

At one moment François would round a curve and see Hintza hurdling on the crest of the curve of a great leap into the

116

air, worthy of the graceful red impala that are Africa's greatest hurdlers, and see him soaring over a saffron-yellow cobra sitting upright, its hood erect and vainly striking at the tawny body flying over it, before collapsing for a moment inert like a coil of rope in the track, as a prelude to wriggling despondently into the bush. At the next, as he pressed a tree, a sparkling black mamba, bird nesting but suddenly frightened, hung by its tail from a branch to take a quick swipe at François, and he would dodge its fangs only just in time. Yet a second later he would not be certain whether it had actually happened to him, or merely part of the general delirium of the day. He found himself bounding over lethargic adders lying still and shining, coiled like Aztec bangles in front of the yellow grass; emerald tree-snakes hung like Maya necklaces round the head of a bush of thorn swaying in the heat, and black cobras with rings of ivory on their throats darting erect, frightened by the vibrations his running sent through their pillow of earth, and spitting poison spitefully after him as he ran on. At one place he had to stop and wait while an enormous sluggish python, looking like a stuffed football stocking, pulled itself slowly across the track up into a tree. But somehow none of this retarded him, because he knew that on the whole snakes and pythons too observed the law of necessity in the bush, and that if he stuck to his own necessity in the middle of the track, they would not come at him wilfully.

Even so, he was compelled, after some two hours, to call Hintza to him and rest, gasping, in the shade of a boulder, while some fever birds with their monotonous voices wearily took up the desperate theme where he had abandoned it on the track. He sat there for some twenty minutes which felt like seconds to his exhausted self. Yet, short as it felt, he recovered enough to reckon up his progress so far. Even his desperate self could not help being somewhat comforted, for he found that he was already just over half-way to Mopani's camp. He began to feel more confident that he could make the camp well before the enemy behind caught up. Yet he sent Hintza scouting back along the trail and watched the bush behind for signs of unusual movement but noticed nothing to disturb him and was all the more reassured when Hintza too returned without any intelligence for concern.

François was about to resume his journey with a slightly lightened heart, therefore, when away to the west in the direction of the Punda-Ma-Tenka, the great Hunter's Road, he thought he heard a series of short studs of sound grate upon the silence. These, he was certain, were not part of the hallucination of heat and exaggeration of fatigue in his senses, for he noticed that Hintza had heard it too and was looking at him with a large question in his alert eyes, which were a deep purple there beside him in the shadow of the boulders. He waited for longer than perhaps he could afford to do in case the sound repeated itself, uneasy because the sound was not unlike the sound of controlled rifle fire at a distance. He could only blame fatigue for the fact that until then he had completely and culpably forgotten the Punda-Ma-Tenka and the road which branched off it to Mopani's camp. Of course the enemy could have rushed patrols fast by truck along it and set up a screen of guards between him and the camp long before he could get to it. He could not imagine what else these sounds could foretell or what he could do about them other than to press on harder and more alert than ever, knowing Hintza would be aware of the enemy before it could be aware of them. He was starting to do just that when a longer and more pronounced intrusion of sound on the silence occurred way back on the track on which he was travelling.

This intrusion lasted much longer and sounded less ordered than the one before, ceased and then came back sporadically before it finally stopped. François looked deep into Hintza's eyes as Hintza was looking back into his and fantastic as it may seem in the telling, he had no doubt that Hintza suspected as he did, that what they had just heard was a burst of fire from pursuers coming from Hunter's Drift. It could only mean that they must have stumbled into the pride of young lions sunbathing in the clearing. François assumed that with none of his scruples, they had opened fire on them and in the process not only warned François of their coming but retarded their own rate of advance.

The encouragement given him by knowing from the sound that he had at least a two-hour lead on his pursuers and that, tired as he was, he could make Mopani's camp before they

118

could catch up, was qualified only by the fact that the sounds he had heard from the direction of the Punda-Ma-Tenka, proclaimed the probability that soldiers much better led than those behind might already be deployed in part of the bush ahead.

Pausing just long enough to put in Bushman words for Hintza's benefit the basic facts of what he feared and repeating the phrase again and again that it was 'strange men' and not animals or reptiles that he had to look out for now, he ordered him ahead and followed quickly after. They travelled thus without any unusual incident for another hour, except the exactions of delirium and hallucination which running in what was more and more a sleep of fatigue increased, was joined by a weariness of sinew and muscle in his body like an acute pain, as if exhaustion had produced an advanced rheumatism of its own in his blood and bone. As a result he had to call Hintza back and rest for some fifteen minutes in the shade of a great boulder. When his breathing had become more normal he found he was stroking the boulder with his hand, as if even contact with an inanimate old stone made him less abandoned and alone. He would have liked to rest more but despite his aching body and smarting eyes, he started on again, because even if his lead of two hours were still maintained and he got by the patrols in front successfully, two hours were not long to prepare Mopani and his staff against the sort of attack that might be launched against them that day.

The thought was so alarming that he had to prevent himself taking the next lap of his journey at a run, and only just managed to limit himself to the rhythm of that fast trot which he knew from experience was the only pace he had any hope of sustaining.

They travelled like this for some three-quarters of an hour, when he came out on the bank of a little stream he knew to be only eight miles from Mopani's camp. There he paused to let Hintza have a good drink of water. He allowed himself a drink too, but a much more sparing one, since too much water in the middle of the day added prodigiously to one's sweating and the sweating to one's exhaustion.

He had just finished his spare draught of water when from the track on the other side of the bush he heard voices. With that

119

immediate speed of reaction which was one of his most marked physical attributes, he had his rifle in his hand, safety catch released, and in the same movement dodged in behind a huge boulder in the bed of the stream, and was down on his stomach, in a firing position facing the far bank. It was only then that he realized that something vital was missing. That something vital, of course, was Hintza. Despite all his training and loyalty Hintza had not followed his example.

Acutely alarmed he peered round the boulder and, thank Heaven and Heitse-Eibib, he saw that Hintza had not moved from his position by the flashing sheet of water. He had merely stopped lapping up the liquid which François knew was his dream idea of champagne and was staring straight ahead in the direction of the sound with his ears erect. But what was far more significant than his stare, his tail was wagging, and François knew it could only be because he had recognized the voices and knew them to be friendly.

Nonetheless he was not in a mood to take anything for granted that day, even so well tried a form of radar as Hintza's tail. He called him back sternly in a whisper and made him take up position beside him in the shadow of the boulder, lying there hidden and listening to the voices gradually coming nearer. He too became convinced by their ease and fluency, and the fact that the ardent beetle chorale in the bush around him was going on uninterrupted, that they must be the voices of people who were known to the bush as well. This assumption was hardly reached when it was proved, and François watched five Africans in the uniform of Mopani's company of rangers, coming in single file round a curve of the track and unhurriedly walk out into the clear on the blue gravel of the bed of the stream. What is more, he recognized the man in the lead. He was one of Mopani's most experienced and trusted rangers, a corporal called Kghometsu, whom he knew well.

A desperate imagination will grasp at what rational man secure in his armchair will dismiss as meaningless trifles. François attached the utmost significance to the fact that the man was called Kghometsu. He was a man of the Sutho peoples, who inhabit the fringes of the great desert to the West from which Xhabbo had come; and in the Sutho language

Kghometsu meant 'Comfort'. Kghometsu had been called Comfort because long after his mother had given up hope of bearing her husband a son (she had had nothing but daughters before) he was born and so inevitably was the 'comfort' that ended her despair, and he was known as such ever since. Stranger still, Kghometsu was married to a woman called Mokho. She was a woman of the Makoba people, who inhabit the vast swamp on the far side of the great desert and her name had a significance of its own. It meant 'A Tear' and had been given to her because her own mother had died giving birth to her.

All this meant much to François at the moment, because it brought back vividly the time when, after his return from his journey to uLangalibalela and that strange encounter he and 'Bamuthi had had with the Men of the Spear, he had been greatly tempted to break out of his secrecy and tell Mopani about the incident. It happened when Mopani had spoken to him about this very Mokho, telling him how Mokho had returned from a visit to her people with a story about the great Tree of Life which they worshipped and which stood in the heart of the remote swamp where only the most dedicated of witch-doctors penetrated in order to acquire a gift of prophecy on behalf of their people. This was the tree, according to Mopani, that figured in one of the greatest myths of Africa and was an article of unquestioned faith to millions among the great tribes to the west and up north in the bush of Angola, the jungles of North-Western Zambia and the Congo. Once it was a singing tree and spoke direct in song to the peoples who worshipped it. But it was said to have been silent for centuries and would remain silent until it could announce again that the moment had come at last when all the tribes of Africa could unite and drive back into the sea the white men who had come from the sea to subdue them. It was almost as if François, thinking of all this, could hear the gravity in Mopani's tone when he told him that Kghometsu's wife had just brought back word that this tree had started its dread singing again.

Of course, all this too came to him far more quickly than it takes in the telling and the moment he recognized Kghometsu, he stood up to step out from behind the boulder and call out his greeting:

'Old father Kghometsu, I, Little Feather, I see you.'

He heard with a delight that almost unmanned him Kghometsu's measured but warm response in that deep bass voice of his that always came from the pit of his stomach, 'Little Feather, I too, I see you there. Yes, I see you!'

Kghometsu was following up his grin with a wide smile of welcome. But the smile vanished when François quickly stepped from stone to stone across the shallow shining water and stood before him. A look of anxiety, if not horror, came over him, for it was not the François he had last seen, looking so fresh, upright, fastidious and unusually composed for his age, his blue eyes always wide and bright and his tanned skin with its urgent state of health, which had never known physical sickness, like the sheen on a new-born calf. He saw instead eyes so deep in the shadow of fatigue that their blue was lost, the young face lined and drawn and streaks of sweat and dirt like the pattern of utter exhaustion itself tattooed on his skin. His bush shirt was creased, slack and wet with sweat and his whole expression as of some steel of keen sorrow newly forged in fire.

In a voice tender as a woman's with concern, he asked, 'Oh Little Feather and Son of our hope, what lion have you had by the tail this day?' – this was a Sutho proverb for someone who has had to wrestle with great misfortune – 'and what trouble has set fire to your house that you should stand before Kghometsu thus?'

Although the use of the word 'fire' was purely symbolic, it nonetheless was so close to the literal truth that François almost felt as if the worthy, solid, respectable, dependable Kghometsu had acquired the gift of second sight.

He replied slowly, a slur on his tongue, 'Oh father Kghometsu, I have had more than a lion by the tail, more than fire in my house. Come quickly, you all, and sit hidden behind this boulder with me because Umkulunkulu alone knows how long we can stay here safe and unobserved. A world of evil men are coming up fast in the track behind me and many of them might already be spread out in the bush coming from the Punda-Ma-Tenka and covering the roads back to your father Mopani's camp.'

Kghometsu was so overcome and concerned by François's

tone that he paused only to summon the rest of his men to him, saying obliquely, 'It was indeed as I thought then, the shooting we heard was no shooting of an innocent kind.'

When they were all seated in a close half circle in the shelter of the boulder round François and a panting Hintza by his side, all five pairs of eyes wide with the fevered curiosity of fear and concern on him, François began by asking, 'My old father, tell me, is our father Mopani back yet from the country over the great water?'

Kghometsu shook his head gravely and answered that not only was he not back but that according to the Major, a message had come the evening before to say that Mopani would not be back for another five or six days. The Major was a very experienced old Matabele sub-chieftain who had been a sergeant-major in the British army and had for many years now been in charge of Mopani's African rangers. He was known just as 'Major' to everyone.

François was aware that the news filled him with dismay, although he had no real time for such subjective reactions, and so forced himself quickly to ask, 'But old father, is the Major himself there, and would he be able to speak to the Government on the telephone?'

Kghometsu nodded and said he reported to the Government at least twice a day, at sunrise and sunset. 'Then, old father,' François went on, as Kghometsu, more and more perturbed, was about to resume his questioning, 'with your agreement, this is what we must do, without delay. You, father Kghometsu, will please stay with me here so that I can talk to you at great length and you can advise me what we are to do in the future. But before then, each one of your brothers here please must go by a different way now, as fast as they can, back to the camp. But they must also go carefully, looking well around them because by now the bush in front might be full of evil men. I will only tell you, so that you can judge the evil for yourselves, that at dawn yesterday morning they came out in their thousands from the banks of the Amanzim-tetse and the bush all round and killed everyone whom you know at Hunter's Drift.'

The look of disbelief matched the horror on all the faces, except perhaps Kghometsu's. Indeed so great and vivid was the emotion that from all the throats, even Kghometsu's, there broke out a deep exclamation of '*Aikona!*' which is their most emphatic and irrevocable 'no' to things they cannot accept in their everyday awareness of the order of things.

'I'm afraid there's no *aikona* about it,' François continued. 'All ... your great chief and father 'Bamuthi, your brother Mtunwya; all their wives, children and grandchildren and smallest babies; our Princess of the Pots, the Lammie of my house and others you know not of, yesterday morning before the sun showed itself above the hills of the Amanzim-tetse, were all killed by these evil men who are on their way now to kill you all. So hasten and tell all this to the Major. Tell him to let the Government know at once that a great army of destruction has invaded the land far and wide and then to collect all rangers and make ready in the way he as an old soldier will know best, to prepare to be attacked and outnumbered. Go, in the name of Umkulunkulu, while I tell Kghometsu more and he and perhaps I too will presently come and join the Major and you all.'

For a moment they all looked as if the horror of it all would keep them motionless there under the sheer weight of it, pressing on their warm, instinctive hearts. But Kghometsu, who had reasons of his own of which François had a suspicion did not doubt the news.

At once he looked at his four companions and in his most authoritative manner called them out each by name, saying, 'You go by this track, you by that!' and so on and on until they all had their directions clear, before ending with the inevitable military command of urgency so full of associations for François, and so strange in English among those sonorous African syllables, 'And see that you go at the double.'

For a moment after they had gone François did not speak. His thirst quenched, he suddenly realized how long it was since he and Hintza had last eaten. He unslung his haversack, took out some biltong, began slicing it up with his sharp hunting knife and fed himself and Hintza alternatively, as he spoke. But first he apologized to Kghometsu for not offering him any of the pink and pomegranate-red meat. He explained how he had not eaten since early the night before and that his supply of food was small and there were others with whom all he possessed would have to be shared. The apology was unnecesary except in so far as manners, always meticulous in the world of the primitive, demanded, for Kghometsu at once spread out his hands wide in a gesture, stressing that François should not even have explained. Besides, his attention had immediately fastened, to the exclusion of all else, to the word 'others'.

'But, Little Feather,' he exclaimed, 'what others can there be except you and your dog? Did you not say that all our brothers and friends are dead?'

Putting the fact for the first time into words himself, only now, perhaps, because his senses for months had been partially prepared for disaster, the full impact of what had happened penetrated Kghometsu's composure and his eyes became blurred with tears. Unashamedly in the natural, uninhibited fashion of his people, when confronted with real cause for grief, great tears ran down his cheeks and he began to sob like a child. So much so that François, who felt as if he had lived with this black tragedy already for years and had his own dark night of tears behind him, found the strength in himself to take Kghometsu's hand in his own and try to comfort him as he had longed to be comforted before, saying, 'Oh thank you, my father, for weeping for them. Your tears will not fall unnoticed to those who watch us from the mountains where the shadows of the evening gather. Be glad, my father, that thanks to your Umkulunkulu and mine, there are three others left alive; the young daughter of him whom you knew as Isi-Vubu, the Great Kingfisher, and two others of whom I have no time to tell you now and whom you do not know. They are, I think, safely hidden far back near my burned-out home. Soon I must hasten to rejoin them. But before I go, listen please, my father, listen carefully, to what I have to say, so that not one word of it will be forgotten when you come to tell it all to our father Mopani.'

François then gave Kghometsu a full account of what had happened and why he was there, omitting only the fact that the other two of whom he had spoken were Bushmen; an omission in his description Kghometsu would not notice among so many other facts of obviously greater importance.

His only comment at the end was one of a kind of dismay mixed with outrage. 'Little Feather, I warned our father

Mopani of all this months ago. I told him how Mokho had just come from her people and said that the tree of life had started to sing again and what was more, had started to sing with a voice of the people who came out of the sea.'

François recognized this phrase, 'the people who came out of the sea' as the description which the Makoba and all the millions of Africans who worshipped the tree had given to the Portuguese, who some four hundred years before had indeed come out of the sea to invade their great land. The significance of this was not lost on him as he begged Kghometsu to go on.

'When I told our father Mopani about the singing of the tree in this voice of the people of the sea, I told him how important that manner of singing was, because from the moment the tree first went silent and refused to sing to its own people, the greatest prophets foretold that it would only sing again when it could sing in the voice of the people who came out of the sea. It would sing thus according to the prophets as a token that the power of the spirits, which, for far back in time had gone over to the white man had now returned to the men of the tree and grown so great that the peoples who came out of the sea and all the many red strangers who had followed in their tracks, could now be driven back into the sea. Our father Mopani told me then, when I had finished, that "he had heard". But if he had heard indeed, Little Feather, why did he not foresee and forestall all this? Why, Little Feather, why did he not do anything when Kghometsu for many moons now could not sleep because of it?'

François, who as one knows was already obsessed with his own crime of omission in this very regard, could only say quickly, 'Oh my father, if you had seen the thousands, armed with guns, travelling with trucks and led by red strangers and other kinds of strangers who have also come out of the sea and never been seen here before, you will know that not even our father Mopani and the Government in the capital could have prevented what happened at dawn yesterday, and is about to happen around us now.'

Kghometsu was not convinced and the agony of it all clearly hurt as much as ever, which was not surprising as François himself was not entirely convinced by his own words, believing that even he could have done something to prevent it. So he hastened to concentrate for both their sakes on the immediate and overwhelming practical significance of his news.

'I know, my father, I know,' he answered. 'I too could have helped our father Mopani to hear as he should have heard you, but all that is a river run dry behind us now. What matters, please believe me, is that we have no time to lose. I will sit down and write a letter which I want you to give to our father Mopani. You can tell him that I must go back to the three I have left behind in hiding. Tell him I think we can stay there safely for some three to four weeks but no longer. If in that time he cannot come to us, I shall somehow try to come to him or make my way to safety where I can best find it. I can't do so before, I'm certain, because from now on every track in the bush will be watched. You all may even be forced out of your own camp and made to run for your lives towards the capital, until the help that will be organized there can be rushed to meet you, for you are only a handful and the enemy a host of many impis. Just make certain that you tell all to our father as I have told you of the enemy's plans, and give him this letter I will now write, to tell him how he can try to come to us and find our place of hiding. Then hasten, hasten please to help the Major.'

Kghometsu protested vehemently at this. He argued that François should come with him and leave his friends well hidden as François had told him they were. François might have been tempted to give way for the sake of talking to Mopani himself, but with Mopani away the clear call within him was to hurry back, because he knew how his absence would add to the terrible anxieties and difficulties of Nonnie and Xhabbo.

When he could not be persuaded, Kghometsu stood up, and with a clenched fist on his broad chest he announced that in that case, he would accompany François, because every child knew that two guns were better than one and that his grey hairs were not grey for nothing, and the experience that had made them so, would be like an ox-hide shield before François. Deeply moved though he was, François refused resolutely, arguing that one had less danger of being seen by the enemy than two and that Kghometsu was needed more as the only letter-bearer, guide and counsellor to Mopani.

So, his ration of biltong finished, he pulled out his dispatch book and wrote a note. He wrote it deliberately in Afrikaans in case the letter fell into enemy hands. He described carefully how Mopani could find the hill where they were hidden, without mentioning the cave or the manner of their hiding. He merely directed that if Mopani got to this hill unobserved and uttered in daylight three times the call of the fox followed by the piping of a night-plover he, François, would appear and guide him to their refuge. His heart was full of many complex emotions and things he would have liked to have uttered, but he knew that in Mopani's case these were unnecessary. All that Mopani would expect from him and would have time for were facts. Facts would be more welcome to his experienced old heart than dreams to a deprived soul, and all that he needed for instant action.

His factual note accomplished, therefore, he stood up and handed it to Kghometsu saying, 'There, old father, go and go in haste, I thank you, I see you and I praise you.'

For a moment it looked as if Kghometsu would once more argue but in the end he just gave François a long, steady and caring look, the same sort of look which Xhabbo and Nuin-Tara had given him in the cave, as if he too were looking on a son of his own for the last time. Then as if it were almost too much for his worthy, manly and disciplined self, he quickly raised his hand high above his head in that Roman salute of farewell of his people, and turned smartly about, to go off swiftly in the direction of the camp.

François saw him vanish without a backward glance. As Kghometsu went, he felt for the first time a certain relief that now he had cause for definite hope of the future, provided he and Hintza played their part in what was to come. Making his slight preparations to go, he whispered in Bushman to Hintza, who was always the best of listeners, 'Hin, we can't go back the way we came. We can't go back by day either. We'll have to travel by night. So you and I must quickly go and find a place where we can hide and sleep and rest till it's dark. When it's dark, dear Hin, you must go ahead and lead me safely back to Nonnie as you have brought me safely here.'

With that, François was ready for the trail. Knowing the

bush as he did, it was already obvious what he had to do. He had to make for an obscure track, rarely used, except by game, and so unlikely to have been discovered by any of his enemies. The track had only one possible disadvantage. It was perhaps too close for comfort to the point where the road to Mopani's camp forked out from the Punda-Ma-Tenka, but was that, he asked himself, quite the disadvantage it appeared? Could it not be perhaps that the last course of action the enemy would expect of him would be to choose a way so close to their own main route of advance? He thought yes, and so retreated back just far enough into the bush on the banks of the shallow stream to have some cover to travel towards it unobserved. More important, he kept close to the banks so that he could walk on the outcrop of stone – there was, thank God, no need for running any more – ensuring that neither he nor Hintza left any spoor of any kind behind them. Half an hour later he found the track at a point only a quarter of a mile from the great Punda-Ma-Tenka and once in it he scouted round and soon came to a deep, dark dense circle of thorn bushes, like a wreath around a huge boulder. Promptly he and Hintza crawled underneath it and in a bare patch by the stone stretched themselves out on the ground. It seemed that even in the stretching they both fell asleep.

How long they slept he could not tell immediately, though he felt it had not been long, when he was woken by what he thought was a sustained outburst of rifle fire in the direction from which they had come. Although it could not be unexpected, it filled him with a particular acute sense of alarm. Yet since there was nothing he could do about it and he was so tired, he fell asleep again with the greatest ease.

When he woke again, it was dark all round him. At least it appeared to be dark to his eyes as he lay on his side facing the stone, with Hintza snuggled closely up to him. But when, painfully, he forced himself to sit up, feeling the time had come to start back to the cave, he looked around and was startled to see not far away a glow as from firelight beyond the screen of thorns. Watching the glow intently, he heard voices, faint but amazingly clear, considering the barrier of brush and leaves in between. Although he could not distinguish separate words, the tone and deliberation of them indicated that they were not African.

At once he was wide awake. He felt that Hintza's coat was a-bristle under his hand, and already that supersonic whimper of his was vibrating at his ear.

CHAPTER SIX

The Way of the Wind

'Thank you, Hin, I can hear and see them too. Thank you,'
François whispered back reassuringly to Hintza, stroking and
restroking his back to calm him, as he felt the skin under his
hand shivering like an ague of fever with the intensity of warning of something outside Hintza's experience. It was equalled
only by the warning conveyed to him so long ago, just before
the first light of day broke over Hunter's Drift to announce the
coming of Xhabbo into his life.

Still aching all over with fatigue but wide awake since his
own senses were refreshed by his long sleep and raised to their
highest pitch of perception by what he had been through,
François looked hard in the direction of the glow, faint and yet
real among the black leaves, the black thorn, the black trees in
their black envelope of night. He hoped that sitting thus he
would be able to sieve the mass of sound into grains of separate
words, but he failed utterly. All he could tell was that the
owners of the voices must believe themselves to be unusually
secure to be so relaxed and talking thus.

This conclusion was reinforced by the fact that some of the
natural noise of the night had returned to the bush, because
down by the stream he heard some of his favourite sounds; the
great bullfrogs of Africa booming as if they were the bass section of the classical choir of night, followed by an owl introducing a note of fate into their theme, and the bright cricket
sopranos along the banks of the stream high and clear to the
stars. From far away there was a crack like a rifle shot, as some
old elephant tore a strip of his favourite bark from a tree, and
nearby, very nearby, the authentic reveille of courage from the
bravest voice of them all: the spotted little bush-buck of Africa,
barking his defiance of fear. It was almost as if the bush were
demonstrating in its own way what life has always had to do

131

from the beginning. After impediment of tragedy it hastens on round the cataclysm like a stream round a rock, broadening out into a full river impatient to reach the sea. It seemed as though the music were specially contrived for him as an example to follow, so that by taking courage from the singing he would be joining in the rhythm of everything he loved and have a new heart for setting about without delay on his own urgent business.

François allowed himself only moments to give Hintza and himself a little more food and pour some water from his flask into his hat so that Hintza could drink. For the first time, since it was now cool, he too drank long and deep from the flask. Then, almost like a lone survivor fleeing from the burned-out city on the great plain of Troy pouring a libation of wine to the god under whose protection he fled, he decanted water on to the ground at the foot of the boulder, made a little paste of the earth there and once more rubbed it all over his face and hands, so that his skin would not show up unduly in the dark. Gathering his little bundle of baggage and making certain that there was nothing that rattled, and that his rifle was ready for instant fire, he crawled very slowly without a sound, back into the track, not even pausing to warn Hintza of how carefully they would have to go because Hintza, he was certain, was aware of that necessity as much as he.

But once on the faint, rarely used track, clear of that thick circle of thorn, he was amazed how bright and near the glow of firelight was to him, and how much louder the voices sounded. Part of him wanted to ignore the voices and hurry on but part of him, the most insistent part and unfortunately one that filled him with apprehension, was urging him to creep forward and listen in to the voices as he had done so profitably in the pantry of his old home the night before.

Perhaps he would have resisted this half of the urge within him, if it had not been for the fact that somehow its argument seemed to be connected with the shooting that he had heard in the earliest and lightest phase of his sleep by the boulder. This connection made him realize how deep the anxiety caused by that burst of rifle fire had gone into him. For the mere suspicion that it might be the begetter of this dangerous impulse which would send him off in the direction of the glow released it alive and great as ever in his mind. It was as if the impulse had become his own version of the kind of tapping of which Xhabbo had spoken; a tapping so loud and vital that it seemed to come from the accelerating beat of his own heart. He remembered Xhabbo warning him, 'Foot of the Day, we Bushmen have always said that only a fool will not listen to the tapping within himself.'

This recollection of the voice of Xhabbo who had saved him and Nonnie from destruction, was decisive and made him lie down flat in the track, put his arm around Hintza and press him close against him to whisper. 'Sorry, Hin. Sorry. I must go and see what that fire is about, and you must come and help me, so that I don't crawl into any of those strangers.'

Just for a moment, before he crawled on, François looked up through the gap which the game track inevitably made in the roof of the bush and examined the stars that were quick, bright and pointed as ever above him, so that he could read them for the time. It was, he noticed, already after nine so that he had not much slack left if he were to reach the cave before sunrise. That made him even more grudging of the time needed for his task, and consequently he had difficulty in being patient enough for safety in his approach. Yet he managed to crawl forward without a rustle or even the faintest intimation of a rattle from his equipment, until he came to rest by a slight outcrop of stone and brush. There he looked ahead into a clearing he remembered well.

It was a recognized resting place just off the Punda-Ma-Tenka road. In the middle of the clearing a spire of flame rose straining from one of the most extravagant fires he had ever seen, utterly disproportionate even in that world of the bush where firewood was plentiful, but where its natural inhabitants would use it only with their native sense of proportion. Beyond the fire he could just make out the dark shapes of a number of trucks. Between the trucks and the fire were huddles of what he took to be sleeping men. Just on the margin where firelight and shadow of the bush met were the silhouettes of two sentries, perched on stones, one at the Mopani camp end of the clearing and the other in the direction of Hunter's Drift. More important, dangerously close to him and clearly visible in the light of the great fire, were two more men.

They were sitting relaxed, facing each other on two boulders and talking without reserve. One was smoking a pipe and the other a cigarette. It was the cigarette-smoking face, as it showed up like a strange, vivid Goya impression, painted by a brush of flame on one of his blackest canvases, that first caught François's attention. The face was long, lean, drawn and looked worn not so much physically as in a strange, inward way. Absorbed as François had naturally been in the past of the France from which his own ancestors had come, he recognized in it what he always thought of as basic Gallic features. Only it lacked the animation and quickness of expression which François's reading had made him assume normally went with such French faces. One particularly bright brush stroke of flame across it revealed a special dominant of experience, utterly beyond François's own comprehension, which was clamped like a mask on the features. What was more, the firelight glanced so cold and sharp from the eye nearer the flame that it could only be made of glass. Once when the fag-end of the cigarette had to be thrown away, the Frenchman immediately leaned sideways to fumble for a packet of cigarettes in the pocket of his tropical military tunic and took a fresh cigarette from it to put to his lips. The arm that came up to steady the match-box which followed had not a hand but an iron hook to it. Some instinct suggested to François then that the mask clamped on what must have been once a proud and sensitive face, could only be a mask made to measure in a life exclusively of war so that even the pride had superimposed on it a look of iron resolve.

The other man, also in the same uniform, was smoking a pipe which in between puffing he held in his hand in front of him and from time to time turned to point the stem at the French-man as if it would help to inject his meaning into the resistance he was encountering there. The face behind the pipe was rounder, the nose less prominent and the features more symmetrical, but the head was well made and round and the hair above a wide forehead long, thick and somewhat curled. François regretted that he could not see the eyes, because he suspected that the expression in them would have been even more important than the words; words that were still round, warm and lively, as if the speaker had something of a poet buried in him. Whereas even the voice of the Frenchman sounded tired and not disillusioned so much as unillusioned and out of love with life. The voice, though clear, seemed to come from far away in the spirit of the speaker and it was the same voice of course that François had heard the night before. The other voice was the Scottish voice raised in argument at the same hour at Hunter's Drift and the one which had called out the guard just before François's home went up into the air.

Just then the Scottish voice was saying, with a certain sad urgency, 'But I tell you, mon, the pity of it, oh the pity of it, is that I don't believe we'll ever get these men of ours to stop and think before they shoot. I'm afeered I've come a long way since yester'morn and think yon creatures have so great a hatred and a wish of death in them that they're only interested in killing and more killing, and not in the life of any living thing except their own.'

'You are wrong *mon cher*,' the French voice replied as if already tired by the obviousness of what he had to say. 'I understand why you should be angry but I assure you of it: few of these men are just killers. For example, if they were nothing but the killers you imagine, would I have had the trouble I had to make them do the killing we had to do from morning to dark yesterday? I think not. I saw many of them sick with *mal-de-guerre* like *mal-de-mer* afterwards, no? On my rounds after I saw many who could not sleep because of that. It is only the experience they lack. I assure you that in thirty years of war in Africa of the north, the Orient and Europe I have seen material far worse fashioned into as good and disciplined soldiers as any European.'

The unbelief with which the Scot greeted this reply was razor sharp.

'You yourself, my guid officer and gentleman of France, are too used to killing to see what I have seen there. You seem to forget that you ordered your men clearly as I did mine that on no account were they to shoot. Knowing you and your French obsession for saying things clearly, there is no reason for assuming they did not understand your orders. And yet at the moment when they themselves were not threatened, they opened fire on one lone man who came running out of the bush into their midst. They could easily have called him to a halt and held him in a ring of their bayonets so that we had him alive for questioning now. But what did they do? They didn't even have the excuse, not that I find it excusable, of that lot of mine, who opened fire on a pack of lions we found in our way, because lions after all are dangerous. But this man was not dangerous to anyone and overwhelmed with surprise. Yet the moment your chappies saw him, they fired not just a single shot but, judging by the sound, some fifty bullets into him. And so what do we have as a result? He's there lying dead in the bush; the men are all back with us, fast asleep and snoring as if they were as innocent as babies. And the two of us are left with a piece of paper in our hands, scribbled all over in a tongue neither of us understands!'

'I am of a complete accord, *mon cher Écossais*,' the Frenchman replied, unmoved and in the same colourless tone, without feeling or haste. 'It was a *gaffe épouvantable*. I will beg it of the Chairman myself to make it his affair when he joins us presently, to see it does not happen again. That I assure you of. But . . .'

He was interrupted by the Scot who came to his feet with exasperation, his pipe pointed like a pistol at the Frenchman. 'A *gaffe*? You call that unnecessary piece of killing just a *gaffe*? It must be the greatest under-statement ever made in all the long and glorious militarydom of France.'

But even the charge of sarcasm with which the phrase 'glorious militarydom' was packed made no emotional impact on the Frenchman. He merely shrugged his shoulder with an elegance strange in that place because it pre-supposed a *salon* rather than the bush, and repeated, 'Yes, *gaffe, mon cher*. These are technical matters that should be approached in a technical spirit and not have emotions unnecessary added to them. I doubt it of myself whether the sound of shooting in this remote place will have done any damage, militarily; that goes without the saying of course. Also we have the note. We know it is from the boy. It will, I am sure of it, tell us all we need. Remark well, *mon cher,*

136

that boy there for some reason chose a messenger to go to this place we have to attack. Now why? That question there is of a significance *formidable*, is it not? The letter will tell us all, I do not doubt of it myself. You yourself said it is in the language of the despots of the south we have come to fight. Now come and look, is it not so? Surely we are of an accord in this?'

'Aye mon, aye, because here, staring me in the face is the word *Oom*.' The pipe stabbed at the space between like a dagger. 'And beside it there is another word, *liewe*. The first one I know well from the colonial history of Britain in which this word has figured prominently, that it is the South African Dutch for uncle. Oom Jannie, that's what the South African soldiers with whom I fought in the last war called their great General Smuts of whom no doubt you, with your experience of war, have heard. We know that this Oom of the letter can only be that Colonel Théron who is in charge of the camp we have encircled, and are going to attack at first light. And that other word, is the word for beloved. But that mon, can't you see, is what sticks in my gullet. All day long we've been killing men, women and children who are the beloved of other human beings with a right to live just like any of us and no part of the tyranny and injustice we have come to overthrow.'

At this point François knew he had heard all that he needed to know. Kghometsu had been intercepted after leaving him, was dead and his own letter to Mopani describing in detail the hill in which the cave was situated was in the hands of his enemies. He should withdraw at once and hasten back to get them all out of the cave before the enemy could occupy the hill and make it impossible for them to escape. They could no longer contemplate hiding in the cave until the enemy moved, and there was obviously no hope now of Mopani coming to their rescue. And yet he could not get himself to leave. He excused himself by arguing that it would take time still for the 'Cape-coloured gentleman' who knew Afrikaans to arrive with his intelligence unit and decipher his letter, so that he could afford to watch and for a while longer listen with profit to the two officers.

There was, however, another and subtler reason, and more important to François's new self that was so slowly and painfully being born. It was something of which he was unaware in his thinking but nonetheless was a decisive factor as an ingredient of the raw material of greater being which suffering and disaster become when they are accepted and endured without evasion. It was simply that in watching the two officers sitting there portrayed so vividly and timelessly in the paint of that Promethian firelight, they ceased to be the monsters they had been in his mind and were becoming only too human.

He was, in fact, beginning to see them in the sense conveyed so simply and meaningfully in the greeting of 'Bamuthi's people, 'I see you! Yes, I see you!' For this greeting acknowledged with even greater implications than can be expressed in words, the primitive awareness of the importance of looking at all men, even the strangest, always as people and saluting their common humanity by an affirmation of seeing. It was not that his bitterness and anger against the men who had massacred the people he loved was not as great as ever. It was merely that the two officers by the fire were slowly moving out of the focus of his anger, which was shifting to the 'Chairman' they acknowledged as their superior and to the forces at the back of the Chairman, which was not difficult, since none of them was there to be seen.

Meanwhile, the French officer had ignored the Scot's reaction. François suspected from what he had heard last night that they had had differences before – differences which the Frenchman, one pre-supposes, had already disputed within himself over some thirty years or more and of which he was utterly weary. He was answering accordingly as if he had not heard the last part of the Scot's statement, merely confining himself to military essentials, 'And so what reason to disquiet yourself, *mon cher Écossais*? The man may be dead. But all that we have to do is to wait until our Chairman and that coloured gentleman from the Cape of Good *Espérance* join us as they will any minute now, and we will know all.'

The Scot's reply was sharp with exasperation. 'Och, I know that, mon. Meanwhile, to confine myself to the military essentials you love so much, the lad and that hound of his are still about and as long as they are, I do not think we're altogether safe. I need not remind you of what he did to us last night.'

138

The Frenchman this time was quick to reply, the voice somewhat animated now, since it had an opportunity of indulging both an individual and national gift of irony, 'Is it that I detect in you a *volte-face, mon cher?* And you are now out of love with last night's cause, and come to the end of a romantic affair? It would be not unwelcome that it should be so because I, and I think our Chairman as well, feared you favoured enough the boy and would not like to see him caught.'

The Scot did not answer at once. He puffed at his pipe so that the glow in the bowl fell on his brow and once or twice he half-kicked the ground at his feet, before he resumed, 'I have nae changed my view about that laddie one wee bit. I tell you, as I told our Chairman back there, that whate'er the consequences, I would not stand for his killing except in fighting. But as long as I'm an officer in this terrible army of yours I have no option but to think of the safety of even our murderous rabble!'

'A murderous rabble, *mon cher?* And our army and not yours?' The question mark in the voice was so clear that it almost stood visible, scribbled high and bright in the dark above the firelight between the two officers and François. 'Is that what this army of freedom and liberation has become for you? I have a regard exceptional for you I would not like to lose. I might understand your hesitations but I would not like to hear you talk like that before the Chairman again. Above all, *mon cher* friend *Écossais*, I would beg it of you to pay attention to what you say aloud. I beg it of you as a comrade in arms that when we catch the boy – as catch him we will, of that I do not doubt myself – you will not try to protect him, not in the smallest particular of speech or action, because if you do I am not sure that your own life will be your own for long.'

All this was uttered with such seriousness that it came near to touching on a long suppressed world of emotion in the French officer, as if he himself was afraid of what he might be called upon to do if that situation came about.

The Scot, who struck François as not only articulate but extremely observant, fastened on to it at once as if there were hope of support in an underlying ambiguity in the mind of his fellow officer. He asked almost gaily, which one imagines was his characteristic way of defying situations of peril and preventing them from depriving him of his self-control and vision. 'Do I detect a warning, a threat, a promise or all three in what you say, my guid gentleman of France? And may I add that you do surprise me. We in Scotland were always brought up to think that the officers and gentlemen of France first brought chivalry into war in Europe and were models of how this un-civilized business could be done in a civilized way. I would have thought you would be the one person to be on my side. I can only tell you that the history of Scotland is full of stories of young lads just like this lad we are hunting. I tell you the Scottish people would not be what they are today if there had not been in every generation, ever since it occurred to the Scots to think of themselves as Scots, plenty of laddies prepared to behave just as this one has behaved. He's a bonnie fechter and a breed we honour even in our worst enemies!'

There was a long silence before the Frenchman answered, ignoring the last part of the Scot's declamation and concentrating only on what was obviously of great concern to him, 'You asked whether you detect a warning, a threat or a promise, *mon cher*. Well perhaps all three. The warning is from me, your comrade in arms, but the threat is from the situation and the promise in that . . .' He paused before drawing back as from the edge of an abyss in his own mind to return gravely to his first point. 'Perhaps I should explain how serious I find your situ-ation. If our Chairman found that you had become a danger to what he calls the wider plan that has brought us here and ordered you to be liquidated and I was told to do the liquid-ating, evidently it goes to say of itself, it would be extremely distasteful.'

For a second time in one sequence of thought he did not finish a sentence and even for François, perhaps, there seemed a greater menace implied in this failure than there could have been in any threat that he could have openly expressed.

The Scot replied, too gruffly to suggest that there was any great degree of comfort for himself in his own words, 'I do not believe you, mon. I came into this freely and feel myself a free man who can go freely if I find that this army is not the army I came to join.'

'How naïve is it that you can be?' the Frenchman observed,

more crisply, now that he was dealing with the irony of their situation itself. 'You heard the Chairman say last night that only our version of what has happened here must be allowed to go out into the world. Do you think he will permit an officer who permits himself the bourgeois luxury of differing with his political superior, to return to the world to give it his version – a far more fatal version than even that young boy could manage?'

'But dammit, mon, if I give my word of honour that I wouldn't speak of what has happened?' the Scot asked, concerned as he was baffled by the Frenchman's persistence. 'Vile as I might think the things are that we've done, I'm not going to add another level of vileness to it by betraying myself even more than I might have done already!'

'I repeat, how naïve is it that you can be,' the Frenchman's tone was reproving now. 'That is a risk which our Chairman will be incapable of taking; an example he cannot permit. At the first sign of public dissension from you he will take a view most grave of the affair. I will tell you why. Dissension in an officer so well liked as you is dangerous especially because to the contrary of what you think, eighty per cent of the men we lead, amateur soldiers that they still are, are as full of amateur emotions as you over what has happened and your example could be as infectious as the pest. He will, I assure you of it, have no alternative but to make an example of such an example, and without hesitation at all make to liquidate you.'

There followed a silence which may not have been as long as it felt to François, guilty of lying there fascinated in this new, strange way and not getting on with his own urgent mission and call of duty. It was significant that the pause apparently was over-long for the Frenchman's liking as well. For a while he watched his opposite number intently, his glass eye fixed in one unchanging glitter in the firelight, as his life had been fixed on a single course within, while the Scot sat there puffing with a measured calm at his pipe, that was also significant considering how quick his responses had been before.

Clearly he was taking what he had just heard most seriously, pondering it with a native shrewdness that made the Frenchman's charge of *naïveté* a strangely limited and technical one,

141

and wondering perhaps whether he had not already told his fellow officer too much about himself and whether he should continue to tell him more. He was obviously not going to talk until he had answered a range of new questions and doubts to himself.

It was the Frenchman therefore who spoke first, this time with something almost warm if not pleading in his travel-stained voice. 'I know, *mon cher*, that you do not like our Chairman. I think it is only because you do not understand him and know him as I do. For example, believe me he was of a sincerity absolute when he told you last night that he is taking life on such a large measure now because he wants to save the taking of far more life later.'

There followed a long military exposition by the Frenchman in support of the Chairman's actions. It dwelt on the need for gaining time for the vast supplies and reinforcements coming up behind them to catch up without being observed; the absolute necessity of complete surprise for attacking and over-whelming the great mining city so that it could be held as a self-contained base for future operations; also the capture of the railway line so that they had a line of supply to the Congo, to Zambia and Broken Hill on the Tanzanian border, and from there on to the ports of the East Coast of Africa. That done they could settle down to a long 'gentleman's war' and take proper prisoners and care for the wounded, which would satisfy even his Scottish friend's tender heart. But until then they had no option but to kill everyone in their way. In that manner far less life would be lost than by sparing people in what his Scottish friend most misguidedly thought was a merciful and humane way now. Was there not an English expression about being cruel to be kind? Well, this was what it was all about.

The Scot listened without interruption and, even then, hesitated before he said, François thought rather bleakly, 'What you say, my guid friend – I recognize how guid a friend you're trying to be – what you say may be logical in a purely military sense but this is more than a military matter. You see, like so many of your countrymen I fear you have a genius for being logical on a partial, or even a false hypothesis. Therefore the conclusions you come to inevitably are only partially true, if not wholly false. The trouble not only with all you militarists but you French today is that you know only a logic of the mind and forget the logic of the heart. You seem to have forgotten what one of your greatest, Pascal, once said, 'the heart has reasons which the mind does not know of'. You see, once the French spirit was important to us Scots, especially one like me who studied philosophy and the humanities at university. It seemed to be so complete. For instance, among many other great instances, it had not only Descartes to speak for reason as reason must be spoken for; it also had Pascal to speak for the heart. But you have all thrown Pascal out of the window, and kept only the Descartes of yourself by your dying national fire.'

The Scot paused perhaps as if he felt he had said enough, but on reflection went on. 'Would it make sense to you if I told you that it was not just for reasons of the mind but also of the heart that I came to join you? Like you I have fought in one world war because I hate tyranny and want to see men free and equal everywhere. Having grown up in the slums of Glasgow as I have, I came out of the war determined to help create a world in which no social or racial or religious discrimination or injustice could exist. Would you believe it if I told you I came here because I was urged by a new movement in the church of my country to . . .'

'You would not surprise me at all, my friend,' the Frenchman hastened to interrupt. 'The churches have always been highly professional in persuading men that they can kill others in the name of God. I have the greatest admiration for their skill in this regard. That goes without the saying of it.'

'Ye canna be thinking of the church as I do,' the Scot was stung where he obviously liked it least. 'Of course the churches have often failed the purpose for which they were established. I dinna speak of those. I speak for a new church to come that will serve its original religious purpose by creating a new brotherhood of men, through a total involvement with the lives of the exploited and oppressed. And I promise you it was this new voice that assured me I was needed for a campaign of limited violence so that a better order could replace the old. That is why I am here. But how can a better order come about if we begin it in this brutal way? Even you must see the nonsense it is,

143

to say the least of it, when you count and consider all those babies and women we killed, all those people we've destroyed these last twenty-four hours who I am certain have never even heard of the injustice, let alone experienced the injustices under the class systems and tyrannies we have come to overthrow. None of them could ever have constituted any danger to us, in spite of what our Chairman says. Unless this becomes from now on the campaign of limited violence I was promised, I shall . . .' The Scot paused as if warned just in time that he had said enough and ended, François thought rather conscious of being feeble and afraid, 'Well, I shall just have to think again.'

'Think and think again as much as you like, *mon cher,*' the Frenchman commented as if encouraged by this obvious sign of caution in the Scot. 'But please, I beg it of you confine yourself to thinking.'

The Scot behaved as if he had not heard him and added earnestly, 'I shall look upon this attack in the morning as a test. Help me to see it is carried out as a proper military operation that can stand up to examination in the light of any world day, let alone our own conscience. Surely we can now give our enemies a chance to surrender, take prisoners-of-war and proper care of the wounded. If we can do that tomorrow I shall know we are engaged on the campaign of limited violence to which I am pledged. And . . .'

He got no further. A third, 'How naïve can you be?' broke from the Frenchman, who sounded not so much impatient as in a state of intellectual despair. 'A campaign of limited violence? Oh *mon cher*, once you start on the way of violence there is no limit to violence until the greatest violence of all has subdued the lesser violence. You talk almost as if there are villains in the piece of life that is our lot and fail to see that it is the life itself that is the villain. I am afraid all my experience tells me that we human beings can only ever be cured from using violence by some system so strong that it can unite the world by force into one powerful society and keep it united and disciplined and in a state of order by force. That is why I am here. That is why I came from the Orient with our Chairman because I know that he represents the one force in the world which can unite the world in this way and that once he has accomplished his objective, you will be amazed by the moderation and tolerance the men he serves will bring to the life of the world.'

'So we are to be like a "tea-leaf" who cracks a safe,' the Scot answered wryly, 'and justifies his stealing by saying it was so that he could live honestly ever after.'

The French officer started as if to protest but was stopped by the Scot saying, quickly, 'Forget it, mon, it's not important,' and hastening on, apparently now fully aware of the danger of prolonging the discussion on a personal plain and so seeking safety in generalization. 'I think you are uttering one of the oldest heresies in life, thinking that you can achieve the right end by the wrong means. I remember reading at my university that, long ago, one of the great men of this China you admire, said "the right end can only be achieved by the right men serving it in the right way and at the right time". I would agree with you that we all have the right end in mind but are you certain that we are serving the right men in the right way, let alone at the right time? The question is important to me, you see, because I came into this as a matter of conscience and nothing else, and let us leave it at that.'

However, the Frenchman, who obviously had come to care what the Scot thought of him, would not leave it at that but asked surprisingly tentatively in one so accustomed to command, 'Would it surprise you if I told you that it is a matter of conscience to me as well?'

'Aye, it might, or it might not but I expect it will in the end,' the Scot replied. 'It depends what you mean by conscience, mon.'

'The conscience of duty,' the Frenchman answered promptly and for the first time with some show of emotion as if he were touching on something beyond reason in himself at last. 'The duty of a soldier to be obedient to higher command. The conscience of duty that comes out of the knowledge that always war is organized chaos and that it relapses into greater chaos if there is no obedience to higher command.'

'That, mon,' the Scot said rather sadly, 'is too partial a conscience for my definition. I do not want to sound a prude but a conscience is not a conscience unless it is entire and includes sensibility of the highest values of which life is capable. I had an old professor of philosophy at my university who defined conscience as the voice of truth in man calling on him always to see life steadily and live it whole. Unless your higher command is so high that it is no longer of this world I might find your conscience somewhat a cripple of a conscience. But let us forget it, mon,' this last said with a return to a bantering tone and a certain pleading playfulness.

'I would willingly forget it, *mon cher*,' the Frenchman replied almost as if speaking to himself, 'but there is something in all this that will not forget me. Look, I have often asked myself why I go on being a soldier and do not leave it all, for there can be no one on this earth alive who has seen more of fighting than I have seen, and believe me I do not like the killing part of it. I am a professional and pride myself on killing no more than is absolutely necessary for the purpose. I do not even hate the people I fight against. Hate and killing for killing's sake, mass slaughter and war on civilians, only came to war when the civilians themselves and their self-righteous amateurs joined in. But that is by the way. What I would wish to say is that very early on in life I found I had a gift for war. It is not a gift that I chose or a gift I sought. It is a gift that chose me. A gift inextricable, as Virgil might have said. You see why I say it is life that is the villain?

'In the beginning I thought I would follow this gift with honour. I come from what you would call a family very *Catholique*. Contrary to what people think, in the army of a republican and anti-clerical France, it was a disadvantage very great to be not even very, but just a little *Catholique*. All the best careers were given to officers of the people who were anti-religious and sons of the anti-clerical establishment of the Republic. That is why I was forced to find a career not in the regiments in which my family had served France for generations but in the Foreign Legion in Africa. Even so I did it enthusiastically because there I thought this gift of mine could serve both God and France. I need not go into the details but in the fighting in North Africa before many years, from what I saw, God as far as I was concerned was the main casualty. Yet there was still France. I still believed in France and all that France stood for, the highest kind of civilization I could serve with honour. All the feeling I had before in God now just went into believing in France. I cannot tell you how this belief was shaken by the capitulation of France in the last war, and by Vichy. But still as part of the Resistance in France I found still beating a pulse of the France in which I believed. But when the war was over and I was back with the Foreign Legion serving in Indo-China, there France became the second great casualty, and then there was nothing.

'I will not overburden you with the details, but permit me to give you one example how France died there. I commanded a unit of parachutists. We were parachuted into Dien Bien Phu during the great siege. Do you know that twenty-five per cent of my men were killed parachuting because the parachutes were faulty? They had been sold and bought with full knowledge of the fact. The manufacturers and armament profiteers in my country bribed the ministry of a corrupt régime to overlook that they were faulty, knowing that thereby they were risking the lives of thousands. And do not think it happened only with parachutes! It happened with many other kinds of vital war materials and happened because the State and the civilians in France did not care about us who thought we were dying for France. They were either indifferent or cared only about the money they could make out of the war. It was common knowledge among all us soldiers. I had known of it from the beginning. But that day when it happened to my men who trusted me to take care of them in battle, France died, and I was left with nothing, and nowhere to take this gift of mine.

'And so,' the Frenchman concluded wearily, with a turn to his more prosaic military self, 'in the end I brought my gift here where you see me, because as a prisoner-of-war in Indo-China I met our Chairman and his masters. I found them in need of my gift. I found also a cause devoted to compelling this villainous life of ours into being good and just to all.'

'You, *mon cher,* may ask, what is there that is so important about such a gift? But I can tell you there is everything in it for me. It is only in the face of danger, the more extreme the danger the better, that I, Jean Armand, become something more than myself, that I am rescued from a self I despise and that fatigues me greatly. When all men are frightened and dying

147

around me, I find myself in a state of exaltation unbelievable with a clarity of mind and capacity for seeing and taking decisions that is extraordinary. Often in the midst of battle, a calm that passes all understanding possesses me and I do not hear the noise of battle and all is so quiet within me that I can hear something like a voice saying to me, 'Jean Armand, for this you were conceived, unto this end you were born.' So great a feeling of peace comes to me then that in the silence after the voice and beyond the sound of battle, I hear a distant music yet great and distinct, that I never hear in other music, and I see a beauty *éblouissante* seen in no work of art on earth. I see the beauty of the courage in man which is the only thing that makes him free. I see men you would dismiss as negligible transfigured in battle and noble with this beauty, and I feel myself no longer alone and unwanted but in a great company of many more than are fighting with me.

'You would not call me superstitious but it is as if I hear the tramp of all men who have ever fought for life since the beginning of time come marching up from the other side of the world to stand at my side in battle.

'It is only when the battle is over and the war is finished and this gift is no longer needed that I, Jean Armand, feel alone and know fear that is like a physical pain of which I cannot speak. Then suddenly all that is extraordinary in life is gone and there is no beauty and music left, and the world is drab again with ordinary men full of extraordinary greed, and I am afraid, not only for me but for all of us. Even now, I confess, I do not want this conversation to end although we have said everything that we can say to good effect. Because then the silence will come at me and this silence is not a silence so much as a voice of fear that I do not understand and know not how to solve.'

The Scot, who was amazed by the eloquent outpouring from his disciplined colleague, so spare in mind and spirit, put out a hand as if to comfort him, but paused half-way as if he knew how inadequate and even perhaps unwelcome the gesture could be to such a seared and enclosed personality. He spoke instead in a voice warm with sympathy, 'I understand, I think, more than I have understood before. But, you see, there speaks the rejected Pascal in you.'

'Pascal? I do not understand what Pascal has to do with it,' the Frenchman exclaimed, as if he felt the flow in his thoughts stopped like a man tripped up in full stride.

'Yes, Pascal, mon,' the Scot replied even more warmly, since the sympathy he meant to convey appeared to have been obscured by the surprise caused by his remark. 'The Pascal who said somewhere in his past – how he too was frightened by the silence eternal of those infinite spaces.'

As he finished, the Frenchman lit yet another cigarette and sat there looking into the darkness, the firelight red in his glass eye, while the Scot opposite leaned forward, slightly puffing away at his pipe.

Down by the river it seemed to François that the frogs had never sounded so loud, and night sounds were now more highly orchestrated by the addition of new instruments; the far-off voice of a lion, the cough of a leopard nearby and the whimper of little bush-apes sent to the tops of the tallest trees by fear, and the long black-sea call of the plover like a bosun piping the Dog Star on deck for its watch on the wake of the night that is the Milky Way.

He did not know enough yet to realize that they might have sounded so loud and meaningful because they were witnesses to another round of what is perhaps the oldest and least resolved dialogue in the heart of man. That it might indeed have been on some such night that Aristophanes was induced by the Brek-ke-keks-keks-koax-koax of the prototypes of frogs to set two of the greatest specialists in the workings of fate to argue out, in an underworld of the dead, the meaning of suffering on life on earth.

Yet the oldness implicit in it all made François instinctively turn to what was oldest in his young life. For despite a certain glimmer of recognition of some humanity in the scene which had come to him in the beginning, it had slowly reverted to resentment and then grown to an anger which he thought, wrongly at the time, was reflected in the stirring and restlessness of Hintza, who kept putting his nose to François's cheek and nudging him repeatedly.

The anger, produced by what he had heard, came to a boil. Had he been capable of putting all of his emotion into words, he might have cried aloud, 'How could two men like you come to such killing before you had settled this argument in and between you? The least one might have expected from the lot of you was that you should have been absolutely certain in your own minds that you were right, before you robbed people of their lives forever. It's unforgivable that you can still sit there arguing about the rights and wrongs of it all like members of a debating society and not the leaders of a band of the killers you are. And oh, so sorry for yourselves. You seem to be more concerned about your own emotions to your killing than the killing itself. Dear God, those frogs by the river make more sense than you. For they find a frog's life in a world full of enemies cause enough for a gratitude so great that they are compelled to break out in song and tell the stars how full of it they are!'

All recollection of how the Scot had, after a fashion, pleaded for him and the humanities vanished, and the tide of condemnation turned to run fast in François. The contrast between what these men had done and the well-beloved night of Africa, which was wrapped like a blanket around him, was overpowering, because no other night on earth is so instinct with love as the night of François's Africa. Even at that tragic moment in his life, it had come tall and bejewelled, to sink to its knees to the ground like a mother by a hurt child, to remove all the pain of the sun that had scorched it, and so to enable the earth to forgive the day its fire. It was a natural moment of infinite compassion that made the lack of compassion in others incomprehensible and unendurable. It joined what was the oldest he had in himself, and that was his dead father, Ouwa, resurrected in his memory. It was almost as if Ouwa were there beside him to remind him that the debate he overheard was slanted and incomplete. There was a third voice not yet heard in the debate and, as far as François was concerned, it was a voice that was decisive. It spoke through all sorts of things Ouwa had said over the years in connection with this very cause those men by the fire purported to serve. He remembered with a pain which blurred his eyes with tears, that all the many dear people as well as brutal enemies who had been killed in the bush in the last forty-eight years were not the first casualties in this particular war. His father, Ouwa, was the first. He had been the first, as far as François knew, to take up this cause and the first to die, killed by the common enemy of all three of them. Yes, he had to admit it; Ouwa, the Scot and the Frenchman had the same enemy and were on the same side. That was the irony of it. Ouwa himself had been murdered, as he saw it, by the people the other two called the 'tyrants in the south', killed simply by their turning their backs on Ouwa, rejecting him irrevocably because he had recognized error in their way of life, and was trying to put it right in the only fashion that life could ever be put permanently right.

Fragments of all sorts of related things Ouwa had said came to him in words so full of illumination that they shone like fireflies before his eyes, coming red and glowing out of the darkness of the past and vanishing in an up-down, down-up little rhythm into the darkness of what was still to come. For instance, he recalled Ouwa talking to his mother, Lammie, so far back that he did not understand all of it at the time but in words that had stayed with him because he knew from the tone of his parents' voices that they were words of overwhelming importance.

Lammie had been asking Ouwa if they were not wrong to be so uncompromising and should they not modify their attitude to the people who had turned their backs on them, and Ouwa had answered, 'It isn't any good because you see every human being has his own inborn sense of contract with life. He has, it is true, also an important sense of contract with the community into which he has been born and its system of ethical rules and other obligations with a validity he cannot reject lightly. But above that is his own special contract with life itself. This contract is entirely between him and life and nothing, not even the community, can be allowed to suppress it, if it should drive him into conflict with it. This contract is in the keeping of its own voice – a voice we call conscience and no man can refuse to disobey this voice and ever know any peace again. Believe me, this unease, this disquiet and enmity of neighbours that has come into our lives, because they found us guilty of having broken our contract with society, is a peace that passes all understanding in comparison with what would happen to us if we broke the special sense of contract that you and I have with life itself.'

There were many other memories, now that the past was in full resurrection. There was Ouwa again saying that it was only by education and re-education and patient exhortation and evocation and change of heart and imagination that men could be permanently changed. You could not punish men into being better; you could not punish societies into being more; you could not change the world by violence and by frightening people into virtue by killing off their inadequate establishments. The moment was upon us when we had to accept without reserve that the longest way round in the human spirit was always the shortest way there. How Ouwa's tongue relished the irony implicit in the paradox. There was no short cut to a better life on earth. Impatience and short cuts were evil and destructive. There were no short cuts to the creative, there was no magic in creation except the magic of growth. Creation was growth and growth was profoundly subservient to time laws of its own, which could not be broken without destroying the process and bringing down disaster upon all. And here the sonorous voice of 'Bamuthi joined that of Ouwa, the deep bass echo coming from the cliffs of Amageba where the evening shadows gather in the ancient mountains and where his spirit was believed to have gone, reiterating again and again, 'Remember, Little Feather, patience is an egg that hatches great birds. Even the sun is such an egg. Hamba Gashle! Go slowly, because if you go slowly, good things will come to you and you will walk to the end of the road in peace and happiness.'

Then again there came the measured, slightly pedantic voice of Ouwa urging that the real art of living was to keep alive the longing in human beings to become a greater version of themselves, to enlarge this awareness of life and then to be utterly obedient to the awareness. Obedience to one's greater awareness, and living it out accordingly to the rhythm of the law of time implicit in it, was the only way. Unlived awareness was another characteristic evil of our time, so full of thinkers who did not do and doers who did not think. Lack of awareness and disobedience to such awareness as there was meant that modern man was increasingly a partial, provisional version instead of a whole, committed version of himself. That was where tyranny, oppression, prejudice and intolerance began. Tyranny was partial being; a part of the whole of man masquerading as his full self and suppressing the rest. All started within before it manifested itself without and tyranny began within partial concepts of ourselves and our role in life. Hence the imperative of obedience, obedience to our greatest awareness and the call always to heighten it still.

All this, Ouwa would add, meant living in terms not of having but of being; a difference which in his own inimitable, ironic way he always stressed was something our civilized superiors could learn from their primitive inferiors. For what, he often asked, was the difference between the 'Bamuthis of this world and the Europeans of Africa, if not that the Europeans specialized in having and the 'Bamuthis in being.

At that flashpoint of memory both Ouwa and 'Bamuthi were joined first by what his old nurse Koba had told him of the Bushmen and then above all by the figure of her dispossessed kinsman Xhabbo, poor in everything in which the Europeans and the Africans were rich, but rich in a way in which they were poor and deprived; rich in a sense of belonging. Though naked in body Xhabbo moved brightly dressed in François's imagination in his own vivid, unique experience of life and not in the second-hand experience that passed for living in the civilized world without; never alone and unknown but always feeling known and part of life and travelling in the company of even the remotest of the stars.

And then he remembered Ouwa saying that that was why any real change in life could begin only by example and the texture and quality of being brought to it. Hence no one could take others further than he had taken himself. The meaning of one's life depended on the element of becoming in the midst of one's being; the process of becoming a more authoritative expression of new possibilities and qualities of life.

This was followed by Ouwa's insistence – if one could use so emphatic a word for the expression of the thought of one who hated emphasis – that this special contract which a man had with life itself demanded that he accept without reservation or resentment the whole of his past as the raw material for the being he accomplished in the here and now, as material for becoming something more than life had been either in the past or present. And he remembered Ouwa saying with unusual tenderness that the life of any human being or any animal, even the smallest of insects, could be taken only in defence of life conceived in some terms such as those and never for any other reason.

Watch your dislikes as much as your likes, he would add, and remember all men tend to become the thing they oppose. The greatest and most urgent problem of our time was to find a way of opposing evil without becoming another form of evil in the process. Hence the New Testament's enigmatic, 'Resist not evil'. One had just to pray, or as 'Bamuthi would put it, to ask with one's heart, to be delivered from evil and try to be something that was not evil and more than good; something he called whole.

One had to reject corruption by suffering as much as corruption by power, be equally uncompromising and unsentimental about both. These two were the main sources of corruption in man, although there was a third, increasingly desperate contributing factor; corruption by numbers, our tendency to allow collective values to become man's greatest values. Had Lammie and François ever thought, he had asked with a subtle, ironic curl to his lips, that when Christ referred to 'Where two or three are gathered together in my name' he might have been expressing a maximum and not a minimum? Had François and Lammie thought how significant it was that Christ's real work was concentrated on only twelve disciples? He had spoken to thousands only once to deliver his Sermon on the Mount; but thereafter mostly to the public in as small numbers as possible. Even so, one of the twelve had proved a wrong one, though perhaps not by accident but by design.

The time had come, Ouwa had suggested, to change the group approach, to make the collective individual and the universal specific, and to avoid mass solutions and the abstractions of numbers like the plague. Men and their meaning were in danger of drowning in a flood of the collectivism of numbers greater than the world had ever experienced, and all creation depended now on the speed with which men could be detached

154

from it, breaking it up by being their own unique selves. Something along these lines, he thought, would make one a modern man. Did François and Lammie realize that so far there had only been one truly modern man, and he had been crucified two thousand years ago?

He, Ouwa, had been told that all this was no use and too late, for the final disaster was already upon us. Ouwa disagreed. One must live life, he thought, as if disaster would never come. It should be one's own finest point of honour never to accept disaster, if for no other reason than making certain that when disaster did come it was the right kind of disaster life needed. It could be that for the moment the greatest victories were only to be won by losing in such a way that losing became a form of winning. Here, unsolicited in François's memory, came a kind of pagan Amen in an echo of 'Bamuthi's deep bass voice: 'Little Feather, the warrior who returns to his kraal from battle without purifying himself first of the spirit of killing that took him away brings the vanquished back with him and the vanquished will conquer him in their turn.'

François was near weeping as he remembered this and above all that flourish of defiance from Ouwa that had preceded it and was revealed to him and Lammie in Ouwa's dying days. It flew bright over all other memories as if it were a flag of union before being nailed to the mast of a ship sinking in a battle against overwhelming odds.

All of this struck François quick and bright as lightning and hardly had the truth within himself been resurrected and the silence between the two officers still not broken, when he felt Hintza not only nudging him in the cheek but lashing him with his tail as well. That brought him alert back into a world where he was lying flat on the ground, and he realized at last that it was not a participation in the turmoil of his own emotions that had made Hintza so restless but a strange harsh murmur of sound coming out of the darkness towards them from the direction of Hunter's Drift. As he heard it the sentry posted at the Hunter's Drift end of the camp jumped from his perch on a boulder of stone, came striding fast towards the pair of officers, stood to attention before them and blurted out: 'Trucks to the right of us, sir!'

155

The two officers looked at one another as if they were coming out of a trance of their own. The Scot was the first to find his voice and break the silence with a bantering, 'Ah, our Mr Chairman, I presume,' hesitated, but could not resist adding, 'no doubt bringing up a full complement of his thoughts as well.'

This drew a quick comment from the French officer and although François had already turned about and was beginning to crawl back the way he had come and so could not see the scene, he could imagine the severe expression that went with his comment, 'You can make a mock of yourself of the Chairman as often as you like, *mon cher*, provided you remember that his thoughts have a habit of becoming deeds as well, and if you would permit me of it, since you quoted an ancient Chinese saying to me just now, I will return the compliment and remind you of another: "The master speaks but once".'

The Scot sounded unrepentant and answered like one uttering a truth in jest, 'It depends on whom you consider your master to be.'

François heard no more. He was crawling back the way he had come as fast as he could and the camp by the fire at once was loud with the sound of men being summoned to prepare for the newcomers. For François this was a welcome sign of inexperience in his enemies which, slight as it was, encouraged him. They obviously had no idea how far sound could travel at night through any gap in the bush and this sound might just be audible to any scout which the experienced old 'Major' at Mopani's camp, warned by Kghometsu's messengers, surely would have sent out as soon as it was dark. Then, man-made sound, particularly mechanical sound, travelled farthest of all so that François knew the trucks were further away than they sounded. It would be an hour if not more before the loose, earthy beloved old Punda-Ma-Tenka road would allow them to get to their destination. And even when they arrived, surely it would take some time before they came round to explain to the Chairman all that had happened, sorting out the priorities of the situation and getting their intelligence unit working on his intercepted letter.

However, François was by training not inclined to be overoptimistic and in matters of life and death in the bush he always remembered one of Mopani's maxims, 'a hunter should always remember that a comforting belief in everything being for the best often does not prevent the worst somehow from happening'. Accordingly he prepared to hasten back to the cave. First he turned on his back and looked at the sky. From the angle of Orion, which had started to dip somewhat towards the West, he realized that he had been lying listening to that debate by the fire for close on an hour. That did not dismay him perhaps as much as it should have done because somehow it had seemed a great deal longer – a length that could not be counted in hours or even days.

Yet to return to the immediate practical issues, even the loss of an hour of darkness could be serious. If he were to reach the cave before daylight there could now be no question of following that faint, inadequate game track as he had intended to after parting with Kghometsu. The shortest and easiest way back was by the track he had followed in the morning. Once certain that he was deep enough in the bush to eliminate any risk of giving his presence away, he came to his feet, put Hintza in the lead and followed an old rhinoceros trail that led him to it, somewhat perturbed by the pain of moving even at the slow pace imposed on him by the difficulties of so contrite a trail.

There was risk of course in what he proposed doing. He could run into some kind of guard left there by his enemies, but somehow he thought that most unlikely. From what he had heard and now knew of the invaders, he was certain that all the troops in the vicinity would be regrouped in overwhelming numbers for the attack on Mopani's camp, which his action the night before had precipitated, because the original plan had been to regroup and rest at Hunter's Drift before moving forward. But even should they have left a guard on the trail, he had no doubt that with Hintza in the lead, they would spot the guard before he spotted them.

It is an indication of what the nature of the night of Africa does for those who belong to it as François did, that it never occurred to him that he might have cause to fear any wild animals as he had in the morning. It was just a fact of life in the bush that unless one were born to be the natural prey of the few animals who made a speciality of hunting at night, one had less cause for fear in the dark than at any other time. Hintza perhaps was a disquieting exception to the rule because of the love of leopards for the flesh of dogs. Leopards were supremely of the night. But they felt so at home and secure in it that they were far less aggressive then than when dazzled by the day. In any case they were methodical animals who liked to work out a plan of campaign before they did their killing of carefully pre-selected prey. It was extremely unlikely, even should he run into a leopard, that it would attack, and at the speed at which François proposed travelling he and Hintza would be in and out of even so wide an area as a leopard's awareness before it could be tempted to form a plan for attack. His one instinctive precaution was to insist that Hintza did not travel as far ahead of him as he had done in the morning, and he gave Hintza an explicit operation order in Bushman to this effect before setting out.

At first it was difficult to supervise Hintza's movements be cause the hour or so he had spent staring at that immense fire of his enemy had dimmed his vision, but soon it began to recover and improve at such a rate that he was astonished at what a distance he could keep the fast moving shadow of Hintza in view. When the shadow tended to get lost along the track, so still was it, that a whispered command which died immediately on the leaves of the dense bush hemming them in, would bring Hintza back closer towards him.

By eleven he was once more in the broad, well-used trail. There he paused, rested and fed himself and Hintza. Above all he listened in with the utmost care to the night. Apart from the far-off sound of the military trucks moving up on the road to the West, he heard only normal sounds expressed in such a free, un-selfconscious manner that he was relatively certain no ab-horred beings were about in his part of the bush. Even more than listening carefully, he observed Hintza closely. Hintza was sitting on his haunches erect and close beside him, the best natural radar system of early warning a human being in the bush could possibly have. The scrutiny, close as it was, not only reassured François completely but did his heart good. Hintza was so without apprehension now that he was almost entirely preoccupied in the many varied and sensitive ways he had of showing François affection and letting him know how much it meant not having to share him with others, however briefly, and being at their ease alone together after all those brutal separations and alarms of the past two days. He did this with such eloquence and delicacy that François had to respond. He put his arm round him, pressed him close against him while giving his mind to consider the rate at which they would have to travel. He remembered that it had taken him between four and five hours travelling at the limit of his capacity to reach the stream where he had met Kghometsu. He had now rejoined the track some three to four miles nearer to the cave and by his reading of the stars still had some six and a half hours of darkness left.

That of course gave him more time than he had taken in the morning. Yet, considering that it was night and that his whole body was aching with fatigue he assumed that he would not be able to go as fast as he had gone in the morning. He really had no time to spare at all. Once he was sure in his own mind of what he had to do, and the last of their rations eaten, he set out at his fast, long-distance hunting jog.

At first it was even worse than he feared. The reaction of his aching muscles and legs was so violent that he doubted whether he could go a furlong at that pace, let alone keep it up for as long as necessary. Yet he forced himself to continue with an immense act of will and as he began warming up, the pain and the stiffness began to diminish. All the natural resilience and reserves of energy of someone who had led so active a life joined in the process so that his movement found a natural, almost self-generating rhythm. His second breath came to him with an ease and steadiness that surprised him. Moreover the loss of vision brought about by the dark impeded him far less than he had anticipated. It was almost as if the soles of his feet had within them a clear memory of the track they had travelled so often in the past that he hardly needed his eyes to direct them. A strange, yet definite kind of reassurance entered him through the soles of his feet from the track itself, as if all the countless feet of the forgotten men who had trodden it over the years still lay there in the bush defined like a line in the palm of a black hand, had imprinted upon it the message for their successors that however winding, casual and tentative the track might appear to them, it was the certain way from life to life as it always had been for them.

What astonished him most of all, however, was the difference made to fatigue by the fact that the night was so cool, whereas the day had been so hot. It was another fact of all the love implicit in the night working on his behalf, lending a clarity to all his senses and breathing hope in him, so that if anything he travelled faster and with less labour than he had done in the morning.

The exhilaration produced by all these unexpected factors warmed his blood like wine. He passed the boulders and places where he had rested in the morning without even being tempted to do so again, merely saluting them in his heart as friends and thanking them for the shelter they had given him. Soon, much sooner than he had ever dreamt possible, he passed the place where the old elephant monument had stood and, only a few hundred yards further on, the sun-parlour of the pride of young lions. Even in the dark he saw that the surface of that lovely grassy little clearing was torn and littered with leaves, twigs and shattered branches, no doubt from the outburst of shooting to which the Scot had referred. But beyond noting it, he did not pause, afraid that since his body and stride had now found their own special rhythm he must not abandon it or he might never be able to recover it again. From time to time he glanced quickly up at the stars that were sextant and chronometer to him, and was relieved to see that his fears of running out of darkness were not going to be realized. A faint feeling came to him that a tide of fate might have turned for him. But in true primitive fashion he did not allow himself to take it for granted, in case Providence found him presumptuous and reversed it again.

Only one immediate problem perplexed him more and more as he drew nearer the place where he had to branch off for the cave. Would he be strong enough to carry Hintza as he had done the previous morning, so that no tell-tale tracks were left on the ground? He would have to try and though he could go on jogging along for a considerable time, to stop, pick up and carry Hintza in his arms, seemed beyond the powers of a profoundly exhausted self.

Close to the place where he had to branch off, he called Hintza back in a whisper. Hintza, immediate as ever, had hardly joined him when there rose up on the silence about half a mile ahead the clear and urgent call of a plover. No plover's call could have sounded more like a plover piping an outward-bound summons to the night, but there was something about it that made François suspect it came from a plover that he had, as it were, known personally. Also, to his amazement, Hintza, instead of watching him had turned sharply about and with ears erect, nose up, was sniffing and re-sniffing the air in the direction from which the call had come. Most significant of all, his tail had begun to wag tentatively.

François's thumping heart beat even faster. Either one of them had made mistakes in anticipation in the past. But the two of them together had never yet been wrong. But for once he was almost certain that out of desperation they were imagining wishful things. Then the plover called again. The call sounded somewhat nearer and so realistic and urgent that a mile away somewhere near his old home, another plover felt compelled to reply. François knew then that he had to investigate the call, particularly since Hintza was already in such a state of conviction that he was not wagging his tail so much as being wagged by it.

François instantly knelt down beside him and whispered, 'Yes, Hin, I think you're right. Go and find him but go carefully in case we're both wrong.'

Hintza bounded off while François waited for what seemed to him a very long time, his gun unslung and at the ready, his chest heaving and himself doubtful whether he could shoot straight if he had to. But it could have been no time at all really before he heard, first very faintly, the pad of Hintza's feet bounding along the track. The sound of the rush of his dog's approach had hardly reached him when Hintza's elongated shadow appeared, and, wildly impetuous, threw himself at François, put his paws on his shoulders so that he could look him straight and deep in the eyes. That done, he jumped down, whisked about and led off down the track again. This time François had to follow as well, all the pain and stiffness in his body rushing back after even so brief a pause. Two turns in the track further on he saw the shadow of a person coming sound-lessly towards him until there, remarkably clear under the star-light, was Xhabbo.

'Oh Foot of the Day!' Xhabbo exclaimed softly, the emotion running deep in the still tone of his voice, 'I heard you coming from afar and hearing felt myself living again so that I came hurrying to meet you.'

François did not pause to reflect that either this was an implied criticism of the manner in which he and Hintza had travelled along the track or just another startling manifestation of Bushman powers of perception. There was no room in him for anything except relief that he had achieved what had seemed unbearable and impossible only a few hours before and was back with a beloved helper and friend. With the relief, the long-rising flood of suppressed weariness broke through his re-sistances and threatened to overwhelm him. Suddenly he was without breath enough to respond properly, and could utter only half the greeting a well-brought-up Bushman would have thought appropriate: 'I too, Xhabbo, live again in a way I never thought I would ever live again.'

At that a kind of dizziness came over him on the track and Xhabbo blurred in his eyes. He was so unsteady that he put out a hand to Xhabbo and wanted to sit down there and then in the track. Xhabbo knew what he longed to do and caught him by the arm, steadying him but also stopping him saying, 'Foot of the Day, we cannot stay here to rest, however much you need the rest. We must hasten back to Mantis's place as we have never hastened before. All day long I, Xhabbo, have been sit-ting apart, listening in to my tapping and oh, Foot of the Day, the tapping has been so clear that Xhabbo could follow you almost as if Xhabbo were seeing you with his own eyes, feeling himself utterly to be wherever you were going. The tapping, yes it was so loud and clear that Xhabbo felt himself suffering with you and feeling great fear with you. By sundown he was feeling utterly dark with a feeling that you had utterly gone and would never return. But then in the middle of the night the tapping showed Xhabbo you were turning back on your heels and told him how he and Nuin-Tara and that utterly your woman must hasten to prepare for your coming, because the danger coming up behind you now was new, great and terrible, and that we all must hasten to leave the place of Mantis our father for ever, and go the way the tapping would at last tell me to go.'

François wanted to protest and plead that surely they could afford just the briefest segment of time to let him get his breath back and reassure his straining body, which was hurting as it had not hurt before. But the tone of Xhabbo's voice was so grave and urgent and convincing that his recollection of how only obedience to this voice in the past had saved him and Nonnie, made him obedient to it again without reserve. Some of the instinctive self-respect of the natural world of Africa and its inborn aristocracy of living spirit which compels its children never to admit defeat this side of death glowed in him and, short of breath as he was, he said 'Xhabbo, you lead and I will follow. I know our danger is great as you say. I will tell you more as we go along, though I do not feel it is as immediately as you feel it. But what is this way your tapping would tell us to go?'

'Foot of the Day,' Xhabbo began obliquely, 'I cannot tell you yet what form this danger will take. But I feel utterly that it is almost upon us. We cannot wait. All Xhabbo knows and feels utterly within himself, is that this tapping tells him that we must all be gone from the cave before the Foot of the Day has stepped clear of the trees and brought the day into the sky. In Mantis's place all is ready for our going. Like you, Foot of the Day, Xhabbo felt himself feeling at first that it was not a tapping speaking but just fear telling him to go and he would not listen to the tapping and say yes to what it was telling him to do.'

That Xhabbo, with all his instinctive respect and his implicit obedience to the commandments of his tapping could have questioned the process in himself, was frightening testimony of their desperate plight for François. Dismay rushed at him, making him utter in a kind of silent prayer to himself, 'Oh dear God, if even Xhabbo's tapping is to be confused and doubted, what is to become of us? Where are we to turn for help and where to go? You've just got to help us now!'

But aloud he merely said, in a voice strained and thin for him, 'Oh Xhabbo, how could it be so that you questioned your own tapping? Was it then in the end not so loud and clear as at the beginning?'

'No, Foot of the Day,' Xhabbo replied, 'it was louder and clearer than ever but it was telling me to go a way that I, Xhabbo, did not want to go and a way Xhabbo feels is more dangerous and difficult than the way Xhabbo wanted to take.'

'And what is that way?' François asked anxiously, knowing how much depended on the answer. For only he knew now that they had no alternative. The five of them were on their own and utterly dependent from now on, on themselves. The telephone lines from Mopani's camp to the outside world were cut. The camp itself, was doomed and bound to be destroyed within a few hours, however valiantly Mopani's men under his old sergeant-major would fight back as he was sure they would do. It was true there was a possibility that finding the telephone lines cut the old sergeant-major might have been able to get a messenger out to the outside world for help before his camp was totally surrounded. But the outside world was far away, and even pre-supposing his messenger got past the patrols covering the trails and roads to the world beyond they would take a week or more to reach it on foot. For the railway line and access to the great mining city were, he knew, effectively sealed off from them all. They would have to go round to the far south where the next city was some two hundred miles away. And the bush in between would be swarming with well-led and alert enemies, while from what he had overheard their numbers would be swollen all the time, by the reinforcements coming up from Angola and the other territories to the north.

Only Xhabbo and his knowledge of the bush and desert and above all his tapping could now direct them to some natural sanctuary. And yet this tapping had prescribed a way and course of action which even its high-priest and faithful servant Xhabbo found doubtful and dangerous.

All this mixed with François's terrible weariness made him hear Xhabbo say as from a distance, 'For look, Foot of the Day, look! The tapping clearly says we go the way of the wind. And go the way of the wind we must, without feeling ourselves to be afraid.'

As he said it François was compelled to open wide his eyes,

164

which were screwed up with fatigue. Clear against the starlight was Xhabbo's arm pointing to the north-west. Significantly the finger with which Xhabbo was pointing was not fully extended but folded back at the joint. It was fantastic how great a meaning that had for François. Bushmen only pointed their fingers like that at things they regarded as sacred and would not dream of offending, as they would have done if they had extended the finger to the full, since that was the rudest way of pointing of which a Bushman was capable. Xhabbo's reverent manner of pointing now, François realized, was so because he was pointing in the direction of the one wind that brought up rare, life-giving rain to the desert.

Overawed by this fact, he put his hand on Xhabbo's shoulder to say, 'I see then we are to go the way of the wind that brings the rain.'

He paused, before uttering what is perhaps the shortest but greatest of all the Bushman forms of prayer, or asking with their hearts from the heart of life itself as 'Bamuthi would have put it, 'And may the rain fall upon us too.'

A kind of Bushman Amen broke from Xhabbo before he commanded, 'But now, Foot of the Day, hasten to Mantis's place, hasten because the danger is great and nearer than ever.'

He would have stepped forward after Hintza, who seemed to have understood the urgency of the words and concluded for himself that speed and more speed were now needed. For once without any need for instruction he had bounded into the lead. But a new sound coming from the west stopped him. He whisked about, light as a leaf, and looked at François. François's feeling of imminent danger, stirred already by Xhabbo's exhortation, became all the more acute because it was clearly the sound of a truck. Moreover it was coming from the direction of Mopani's camp, its engines racing. Already the glow of headlights was visible fanning the fringes of the bush.

It could only mean, he was certain, that his letter had been deciphered and that the truck was hastening to Hunter's Drift, to ensure that the hill of the cave could be surrounded at dawn and the hunt for them pursued to a methodical and successful end. Prepared as Xhabbo was by his tapping, even he was obviously startled by the sound. François just intercepted the question that was on his lips, saying, 'I hear it too and I know what it means and will explain on our way but that sound, please Xhabbo, feel as I feel, is proof of how true your tapping has been and how we must hasten to obey it. But, Xhabbo, could you pick up and carry Hin for I no longer have the strength to do it and I feel we must not leave his spoor here for the enemy to find.'

Xhabbo without a word stooped down, gathered Hintza to him, lifted him and led the way to the top of the hill with a speed and ease which to François's exhausted self seemed miraculous. There by the last boulder of stone guarding the narrow entrance on a bed of gravel François begged Xhabbo to put Hintza down. Hintza at once stood up expectant, obviously anxious to be the first to go into the cave and François did not have the heart to refuse him. He knelt down and ordered him, 'Yes, go, Hin, go and tell Nonnie we're back.'

He did this knowing that they had to do everything possible, however hopeless it might appear, to prevent his enemies from discovering this first temple of man in Africa and blowing it up in another act of negation and revenge when they found how it had sheltered them, for he was certain Hintza's tracks over so short a distance could be as easily erased as the Bushmen had their own for centuries.

As Hintza vanished, he looked deep into the night over the West. That light truck on the Punda-Ma-Tenka road was coming up with alarming speed. It could do so he believed only because it carried nothing but the dispatches necessary to organize the final hunt for them. Its lights were flashing ominously high in the sky, and the need they emphasized for speed on his part was about to send him down on his knees to crawl into the cave when he suddenly left the first air of the morning cool on his hot face.

Instinctively he put his finger in his mouth and wetted it and held it up high above his head as 'Bamuthi and his people always did when they emerged from their kraals at their beloved 'Horns of the Bullock' hour. Once, when he had asked 'Bamuthi why they always did this 'Bamuthi had said, 'Do it yourself, Little Feather.'

He had done it and was amazed how cool and alive the air

had become on the side of his finger. Noticing his amazement 'Bamuthi had instantly said, 'Ah! You always do this, Little Feather, and you will feel the breath of the first spirit on you for the day to come.'

It was of course, he realized then, an act of prayer and most strange of all, joining in it now as he had done so often in the past, he felt the wind of morning on his finger even more clearly than he had done on his cheek and could tell· exactly from where it came.

He had to put out his hand impetuously to Xhabbo, grasp him by the arm, pull him towards him and exclaim, oddly up-lifted, 'Oh Xhabbo, do you feel what I am feeling now, the wind of morning on my face and finger, breathing and feeling itself utterly coming down the way of the wind your tapping has told us to go?'

And with that they both went down on their knees and crawled towards and into the cave.

CHAPTER SEVEN

An Order of Elephants

Although the cave was lit only by candle-light, after the dark of what François felt had been a dash to the end of the night and back, the light was dazzling. He came out of his crawl and slowly up to his full height, to stand beside the entrance blinking for a moment, unable to take in the scene and aware only that a smell of warm food had come to meet him. It was a complex smell but its dominant ingredient was the best scent of all to welcome an exhausted, thirsty, hungry and healthy young person: the smell of hot chocolate. François's associations with this smell were so many and went back so far in time that a feeling of home-coming possessed him. It was reinforced, as his eyes became capable of grasping the detail of the scene that was being enacted in the centre of the cave.

The four halves of two of his dixies were there gleaming like silver and arranged on the improvised hearth he had invented the night before, four stones supporting each of them and four sets of candles burning underneath. The light by the hearth was clearest for the glow from the candle ends was reinforced by that of eight long candles stuck in the sand further back. The yellow dome above and honey-coloured stone around, reflected and magnified the light so that all was clear and contrived as in a painting of a fastidious Dutch domestic interior.

To the left of the hearth, a hood of shadow around her head, was the beautiful archaic face of Nuin-Tara, her slanted, dark Mongolian eyes wide and brilliant, shining with light as much from within as without. Somewhat more indistinct on her left where the shadows lapped at the rim of light, was Xhabbo, the little finger of his right hand hooked in Nuin-Tara's left. In aristocratic Bushman fashion, Nuin-Tara was waiting for François to greet her before she as a woman could feel herself free to greet him, although that light in her eyes, one has mentioned, was already greeting enough for François. She could tell this immediately from the way François's own tired eyes came alive. She began to smile and the smile quickly became wide and dazzling. Instinctively, in case she should be thought indelicate, she raised a long hand which she held oddly penitent and shy in front of her mouth so that she could go on smiling out her own feelings of relief behind it unobserved and, above all, unprovocative of more feelings in circumstances already over-charged with emotion.

Behind her François noticed the haversacks with which he had stocked the cave as well as the one he had given Xhabbo months before, arranged in a row and bulging presumably with the supplies he had enumerated in his letter to Nonnie. They were strapped tight and obviously ready for instant travel. Close by them their field flasks of water darkened the yellow sand. And at last, on the far side of the fire, there was Nonnie on her knees, her arms round Hintza and her face pressed against Hintza's shoulder. She must have known he was there and yet did not look up at once to greet him.

For a moment François resented the fact that, although Hintza had been the first into the cave and had already received his own abundant ration of welcome, Nonnie was persisting in putting him first and apparently not ready yet to welcome him. Pre-warned as she was by Hintza's arrival, he was inclined to feel the least she could have done was to be on her feet, as eager to greet him as Nuin-Tara had been for Xhabbo and himself. But before he could allow his exhausted feelings the slight luxury of so understandable a subjective reaction, all temptation to resentment vanished when he overheard some of the words rushing out of Nonnie.

The words were apparently intended for Hintza, who was wriggling, twisting and waggling with pleasure, in spite of the fact that he was held tightly against her. Hintza clearly wanted to interrupt her, convinced it was his turn to get in a welcome edgeways. He was trying to push his muzzle under her chin and to lift it up so that he could lick her cheek. But as so often in the past, Hintza was being royally welcomed not just for himself but as a unique plenipotentiary. François, who Nonnie often found oddly slow in perceptions of this kind when he was unusually observant and sensitive in so much else, for once understood, and the tone and quality of Nonnie's address to Hintza affected him deeply. In a manner so characteristic of the Nonnie he had known in the age before the disaster, she was desperately trying to tame her quick, spontaneous and passionate nature by teasing Hintza, François and not least of all herself. The courage of it even more than the concern for him concealed in it, went straight to his heart.

'Yes, darling Hin,' he heard her say almost as she would have said on any one of those brief, golden days in darkness behind them. 'Yes, I'm glad that you agree with me. It was a wicked, wicked thing to do, corrupting someone as trusting as me with drugs so that I was not there to say good-bye. I think he's really just an old drug pedlar at heart, don't you? We'll just have to report him to the first narcotics bureau we get to, won't we?'

And she went on in that strain until her eyes felt sufficiently unblurred and her feelings calm enough for her to look up at him without danger of falling into another round of tears.

The new words of banter that she was wrenching out of herself went silent on her lips as she saw François there with that tender old painter's candle-light full on him. The record of all he had been through since she had last seen him was on his face, in his eyes and even his way of standing, so obviously that even the blindest of blind in these matters could not fail to read it. François always had a somewhat grave look about him, not because of a lack of zest or sense of fun but due to that instinctive, long-distance view of life that tended to overawe him at times with immensities ahead. It was a gravity implicit in the human heart at the beginning of the journey and not its equal born of intimation of its end. And all of this now had been underlined by a look of new suffering and signs of exhaustion on François's face that would not have discredited a runner who had just brought the news across the mountains of the arrival of some new Persian Armada on the coast of his beloved Greece. She was horrified to see how thin he had become in just twenty-four hours, how hollow his cheeks, how elongated his features and how far back his eyes had receded and how in a shadow of their own they seemed wider and brighter than ever, as if burning with the fever of a fatigue she could not possibly imagine.

She wanted to push Hintza away from her, jump up and rush towards him. All that was latent and maternal in her flared into a quick flame that threatened to destroy her strained self-control, since she had never experienced anything comparable before. It was her first clear annunciation of the role in which women are compelled at one and the same time to be both mistress and mother to their men. All the unschooled feelings released by the sight of François, combined with relief and gratitude over his return would have been irresistible, had it not been for one factor: twenty-four hours alone with Xhabbo and Nuin-Tara had taught her much. Her quick, sensitive and impressionable self had recognized from their example how still and calm the human spirit had to strive to be on occasions such as these.

All day and night long she had been impressed to the point ot being wretched and dissatisfied with feelings of her own inadequacy by the behaviour of those two. They were, she recognized, professionals in disaster and the art of how man and woman supplemented one another when all life seems to be against them, so that moving as one they find a strange, still centre in the storm of chance and circumstance raging around them. She had concluded sadly that she was by comparison not even an amateur so much as a child entering some kindergarten of the school of tragedy.

Her heart was crying out: 'Oh what have they done to you, François, these terrible minutes and hours, these long, long years when you have been out there alone where I could not follow you and help and comfort you. Oh come here quick and let me . . .' But in the very act of listening in to her emotions, she was aware that Nuin-Tara's eyes were on her and that once more she was being appraised and measured as to whether she was capable of being the kind of woman Xhabbo's Foot of the Day deserved in so great an extreme of crisis.

Pushing Hintza aside, she came lightly to her feet, walked over to François and took him by the hand as she had seen Nuin-Tara take Xhabbo by the hand to say in a voice tight with this new grip on her feelings, 'Oh welcome, François, welcome back! Come and see what I have cooked and long kept warm for you.'

So remote were the words from what she really wanted to say that she sounded like a total stranger in her own ears but when she forced herself to look up into his eyes so close to her own, she very nearly lost all that she had gained by resolution. She was grateful then for the help of a distance which divided herself against herself, so that she was weak enough to be ruled by her reason. She noticed that the dark streaks on François's face which she had thought a trick of candlelight were in fact zigzags of white skin exposed on his face by the sweat that had run like water down it, washing runnels in the paste of earth he had rubbed on it to blacken it. The appearance utterly belied the vivid image she had formed of François all day. For in all she had imagined him to be doing that day he had been good and immaculate. If life were obedient to one's subjective feelings he should have been standing there bright and unstained too.

Yet there he was as if deliberately made up to look more like a clown than a hero. This element in his appearance, however fortuitous, affected her profoundly. She had no direct experience to instruct her in the matter. She knew only that it was more than a consequence of a feminine gift for seeing the rejected and uncared for in life behind the dirt, the rags and tatters. It was more than an instinct for taking all that under her care and protection. Men may be the defenders of faith and the promoters and guardians of ideas; but women are the natural trustees of the wards in the chancery of life. So that the only clue to the new dimension added to her response was in the thought of the clown which came unsolicited to her, since the clown is perhaps one of the most telling images of the mockery fate injects into its greatest tragedies, for the surprise that human beings express when confronted with death and disaster is so unwarranted as to be as comic as it is moving.

Both are common ingredients of the lot of us all. And yet we go on behaving as if we are to be the exceptions to prove the rule of suffering in life, so that when death, which is no stranger to our neighbours, darkens our own little orbits, we are as outraged, complaining and surprised as any clown by his petty mishaps in a crowded circus. And it was precisely here that the child in Nonnie had pushed roughly aside the person crossing the frontier between woman and girl in her. François in that unprepossessing state was more heroic than any figure of medieval chivalry in full armour could have been. Suddenly Nonnie was the child in all of us again who sees its first clown as an object of compassion rather than fun, and is more horrified by his mishaps than moved to laughter, because the child is in itself a clown, tumbled and laughed at in the circus of a well-trained, grown-up world.

The child's experience, long before its mind, knows how the clown is rehearsing a role all are contracted to play and that in his willingness to be tumbled and humiliated again and again, the clown, armed only with his fooling, is out-laughing fate and asserting a braver and more subtle form of courage than that of any professional hero armed and schooled for the role.

She could just rescue herself from a display that she knew would undo such esteem as she had laboriously acquired in the eyes of Nuin-Tara, by pretending to a brisk and practical version that she did not feel. Tugging at François's hand she urged with a surprisingly commanding tone, 'Now come on, Master Joubert! You're already much too late for your supper. You can't go on standing there all night. Let me get some water and wipe that dirt off your face and hands.'

François hardly heard her, moving obediently after her towards the hearth. The disguise of the tenderness that Nonnie was feeling for him, was transparent as glass to François, but his reaction to it was overlaid by an emotion of his own too full for him to give her an immediate answer. Seeing Hintza, Nuin-Tara, Xhabbo and Nonnie reunited there in profound shelter by a fire of their own and food and drink ready to be eaten and drunk, the irony of the reality concealed in the innocence of the appearance was almost too much for him. Appearances were calling on him to exult and cry out, 'You've come home François. You're back again with all that there is left for you in life to love and you can now rest and relax, and be at one in your love.'

It needed only a glimpse of those haversacks and piles of water flasks near to them, to expose the illusion of appearances.

He knew more clearly even than Xhabbo and Xhabbo's tapping, that this beloved cave and temple was neither home nor anything now except the briefest of shelters. They could just use it quickly for refreshment and reprovisioning as at a wayside hospice lost in the bush of Africa. And then as soon as possible, return to the dark outside and continue on a way that was without foreseeable destination or end. In the midst of this turmoil of feelings he noticed on the far perimeter of the light, the picture of St Hubert, his little altar of stones underneath and above it on the yellow sandstone the red cross painted those thousands of years ago by a Bushman hand.

At once the scene was transformed into a setting of which he had never had any experience himself except the vicarious one of having encountered it in many readings from the Bible by lamplight. It was a Passover scene; a microscopic version of the great Passover in the Pentateuch so beloved by both Ouwa and Mopani and particularly relevant now. There the chosen people stood fearful in their homes, ready for their exodus from persecution and bondage into the unknown, knowing that as they were waiting there afraid, all that protected them from destruction was a cross marked above their doors outside, so that the angel of death who was visiting everyone in the city that night would see it and seeing it pass them by.

The impact of the recollection and the comparison evoked a feeling that they too were on an authentic journey not without protection. Despite all the conditioning of history in his Huguenot self against such a response, he found his one free hand involuntarily going through the 'Papist' movements of describing the sign of a cross. Nonnie, knowing the hard Protestant core in him, was startled and moved, and was nearly trapped into commenting on it.

Just in time she took refuge in an expression of her father, which she had never properly understood but knew was intended to overcome the inhibitions of over tentative guests.

'Now come on, François,' she spoke up, imitating as best she could her father's tone of command, 'No heel taps please. I gather from Xhabbo and Nuin-Tara that we've no time to lose.'

She pronounced the name 'Nuin-Tara' without any accent. She even reproduced the very difficult click in Xhabbo's name so precisely that a real glow of pride joined the tumultuous variety of François's feelings. Even more, to his joy, she had said it so easily and well that the same pleasure he was feeling himself appeared on Xhabbo's face, strained and preoccupied as he was with the tensions of his awareness of imminent danger, the extreme need for haste and doubt whether there was even time for François to eat and drink.

And then he was by the hearth, with Nonnie urging him to sit while she fetched some water to wipe his face and hands so that he could eat without delay. But quickly he stopped her. His sense of the need for extreme economy in the use of supplies imposed on them by their plight, had already been disturbed by the display of candles which had greeted him and he would immediately have put them all out, had he not suspected that it was something of Nonnie's contriving to celebrate his return. In any case they could do without candles if necessary but never without water.

'Please Nonnie, please!' he answered as gently as he could. 'You must just let me go dirty for the time being. We can't waste any of our water. We might still be forced to come back here and need all the water that's left. Besides, as Mopani says, a little honest dirt is good roughage for the system and gives us despised bush-dwellers immunities against infections that no citizen of the hygiene-made world outside possesses.'

His tone was light, trying to follow her example to lift their minds above the many negations evoked by their plight. Nonnie, who could have been abashed by this defeat of her impulse to take special care of François and to do something that would have made her feel less ineffective than she had been feeling all day, responded to the tone particularly as for the first time since this dark new era began, a smile came to François's tired face. She smiled back at him, hearing him add, 'Come and sit beside me here and have something to eat yourself and . . .'

Nonnie interrupted. She could tell him happily that she and Nuin-Tara had already eaten and drunk as much as they could, so that they would not delay him and Xhabbo on their return. Indeed already she was so full of food and hot chocolate herself that she was certain she would have the severest indigestion before long. She clutched her stomach and conveyed in a parody of words and actions an over-full state that brought a look of amusement to Nuin-Tara's and Xhabbo's faces, for what they had failed to follow in words was plain to them in the artless pantomime that accompanied them.

'Well done, Nonnie! How wise and thoughtful of you,' François exclaimed with a warmth that uplifted her. 'I'll tell you what you can do then. Give Hin lots of hot chocolate as well and please fetch a couple of those tins of condensed milk in our store and give him one to himself. It's his idea of Heaven, and Heaven knows, he's deserved it, because without him we would not be here alive today.'

Nonnie, over happy to have something to do, rushed to the back of the cave, returned with the two halves of their last dixie, half-filled them with steaming hot chocolate, opened two tins of condensed milk, divided the contents of one between the two halves as François had directed, and kept the other for him.

Hintza, of course, had no doubt that it was all for his special benefit. François always saw to Hintza's wants before he took care of his own. As a result Hintza was already on his stomach, stretched out in a dog's attitude of ardent supplication in front of Nonnie, his tongue extended, and his mouth dribbling shamelessly at the corners, while he was beginning to pant with an uprush of thirst and hunger.

But Nonnie held him firmly back with her hand, reproving, 'Not so fast, darling Hin, not so fast, or you'll burn that lovely long pink tongue of yours. Gosh, you'd better be careful or it will come unstuck at the back!'

She held him thus, stirring the chocolate and condensed milk round quickly so that the heat could evaporate while she tested the dark steaming liquid with her finger from time to time until it was cool enough for Hintza to drink. She then pushed both the halves towards him. Her hands had hardly come back folded in her lap, or so it seemed to her, when all the chocolate vanished, and the dixies were empty and clean as if polished by a conscientious servant's hand.

'Dear Mother in Heaven, Hin,' she exclaimed, 'you're an even greater genius at gulping than your master. Is it a case of like master like dog, or like dog like master? Which of the two

of you, you irresistible beggar, started so outrageous a habit?
Be careful or you'll hiccup yourself to death one day. Yes, to
death you greedy creature. D'you know, and I hope your
master is listening too, there was an infallible Pope once, protected by all the blessed angels in Heaven, who hiccupped himself to death in spite of the prayers of a Convocation of
cardinals. And all because he would not stop gulping his food
so that he could get on with his praying. But I don't expect you
know about Popes, being such a keen young Huguenot dog
yourself!'

But Hintza for once failed to detect the affection wrapped
in the teasing. How could even a human expert at inhumanity
as only human beings can be, be so lacking in the little
humanity they possess to find so desperate a matter a subject for
joking, particularly such a beloved human as Nonnie.

Once certain that he had licked the last drop of liquid out of
the dixies, Hintza looked into Nonnie's eyes with an expression
as devastating as no doubt it was intended to be, so that she
broke off her teasing. It was a look of infinite tragedy, as if with
that last drop of liquid life had lost all its meaning, chaos and
old night were about to descend upon him for ever, and there
was nothing left under the visiting moon he loved so well.

'Oh Coiske,' Nonnie called out, convinced that two tears like
two great Pacific pearls were forming at the corners of Hintza's
purple eyes. 'Can't I make him some more chocolate? I can't
bear to see him looking so hurt.'

François, who had suffered under that eloquent look of
Hintza's ever since his puppy days and had long since come to
terms with it, was, Nonnie thought, rather heartless. For he just
said firmly, 'No Nonnie, no. The little skelm knows he's got
enough of that sickly sweet stuff in him to last for days. He's not
had such a feast since last Christmas. He's just an artful and
greedy little dodger. But I'll tell you what you can do. Please get
some more biltong from our store. Here – take my knife and
slice it up and feed him with as much of it as he can eat, so that
he has something solid in him as well. But please be as quick as
you can, we leave in minutes now.'

Meanwhile François himself had got Nuin-Tara and
Xhabbo seated by his side. He divided the food in front of him

177

between Xhabbo and himself in the proportion of one third for himself and two thirds for Xhabbo. Even that third was more than he could manage. The chocolate with which they began had been so warming and satisfying that it felt a full meal in itself. In any case, he lacked appetite, both from exhaustion and the ache deep at heart that ran swollen and full like a great river in the underground of his being. He felt almost too tired to chew anything at all. Indeed it is doubtful whether he chewed the mixture of corned beef and tinned beans which Nonnie had prepared. In between gulps, he questioned Nonnie about the supplies she had packed in their haversacks. She had done it so well that he congratulated her warmly and could think of only a few refinements of his own to add which she could not possibly have known about. The moment he had finished his food, only slightly ahead of Xhabbo, he got up to see to them, explaining to Xhabba that he was almost ready to leave.

The relief on Xhabbo's strained face at this announcement was obvious. He was on his feet at once and telling François that he was just going outside for a moment to look around. When he came back he counted on them being ready to leave. He was at the entrance and out of the cave with astonishing speed.

One of the most important of Francois's refinements was changing the gun he had carried with him all day. It was his favourite rifle: a large ·375 express. The cartridges for it were so long and heavy that he could not carry as many rounds on him as he had now concluded were necessary. On the way back, hard as he ran, he had been thinking how disastrously their situation had deteriorated since all chance of help from Mopani's camp was destroyed. Instead of counting on relief as he had done in a matter of weeks or at the most months, he had now to face the possibility that it might be a year or more before they could find a way across the desert or the bush to safety. For there was no other way left for them to go that was not now swarming with enemies. And either through bush or desert the nearest places of safety were a thousand or more miles away.

Fortunately he had, in the reserve he had built up over the months, not only that lovely old muzzle-loader with which he had begun his life as a young hunter but a lighter, high velocity

178

all-purpose gun. That of course would not be so effective a weapon if they were ever charged by elephant, lion, leopard or rhinoceros but none of those figured on François's black-list of enemies. Their main enemies from now on would be the men outside, and hunger and thirst. More, he knew that this rifle, accurately used, was powerful enough to kill men as well as the buck and birds they would need for food without shattering the smallest of them. Above all, for every one of those long heavy cartridges of his ·375 rifle, he could carry several rounds of ammunition for the lighter gun.

The exchange of rifle and ammunition took no time at all and instead of the fifty rounds he carried in his cartridge belt, he now had two hundred rounds divided in two satchels, one for himself to carry and one for Xhabbo, enough to last them for two or three years and, unless they were extremely unlucky, even longer, considering that they had so great a bow-and-arrow hunter and trapper as Xhabbo with them. Indeed, he would have taken less ammunition had it not been for the fact that he had to be prepared at any moment for something he had not yet experienced: fighting off an attack by human beings. And that was something he had gathered from Ouwa's and Mopani's accounts of their experiences in war, which used up ammunition at a devastating rate, particularly by the inexperienced.

That done, he called Nonnie over to him, made her unbutton the flaps of the four pockets on her bush shirt and stuff them full of dried fruit he had surreptitiously extracted over the long months from Ousie-Johanna's store. At the same time he filled the spare spaces in his own shirt with more biltong and the last of Ousie-Johanna's rusks. He was tempted to add just a few tins of delicacies but their weight made him reject the temptation as soon as it was born. He did, however, take a bottle of the oldest brandy he had stolen from Ouwa's store for medicinal purposes, filled one field flask with it and found he had still a third of a bottle of the rich amber liquid left.

At that point Nonnie interrupted him with a sudden plea which however lightly uttered was deep in earnest. 'François, d'you think that you could do something for me that you may not like, and even hate?'

François stared at her in amazement. 'But, of course, Nonnie, provided it doesn't take long.'

Without a word then, she drew him a few yards to the left of the store to face the picture of St Hubert and the cross on the wall. Would he, she asked with a certain embarrassed determination, please kneel in front of that place with her? In the act of doing this she did not speak again. She could not even get herself to put all she meant by the act in silent words to herself. She just somehow wanted to affirm in the deed of their kneeling before the power of which the painting and the cross on the wall were such clear evidence to her, that though they were kneeling before it as two, they were there as one. She felt this so deeply that instinctively she took Francois's hand in her own and for once without hesitation he clasped it so firmly that it hurt. Utterly silent, she just let feelings beyond measure or knowing plead for her. If the *one* she felt them to be had to be divided into *two* again, would the reality that was represented by the signs in front of them, her heart was asking, protect the part that was François as greater than the part that was herself? Yet if it could, oh yes, out of mercy and in recognition of what they had lost and were learning through suffering, could it, would it protect both so that one day they could come together again and forever be the one they were before it now?

Her heart had barely run the full course of this unutterable longing and cry for help when there was a rush through the entrance of the cave and there was Xhabbo calling, 'Foot of the Day, we must altogether go now and utterly at once. The danger is near and could be greater than Xhabbo feels.'

Xhabbo's entry was so abrupt and his call so urgent that François and Nonnie jumped to their feet and turned about to face him.

'Yes Xhabbo, we're ready, and we come,' François answered firmly, striding towards him, half a bottle of brandy still in his hand, 'But come to me first quickly with Nuin-Tara. I have some magic water here for the journey that we must take.'

He turned to Nonnie, whose pulse was racing with the shock of Xhabbo's intervention and all it foreboded. She tried to rally herself while he continued, 'Now now, no heel-taps in your turn. Have a great swig at this. Quickly, please!'

180

In spite of the fact that drink was one of her great dislikes, Nonnie obediently grasped the botle and swallowed a draught of brandy that left her gasping. François took a much bigger and longer draught from it, knowing how much more his exhausted self needed a boost than anyone else's.

Then he handed it to Xhabbo, saying, 'Xhabbo, divide that between Nuin-Tara and yourself, knowing that you are drinking the water of the spirit of your father Mantis and that it will give you warmth against the cold of morning and power against our enemies outside.'

To his amazement the name of Mantis made Xhabbo briefly hold the bottle towards the light as if instinctively preparing a toast to a king. The glass and its dark liquid were gold with candle fire before Xhabbo raised the bottle high for a long swallow. Then he handed the bottle to Nuin-Tara to empty.

The shock of the brandy on the palates of the two of them, who had never tasted anything like it before, was even greater than it had been to Nonnie. But it was followed by immediate warmth and exhilaration. On the arrival of the spirit in their stomachs, both faces were transfigured with wonder and François was certain that at any other time they would have danced a little dance in gratitude that the Bushmen prefer to dance out rather than express in vain words.

Then they went over to the haversacks. Xhabbo was made to shoulder one of the two heaviest, the other of course was for himself. In addition he gave Xhabbo one satchel of precious ammunition to sling round the other shoulder and handed him a field flask. Nonnie and Nuin-Tara got the lightest of the haversacks, filled mostly with medicines, bandages, odd bits of spare clothing and cloth that François had accumulated over the months, including some old face towels and biltong and rusks packed in their dixies. Quickly he adjusted the straps on their shoulders, not only to ensure that they were comfortable but that they would not chafe their untried skins underneath. Noticing that the laces of Nonnie's ankle boots were tied in an over-long single bow he knelt beside her and shortened them by doubling the bow, muttering an explanation that once years before he had nearly fallen in the path of a charging rhinoceros by tripping over his own laces. He had been saved only by 'Bamuthi roughly pushing him into the painful safety of a thorn-bush at the side of the track.

'There, Nonnie,' he exclaimed, 'out you go now. I'll follow in a second.'

Shouldering his own loads, easing his hunting-knife in its sheath and loading the magazine of his rifle to the full, he put out the last of the candles and crawled quickly out into the dark after her.

He found the three of them close together, with Hintza beside Nonnie, standing just beyond the great old bush which covered the entrance to the cave. His eyes, already recovering fast from the impact of candle-light, showed him Xhabbo in the act of turning about and then getting down on his hands and knees to smooth out the marks of their crawling and Hintza's feet on what there was of ground around the entrance to the cave. That done he scattered dried bits of grass and leaves over the places to look as if they had just been dropped there by the casual night air of the bush.

It was all over in a matter of moments, and Xhabbo was whispering to him, 'Foot of the Day, come quick and look and tell me what you feel we are to do.'

Stepping carefully from stone to stone until they reached the great boulder which marked the far end of the concealed approach to the cave. They came upright behind it and looked over it in the direction of François's shattered home below. François noticed that the truck which he and Xhabbo had heard had apparently arrived and was standing there with lights blazing to reinforce all sorts of other lights and fires that had been lit in what at the moment of his return to the cave had been an area of complete darkness. Indeed, there was an expanse of light stretched taut across the black like an immense piece of yellow fly-paper, against which the dark outlines of men appeared stuck frantic with movement as insects struggling to free themselves.

Obviously the enemy was so sure of itself that it was making no attempt at concealment. The clamour of soldiers preparing for action at high speed was loud and clear in the still morning air. Ominous as it all was, it was so much what François had expected, and the distance between the hill on which they were standing and his old home was so great, that he would not have been any more alarmed than before, had not Xhabbo whispered in his ear.

'Foot of the Day, all that your eyes feel themselves to be seeing down there is not all. Xhabbo knows that when he first came to stand by this grandfather of a boulder, his eyes were altogether full of men moving up along the river and spreading out round the hill down there below. Xhabbo had a tapping that tells him that some of these men are already near and others going round to the back of this hill towards the way we have to go. Look, see how high the Foot of the Day has stepped into the sky and how small a darkness we have left. But tell me, how are we to go? I, Xhabbo, knowing the way must go first, and you should come last to make us safe from the men coming up the hill. But I feel I need you for a greater danger in front and . . .'

Xhabbo was interrupted by a rush of sound behind them. There, unbidden, was Hintza, leaping at François as he would never have dreamed of doing unless some imminent peril had freed him from professional obedience to orders and forced him to take so unusual an initiative as to leave his allotted place of duty by Nonnie's side. As it happened the warning he had come to deliver was unnecessary because as his paws came to rest on François's shoulder, there came from the far side of the hill three sharp, distinct barks of a fox followed by a long sustained piping of a night plover, exactly as François had requested in his intercepted letter to Mopani. The call came obviously from an expert in these things but not expert enough to deceive Xhabbo or even François because both turned instinctively to each other to confirm the deception.

Xhabbo got in first with a Bushman idiom that would have made François laugh with delight at any other time. 'Foot of the Day, those are not a fox and a plover feeling themselves to be men but a man feeling himself to be both fox and a plover.'

It was unnecessary for either of them to comment on the danger to which it testified because it could only have come at a moment when their enemies were certain of their position. What was far more serious, it had come from behind them, proving that Xhabbo's eyes had not deceived him when they had seen the dark shadows of men deploying at the base of the hill.

'You're right,' François told Xhabbo urgently. 'We must go ahead and our women must follow, Nonnie behind and Nuin-Tara last because Nuin-Tara will feel any danger coming from behind us long before Nonnie. But I can't help feeling we cannot go on like that for long. It will be difficult for the four of us and Hin to get by the enemy without being seen and even if we do get by we shall leave so great a spoor that they will have no difficulty in following us. And I'm not sure that someone like Nonnie can travel fast enough with us all day long keeping ahead of the enemy. Is there not something else we can do? You see Xhabbo, I have not told you yet but the enemy does not know about you and Nuin-Tara and Nonnie. I am certain they only know about me and Hintza. Would it not be best if we could somehow make the enemy go on believing that?'

François was speaking purely out of instinct. It was an area of life on which he had no experience and he felt that he should turn to Xhabbo who must have experienced similar dangers many times and would have been minutely schooled in the tradition evolved by the Bushmen throughout thousands of years of persecution in all the best ways of dealing with such a situation.

From the way Xhabbo grasped his hand and pressed it, he knew at once how right he had been. Words softly uttered flowed from him; the clicks that are the Bushman consonants crackled like electricity on his lips as he said that he knew his Foot of the Day would be feeling as he, Xhabbo, was feeling. Foot of the Day was right, there was only one thing to do, the Bushmen had always found in these circumstances. Feeling themselves to be utterly surrounded by their enemy they would choose one or two of the fastest and best among them to show themselves so that the enemy seeing them would go after them and give the main body a chance to escape. There could be no faster and better than Foot of the Day and Hintza, except that he found himself feeling full of longing to come with them. But someone had to show the women the way. Only he, Xhabbo, knew the way. Not even Nuin-Tara had ever travelled the way they were going now. So he would beg his Foot of the Day, once they were safely over the top of the hill and half-way down the slope, to branch off away to the south. Branching off he would show himself to the enemy but show himself only in a way that looked not deliberate and, above all, not so much that the enemy could kill him with those weapons that killed at so great a distance.

Did Foot of the Day, Xhabbo asked obliquely, know a deep gorge that if they starting running now they would reach just after sunrise? It began where a little river feeling itself to be only a little river, joined the great river they all knew, and the great river feeling itself to be great took the little river under its arm and carried it safely to the great water on the other side of the bush and hills. Did Foot of the Day know far up this gorge, a great mountain crowned with a wreath of cliffs the Bushmen called 'Lamb-snatcher's cliffs' because they were favourite roosting places of the 'lamb-snatchers', the greatest of all African eagles?

Yes, François assured him, he had twice been on patrol in this gorge with Mopani and knew the cliffs. Though he did not say so he marvelled at Xhabbo's choice because it was just about the wildest of wild places in this area, over-populated with leopards, nyala, bush-buck, wild pigs, pythons and snakes, densely covered with bush and the ground so broken that few human beings ever went there by choice.

Well then, Xhabbo continued, obviously relieved that François knew the place, underneath the greatest cliff there was an imperceptible track among great boulders, standing almost shoulder to shoulder and protected in between by broom, blue-bush, wild juniper and raisin bushes. Foot of the Day and Hintza, having made certain that they had utterly deceived the enemy and sent them on a false trail, should make their way back to this place by nightfall. He would find Xhabbo waiting there on the edge of the track to take them to another Bushman place of rest.

Meanwhile Foot of the Day was not to be afraid for that utterly woman of his. Once certain that the enemy was following Foot of the Day and Hintza, he would lead them down to an old hippopotamus track hidden in the rushes and papyrus on the banks of the great river, and so on to the black gorge where, stepping from stone to stone, they would leave no spoor behind and find shelter on Lamb-snatcher's Hill.

'Yes, Xhabbo, yes,' François replied, praying that somehow he would not fail and that from somewhere, Heaven knew where, he would find the strength to do what he had to do. 'You are utterly right. All I would ask is that the three of you take great care even now not to leave any spoor. As you say, the only spoor they must see now is mine and Hintza's. And I am feeling full of a longing that finding our spoor leading the other way they will not stop to look for any other signs that might take them to the place of Mantis. I am feeling utterly that this place must remain as it has remained, and that I will not have betrayed it to your enemies.'

François had hardly spoken when the fox and plover once more proclaimed their false announcement of Mopani's coming but this time somewhat nearer, clearly indicating that out there in the darkness at the foot of the hill on the far side, their ring of armed men had been tightened. Also the sound had a new and imperious quality as if the person who uttered it could not understand why François had not yet showed himself, as he had promised to do in his letter to Mopani.

They hastened then to rejoin the women. Xhabbo whispered his instructions to Nuin-Tara while François explained his to Nonnie, stressing that whatever happened she had to keep station between Xhabbo and Nuin-Tara. He told her as nonchalantly as he could that he and Hintza were moving out to the right to cover their flank and that she must not be at all alarmed if she did not see them for quite awhile. He begged her to go on as she had so admirably started on her own in his previous absence, and to study Xhabbo and Nuin-Tara in everything. And he added, with a tenderness that only comes to people in moments of disaster, 'You've been wonderful Nonnie in all this, far more wonderful than I ever imagined any girl could possibly be. I know you will end up by doing all even better than Nuin-Tara. So off you go and stick as close as you can to Xhabbo, and all will be well in the end.'

Nonnie had no idea how she managed it for she had her own shrewd concept of what François's comings and goings could mean. But she could just utter what sounded to François a convincing reply, however unsteady the words felt in her own ears, 'All right. And thank you. I'll be seeing you. But please, please take care.'

She turned quickly, before she could betray the fear clamouring within her, and following Xhabbo's example she stepped out lightly from stone to stone after him with Nuin-Tara, close and graceful as a klipspringer behind her.

François and Hintza, making no effort to conceal their spoor, moved off quickly to take up their station beside Xhabbo. Silently they went lightly, and all together, over the hill and down the far side as fast as they could. Half-way down, that faked Mopani call went up and out for a third time, more imperious than ever and so close that François knew they could never get by the men who must be circling or the person simulating the call unless he and Hintza diverted their attention as Xhabbo had suggested.

'I go now, Xhabbo,' he whispered, oddly rough in tone out of anxiety and sense of haste. 'I go. But please, whatever you hear, do not walk from your path or let either of the two women walk from the path either. Go! And your father Mantis goes with you.'

Xhabbo did not reply in words. He paused briefly in his tracks just to raise his hand to his shoulder, palm out, in a final salute, a kind of Bushman hail and farewell, which François could only just read across the lengthening gap of darkness between them where he was already bending over Hintza ordering him to heel before they branched away fast towards the south. A quick glance over his shoulder showed him the shadows of Nonnie and Nuin-Tara, hurrying to catch up with the fading shadow of Xhabbo. Then the combined shadows vanished as presumably on Xhabbo's command they sank to the ground, in order to try crawling forward unseen.

He himself took great care to heed Xhabbo's warning not to make himself over-conspicuous. He allowed himself only a measured ostentation, suggesting a carelessness produced by exhaustion rather than design. When he had gone a hundred yards or so away to the south, he paused and crouched down to look carefully around him. The morning star was high but the 'Horns of the bullocks' hour had not yet come. It was darker than ever. The starlight was clear and the star murmur, so quintessential an element of all experience in François's world, sounded as though it were the universal equivalent of a Greek chorus in a theatre of fate summoning the day from the wings of time to play its part in this new act of the play in which he had been so brutally cast. The whole declining outline of the hill, its fringe of boulders and bushes behind him were clear cut against that sky of stars and there was not a sign of Xhabbo or the two women, nor any sound of movement in that direction. And all that was good and encouraging, until there came a characteristic warning from Hintza at his side.

Hintza was standing, ears erect, nose and tail aligned, pointing away to his right where François at once made out the shadow of a man crouched forward and low, moving foot by slow foot up the hill. Some fifty yards away to the left another shadow moved likewise. The moment Xhabbo had foreseen had come. François felt over the straps of his haversack as if by reflex, tested his hunting knife to see that it was still loose in its sheath, quietly slipped the safety catch from his gun and with his free hand made certain that all his loads and buckles were firm and safe. Thanks to that long draught of brandy, the stiffness and aches in his body seemed to have been anaesthetized for they vanished completely at that moment. The relief of it, joined with the cool air of the morning, made him feel unbelievably refreshed, as he said to Hintza with a will, 'Now listen, Hin, no fighting unless it's necessary. I see those two men. Yes, I see them, you dear, blessed dog of dogs, and thank you for telling me. We're going to try and get by in between them. I count on you to tell me if there are any others ahead. So now you step straight out in front of me as if you are stalking a leopard and I'm following close behind. As fast as you can, boy.'

Hintza whisked about and went into the relevant attitude almost gaily, as if this were just a continuation of the series of hunts he and François had conducted so successfully in the past, and led off with incomparable skill. Even François found it hard to follow his shadow, so that it took barely a minute for them to arrive mid-way in line between the two men coming up the hill.

There François stopped, put his hand on Hintza's rump as a sign for him to crouch down and lie still while he went down on his stomach as well with only his head raised to look up and along the slope of the hill. To his joy, the two men were moving now even more slowly and carefully than ever, straight towards the summit. Both to the right and left of the two he heard faint sounds that suggested they had companions out on their flanks. But thank Heaven, no sound of any sort had come as yet from where Xhabbo and the two women were moving. Yet he was certain that he could not count on them remaining undiscovered for long unless he did something at once to distract the enemy. He jumped soundlessly to his feet, whispering urgently, 'Here now, Hin, here! Straight down the hill as fast as we can. If anyone tries to stop us now, fight as much and as hard as you like.'

Hintza leaped forward and down the hill, and François bounded after him, not with a clatter but nonetheless a thud from stone to stone, at that speed loud enough to be audible some distance away. His enemies heard it almost at once. In that impulsive and inexperienced way of theirs which both the Scot and the Frenchman had condemned, the men nearest to François, in whose ears the sound was therefore loudest, began calling out warnings for everyone to hear far and wide. Then it was as if the hillside around them was a great graveyard with its moment of resurrection arrived; wherever he glanced as he ran men were coming up straight out of graves of darkness alarmingly upright and alive, armed and ready for attack, because the air was light with the phosphorescent glint of stars on the steel of many bayonets.

Yet quick as the enemy reaction was, to the right and left of Francois, there still remained a wide gap in their line which he and Hintza, he felt, could get through with relative ease, provided they moved at their greatest speed. So they ran for it all out with no effort at concealment.

'Go, Hin, go to it!' he called out, perhaps more in encouragement to himself than to Hintza, who was tireless. They were almost safe at the far rim of the gap, close to where the dark fringe of the bush impinged on the hill, when one of the enemy must have seen him clearly enough to shoot, for suddenly bullets went by like angry bees at his ear, followed by the rasp of automatic rifle fire. From all around and behind the hill men began shooting rapidly and long so that it sounded as if a full-scale battle had broken out there. Miraculously, still unhit, François reached the foot of the hill and was beginning to feel certain that everyone would be rushing to the place of the shooting so that Xhabbo and the women would be safe, when a large black figure jumped out from behind a boulder directly in Hintza's path. A dagger of flame stabbed at the dark and a shot rang out. Thank God! He could tell from the sound that the shot had not found a mark, but had merely gone close enough to make Hintza swerve from his course. François was already near enough to see a gun with a bayonet at the end thrusting at Hintza and the long, speed-taut shadow of Hintza flying, it seemed, almost directly into the point of the bayonet.

François went black with despair for he could not imagine how Hintza could not be impaled on the bayonet or, if not, hurt severely, perhaps fatally. But as he felt it, a rifle clattered on a stone ahead, and the shadow of the man fell over. Sounds of a violent struggle came up from the ground nearby and then there, almost at his feet, was a man not only fighting for his life and grunting as he was trying in vain to call for help. Yet no sound of any kind came from Hintza, which he knew was a sign that Hintza had a mind for nothing but killing and was not going to waste any breath and energy on noise.

How wise Hintza was in concentrating on this single issue was immediately clear to François as he slid to a halt beside the struggling pair. Hintza had his teeth firmly fastened just above the place where the neck joined the shoulder of his enemy and was desperately trying to keep a burly man pinned down to the earth until he could strangle him with his teeth. The man was obviously powerful and filled with the energy of desperation. Somehow he had managed to pull out a long jungle knife from his belt and was just bringing it up to stab Hintza low down in his side.

Without hesitating, François shot the man through the head. Doing so he had no feelings of any kind except relief that he was in time to save Hintza's life, and that they had to move on at once if they were to get away safely.

'Come, Hin, quick. Follow me!' he called out. But Hintza was still sunk deep down in the profound instincts involved in a dog's fight to the death for his and François's survival that he went on savaging the throat of the dead man as if he could still come alive again. And for once he did not heed François's call. François was forced to lose invaluable moments, kneeling by him and whispering in his ear, almost like a mother to a hysterical child, 'There now, Hin, there now, boy, it's all over. All over now and nothing to fear. We must go at once. There now, Hin, come and look, he's dead. Oh come at once, at *once*! Do you hear me, sir?'

This last 'at once' and its sequence were uttered in his severest tone and it was only then that Hintza let go and responded. To François's horror, he responded on only three of his four legs. François wanted to see to the other leg there and then, but the shooting was louder and wilder than ever and the air above them filled with the sound as if all the wild bees in Africa were swarming for a world war.

There was only one comfort in all that noise. He believed the sound of his own shot would have been lost in it. For all he knew, with such careless and wild shooting his enemies might not only be shooting at shadows but at one another. He was amazed to find that the thought of such a possibility became a kind of prayer for them indeed to shoot and kill one another until not a single person was left alive. Yet he knew the prayer was vain and that he had no time to lose because sooner or later sanity would return to the scene. With the day near, his and Hintza's spoor would be found and they would once more be pursued, this time even more ardently and in greater numbers than the day before.

For the moment he had to suppress his concern for Hintza's condition in the greater concern of finding a safe place in the bush ahead where he could attend to the wound, saying to himself over and over again as he concluded this, 'Dear God, please make it only a wound and not a broken leg. I might be able to deal with a wound but with a broken leg, neither Hintza nor I can ever hope to get away.'

In this manner he moved as fast as he thought Hintza could follow along an old game track that led deeper into the bush and along the foot of a range of hills running to the south, parallel and between the great gorge to which Xhabbo was travelling. Once deep in the bush, just as soon as the first light exploded over the hushed bush, he stopped to look and listen carefully. There was still some spasmodic shooting in the distance far behind him but as yet no sound of pursuit or startled flight of any of the many birds of morning to suggest one. He could turn at last to Hintza who was bravely still at his heels, without a whimper of protest. Kneeling down, and in a voice gentle as a woman's François said, 'Oh come now, dear Hin. Let's look and see what he did to you, that terrible man!'

The light was good enough to show that Hintza had a deep bayonet thrust in the soft part of his left back leg. Fortunately his healthy young blood had already begun to congeal and was only very slightly oozing from the centre, so that François knew no vital artery or vein could have been cut. Gently he felt the crooked leg around the wound, fingered the muscle and sinews, and softly caressed the bone up and down from the paw to where it joined the body.

Hintza shivered with the pain of the contact, gentle as it was, but stood still without a sound. Thank God! The bone was not broken, and though the wound itself seemed terrible enough François felt now he could deal with it. He hastened to extract from his pocket one of the field dressings he always carried on him, clamped it on the wound and bandaged it firmly in position. The wound, thank Heaven again, was in the one place where he could bandage it with the certainty of it staying in position, for he found he could knot the bandage both underneath the groin and again on top of Hintza's spine.

That done, he took some of the aureomycin tablets he carried with his field dressings, and poured some water from his flask into his hat. He opened Hintza's jaws, pushed the tablets down his throat, held his jaws together and tilted his chin for just long enough to be certain that the tablets had gone down.

'Good Hin, Good,' he said. 'There's some water for you.'

Hintza needed no urging and lapped up the water. When he had done, he looked up in a way so like the look on his face when he had been pleading for more chocolate a few hours before, that François could not say no. Knowing that there

192

was a stream ahead, he poured all the water left in his flask into his hat and happily watched Hintza drinking it all up, scolding him as he did so in the excessive jest of relief without bounds, 'You ought to be ashamed of yourself, frightening me like that. Shame on you, you miserable outrageous little hound. Yes, frightened me to death, you terrible old *goggatjie** you!'

At that Hintza, quick to detect a note of reproach even in jest, looked so abashed that François put his arms round him, pressed him to him and for a moment held his own cheek against Hintza's saying, 'Of course you know I don't mean a word of it! You've been a wonder. Without you I would have been on the end of that bayonet and not you. Now come, let's get away from this place and all these terrible people. I'll go as gently as I can.'

He started off on the same track, still bearing south of Xhabbo's course, first at a fast walk, repeatedly looking over his shoulder to measure if it was not too much for Hintza. But as he noticed that Hintza was keeping up with ease and no obvious increase of pain, he began jogging along, gradually raising the pace to the speed necessary for putting a safe distance between him and his enemies, before the heat of the day made travelling over-exacting. He was reassured to find that even so Hintza was keeping up well. Nonetheless, the sight of him bravely coming along on three legs just as if he had his usual four in use so moved François that he could not help stopping after a while. When Hintza came up to him he said in a voice harsh with affection, 'You know what, you little old insect, you're a bloody marvel! I'd like you to know I'm only doing this so we can have as great a gap as possible from our enemies and find a nice place ahead for you to lie up and rest.'

The sound of the shooting had vanished and only the silence of the bush told him that somewhere far back something utterly foreign of which it heartily disapproved had entered it. Indeed, so still was it just then and so listless had the wind of morning become that he no longer heard as much as a whisper from the leaves, but only the beat of his heart drumming at his temples.

* *Goggatjie,* diminutive of *goggo,* the Bushman generic term for insects of the creepiest kind, and paradoxically the greatest form of endearment.

He was about to go on when an odd new sound reached him from some hundred yards to the north-west of the track, towards the way of the wind that Xhabbo was following. Faintly at first, but growing gradually louder, he heard a strange rumbling, as if numbers of vast witches' cauldrons had suddenly been brought to the boil. He thought he knew what it meant, but it sounded too good to be true, and he was compelled to make sure.

Just ten yards away there stood a dead giant of a tree and instantly he made for it. Its bark was ragged and the trunk deeply scratched by the claws of many leopards who obviously used it as a nail-file for sharpening the points of their crampon claws as well as the top for an observation post. He had no need to tell Hintza of his intentions, as Hintza had often enough seen him doing what he was about to do. He climbed up the tree, noticing as he went higher how well the leopards had pioneered the way for him. Almost at the top he found a fork high enough to show him the bush spread out like an immense sea of green and gold around him. It was as if he were there at the mast-head of the morning and could look back to where the hills above his old home were purple with shadow below, but with their bushy heads ringed with crowns of diamond-dew light. There was no sign as yet that their tracks had been found and that they were being pursued, because there were by now enough birds, baboons and apes awake for warning if that were so.

Concentrating on the area to the north-west where the volume of rumbling was greatest, he noticed that the immense surface of the bush was mysteriously agitated, leaves trembling, branches waving and some of the tallest tree-tops shaken as if caught in gusts of wind in this utterly windless moment. François, of course, had never seen the sea but had read a great deal about it, and in that kind of crow's-nest of the bush in which he found himself, he had a feeling as if a school of enormous fish were on the move over there.

This impression was heightened when in gaps in between the greatest of the trees, one immense marble back after another began showing itself in a slow arc of surrhythmic movement as it passed over the smoking crest of early light, drifting like spume and spray of the swell of the seagreen forest deep, before van-

194

ishing in the trough below another vast wave of shadow looming beyond, in the way that the whales of his picture-books
seemed to love to show their backs above the swinging sea. And
then of course he could not doubt: they were to the ocean of his
bush what whales were to the sea. The superfluous confirmation
came when all round him the slender ends of the long blue-grey
trunks of elephants emerged elegantly from the ocean of
shadow to sniff the sun-dipped tree-tops and burning tips of
branches until they found a sprig to the taste of their gourmet
palates. Their trunks would curl round it then like the tendrils
of some vast convolvulus, wrench it off with an audible crack
and pull it down into the ocean of shadow below, without the
bodies that powered the process becoming visible, so that the
disembodied scene had a strange Merlinesque quality about it.
But soon he saw trunks and great marble backs plunge on reunited and at last the gleam of ivory tusks, incandescent, warm,
knightly above a caparison of purple shadow, forming altogether a vision so numinous as to take command of
François's senses.

It had always been one of his favourite sights but his familiarity with it had never bred any feelings of contempt. Indeed
this morning it was as if he were seeing it for the first time, and
he was strangely uplifted, for in the presence of this great assembly of the lords of his bush, he seemed to have rediscovered
a moment of innocence in his life, free from fear and malice.
Utterly without fear themselves, in their giant strength unusually tender and wise, loving in their relationships with one
another, and considerate of other forms of being, even if to a
plant somewhat large of appetite, they seemed to him to be
breakfasting so at peace and at one with life and their companions that the 'I' in him became a one too.

This 'one' just could not help feeling that what had happened
back at Hunter's Drift was an aberration which would never
happen again, and it had only to seek admission to this noble
and most ancient order to be at peace and at one with itself as
well. But even more immediate to the François of that
moment, was a feeling that he had only to accept this assembly
of peers as his guide now and they would direct him to a stream
of running water where they went daily, not only for refresh-

ment and delight but out of a sense of cleanliness that was next to the great feeling of godliness they gave out at that hour.

François knew at once what he would do. He would put himself and Hintza in the protection of this great company, swimming so it seemed in the ocean of shadow since no legs were visible as yet to explain their movement. The resolve became all the more ardent when in a vacant patch nearby there appeared the largest old elephant ever seen in that part of the bush. François knew him well and treasured him above all others. He came from Mopani's reserve, like the immense following of which he was king-emperor. Over many years in which he and his people had been scrupulously protected by Mopani and his rangers, he had lost much of his hatred of men and came near to acquiring a relationship of trust with them. He was so conspicuous and remarkable an elephant that in the manner of the bush he had to have a name of praise. The Matabele rangers gave him one of the greatest in their history: they called him Mosilikatze.* But for François he had always been Hannibal the Great.

That was sign enough to send François slithering down the tree. The rumble of stomachs now was very near. If not careful, he would soon be caught in the middle of the herd itself, when what he really wanted to do was to travel with Hintza just slightly ahead of them, keeping touch through the sound of their boiling, bubbling stomachs, staying always close enough to know at once if anything happened to alarm them. He knew that provided he and Hintza kept only thirty yards ahead of the elephants, they would be in no danger of being seen because elephant eyesight is notoriously bad. He was not even afraid that they would pick up his and Hintza's smell, although they have the keenest sense of smell of any animal in the bush, since what little breath was left in the wind of morning was stirring from them towards him.

Even should they pick up a whiff of his and Hintza's scent, they were so discriminate and had such incredible memories that he believed they would recognize the scent as that of old and proved friends, and whether they saw or smelt, they would not attack but merely move circumspectly aside, which was the

* Founder of the Matabele nation.

one thing above all others François wanted to avoid. He wanted them to move directly after him so that the elephants would eliminate his and Hintza's tracks. Although his enemies would certainly find his and Hintza's spoor sooner or later merging with the great satin imprints elephants made on the rough red texture of the earth, no tracker could possibly imagine that a boy and a dog could have done anything except give way as quickly as possible before the advance of so great a column of beasts. Should the enemy be bold enough to press directly after the elephants and try to disperse so great a herd, they would not help themselves thereby, because he and Hintza would be warned by such alert animals, long before the enemy caught up with them, and have time enough to find a good place of hiding.

Accordingly François hastened to break the good news to Hintza, who of course already knew all about the presence of the elephants despite his reluctant pre-occupation with his own pain. In the telling he put his hand to Hintza's nose, afraid that he might find it hot and dry with fever from the wound. To his amazement it was still faintly damp and cool. Considering the long distance Hintza had come on only three legs, this, even more than the brigade of imperial guards covering their withdrawal now, raised François's hopes, for it suggested that the tablets he had given Hintza, as once he had given them to the wounded Xhabbo, were doing their work and preventing fever and infection from his deep wound.

When he judged the nearest rumbling to be only ten yards away, he led off down the track again. Elephants even when browsing can move so fast that François was afraid they would have to travel once more on the run. But their protectors appeared to be finding the food so much to their taste that they were unusually leisurely in their advance. Whenever François looked behind he would see one great granite shape after the other, pause to extract a bouquet of succulent green leaves from a tree anointed and dressed with sun and insert it like the finest of French salads with aristocratic precision into their mouths. Most reassuring of all, Hannibal the Great himself was so full of the peace of the morning and so conscious of the dignity his high office demanded that he was not only eating

197

more slowly and fastidiously than the rest but in between one dish of green and another, one course of sweet wild berries and another, was leading his formation at his stateliest pace, so that it took François and Hintza two hours to reach the stream, when normally he could have done the distance easily in under an hour. But that, considering Hintza's plight, was all to the good.

Since the stream there was particularly shallow, or 'feeling itself to be only a little stream' as it would have been put by Xhabbo, who, pray God, was by now well on his way to safety, François crossed it easily and without hesitation so that Hannibal the Great could exercise his imperial prerogative of having the shaded banks for the refreshment and ablution of himself and his subjects. On the far side he found shelter and shade for themselves behind a slate blue boulder under an umbrella of some vast wild fig trees. For the bush stepped down on to the edge of the stream and raised its greatest columns there. Should the need arise, he had cover abundant and to spare at hand for his and Hintza's safety.

Settling Hintza down in the smoothest patch of ground he could find, he went at once to the stream to fetch one hatful of water after the other, watching the elephants come glistening with dew out of the shadows of the bush, their young rushing eagerly ahead with trumpet-squeals of joy at the sight of the stream, while their parents followed like Patricians about to take to Roman waters. Hintza lapped up his water with obvious gratitude and François then allowed himself a hatful, refilled his empty flask and prepared to bed down beside Hintza for as long as the heat of the day lasted. But just for a moment he sat up. Yes, his eyes had not deceived him; there, only a mile to the north-west of him was the summit of Lamb-snatcher's Hill. He had not been wrong in concluding that the elephants were following the route from the reserve which he and Mopani had taken when they themselves had gone on patrol in the gorge on the far side of the hill.

Again a feeling that a tide had turned in his affairs came rushing back at him, so intoxicating that he rebuked himself for it in a typical African way, spitting out the thought on to the ground beside him before it could unbalance him and saying to himself, 'Now remember, François, remember, the eye crosses the swollen river days before the body can.'

Nonetheless he lay down comforted on his back, his haversack as a cushion under his head. Just before closing his eyes he looked up and saw the jet black face of a little bush ape with a fringe of shining silver hair round it and quick sparkling amber eyes, looking unbelievably wise and old, under a forehead wrinkled like that of a Chinese sage. It was staring down at him only two feet away, as if to say, 'Now if I were you, I would not be sleeping there.' And then a fatigue that no anaesthetic could equal put him instantly to sleep.

He could not tell how long he had slept when a high-pitched, urgent elephant trumpet call to arms woke him. Gun in hand, he was on his side and crawling round the boulder to look across the stream. The immense herd of elephant were still in the water but the scene was no longer as he had last seen it. Then the young baby elephants, shrieking and spluttering with delight, had been splashing round their mothers and he had seen one elephant mother proudly nudging another and pointing to her young as if to say, 'Don't you think he's marvellous? Have you ever seen so young a child so advanced for his years and prodigiously intelligent?' Others had been scrubbing their young vigorously behind the ears and the old and young bull sentries dotted up and down the line of bathers at a respectful distance from Hannibal were squirting fountains of water over their massive shoulders with their trunks until they looked clean and dark enough to have been carved out of Nubian granite for the hope and glory of the vanished Carthage.

Instead, they were all standing motionless now in the pools of water, even and bright as glass polished by the heat of the day, and only their trunks were up and out searching the air for a whiff of whatever it was that had sent up that signal of alarm from Hannibal the Great. François had barely seen them thus, when Hannibal lifted his huge trunk once more to a sky white with heat. This time there could be no mistaking it. It was no longer a trumpet call to a stand-to but to scatter and be on the march, and on the march, moreover, at speed.

Hannibal immediately set the example by rushing down the stream towards the main bulk of his herd, trumpeting and trumpeting again, but with his subjects bunching like sheep instead of scattering, as they headed for the only easy slope out of the bed of the stream into the bush above the steep bank. They were just beginning to enter the forest like a river of ink, when a score or more African soldiers led by an officer who was neither European nor African but of a race François could not recognize, appeared on the edge of the stream, just where Hannibal had been standing. Worse, barely a quarter of a mile below the herd struggling to escape in the narrow gap, another group of African soldiers came sliding out of the bush down the bank and filing out along the bed of the stream.

François had no doubt then that his enemies had found his and Hintza's spoor and more, found what he had feared most of all, the blood that must have dripped on to the grass and leaves in the beginning from Hintza's wound. They would not have been able to tell whether it was his or Hintza's blood but would have obviously been encouraged by the discovery to believe that with either one of them seriously wounded, they could not get far away and must be hidden somewhere near at hand. So that when they came to where the spoor of the two of them was rubbed out by the spoor of the elephants, they had not given up the search but had spread into two groups, one travelling to the left of the column of elephants, and the other to the right, convinced that somewhere on the flanks of the herd they would find traces that would finally lead them to François and Hintza. It was a terrible blow to his newly-born hopes, for it could only mean that the pursuit was not to be broken off until either he and Hintza were found, or the enemy was satisfied that they had made off in a direction of country in which they could not possibly survive for long.

François had confirmation of this from the manner in which both groups moved out to the gravel in the bed of the stream, tired, frustrated and in a bad temper because they had not yet found their quarry, and were clearly perplexed over what next to do. Obviously they blamed even the elephants for their failure, for once they were all standing in a ragged line on the gravel, they did not wait for a command from their officers, who had produced field glasses and were methodically examining the bed of the stream up and along its opposite bank.

Suddenly, in a way which may have surprised their officers, but not François, they started shooting at once into the herd of elephants struggling desperately up the banks towards the shelter of the bush.

It was typical of Hannibal the Great that, as head of so great an order, responsible for so many women and children, he turned without hesitation to their defence. Up went his trunk and a sound of defiance burst out that thrilled François through and through with its lightning manliness, and brought Hintza up on to his three feet, the hair on end all along the ridge of his back and his long lips snarling and white teeth bared so that François had to put his arm round his shoulders to hold and calm him. Together they watched the great trunk swish down, immediately roll itself up to be tucked out of harm's way firmly underneath Hannibal's great chin. That done, Hannibal charged out of the water straight over the gravel towards the shooting men, his long tusks curved and gleaming in front of him.

François had never longed more for some knowledge of the elephant language, which according to his old Bushman nurse Koba, was one of the most eloquent languages of the animals of the bush, so that he could have called out to Hannibal not to be so wonderfully and heroically foolish, but for the sake of them all to be brave in a new way and discard his pride of manhood and humbly go after his disappearing subjects. But knowing not a word of the only language that could have helped, he could just ask with his heart, as the Matabele say, for a miracle from life to deliver Hannibal from their common enemy. But it was asking in vain. As he asked it Hannibal slithered to a halt. Shaking his great head in confusion and staring with sheer unbelief at his knees that were beginning to buckle underneath him, he looked so unfairly and treacherously brought to judgement that tears came to François's eyes. But from somewhere, from a depth of life François suspected such enemies could not be aware Hannibal summoned the power of the courage that is the core of the honour of the male, whether in plant, insect, bird, beast or man, to move to the attack again. But this time he just came to the edge of a pool François knew well as the pool he and Mopani had christened the 'sea-cow pool', after the name for hippopotamuses in their language, when scores of bullets hit him again. Only then did that vast marble head sink down on his chin. He staggered, halted, shuddered as he still obviously refused defeat, but then fell over into the deep pool, splintering the glass of its surface and sending its sparkling fragments flying upwards into the brilliant air. As his black body hit the water, he rolled over like a shattered battleship foundering and slowly went down and out of sight.

The pity and the futility of it had already brought François close to tears but from somewhere deep in himself the feeling deposited there by 'Bamuthi's last great 'To me!' joined his feelings now to ask what could be the meaning of the word – futile – when futility was accompanied by a gesture that would remain with him for ever if he survived. He was certain he would, to his dying day, tell as a memorial of Hannibal the Great and all the countless forgotten manifestations of man in the life of Africa who when even all the odds were ranged against him, refused to aid any end imposed on him from without. For how otherwise could the living chain of being from the remote point in time, where once it only had position but no size or magnitude, remain unbroken up to this perilous sunlit moment that had just witnessed the latest summing-up and transfiguration of the record of them all by Hannibal?

Through blurred eyes François looked beyond the pool into which Hannibal had vanished. There two young bulls were trying with their tusks to help a wounded cow up on to the bank and into the bush where the last survivors were just vanishing. A sustained burst of fire from the soldiers brought them down as he looked, and all three rolled down the bank to lie ashen with dust like bundles of dirty laundry dropped on the gravel for washing in the stream.

'So it's not over yet,' François whispered in the bitterest of tones to Hintza. 'They're obviously going to keep at it until they find us, Hin, so the sooner you and I are on our way the better. For I'm not going to let them. I'm so sorry, you poor little old goggatjie. I so wanted you to have a proper rest before going on and to tell you the truth, I could do with more of it myself. But what can we do with so many rude, uninvited and ill-behaved guests about, except to abandon the party to them and be on our way?'

He deliberately tried to lift his last sentence into a lighter, almost jesting key, but wondered whether it had helped as far as he himself was concerned. Looking at those soldiers swarming towards Hannibal and a score of elephant corpses, knives in hand and obviously preparing, whatever their officers were going to say, for a great feast of elephant meat before moving on, he suddenly remembered the Scottish officer as he had watched him by the fire.

He wished that he had him there beside him, so that he could rub his fine ethical nose in what had just happened, belabouring him with feelings to some such effect as, 'So much for the campaign of limited violence you and your church's conscience demanded! Limited, my tired-out feet! You can't even limit yourself to killing human beings indiscriminately but have to spill over the hatred that's in the lot of you on to elephants that have never done you any harm. Don't tell me they did it for food. One quarter of just one elephant would have fed that lot for days and look, there are twenty or more of them dead. Dear God – not your sociological god, Mr Conscience Scot, but the God that is also in Mantis and Umkulunkulu and known by a thousand and one names and sounds and colours in this his bush – this dear God of us all, please make an end to this evil and killing!'

Feeling all this and more he came to his knees to gather his possessions for an immediate departure. There above him again was the face of that little, wise, young-old ape, looking down at him but this time with an expression of, 'you see, I told you it was not a place I myself would have picked for a nap. What a pity you humans do not listen more to the apes in yourselves, little cousin, for surely you would not deny now that we have a special relationship, would you?'

The look was as sympathetic as it was sardonic and this slight sign from life that he was not the only witness to disapprove of what had happened helped him out of all proportion to its size.

'Come, Hin,' he whispered, 'follow me. Straight into the bush here and we'll get away long before those men there are ready to follow.'

The track François proposed following led straight up the flank of the range that separated him from the gorge in which

203

Xhabbo should by now be sheltering. Indeed, it should pass right over the shoulder of Lamb-snatcher's Hill itself, if he remembered rightly. Fortunately too it was a rough and stony track. He had no fear that, provided he went carefully, they would leave obvious signs on it for their enemies to find, particularly as Hintza's wound was now so well bound and no longer bleeding. It was true that sooner or later they must find and follow the track itself, because it was the only one out of the river bed for miles around. They would follow it however, he was certain, more by guessing because from what he had seen of their behaviour down by the river, they would be so full of food and frustration that they would take to it not out of any enthusiastic conviction so much as a reluctant sense of duty.

So both for the sake of his own exhausted self and Hintza's wound, he climbed slowly up the winding track. Every now and then he would clamber on a rock or climb a tree where he would survey the river bed below. He would see the smoke of several fires on the gravel under the shadiest banks where the soldiers were no doubt cooking their fillets of elephant steaks. The last vision he had of them as the sun was beginning to sink in the West, was of their fires still smoking. A hope that was clear enough almost to be a certainty came to him that the soldiers might bed down there for the night before re-starting their search in the morning. They could well persuade themselves, in such an over-fed state, that after the blood they had seen, he and Hintza had to be near and ready for the taking.

Once over the saddle of Lamb-snatcher's Hill, he deliberately gave the enemy no further thought, but concentrated on the problem of establishing contact with Xhabbo who would be expecting him from the opposite direction. Fortunately the answer to this one appeared not difficult. Just as the sun was about to go down, red as it had been red on the morning of Heitse-Eibib in the dark ages behind him, at a moment when Hintza for all his lack of complaining had to be forced to rest, because François saw him foaming at the mouth with pain and exhaustion, he came to the edge of the great wreath of rock near the place where Xhabbo should be hiding. There, without hesitation, he stopped and uttered the call of jackal and plover in the succession which had been their own password for so long. He waited and no answer came. So tired was he and so many frustrations and disappointments were behind him that he despaired even of this call on which he had banked so much, particularly when he considered how discredited it had been earlier in the day. It was only with a great effort of will that he could persuade himself to try it a second time. Again he waited and no answer came.

'I might have known it,' he muttered bitterly to himself. 'It just won't work. I think Hintza and I had better find a place to settle down for the night by ourselves.'

He had hardly concluded that when from the side and just behind him there was a thud as of naked feet coming down from a height on to the track. He swung round, his rifle instantly at his shoulder and ready to shoot. There, smiling a smile which François thought was the most wonderful thing he had ever seen was Xhabbo, exclaiming, 'Oh Foot of the Day, forgive Xhabbo for although feeling that call came from you, feeling yourself to be both jackal and plover in a way which fox and plover feel themselves to be so on account of it, Xhabbo had to make certain. Foot of the Day, we all live again.'

CHAPTER EIGHT

Lamb-snatcher's Hill

François and Hintza, responsibility for themselves surrendered into Xhabbo's capable hands, were so overcome, François with an exhaustion as emotional as it was physical, and Hintza both with exhaustion and pain, that they were incapable of taking in any of the detail when they arrived at the shelter which Xhabbo and Nuin-Tara and Nonnie had already prepared deep under a vast overhang of rock near the summit of Lamb-snatcher's Hill.

But there was nothing in the slightest degree vague in the way that the two girls watched their arrival. They had, it is true, come far themselves, and known moments of great peril on the hill, greater even than Xhabbo had realized when the first shouts of warning had gone up from their enemies. They had seen, dismayed, from the place in the earth between the boulders where Xhabbo had forced them to lie down, the dark shadows of far more men appearing from all round them than even Xhabbo and his tapping had anticipated. Indeed they had rushed by them so close and in such numbers that they could not believe that they themselves would not be discovered. But then as the rush receded and they peered between the boulders, and heard not only the silence broken by sustained rifle-fire but saw the dark pierced with the red thrust of the pointed flame that followed each shot, the impossible seemed to have happened. They themselves were safe for the moment but that was of no comfort to any of them. Nonnie's feelings and the heights of which they were capable could only be understood through a proper regard to the depth of anxiety and fear into which they could plunge. She could not possibly conceive how François and Hintza could have survived such cataclysmic shooting. Her spirit which was as bright and brave as any young, inexperienced spirit can be, abandoned her to such an extent that, despite all her conscious pre-determination to the contrary, she had no thought of going on with the journey. She had, instead, an overwhelming compulsion to go out, no matter what the consequences, search for the bodies of François and Hintza and look on them for the last time. Nothing else mattered to her and she had no care or wish for any part in what could lie ahead.

But at this point, she felt Xhabbo's hand very gently stroking the back of her head. After stroking it, the hand turned it sideways in his direction and Xhabbo whispered in her ear a word which she had already learned the previous day from Nuin-Tara: the Bushman word for good, whispered it over and over again and followed all up with a smile wide and white, even in the dark. Also he made signs indicating that if François and Hintza had been killed or found, the shooting would not be going on so furiously as it was on the far side of the hill. All that could only mean that François had drawn the enemy away from the three of them and he and Hintza must be well on their way to safety now.

'Foot of the Day, good, good!' he whispered the words she knew, pressing her hand to his chest to show her how good he felt both François and their situation to be.

She longed to believe him but doubted him longer than necessary, because to have been uplifted into conviction again only to have it denied utterly by facts later on, would have been the end of the road as far as she was concerned. But then, when Nuin-Tara also put her hand on her shoulder to smile a smile of thanksgiving at her, she no longer doubted and before she could give more thought or perhaps more feeling to the matter, the signal came from Xhabbo to be on their feet at once and run as they had never run before.

The relief not only of action but of actually participating physically in something she now believed François and Hintza to be doing as well, somewhere on a line parallel to their own, was as stimulating to her spirit as that brandy warming her within. She felt she could now follow Xhabbo all day to that infinity of time where all parallels could meet.

Xhabbo led off with no effort at concealment, since the shooting clearly showed how the enemy had lost their heads and had poured over the hill, confused and in the wrong direction as he and François had intended. As a result, just as the first light broke, they found without hindrance the old hippopotamus trail in the rushes and papyrus along the river banks which Xhabbo had described to François. From there, hidden from human eyes, they travelled at relative ease and not long after noon, they were installed underneath the ledge of the hill without any sign of pursuit behind them.

After that there had only been one other moment of real alarm and that was when they heard the far-off sound of rifle-fire during the attack on Hannibal the Great and the brutal dispersal of his order. But again, Xhabbo and Nuin-Tara, after listening to the sounds carefully, had made light of it in pantomime so convincingly that Nonnie's heart was reassured – a heart that was with François and Hintza all the more because she had no experience of any kind to support her spirit by enabling it to be with them in imagination as well.

One should not exaggerate, however, and suggest that all her anxiety on their behalf was ended. It remained great all afternoon but it was not comparable to anything she had felt at any time in the cave during François's previous absence because somehow up there on that great hill, with the Atlantic view of the land of Africa uninhibited and urgent, unfolding itself in wave upon wave of light and shadow, flashing river and precious stream, yellow hill and purple valley, levelling out like the spent swell of some sea of summer on a vast foreshore of sand, where the blue of the sky prolonged the blue of the earth a hundred or more miles away, she just could not help a feeling of having broken out of prison with a prospect of freedom at last before her. She could not know then that she was having her first glimpse of the desert that was Xhabbo's and Nuin-Tara's home. She knew only that seeing such abundant and turbulent earth resolved in so calm and firm an horizon did her senses good.

All this was helped along by an instinct which compels life after each encounter with disaster to turn about and reach out towards a vision of what, for all its inevitable remoteness, promises renewal and increase of life. And so begins, however reluctantly, some new movement towards the future. In the primitive worlds of the past whole peoples abandoned the capital of a dead king and hastened on to found a new one for his successor elsewhere. So a similar urge had begun to stir in Nonnie during the flight from the cave to Lamb-snatcher's Hill. Her being had, however intangibly, undergone a change of course and come under the pull of a mysterious force of gravity in the human spirit which determines that a journey into the unknown in the world without produces a movement towards new and unknown areas in our world within. There is a profound interdependence of world without and world within, and experience in either one of them is valid also in the other. Whenever one succeeds in breaking the code wherein their meaning is transmitted from one dimension to the other, this validity is so marked that one wonders whether they are really two different dimensions and not just two aspects of one and the same whole. The visible world being merely the spirit seen from without; the spirit, just the world without seen from within.

If this had not been so, one doubts whether this sense of a new dimension could have been helped as much as it was by Nuin-Tara, once they reached sanctuary on Lamb-snatcher's Hill. From the moment of arrival she began to do her utmost to teach Nonnie a new language as well as a new role in life. She made her repeat new Bushman words after her, over and over again, until she had mastered not only the meaning but the sounds, and clicks. She also trained her in the elementary duties of Bushman housekeeping on the march.

There was first of all, Nuin-Tara showed her by example and pantomime, the importance of preparing the place which was to be home for the night. She showed her first of all how the beds had immediately to be made before it could be too dark to see; the ground cleared of litter, stones, pebbles, twigs, smoothed out and patted down with their hands until it was level and clean. In all this Nuin-Tara was so exacting that it took considerable time. When it was done at last, and Nonnie stood up straight behind Nuin-Tara to inspect the ground at their feet, she had a distinct illusion of having helped to create two bedrooms equipped with two double-beds. Nuin-Tara, by some telepathy of the universal feminine, must have known what she was imagining, for she smacked her lips with satisfaction and pointed at the ground to confirm Nonnie's unuttered conclusion by saying, 'Xhabbo, Nuin-Tara,' and then moved the finger a bit further to the right, to add, 'Foot of the Day, Nonnie.'

She then beckoned to Nonnie to follow her and turned about to make for the centre of the ground under the vast overhang of rock. Nonnie's illusion that she had been helping in the building of a home was by then so confirmed that she felt as if in the act of complying she were walking through a bedroom door.

She knelt happily beside Nuin-Tara, imitated her movements and to her amazement found that the earth was surprisingly soft and supple and that mixed in with it were the ashes of what must obviously have been the remains of the fires of countless generations of Bushman travellers. This sense of others having been there before them, induced a strange feeling of having company in their homely duties. As a result, this part of their work took no time at all. Soon she was following Nuin-Tara outside into the thick bushes, scrub and thorn trees which covered the approaches to their shelter and helping her to gather wood for the fire-place they had just constructed.

There was no scarcity of dead wood on what Nonnie almost thought of now as their door-step, but even so apparently easy a task was made difficult by Nuin-Tara, since she was as exacting and discriminating in doing it as she had been in the making of their beds. The nearest and most obvious of dead wood was not good enough for her. She made it plain to Nonnie that only the driest and thinnest wood would do for a reason which became plain to Nonnie only much later. They made a score of journeys between the brush and the fire-place before they had wood enough to Nuin-Tara's special specifications. Again Nonnie was amazed at Nuin-Tara's minute sense of the fitness of domestic things. She herself would have been quite happy to let the wood lie there in the two untidy heaps into which it had been piled, since it was to be burned up in fire soon enough anyway. But Nuin-Tara compelled her to join in sorting out the wood, breaking it into suitable and more or less equal lengths, and then stacking it row upon row in a large, rectangular pile to the left of their fireplace. Then from a dark corner at the far end of the ledge, Nuin-Tara fetched some flat stones, blackened presumably by the fires whose ashes Nonnie had helped to scoop out of the ground. In a most expert fashion, she built a range of stone around the scooped-out earth and with the air of a Vestal Virgin performing a sacred ritual, reverently laid some carefully selected wood ready for a fire underneath it.

After that it was the turn of the haversacks. For the first time Nuin-Tara made herself take second place with great good grace, signalling to Nonnie that she would be relieved if she would take over this part of the housekeeping. She helped Nonnie only to carry the three haversacks they had brought with them to a platform of stone where the ceiling of the rock curved sharply down towards the earth before coming to rest on a broad ledge some four feet high. She stood back silently while Nonnie unpacked, and watched each article extracted almost as if it were not inanimate matter at all but highly animate and a part of some exciting new drama. Slight as this delegation of responsibility was, it was extraordinary to Nonnie how significant and arduous she suddenly felt it to be. It was as if she had been put on her own special mettle and was afraid that in some way she might fail to do the unpacking and arrangement of their supplies to Nuin-Tara's satisfaction. She already knew from François how few possessions Bushmen owned and would have felt it right to be asked to unpack and sort out what must have appeared an embarrassment of riches to Nuin-Tara, had she not already been overawed by the immensely fastidious example that Nuin-Tara had set in all other things. In her apprehension she fumbled and occasionally dropped some cartons of medicines, happily without damage, on the sandy floor. But in the end she had all their food and medicines arranged in their logical order on the ledge.

Right in front, their folded handles bracketed to the side of the ledge and upside down, she laid the dixies which had been fitted, military fashion, into the pockets provided for them on their rucksacks. They gleamed like aluminium saucepans on a kitchen dresser and gave so fine and authentic a domestic quality to her work that Nonnie should have been reassured. Bandages and medicines at the back, then a row of heaps of preserved fig, peach, apricot, apple and plum, bright as in an impressionist still-life, followed by several rows of biltong, another of thick slabs of sweet milk chocolate and finally, glow-

211

ing brown and gold, mounds of Ousie-Johanna's finest rusks. The ledge was transformed into a model little larder.

Yet she was oddly afraid of what Nuin-Tara's reaction would be as she stepped back to look over what she had done. Also she was remembering a favourite maxim of her old nurse Amelia. Always after she had been made to help in tidying their bedrooms and quarters in the series of government houses in which she had grown up, the vast, statuesque Amelia would admonish her monumentally, 'Now remember, Luciana, before leaving a room, you must always stand back in the doorway to survey what you have done, like an officer in your father's guard inspecting a detail of sentries about to relieve the watch. You will be surprised how often people, yes, although I confess it to my shame, even Amelia has left some important detail undone.'

She stood back trembling inwardly, near to tears at this unbidden thought of her butchered nurse. It was almost as if Amelia were standing behind her. If Amelia had, of course she could not have failed to notice that Nonnie had never been so obedient and conscientious to her commands as now when she was not there to supervise their execution. Nonnie's doubts about her capacities on this occasion were needless, for she had hardly begun her military inspection when Nuin-Tara smacked her lips with delight, clapped her hands and at the same time did the little curtsey Bushmen women do when they are about to begin a dance of thanks. Indeed she tripped a little fantastic step or two of delight in front of the ledge before seizing Nonnie's hand to exclaim, 'Good, good, very good!'

And immediately Nonnie was glowing all over and confident enough to be strangely thrilled by her work. She clasped her hands tightly in front of her and turned round and round to take in all they had done together, feeling for the first time what it must be like to make a home of her own.

Eyes shining, she faced Nuin-Tara to exclaim, '*Merveilloso!* Isn't it lovely? We've got a complete house now, thanks to you. Two double bedrooms, a kitchen–dining-room and now a larder complete with a dresser.'

Nuin-Tara obviously had no idea of the exact meaning of the words but could not fail to take the spirit and the sense for granted. Suddenly, as if she herself had an Amelia within, she placed her legs astride, her two hands on her hips, and now with a look of the utmost gravity re-surveyed the scene. The attitude belonged not only to her and Amelia but to woman everywhere making certain that her duties for the day had been scrupulously discharged.

It would be impossible to exaggerate the good all this did to Nonnie. Nuin-Tara's attitude was implicit with the kind of self-respect that is peculiarly a feminine speciality; a unique form of courage to endure in their care for life and living things, no matter how grim and formidable the circumstances thrown against it. Cities and homes may be pillaged and destroyed. The Carmona of Nonnie's mother had been destroyed, and her mother killed in an African St Bartholomew's Day massacre just as the home of François's Hunter's Drift had been destroyed and his mother in turn massacred beside her father, Amelia, and Ousie-Johanna. But what she happened to be seeing in Nuin-Tara just then was a demonstration of an essential built-in pattern of the feminine spirit which ensured that always out of ashes and rubble, new shapes, new and greater versions of what had gone before would rise. She thought she had never seen any woman look as beautiful to her as Nuin-Tara did just then. Wonderfully lifted out of her wounded self, she went up to Nuin-Tara, put her arms round her and her head between her naked breasts, held her close and let tears of sheer gratitude and admiration run without impediment out of the corners of her closed eyes. Instantly Nuin-Tara's arms went round her, pressed her closer and then freed a hand to stroke the back of Nonnie's head and its long, fine and black Iberian hair with great tenderness. They were still standing like that in that act of communion of oecumenical woman when Xhabbo appeared on the track at the entrance to their shelter.

All the while Nuin-Tara and Nonnie were at work preparing their shelter for the night, Xhabbo had been conspicuously absent. He had been far more disturbed by the sound of shooting than he cared to admit even to Nuin-Tara. He had been often enough under fire from the African impis who annually, after the rains fell, foraged deep into the desert in order to capture young Bushman boys and girls: boys to be turned into slave-herds for their cattle grazing on the fringes of the desert, the girls as concubines for their rulers and headmen, who were inordinately attracted to their light copper-coloured skins. He could tell the difference between the sound of rifle-fire which hit only thin air and the sound of shot that went truly home in its target. Far off as that sound of gunfire was, he had no doubt that many of the shots he was hearing smacked as if they had hit what they were meant to hit. Moreover they were coming precisely from the direction which he knew François and Hintza would have taken in the first instance.

All this would have perturbed him to the point of despair, had it not been for one strange element in the sound of the shooting. Had those shots been aimed only at François and Hintza, he was certain they would not have had to fire so many times to kill the two of them as those shots he heard were killing their targets. Of course, from what both he and François had seen of their enemies and their attack on Hunter's Drift the day before, they were quite capable of going on shooting long after the targets were dead but even so, there seemed to him something unexplained, if not reassuring, about this aspect of the matter. It did not rule out the possibility of course that François and Hintza could have been killed by some of those shots at the beginning. But all in all, the sheer volume of the sound suggested that much more than just a young man had been killed. But what could that something else possibly have been?

In order to seek the answer to this disturbing puzzle, he immediately left the women alone to their duties and climbed to the top of Lamb-snatcher's Hill, taking care not to show himself on the skyline of the great summit. From there he carefully surveyed the scene; first in the direction from which they themselves had come. He observed that there was not the slightest indication that they were being followed, as there would have been by now if that were so. He then surveyed the land in the direction of the shooting. There was nothing unusual to be seen for quite a while, until a mile or so away as the beloved bees flew in the bed of the valley, the blue smoke of several fires suddenly rose in lazy spirals up into the thin, still afternoon air. He could tell that they were cooking fires from the pattern of the smoke and thought that they were fires cooking the food of many men, judging by their size and number. He assumed too that the shooting may have had something to do with providing the cooks by the fires with material for the cooking. But again that, of course, did not exclude the dreadful possibility that François and Hintza may have been disposed of first in so long and sustained an outburst of shooting. Indeed the supposition was supported in Xhabbo's estimation by the fact that their enemies – the longer he walked the more certain he became of his first impression that so many fires could only have been lit by their enemies – were unlikely to have broken off their pursuit of François and Hintza to start cooking a meal so early in the afternoon, unless they had accomplished their mission. His spirit would have been altogether clouded over with despair if it had not been that his strangely acute sense of tapping persisted that François and Hintza, though in trouble, were not dead.

Consequently, he had stayed on watch on the summit of the hill, knowing that if François were still alive and his own reading of the smoke and its meaning were correct, François would be unable to make for the place of meeting on the hill as they had so hurriedly agreed on in the early hours of the morning, but would come towards it from some unpredictable direction. Part of him knew that he ought to be down below to help Nuin-Tara and Nonnie in their preparations for the night. Although they had supplies of food enough with them for the moment, he knew as François would have done, that these were supplies to be drawn upon only in emergencies. The sooner they started living off the land in the Bushman way the better.

His conscience in this regard was quickened by the greatest and subtlest of temptations to which a Bushman could be subjected. A strange, unobtrusive brown and white little bird had come just at that moment to settle on a bush nearby and started to deliver itself of a demonically urgent and maddeningly persistent cry of 'Quick! Quick! Honey! Quick!'

Confident that its message could not fail to penetrate and induce instant compliance, the bird repeated the call on the same note a number of times, but when to its obvious astonishment it appeared to be either not heard or understood, it fluttered out from the bush in a quick, dipping movement and into the open to settle only a few yards away. Recognizing Xhabbo from his colour to be a man of the human species who loved honey above all other edible things; it sat there unafraid repeating its call, convinced that the sound combined with the sight of the unobtrusive livery which only a herald of the greatest distinction could afford to wear, must succeed.

But as even this combined appeal failed, it lost patience and gradually its impatience assumed proportions that threatened to burst its white little throat with the uprush of sound. Quick and wise as birds, beasts and insects are in the ways of men of the bush and desert, as a consequence of their millenniums of natural co-existence, it seemed to know that the copper-coloured shape of man glistening like polished metal in the westering sun between those blue-grey boulders, barely a trembling wing's-stretch away, was terribly tempted to come after it and harvest the honey they both so ardently desired. But to the bird's growing amazement, which soon overshadowed its indignation, the copper-coloured shape made no move in its direction.

After an hour of the most eloquent, the most enchanted and siren-like enticement of which a honey-guide had ever been capable, the call was transformed, and in a glittering silver crescendo achieved a grand finale which amounted to an unmistakable pronouncement that Xhabbo's behaviour had imperilled the most wonderful relationship ever evolved between bird and man, and that it would be compelled to submit itself to an agonizing reappraisal of this ancient alliance between the honey-guides of the bush and copper-coloured man. On this portentous, Wagnerian note, just as the long, level light in the west was beginning to prepare the day for twilight and to throw long shadows all round them, the little bird flew away in a shower of apocalyptic sound.

Xhabbo was as relieved then that temptation was behind him as he was guilty over not having answered the bird's summons, which he would normally have felt in honour and self-interest bound to obey. This partnership between Xhabbo and his kind and the honey-guide, was not only unique in the history of all the many and varied relationships that human beings have with other forms of natural life, but also possessed a magical and rare religious quality. For these relationships, on the whole, are one-sided and imposed by man on the birds, the animals, the insects and even microbiological forms of life for wilful and selfish ends. However much he might try to mitigate these elements in his more enlightened moments, and redeem compulsion by being as considerate as he can in his demands, one has only to look in the eyes of, for instance, the animals he has domesticated, to see that the compensations he offers in return for services rendered, are not enough. For those eyes, when they are not on their guard and focused in the service of his bidding, like those of the dogs that follow at his heels, the horses munching in his stables and the cows in his meadows, amaze and confound one with the sadness glowing at the far end of the long look that goes back to their remote beginning.

For human eyes that are still open to these things, it is a sadness that emanates from a nostalgia for a time when they were not enslaved but were free to be their immediate, instinctive selves. For ears that can hear, this nostalgia is there even in their voices, for what can be less joyful than the bleating of the sheep that is the ultimate in subjection to man? There is the pitiful nicker at night of horses haunted by dreams of their birthright of freedom exchanged for a mess of oats and straw and the security of luxurious stables. There is also the sound of cock-crow that has become part of the music of self-betrayal. In all these there is expression both of a persistent incurable sickness for the wilderness that was their garden in the beginning, and reproach to powerful men who have malformed a natural kinship and put an unnatural totalitarianism in its place.

But this partnership of the honey-guide and man differs from all others because it is voluntary, free and equal, formed out of a sense of mutual obligation to a common purpose of life and love of the honey that is the product of the purpose – honey that in its sweetness and capacity for transforming what is bitter and unpalatable in the raw material of life into something not just palatable but eminently desirable. It is proof miraculous of what life could become when a sense of common purpose and interdependence of all living and existing things is recognized and wholeheartedly served. To see the honey-guide as Xhabbo saw it on that golden afternoon in its great, dark surround of peril, is to observe how free the relationship is and how the tiny bird spoke its meaning to him frankly without fear or favour.

One cannot, of course, vouch for the mind of the bird although the vivid instinct which makes it call on man seems to be evidence enough. But one can speak for Xhabbo and say without reservation that as a result honey to him and his fellow men was more than food. It was a substance of a mystical kind, which in the eating was transubstantiated in the blood of the eater to become a thing of spirit, making him a different person. As one ate, so one became, and for him it was therefore, however instinctive and unconscious the deed, an act of as great meaning as the sacrament in which bread and wine are believed to be transubstantiated into living flesh and blood. This translucent image of the role of honey in this partnership is held without hesitation. It is the bee that produces the honey and whose ways Solomon in all his glory exhorted the men of his day to study in order to be wise. It is itself involved in partnership with flowers, plants and matter, so that it plays a great, intermediary role in bringing together in a single, creative purpose, four dimensions of reality that would otherwise have been separate. For in the act of culling the flowers of which there were so many among the fragrant bushes, plants and herbs that cover so densely the slopes and summit of Lamb-snatcher's Hill, the bee is engaged in labour not just for itself and its own kind but on behalf of all creation. It carries fertilizing pollen from one growth to another, joining the feminine in one growth to the masculine in another, so that if it had not been for it and its detailed, unceasing and minute industry, the flowers and plants would not have multiplied but perished, divided and alone in that great, natural setting.

The end of all considerations, therefore, must be that the honey which enables the bee to provide for the survival of its own kind and the procreation of plants and trees as well as producing food for the delight and sweetening of the spirit of man and bird, confirms that despite all the rigour, the exaction, the pain, the suffering, the insecurity, frustration and defeat momentarily incurred, the business of living can be transfigured in an achievement of meaning greater than either happiness or unhappiness.

All these things of course worked on Xhabbo not as rational concepts or organized dogma, but as feelings derived from the most vivid of instincts of which a human being is capable. The pull of these feelings were all the more powerful because of his recollection of occasions before the brutal African invasion and the ruthless dispersal of his people in that part of the world, when he had as a child spent days with his father and his clan on Lamb-snatcher's Hill. He remembered how, at this very hour of the evening with the sun yellowing in the west, they would follow the honey-guide to one of the many deep crevices in the wreath of the peacock-blue rocks around the summit of the hill, and in the heavy shadows there, hear the strands of its ironstone vibrate with the humming of the hosannas of thousands of bees returning home heavily laden with the juice of a flower in which Lamb-snatcher's Hill specialized. This flower was called the 'Touch-me-not' flower. It was shaped like a long horn, wide at the mouth but tapering towards a deep, pointed end. The mouth was a silky, delicate crinoline of bright shocking pink, elegantly indented along its round, turned-over edges with a warm translucent yellow beyond, so that one could see the shadow of its contents rising almost to the brim. These formed a black syrup that even in its untransubstantiated state was sweet, and the horn of the flower would be so full that should one brush it in passing, it would spill and waste its heavy, quintessential molasses either on the skin of the passer or on the ground at its feet. Hence the name, 'Touch-me-not' flower.

Seeing the flower, all Bushmen would be reminded by the name of its nature and role, and so take special care not to waste contents that were there for the delight not only of the flower but of man, bird, insect and animal. Listening to the final crescendo of the bird about to depart, outraged and bitter with resentment, Xhabbo could see in his memory, the crevices down there below him as they had been in the golden past with the long combs of honey hanging full and dripping from the ceilings, and glowing in the deep shadows like segments of a just risen and full desert moon.

These memories, combined with the grim warnings of what happens to human beings who refuse or deceive the honey-guide, which are impressed on every Bushman from earliest childhood, argued so eloquently inside him for compliance with the bird's summons that he might have been compelled to obey in the end, had he not just then seen on the slope towards the valley, where the smoke from many fires was still standing tall and steady, signs that something unusual was slowly and carefully coming up towards the shoulder of Lamb-snatcher's Hill. That was decisive. Odysseus-like, he bound his straining, honey-inebriated senses firmly to the demands of duty and refused that siren bird, to continue his watch until he was certain, yes absolutely certain, that something unusual was moving slowly up the slope.

He dared not let the obvious hope induced by this certainty influence the extreme caution which his special responsibility exacted. He left immediately to hurry down to the shelter in order to warn Nuin-Tara and Nonnie to leave and hide in the bush around, in case that movement came not from what he hoped but from some subtle members of the enemy who had discovered their secret and were working their way towards the summit.

The need for quick action was great. Yet the sight of Nuin-Tara and Nonnie in that attitude already described, made him stand silent for a moment observing them. He, more than either Nonnie or François, had of course been aware of Nuin-Tara's reservations about Nonnie. He had said nothing about it, not even to Nuin-Tara, but nonetheless, amid all the other more immediate and dangerous problems that confronted him, it had secretly caused him much concern. He knew how harmony between people was vital to survival in such dangerous circumstances. Even in so peaceful a pursuit as hunting it was a closely observed practice not to set out with men whom one did not like much, let alone of whom one actively disapproved, because it was well known that even so slight a lack of sympathy tended to exclude one from the sympathy of nature for one's cause. On dangerous missions when men would be thrown into one another's company for months on end, the members were always carefully selected with this precept in mind. Everyone knew how discord among them would inevitably act as a magnet for the accident and disaster always latent in chance and circumstance in the desert. So he greatly feared the consequence of any lack of sympathy between Nuin-Tara and Nonnie, seeing how closely the four of them would be thrown together if and when they broke out of that terrible trap in which they were caught and started their long and uncertain journey to safety.

So he stood there watching the two of them with relief and true happiness that the person whom he regarded as 'utterly Foot of the Day's woman' at last appeared at one with 'utterly his own woman'. He would have walked away to leave them like that longer if his sense of duty had not compelled him to interrupt softly in Bushman. Softly as he spoke, Nuin-Tara knew from the words, Nonnie from the tone, that something of great significance had occurred. Since all things significant in Nonnie's experience in recent days had had such unpleasant meanings, she drew apart from Nuin-Tara and listened, startled, to their exchanges, eyes wide and bright with new fear. The fear was heightened when Nuin-Tara signalled to her to snatch up a field flask of water. Grasping one herself, she hastened to lead Nonnie off into the bush for some hundred yards down the slope. There she made Nonnie lie down beside her and signed to her to keep silent and still so that not a rustle of leaf or vibration of stem could betray them.

Meanwhile, Xhabbo took up his spear, his bow and arrows and went noiselessly to the point where the track, perceptible only to the eyes of Bushman who had known it, met the clearly defined track leading up out of the river bed over the saddle and into the gorge below. There he chose a position on top of a large, flat boulder, deep in the lengthening sunset shadow cast by the summit of Lamb-snatcher's Hill. Carefully because of its poisoned tip, he extracted his favourite arrow from a quiver full of twelve which he always carried slung across his left shoulder. He took his bow, tested the cord like a harpist the strings of his harp but without twanging it as he would normally have done, in case it could be heard by whatever was coming up the hill. The test was entirely to his satisfaction. He shifted the sling of his quiver from left to right shoulder, so that he could extract arrows from it most easily by just raising his right arm and stretching over his right shoulder. He settled himself on his elbows flat on the rock, his spear ready beside him and the bow firmly grasped in the shooting position in his left hand, his favourite arrow between his fingers and fitted to the cord.

In this position he waited, marvelling at the skill of whatever was moving up the hill towards him. All traces of movement among the bushes and grass had vanished on the slope. Nor were there indications of anything unusual coming from the many highly observant birds, animals, insects and plants all around him, so busy organizing the transport of life from its way by day into another night.

There were many beautiful and meaningful examples of how this delicate transition was ordered in Xhabbo's vicinity and how suddenly even the air began to move in the opposite direction to the one it had done in the morning, as if the life of the bush had decided that after one long spell of breathing out all day, the moment had come to take a deep, long breath in. But there was one transitory portent that overshadowed all others. Watching the slope below, Xhabbo suddenly noticed three great jet black patterns appearing in a place where the sun was weaving some yellow-green satin of grass and leaves, just beyond the frontier of the dark shadow cast on it by the summit. At once he looked up. High in the blue, three great lamb-snatchers with wing-spans of two strides each, the sun on fire on their foam white breasts, were circling despondently in a slow descent towards their homes on the hill. He looked carefully and yes – oh yes, their talons were empty. The omen was the best of all possible omens. One lamb-snatcher would have been enough to make a point; the unusual number of three, coming home empty-taloned, stressed that it was a whole issue beyond any possible doubt. The greatest hunters in the skies of Africa had been disappointed. Clearly it had been a good day in the universe for the hunted and a bad one for the hunters.

And at that moment the call in their own special code went out from François for the first time. He had no doubt at all that it was François. Yet so great was the discipline imposed on his spirit by the experience of life of his kind, that he compelled himself to wait until the call came a second time. He was still inclined to wait when he saw François come walking out of the bush and the bandaged Hintza, on three legs behind him. They were both, he saw, utterly at the end of their resources and at once, full of remorse and concern, he jumped down from the stone and presented himself to them.

For once François did not have it in him to reply to

222

Xhabbo's greeting. It was all he could do now that he had arrived to keep upright. Indeed it seemed to Xhabbo that he was swaying on his feet for he hastened to François and unbidden took his heavy haversack from his shoulders and put it on his own. He was about to take François by the arm and lead him up the slope to the shelter but François, seeing what he intended, forced himself to speak and say, 'No, Xhabbo, let me tell you first what has happened because I am afraid our troubles are far from over. The enemy is just down at the bottom in the stream, in the valley. I think he's down there for the night but I'm not even certain of that. All I am certain of is that he will be coming after me again either tonight when he has eaten, or first thing in the morning. I think we ought to be on our way at once. But look! See what they have done to Hintza. He can't go on just yet and I myself, I'm sorry, I can't go much further. I feel it might be best if Hintza and I find somewhere to hide and rest alone, and you and Nuin-Tara and Nonnie go on now. I just know these men will never give up until they have found me and Hintza, and killed us. I have been trouble enough to you, and you have done more than enough for me. So please hasten on and leave me and Hintza to ourselves, feeling you have done all that a man, friend and brother can do for another. If we escape, which I doubt, I shall come to you some time at any place you feel best.'

Xhabbo had never heard or even imagined that he could hear his Foot of the Day speak in such a tone of despair. But he had experience enough of relentless persecution himself to realize that François was not himself, and speaking far more out of sheer fatigue and fear for Hintza than out of any reasoned or unclouded assessment of their situation.

Feeling that a pause before they did the last steep little climb up to their shelter and some considered words from himself would help, he smoothed a place on the ground for François to sit down and very gently aided the exhausted Hintza to lie on his unwounded side close to them. Taking his own field flask, he gave François some water, and unslinging François's hat, filled the dented crown with water, lifted Hintza's head and held it in the palm of his hand to let him drink as well. Explaining that he had made their women hide and that they would be so full of anxiety and fear that he ought to reassure them without delay, he stood up straight. In the most authoritative and effortless manner he delivered himself of the honey-guide's classical summons: 'Quick, quick, quick! Honey! Quick!' He repeated the call three times, with such clarity and perfection that François, tired as he was, realized the call was the personal code of Xhabbo and Nuin-Tara.

That done, Xhabbo sat down beside him and begged him for a quick account of what had happened. When Xhabbo had heard all, he told François firmly that there was no need in his view for them to separate. It was true, François and Hintza would have been unable to avoid leaving signs that an expert tracker could follow. But from what he had seen of the way François and Hintza came up the hill, they had done it so well that the trackers would find it most difficult to find their spoor and so would have to follow exceedingly slowly. More, not only François and Hintza but they all, needed good food slowly eaten, as well as a proper rest, because he feared they still had many dangers, troubles and a long, exhausting journey ahead of them. So now that they had recovered their breath, he was taking them to the shelter the women had already prepared. There, once they had eaten and he had made certain that François and Hintza were asleep, and resting in the way they had earned, he, Xhabbo, would take over the watch. In the night he would decide what to do.

He said all this firmly and in the manner of one who had taken over supreme command. François did not protest because at last reassurance was complete. He prepared to get up, and indeed was already encouraging Hintza to do likewise, murmuring, 'Well, my little old goggatjie, here we go for the last lap home. Only a few steps now, you blessed little old dog, and I'll hand you over to one of the best nurses a dog could have in the bush.'

Struggling to his feet, he saw Nuin-Tara followed closely by Nonnie, stepping with a long Atalanta stride out from between the bushes. His resilient body had recovered enough for him to give Nuin-Tara the greeting Bushman manners demanded and hear her warm response. He looked beyond to Nonnie to greet her as well, but he could not yet take in the detail of her appearance. He only had an overall impression that she was looking surprisingly refreshed, more relaxed and lovelier than when he had last seen her. Indeed he was convinced he had never seen anything more welcoming than Nuin-Tara and Nonnie hurrying towards them. But that was as far as he got with his feelings. He managed only to begin a feeble, 'Hello, Nonnie! How ...' when Nonnie's face was possessed with horror and then a searing pity as she took in all the obvious signs in their appearance of what they had endured.

In particular, the sight of Hintza, his coat normally so burnished and bright, dull and stained with dirt now, and standing on three legs with that caricature of a white bow in the bandage on his back and bravely wagging a tail, when every wag must hurt, was too much for her. All the preconceived and highly imaginative plans she had formed for welcoming François and Hintza in a manner that would not be spoilt by excess either of warmth or restraint, went hurtling out of the windows of her mind. A strange, quick, fierce feeling that meant in effect, 'To hell with Nuin-Tara. I am Luciana Monckton after all, and have a way of my own too,' took command of her.

She pushed roughly past Nuin-Tara, in between Xhabbo and François, put her arms round François and kissed him warmly on both cheeks and held him tightly to herself. She held him in that way wherein the ancient language of physical contact has to speak for men and woman when words are inadequate and inaccessible. She held him thus for a while which, however long it may have appeared to the two onlookers, felt far too brief for her, before she let go and dropped on to her knees beside Hintza to stroke his up-lifted head lightly and then put her cheek against his, saying, 'Oh what have they done to you, my darling Hin? All these terrible men, what on earth have they done to you, you dear, innocent dog? How could they be so cruel and mean?'

She went on in this uninhibited flow wherein the only reservation allowed came from a determination not to let relief over their safe return combine with distress over the wounded Hintza and make her tearful again. She felt somehow that she had earned the right not to cry in the last two days, and suddenly come of her own true age.

Her restraint was helped by the call for action. Xhabbo was determined to get them all back under the ledge as soon as possible. Ordering Nuin-Tara to lead off, he and the others followed as fast as he thought it prudent for François and Hintza to go. That turned out to be slow, and he stopped to offer to carry François's gun and ammunition for him. François refused, with what appeared to Nonnie to be a rude rebuff, but the bright look of admiration in Xhabbo's eyes after Francois's abrupt gesture made her realize that there was far more to it than she was capable of appreciating. She thought it best to concentrate on helping Hintza and leave François and Xhabbo to each other until they finally arrived at their home where Nuin-Tara was already in royal possession by their unlit fire.

François was incapable of realizing in full the meticulous preparations made for his home-coming but a general impression of order and readiness more vivid than might have been expected had its impact. Ordered by Nonnie to relax and made comfortable by Nonnie placing an empty rucksack underneath his right elbow, he lay on his side by the fire-place watching the fire being lit. Soon the agony of exhaustion began to recede and a more rounded feeling of a healthy physical weariness moved into its place. He made no effort to speak and explain but just let his eyes first go slowly back and forth from Nuin-Tara and Xhabbo opposite him. He was entranced and warmed by a beauty as of another world and age on their faces, full and bright, immanent and overflowing. It seemed to him that the heat and flame of the rising fire evaporated into a mist of saintly yellow that blurred the precise outlines of their features. From them his eyes would go to Nonnie beside him, Hintza's head resting on the edge of her bush tunic and one hand, understandingly not stroking a coat wherein every movement hurt, but just resting lightly for reassurance where head and shoulders met. Gradually the memory of the day and the hurt of it, went from him until the moment became totality, round and complete.

As a result, he revived sufficiently to take on what he still felt to be his particular duty. First, he asked Nonnie and Nuin-Tara to fill all their dixies with water and put them on the fire to boil.

Xhabbo had already assured him that there were ample supplies of water available in a deep crevice in the rock nearby. There the water caught on the summit of the hill during the rains and stored in the pores of stone, leaked out through holes in a gigantic cistern to form pools in clefts below. From there the bees fetched the crystal liquid they used in the making of honey on a scale that made Lamb-snatcher's Hill one of the greatest storehouses on earth of the magical substance. He made Nonnie make hot chocolate lavishly for them all. But just before Hintza was allowed his ample share, two more aureomycin tablets, two sedatives and two sleeping pills were forced down his throat.

That done, he asked Nuin-Tara to select twelve pieces of their driest biltong, while he extracted what he had left of preserved apricots, peaches and apples in his pockets. He set Nuin-Tara who knew the manner of it best, pounding the biltong on stone until it was all loose and ravelled like old rope. But he insisted on cutting it himself into suitable pieces for spreading in the bottom of five half dixies. The shredded biltong was joined with dried fruit and just enough water to lap at the edges of the topmost layers and then given back to Nuin-Tara. Soon a delicate scent from François's improvised casserole drifted on the air, giving it an oddly sophisticated feeling for Nonnie, all the more pronounced in her acute awareness because of so unlikely and wild a setting.

All this while, François hardly spoke to Nonnie, apart from asking her help. His communication with her was through intense looks as if he could not yet believe the miracle that she was really there beside him and Hintza and their company complete at last. Moreover he had great difficulty in keeping open his own eyes, because Xhabbo's calm, experienced presence gave him such a feeling of having been relieved of an impossible burden of responsibility which he had carried alone too long, that he could abandon himself, almost without impediment, to pamper a vast physical fatigue that is a luxury of the senses and balm of mind, and which civilized life has forfeited because it no longer earns or knows how to value it.

In fact François was in a twilight state of being where he was not sure whether he felt awake or was dreaming of being awake. All that he was seeing and hearing of Nonnie was on the margin of a profound crepuscule of awareness, which was like a kind of enriched dreaming. But the feeling of dreaming came abruptly and rather joyfully to an end when, for the first time in his life, he heard a loud snore break from Hintza who normally was the quietest of sleepers imaginable. The snore was so loud that Nonnie, amused, could not resist calling to François softly, in the gentlest of teasing ways, 'Why, François, you do surprise me! Whoever would have thought that you'd keep company with a hound who snored so loudly in his sleep?'

François, happy that Hintza for the first time that long day should be out of pain, was of course not offended by the teasing. And yet Hintza was so intimate and inexpressible a factor in his emotions that he had instant reservations beyond reason or claims of humour about the aptness of Nonnie's tone, however affectionate the utterance. He found himself, therefore, without justification, stung on Hintza's account and as a result responded somewhat pompously, 'There are a lot of things about me and Hintza that you don't know, as you'll no doubt find out in time to come.'

Nonnie asked quickly, 'For instance?' Then without giving him a chance to reply she prattled on. 'For instance, in the practice of administering drugs ...? By all accounts Xhabbo was your first victim. I, the unsuspecting Luciana Monckton was your second. And now this poor innocent dog who has been your sleeping partner all his life. He's been so drugged that he's disgracing himself with a shameless exhibition of snoring, that must be audible even to those baboons barking on the cliff outside.'

François did not mind the re-direction of the teasing towards him. Half-awake as he was, he was somewhat light-headed and oddly confident for once in the world of unfamiliar emotion into which the coming of Nonnie into his life had taken him.

Spontaneously and precisely in the word and tone he had used on Hintza on countless occasions, he said, 'Oh shut up, Nonnie!' And before she could reply, he added, 'But seriously, the little beggar has fallen asleep a bit too soon. I wanted him to have some of that stew before I do what I have to do. But it can't be helped. He'll just have to go on sleeping without it and have it cold when and if he wakes up in the night. But now, Nonnie, would you please take that dixie of his and mine, rinse them carefully, fill them with water and put them on to boil because I deliberately gave him those pills you distrust so that he would be dead to the world while I undid his dressing and saw to his wound, because otherwise it'd hurt like hell.'

While they waited for the water to come to the boil, their own casserole was pronounced ready at last. Xhabbo and Nuin-Tara ate theirs with relish and that sense of the miraculous of all the new food François had brought into their life. They smacked their lips repeatedly with delight and sang little snatches of gratitude to him, Mantis and life.

Even Nonnie thought it one of the best dishes she had ever eaten. The astringent apricot and tart apple blended with bland peach to balance the surprisingly rich meat, which now after a long, gentle simmering proved to have been well marbled with fat, and delighted her palate with its fullness.

'You are obviously as good a cook as – ' she paused deliberately '– as you are a pharmacist.'

François was too tired to carry the banter further, too tired really even to eat any more. The chocolate had been almost enough. Glad that his friends were enjoying food of his invention and barely half-way through his own helping, he offered what was left to Nonnie. When she refused, he offered it to Xhabbo and Nuin-Tara who he was certain could have eaten ten times as much, considering how many days without proper food they had been on the march to come and warn him at Hunter's Drift.

He then leant back on his elbow, silently fighting off his sleep until they had all eaten, and the water for Hintza's wound was boiling.

Nonnie, who for all her objection to gulping was finished well before the others, insisted on helping François. She held Hintza's head gently but firmly in her lap while François undid the bandages. As foreseen the field dressing was stuck fast as with glue in the congealed blood of the wound. Slowly François let the hot water drip on to the dressing, soaking it through and through. Soaking his own handkerchief with water repeatedly, he sponged the skin and hair around the wound.

Still Hintza lay there snoring away as if he were not a badly wounded animal but some natural boulevardier of the bush who had drunk and eaten too well at his favourite café and been overtaken with sleep in the process. The only time he showed any signs of intrusion of pain in that far-off world of sleep where he was so deeply entrenched, was a shudder and transformation of the snore into a quick, odd puppy-like whimper when François cut the hair between dressing and skin and finally pulled away the dressing.

Nonnie was shaken by the size and extent of the wound and the way it was bleeding again, for the dressing had brought away with it the scab which had formed underneath. She had never before looked into a wound like that in any animal or human being. She thought she would be sick.

'Dear Mother in Heaven,' she exclaimed, 'this is too awful! I had no idea it was so bad. How did it happen to him? You haven't told me a thing yet.' Her look and tone were full of reproach.

François was both too tired and emotionally unprepared to talk about so raw a subject. 'It was done by a bayonet,' he said curtly.

'A bayonet? How? Where? When?' she demanded, pale and distraught, realizing how little she knew of the dangers François had been through that day.

Brief and crisp, he told her what had happened and added a tender, lingering grateful afterthought, 'If it hadn't been Hin, it would have been me at the end of that bayonet.'

'But how on earth did you manage to get away?' Nonnie persisted, as she forced herself to go on looking into the wound, feeling that she owed it to them to discover what they had suffered on behalf of them all and marvelling why Hintza's leg had not been sliced from his body.

'I shot him through the head as Hin kept him pinned to the ground by the throat,' François replied.

He sounded strangely casual and concerned only with concentrating on washing away the dirt and dried blood around the wound, obviously unaware that he had not explained fully.

'Oh how awful for you, you poor François,' Nonnie said, brimming over with sympathy, imagining from all she had heard and read about such things that François must be overcome with remorse at having had to kill another human being.

To her amazement François replied, unexpectedly vehement, 'There was nothing awful about it at all. I was only too glad to kill him before he could kill Hin and me.'

All this was so self-evident now to him that he would have left it there, had he not realized suddenly that even the self-evident could be unusual. For all at once, unbidden, there came to him vividly the memory of the day when he had been compelled to shoot his first elephant in the shape of Uprooter of Great Trees – an episode of which Nonnie had been fully informed in the past.

He found himself saying in amazement as much to himself as to her, 'Why it's odd, Nonnie, now that you make me think about it, I felt no regret, none at all. It all happened so quickly but not so fast that I could not feel a strange, sharp kind of pleasure shooting the man. Yet I felt only sad and sorry when I shot old Uprooter of Great Trees. That poor old beast was drunk, old, an outcast and not really knowing what he was doing. But this man and his friends knew perfectly well what they were doing. They were not drunk, but acting under orders from other calculating men determined to kill us. But I'll tell you more about that later. It's a terrible story.'

It was Nonnie's turn to be astonished. Her impulse to be remorseful for François in the matter now seemed to have been shallow. It left her as if it had never been. Instead the woman in her was strangely reassured. She looked at François in a new and proud way, as if deep down in her there was something that had to know that the men who accompanied her through life should be the kind of men who would not hesitate to kill on behalf of life. It was her first private and personal encounter with the uncomfortable fact that life in its extremities has need for death. She was utterly bewildered and deeply moved by the complex of unexperienced feelings rushing at her, so that trembling she took François's hand, pressed it to her cheek and said like a person just woken from sleep: 'Oh bless you, François, bless you and thank you both.'

François hardly heard her. The contact and deed were enough, but he had just then finally cleaned out the wound and

231

wanted to complete the work. In any case, before he could respond, Nonnie spoke up, offering to fetch a new field dressing and fresh bandages from her larder. But François said no. He asked her only for a tube of yellow aureomycin ointment, which she watched him spread thick and wide all over the wound, carefully massaging it into the skin around the edges.

'But surely you'll bandage a new dressing over it?' she asked, bewildered, when he sat back, as if it were all done.

'No, Nonnie. The reason I wanted to dress the wound the moment I got back was so that a scab can have as long as possible to form over it in the night. The scab, as Mopani says, is nature's field dressing, and no man can improve on it. Hin will be far more comfortable with his own natural field dressing and no bandaging to restrict his circulation. If he goes on sleeping and snoring away like that he'll grow a wonderfully thick scab before morning. And he'll need it too! Won't you, you old *goggatjie*?'

He laid a hand that suddenly felt like lead for a moment on Hintza's head and realized that his day had come to an end. He could not go on talking any longer, even to Nonnie. He could not keep his eyes open for any purpose whatsoever, however urgent. He just had to sleep and at once. He could barely say good night to any of them. Through blurred eyes, he looked at the place of sleep prepared for him and the empty haversack at its head put there by Nonnie as a pillow.

All he could manage was, 'Please, Nonnie and you too, Xhabbo, help me to get Hin away from this fire and put him down to sleep with his head on the other side of that haversack.'

Together, they lifted Hintza, carried him over and laid him down in the right position. François stepped back over the haversack and stretched himself out on the other side as if on a bed of feathers. It seemed to Nonnie that he was fast and uncannily asleep in an instant; indeed so deeply asleep that he did not hear another haversack being placed beside his own or feel Nonnie settling down, her arm going naturally round him.

Nonnie, of course, was tired as well, though obviously not as tired as François. The turmoil of what she had been through, particularly the shock of finding François gone, and the fear and anxiety experienced during the long period of inactivity in the cave was still too great to let her sleep at once. She would lift her head from time to time and through half-closed eyes first see Nuin-Tara coming alone to her bed near them, and then, on the far side of the fire, Xhabbo getting up and taking his spear to walk out into the comparative open beyond the shelter. He stood there for a long time, his head and shoulders clear-cut against a segment of sky spattered with starlight. Xhabbo was listening, as she was, to the sounds of the night, the bark of the great baboon sentries on the cliffs above and the coughing of leopards in the bush with a volume and density which, had she known it, impressed Xhabbo as much as it made her fear. Out of her fear she looked at the neat, economical fire Nuin-Tara had built and wondered whether so small a flame was enough and should not be multiplied a hundred times if fire were ever to make them safe in such surroundings. But she already had drawn the relevant lessons from her experience of Xhabbo and Nuin-Tara's apparent infallibility in such things and begun to make it an axiom of her new self not to question them in matters outside her own knowledge.

Xhabbo, she thought at first, was standing there on guard but after a time the outline turned abruptly about, passed along the mouth of the overhang of rock and vanished in the direction from which François and Hintza had come, to let the starlight come down like rain unhindered on their wide doorstep.

It felt many hours before she woke, heard and saw Xhabbo again at the mouth of their shelter and Nuin-Tara on her knees putting fresh wood on their fire. François was still sound asleep. Hintza was no longer snoring but breathing heavily, his nose almost in her ear. The noise outside of leopards coughing and baboons barking had been joined by the ominous howling of the big striped hyenas and the far-off yacking of jackals, indicating that the great glittering wheel of the night dripping with the heavy water of time was turned over remorselessly towards day.

Anxious to be more than just a sleeping partner on the journey in front of them, she forced herself to get up, and sign to Nuin-Tara indicating that she would like to look after the fire from then on so that Nuin-Tara could have more sleep. A wide smile accompanied a gracious refusal, and she was told in no uncertain feminine terms that her place of duty for the night was beside François who, despite his sleep, was showing signs of being aware that he had been left alone. It looked as if his left hand was searching around him, his sleeping self mystified and uneasy. She hastened back to his side. She had barely put her arm round him again when he spoke in a slurred manner, Nonnie thought in his sleep, as she could just hear, 'His nose, Nonnie, his nose!'

She ignored it because it seemed to make no sense to her and she thought any question from her would wake him needlessly. But after a while the words came again, unmistakably in a more agitated manner: 'His nose, please! His nose!'

'Whose nose, Coiske, whose nose?' she asked softly.

She had to murmur the question twice at his ear before the blurred answer came: 'Hintza's nose, feel it . . . feel it quick . . .'

None of it made any sense to her yet; nonetheless, she put up the back of her hand to Hintza's nose and touched it gently. It seemed an extraordinarily active, almost volcanic nose to her, contracting and expanding in a fantastic manner, presumably to provide Hintza with breath enough to keep him from drowning at the bottom of the deep sea of sleep into which he had plunged. Hintza gave no sign that he had noticed the contact.

'I've felt his nose,' she whispered gently in François's ear, 'and I promise you it's still there, good and intact. So just you sleep on. There's no need to worry about it, I promise.'

Her answer came near to waking up François completely for his murmur became more agitated than ever, 'But what does it feel like?'

'Oh just as it always does; rather cool and perhaps a little damper than usual.'

'Thank God,' François sighed with relief as he vanished, words and all, back into the fullness of his sleep. She was perhaps just a little put out that such a glimmer of awareness contained no recognition of her presence except out of his sleep again, 'Please, Nonnie, don't you ever dare to leave me like that again.'

With that a most extraordinary calm came over her and she must have fallen asleep at once. She felt she had slept thus barely a moment before she woke up. The fire was burning brightly. François was up and sitting beside it deep in conversation with Xhabbo. Hintza was hard by them, eating the cold casserole left over for him perhaps not quite as fast as he normally did but nonetheless fast enough. Nuin-Tara too was there tending the fire. Somewhat conscience stricken Nonnie jumped up and joined them, to be greeted not with a polite good morning but an immediate injunction from François to make them the biggest brew of chocolate possible, with what was left of their chocolate, and to bring them a sackful of rusks as well, because they had to eat, pack up and be off as soon as possible.

The atmosphere was so tense that Nonnie had no difficulty in overlooking any lack of graces. She hurried to do her part as deftly as she could. Once all together round the fire, eating their breakfast, all was made clear in the quick précis François gave her of what Xhabbo had been telling him.

Xhabbo had already been down earlier in the night to the stream in the bed of the valley. It appeared to him that the numbers of their enemies had been greatly reinforced since François's retreat from the stream. Xhabbo wanted them out of the shelter and on their way, the way of the wind, as soon as the morning star showed itself above the horizon and that would be at any minute now. Xhabbo wanted it because the track they had to follow was clear and distinct enough for them to travel by starlight alone, and he would like them to be at the place where the track met the river before sunrise. The stream there poured over a wide cataract of stone and at this time of the year the water would be so low that they could step from stone to stone across and along the edge of it. Unfortunately it was something they could not do safely in the dark and it would mean that they would have to expose themselves to the danger of being out in the open and visible to anyone who might be sent there to watch. Xhabbo was convinced that the crossing was accordingly best done at first light and done quickly before the enemy could gather in strength in that part of the world.

He, Xhabbo, was not going with them at once. Nuin-Tara would lead them there and take them across the ford, which she had already crossed once with Xhabbo in their race with the enemy towards Hunter's Drift. He was going down back once more to the bed of the valley to see precisely how their enemy would organize their pursuit of François and Hintza. The moment he knew, he would hasten back to join them. Refreshed as Xhabbo was by good food and the enforced rest in the cave, he was certain it would not take him long to catch up with them.

'But Hin,' Nonnie protested, calling him by his contracted endearment, noticing he was observing her closely and listening carefully, 'But Hin, François. D'you think he's up to going on?'

'Of course he is,' François was somewhat indignant that Hintza's stamina and courage could be questioned, however lovingly and well-intentioned. 'Look at him! Look how he can't take his eyes off your face. He's forgotten all about his pain. And just look at that wonderful scab he's grown in the night! Feel his nose! If it weren't for that leg of his, I would say he's never been in better shape or spirits. Besides, no matter what you say, Nonnie, I'm going to give him pain killers on and off all day while we're on the move. So there.'

His voice was clear, spirited and almost gaily confident so that Nonnie looked and heard him as much with admiration as with amazement. In fact she could hardly believe that the alert, fresh, although exceedingly fine drawn face looking at her across the fire, was that of the same exhausted person they had helped into the shelter the night before. Moreover the fact that she was going to travel on for once in François's company and that Xhabbo was taking on the more arduous and dangerous part of the work for a change, lifted her spirits to one of the highest summits of the long range of her feelings. She set about her share of the packing and followed François outside with a heart light as air to take up her position between him and Nuin-Tara.

Then no more words were spoken. Their hands were just raised in a quick farewell to Xhabbo, for the morning star, spear in hand and arrow fitted in its bow, as the Bushmen say, was already straddling the horizon. Nuin-Tara led off fast, to Nonnie's amazement, without a backward glance to Xhabbo, who had turned about and was making off likewise for the saddle of Lamb-snatcher's Hill.

CHAPTER NINE

Kwa'mamengalahlwa

Dark as it still was, Nonnie and even François were amazed at the certainty and speed with which Nuin-Tara travelled. For all his brave words, François was for a moment uneasy about Hintza. But although still moving on only three legs Hintza, in that cool hour of the day, was keeping up well and, from the way in which his muzzle was searching the air, was resuming some of the duties that were always his when in the bush with François.

The journey to the bank of the river was without drama. The detail of an unknown road was always absorbing to François and Hintza, but all that mattered was that they arrived at the ford just as first light broke, well before the crocodiles could muster for the day. It was an hour so naïve and unthreatened by foreign elements that just a few hundred yards from where they began their dangerous crossing, a well-padded family of hippopotamuses returning from their grazing, without condescending even to glance at them, took to a large pool, stained a brilliant red with the light of a great dawn. On the far bank some white and lilac waterbuck, a vast herd of elegant impala and a lone, majestic sable were drinking up the firewater, lip to lip, from trembling reflections of themselves. The birds were beginning to stir and sing in a way François had not heard them sing for days, in voices that sounded singularly young, pure and acolytic, and they were able therefore to step quietly from stone to stone without haste, making certain of their footing, to music full of a sense of deliverance and devotion. Where the passage of water between one boulder and another was too wide for Hintza to step over the gap, François had more than time enough to pick him up and carry him across.

Just before the sun itself came over the horizon they found themselves back on the track, hidden from human sight by tall

237

reeds and flared papyrus, their tops bright and crackling with vivid electric light. Even so, Nuin-Tara did not stop to rest but led on faster than ever for another mile across the gravelled and stony ground until it found the earth of the bush again. There, obviously afraid of leaving any spoor, she turned aside on the edge of the ridge of stone, and after another quarter of a mile on a curve parallel to the stream found shade and cover thick enough for them to wait for Xhabbo without danger of being observed.

They had barely recovered their breath when from what François judged to be a quarter of a mile away there came the summons of a honey-guide. At once Nuin-Tara was on her feet, giving a faultless rendering of a female honey-guide's reply to a summons from her male. Back came the confirming answer, and soon there was Xhabbo, sweat running like water down his skin, stepping through the circle of bush and trees towards them.

Nonnie thought a man sweating like that would have had to be out of breath as well. But to her amazement he was not only far from it but also physically at ease enough to begin talking at once, fast and effortlessly. It was another of a horde of indications she was accumulating of her ignorance of the kind of people that Xhabbo and Nuin-Tara really were. To add them all up meticulously in an excellent memory was a basis of an understanding that would match her gratitude and growing love of the two of them.

This was emphasized now by one simple fact she had hitherto done her utmost to repress. On their first encounter with Xhabbo and Nuin-Tara she had been appalled by their smell. Even in their desperate race to the hill and the cave, not knowing what was happening and certain only of the fact that they were in great danger, she yet had had time to be troubled by it. When she realized who Xhabbo was and that he was indeed François's precious 'secret', she was ashamed of a disappointment which had time to possess her, despite the pressures of a deadly danger, and made her exclaim inwardly, 'Dear Mother of God, he stinks! Oh why must he stink so?'

As a result of the sweat running from Xhabbo, this smell in that fresh morning air was sharper than ever. Yet, miracle of miracles, she was no longer appalled by it. It was suddenly something so natural, frank and unashamed that her whole being warmed to it. She thought of it as the kind of smell that could come clinging to the root of some great tree drawn from far down out of the dark, secret soil of Africa, and knew she must be right in her appreciation when she saw how Hintza was relishing it. As the greatest connoisseur, or perhaps the most discriminating gourmet of smell and bouquets in Africa, his nose was stretched out to its uttermost length, taut as a cello string and vibrating as it sought to extract all he could of the rare, beloved smell from the air between himself and Xhabbo, expressing his admiration of its ancient quality by lashing the ground with his tail.

But that was as far as she went with subjective reactions to the occasion, for she could tell, as Xhabbo's long account to François and Nuin-Tara unfolded, that it was of great and desperate import. So onomatopoeic both in word and meaning was Xhabbo's language and the tone of his delivery that Nonnie could tell the drift of what he was saying just from the rhythm and the sound and gesticulation.

Xhabbo was in fact describing how he had arrived on the edge of the bush on the banks of the stream in the valley just in time to see the enemy finish breakfasting by large fires. By the light of those fires he saw eleven men take up flasks and fat rucksacks exactly like the ones they were carrying, and come together before a 'chief' who addressed them at great length. When the 'chief' finished, they were joined by two men who, to his horror, he was certain were Hottentots from the country on the other side of the desert that was his home.

François immediately interrupted and cross-questioned Xhabbo closely why he was so sure the two men were Hottentots, so unlikely did it appear to him. But at the end of his questioning he had to accept that Xhabbo was right, particularly when Xhabbo explained how in the far West, Hottentot desert policemen were often used against his people. This made François as concerned if not afraid as Xhabbo was already, because he knew that in all Africa, only Bushmen excepted, there were no more experienced and inspired trackers of game and men.

239

Xhabbo continued then to say that a great number of the enemy meanwhile had left their fires, gathered up their belongings and appeared to be assembling to go back the way they had come. He had not stayed long enough to make absolutely certain that his conclusion was right, because he had hardly reached it when the eleven armed men, with the two Hottentots in the lead, started to cross the river in his direction.

At once he retreated up the hill to another place from where he could watch the track below in safety, and observed how the Hottentots, after a remarkably short time, found the track leading out of the river and up to Lamb-snatcher's Hill. From the way they were examining the track, he knew how right he was to fear them, for soon one Hottentot stood up bright as new copper in the growing light, and called out exultantly to the men behind him. It was obvious to Xhabbo that he had found the kind of special sign they were looking for. He had waited no longer then but left the place, running full out, for it was clear that from then on they had no time to lose.

He had seen enough to know, as his Foot of the Day already knew, that those men were determined to go on looking for spoor and more spoor and would keep on coming after them, until they found and killed them all. They had therefore to start at once, because with those Hottentot trackers and so special and compact a team on their trail, the enemy was now more dangerous than it had ever been.

At this point an old argument broke out again between Xhabbo and François. François thought they had better separate, because the enemy still did not know that there was anybody else to pursue except himself and Hintza. Xhabbo protested and said that coming running, he had thought of nothing but that. He was feeling now that they must not separate on any account. They would be safer and stronger together, should they run into any of their enemies as they might from now on at any moment. He was feeling that they should go back to the track that led in the way of the wind.

Once there, Hintza must go in front, François following and then Nonnie. Both François and Nonnie must take great care to walk over the spoor of Hintza, and Xhabbo and Nuin-Tara, coming last, would take care to walk over the spoor of Nonnie and François. So they would make a kind of blurred spoor which might belong to any of the natural people of the bush who often came and went along such trails. Even if in the end they did not altogether deceive their pursuers, Xhabbo was feeling they could confuse them enough to compel them to travel more slowly than they themselves did.

They had to remember, Xhabbo stressed, that their pursuers would not be their only danger. The way they had to go crossed the great Punda-Ma-Tenka road which the enemy had followed to François's home. Not only this great road but all the tracks for wide distances around it, judging by what he and Nuin-Tara had seen on their way to warn François, would be full of movement of yet more enemies. It was vital that the five of them should be close to this area when the sun was exactly where he was pointing to the sky.

François followed the angle of his hand and made that out to be about an hour before sundown. That would give them time to rest and eat in safety still ahead of their pursuers. Then, in the early hours of the morning, when the enemy would be asleep, they would find a measured way to a place on the road where the enemy was not. He, Xhabbo, and François saw the point immediately, emphasized that crossing the enemy's line of advance must take place before their pursuers could meet their friends, tell them what they were doing and, as probably already instructed, enlist their help to organize a massive hunt for François and Hintza in that new area as well. Obviously such a crossing could only be attempted in the dark.

Even so, François thought Xhabbo should have a brief rest before they travelled on. But Xhabbo had already ordered Nuin-Tara to take up her load and was not even attempting to sit down, but standing there impatient to go. François just had to tell Nonnie to follow Nuin-Tara's example and hasten after the other two, explaining why and what they were doing as they started out on the side-track back to the way they had come in the morning. Once there, on Xhabbo's command, nobody spoke. Hintza, drugged against pain, seemed sufficiently at ease to be proud of being in the lead again with François close behind him. Every now and then, Xhabbo would come up to the front, make the three of them sit by the side of the track while he scrambled up a dead tree and observed the land behind them. Occasionally he rushed up, blurted out a few words of explanation to François and then ran ahead, to vanish along the track, obviously in order to make sure the way was still clear.

Nonnie at first thought she could continue like that for the rest of the day. But as the day became first warm, and then hot and airless in the stifled bush she felt herself tiring, and so thirsty that she reached for her flask of water. But before she could lift it to her mouth, she heard a rush of feet behind her, and there was Nuin-Tara beside her, gripping her arm and forcing the flask back into position, so forcefully that a muffled protest broke from her.

At the sound François stopped and swung round. Before she could explain, she saw him nodding approvingly to Nuin-Tara before saying with a voice full of sympathy, 'She's right, you know, Nonnie. You must be terribly thirsty, because though I'm used to this sort of thing I'm very thirsty too. So is poor old Hin. Just look at him. But believe me it's a waste of water to drink it in the heat of the day. It only makes you feel thirstier then ever, and what's more makes you sweat so much that you get terribly tired. There's nothing so tiring as sweating more than you absolutely have to.'

It is some indication of Nonnie's spirit that in circumstances so unfamiliar to her, she managed to pretend that it was all a kind of joke against herself.

'Ladies, I would have you know, François,' she said, surprisingly clearly out of so parched a mouth, 'perspire, and do not sweat.'

François gave her one of those smiles she had always longed to see more often on his face, and somehow, despite the physical agony of it all, she managed to keep up and to say no more.

She was helped in this before long by a series of unexpected opportunities to rest from time to time. Xhabbo made them all stop by groves of wild raisin bushes, charged with large, ripe sweet, Pinot-noir berries. He made them all join in harvesting the bush and stuffing berries in the empty spaces in their rucksacks as well as scattering some of them on the track. Considering what care they had taken to disguise their footprints, it seemed to Nonnie a careless if not dangerous way of carrying on.

She said so to François, and he replied, 'You know, Nonnie, I feel almost as ignorant as you in these circumstances. I've been the tracker often enough and know quite a bit about tracking but this is the first time in my life that I've been tracked myself. These two know more about it than anybody else in the world and I'm certain there's a good reason for it all.'

Thereupon François spoke to Xhabbo for a while and turned to Nonnie again to give her the explanation. 'They know what they're doing all right. Xhabbo says he hates it all because it gives the people behind more time to catch up, but he says that unless the tracks the enemies will have discovered by now, are made to pause noticeably by bushes of this kind, our trackers won't take the spoor to be that of natural persons going their habitual way. So they do this deliberately to give the impression that we're only unsuspecting people of the bush on harmless business of our own.'

He did not add that Xhabbo had explained to him that if those men on their spoor did succeed in reading their tracks accurately, they would know that all this had been done deliberately by people who realized they were being followed, and therefore could only be a party which included the François and Hintza that they had to find and kill.

After this there were different pauses at places Xhabbo obviously knew and where they branched off the track into little clearings and dug into the ground to extract a surprising collection of edible bulbs, truffles and tubers. François assured Nonnie they were great and nourishing delicacies that he liked as much as the Bushmen did themselves. Digging them out, he stressed, would be far more likely to put the suspicions of their pursuers at rest than anything else.

And so, just an hour before sunset, exactly as Xhabbo had intended, he was able to take over the lead from Hintza and swerve away to the left at right angles from the track, straight over an outcrop of gravelled ground and so on to a ridge covered with great ironstone boulders and in between, heavy broom bushes and huge euphorbias, standing out against the yellowing sun like enormous Byzantine candelabras. They followed the ridge for a mile to its decline suddenly into a cleft with a dry stream bed below, and the bed itself, covered with fine blue water gravel. There it was heavily shaded by enormous storm, black-thorn, acacia, camel-thorn and wild fig trees, and there, Xhabbo exclaimed with fierce finality, throwing off his rucksack in the act, was their place for the night.

That was all he had to say because Nuin-Tara there and then took charge and beckoned to Nonnie. Tired as she was she made her do her share of the housekeeping that had to be done. François was still unburdening himself and preparing to see to Hintza, who, although not foaming at the mouth as the day before, was obviously very tired, thirsty and beginning to feel the profound ache of his wound. Xhabbo called out to him that he was just going out to look around for a while and would soon be back, but meanwhile to lay though not to light any fires until he was back.

It was twilight when Xhabbo returned, a twilight as red as the dawn of Heitse-Eibib had been, one which the Hottentot people, to whom the two trackers pursuing them relentlessly belonged, called the 'Heel of Heitse-Eibib'. They thought of it as part of the god bleeding from a wound of an arrow shot into him, while his back was turned in the process of consolidating the day, by the darkness, his implacable enemy hastening up behind him to do battle again for the mastery of life. The great bush-bats were beginning to zoom about on their zig-zag streaks of flight; a Goliath heron flew ponderously over their heads, followed by a vast hammerhead, the great marginal observer in the Bushman imagination, of all the delicately shuttled transitions of life into death and death into life, recorded at sunset on smooth pages of silky water. Then one great old forest owl started to call out to nature that in his considered opinion and speaking as a being of unequalled experience in these matters, it was now dark enough for lesser owls to emerge and follow him on their lawful occasions. François could tell from Xhabbo's appearance that he was neither satisfied nor dissatisfied and soon understood why. He explained that he had gone back to the main track and climbed one of the tallest trees. Not far away to the north-west he had observed the smoke of many fires, which could only have come from a major enemy, collected on the great road and the tracks leading into it. Far behind him, where the fringe of the bush met the blue of the sky, he had seen dust drifting yellow and bright like a swarm of bees hastening home for the night. The dust he was certain was the dust of their pursuers coming up fast and yet not fast enough he believed, to reach their own turning-off place before the dark.

He was certain their pursuers would be compelled to camp in their turn for the night. Good as that was, it still meant that they were nearer than he had feared because without a doubt they would be able to join the men who made the smoke he had seen by first light the next morning, if not before. That meant they themselves would have to cross the road much sooner than he had anticipated.

They had better therefore light their fires and cook their food without delay. It might be their last hot meal for a long time and then, after a short period of rest, they had better hurry on their way. Although he said all this calmly, if not casually, speaking as he did out of a spirit disciplined by the great necessities of life to avoid any exaggeration of either hope or despair, even Nonnie felt how troubled he had been. She noticed that François, too, must have had a similar reaction because he questioned Xhabbo's decision to light their fires and cook their meal somewhat more brusquely than he would normally have done. At that Xhabbo responded more emphatically than usual, with a pronounced, almost sardonic gesture of hands and shoulders, apparently asking rhetorically why one or two little Bushman camp fires should not live, when so many other Kaffir fires were burning so high and arrogant in the vicinity?

Accordingly Nonnie found herself more deeply and subtly perturbed than she had yet been. Up to now she had been confronted by fear, stark and clear, derived from danger immediate and direct. It had been something obvious with tangible causes which she could recognize and explain unequivocally to her desperate senses. But it now seemed that a new element had entered their situation; unknown, unpredictable, stealthy, deliberate and of a more lasting kind. Somehow she seemed to have taken it for granted too naïvely that once they had broken out of the circle of their enemies round the cave, travelling together, reunited in their foursome, they would quickly leave that danger behind and have only the natural hazards of a journey into the unknown to confront. By now, she realized that danger most highly organized and informed was determined to stay with them. Added to the hazards of the unknown, it meant that from now on the threat to their survival would be greater than ever and a constantly recurring element. For all her courage and a naturally hopeful heart, no matter how hard she tried, she could no longer see how, where and when, if ever, they would have done with this danger.

This awakening to new and greater peril, was inflicted upon her at perhaps the worst hour of the day. Because as she admitted all these new and fearful considerations to herself, the last red spark of light in the West was extinguished, the birds round them ceased singing and a silence almost as deep and black as the night, closed in on them. For all her inexperience she knew from what François had told her, and from those nights she had spent at Hunter's Drift and Silverton Hill, such a silence was totally unnatural and evidence of how the natural world about her felt itself invaded and threatened. Her relief at the sight of the first clear little flame flowering in front of her accordingly was immense. And as the faces of her companions emerged from the dark she tried to draw solace from their nearness and to read their expressions.

She saw Nuin-Tara and Xhabbo close to each other, their faces without any traces of indulgence of feeling whatsoever, except that imposed by concentration on the tasks of tending their little fires and preparing the meal. Nuin-Tara's in particular seemed to be free of any emotional stress, and so absorbed in the practical needs of the moment that Nonnie envied her as she had never done before. The look of unfathomable calm in her eyes and the kind of vestal devotion she brought to feeding her fire, implied an attitude to life that had never allowed any tyranny of either hate or despair to impair it. It was contained in a belief that if one served the small needs of all the living, urgent moments utterly, to use Nuin-Tara's and Xhabbo's favourite word, the great necessities could be left to take care both of themselves and those who trusted accordingly. She wondered what sort of an apprenticeship to life could have produced so rounded an attitude, and felt dissatisfied and hopelessly inadequate by comparison. She just could not suppress a new fear that she would fail, even if the danger did not over-whelm them as she now felt more than ever that it would. Yet without being aware of it, she had progressed so far in this battle with the unknown that she was able to do something of which she had not been capable a bare forty-eight hours before, namely to shape her fear in a direct and uncompromising ques-tion to François.

François had just forced one more aureomycin tablet and one more sedative down Hintza's throat. Hintza was shaking his head and licking his lips, as if trying to rid his palate of some-thing distasteful. Having got rid of it, it was as if he realized it all had been for his own good, because he turned his beautiful head to look at François as if he were some kind of a god. François looked back at him with a naked and unashamed tenderness that nearly brought tears to Nonnie's eyes. That little scene, and the sense of utter acceptance of whatever life had to give implicit in Xhabbo and Nuin-Tara, seemed to her to be so good and true, that a feather of hope stirred in her that no evil could ever be great enough to extinguish it.

'Dear Mother in Heaven,' she cried within herself. 'Let all other things come and go, even our chances of getting back to the world to which I once belonged, and we be compelled to live on here, but let these things go on for ever.'

Hard on that she asked François the relevant question, 'I know that Xhabbo's news was bad,' she began in a grave, small but clear voice, 'But tell me honestly, do you think we shall ever get out of this alive?'

François, whose mind, in the manner not unlike that of Nuin-Tara's, was inclined always to be utterly in the service of the necessities of the moment, had been so absorbed in his concern for Hintza that he was startled by her question. He stared, surprised, at her for quite a time before he answered. Indeed, he took so long that Nonnie was putting the worst pos-sible constructions on his hesitations, before she heard him say in that maddeningly deliberate and prematurely old way of his, 'I don't know Nonnie, if it is a matter for thinking really. If we just have to think about our plight, I guess we might come to the conclusion that it's pretty hopeless. But there's more than just thinking to it. We've broken out of a ring of what I myself believed at one time was almost certain death to us all, and we have in Nuin-Tara and Xhabbo two of the wisest, most experienced and bravest guides we could have in situations of this kind. However silly it is I would back their wisdom and their experience against these evil men swarming all over the place – yes, even against those two Hottentots who are keeping them on our spoor. It's not just a matter of thinking and numbers. You can't just think about things in the bush, as Mopani has always told me. Thinking has its place, he says, but only when one is confronted with known facts and statistics. When you're in the unknown and the dark, as we are here, Mopani says, you surrender your thinking in trust to the feelings that come to you, out of the bush. All my feelings are that, though I don't know how and don't care about knowing how now, somehow, when the time comes and the things start to happen to us, the how of it all will present itself to us and that now, here, by this fire, I promise you by the light of the fire that all my feelings are that we shall manage.'

Her relief at so positive and unusually long a pronouncement from him was so great that she feared it and exclaimed, her eyes wide and her heart beating faster, 'Do you really mean what you're saying, François? You're not just trying to comfort me, are you?'

'No Nonnie, no,' he shook his head vehemently. 'This is what I feel and I'm certain if I asked Xhabbo your question, his answer would be the same. Only I'm not going to ask him. He and Nuin-Tara and, for that matter, us as well, need all we have for this moment and the next step. As 'Bamuthi always used to say to me, "Look after the steps, Little Feather, and the journey will take care of itself." Besides, do you remember that night, it feels a hundred years ago, when our own world came to an end, how Xhabbo said he had a tapping inside himself which told him it would show us a way? I'm not going to insult his tapping by putting such a question to him now. From what my old nurse Koba told me, all Bushmen are superstitious about considering the future unless their tapping does it for them. It's a jolly good superstition and you and I could do worse than copy it ourselves.'

'But, François,' Nonnie protested, 'François, I believe you.

But just in case you and Xhabbo could be wrong, and the worst happens to us, I shall not mind so much if you promise me that you'll be with me when it happens.'

'I promise Nonnie,' he said promptly. 'Because if that should ever happen, I'd find it easier that way myself.'

François might have said more but at that moment the sound of a vast yawn escaped from Hintza. It sounded as if he was bored beyond any tangible measure by being left out of their joint reckoning for so long, particularly for such an unnecessary exchange of thought. If only human beings thought less and used their noses more, it implied, how much better a dog's life would be. The sounds made both Nonnie and François look at him. His jaws were stretched as if they would break apart; his teeth were white and dazzling, his long supple tongue pinker and more beautiful than ever in the firelight, his profound and alert eyes, shut with the strain of such prodigious yawning. So spontaneous and uninhibited was the act that Nonnie, in a swift change of mood so characteristic of her, let the first laugh for days break out of her. Even François had to smile and, stroking Hintza's back, exclaim, 'You see, Hin agrees with me and is feeling that this sort of conversation had better cease.'

Soon they had cooked and all eaten another meal very much like the one on Lamb-snatcher's Hill the night before. The moment they had done so, Xhabbo ordered Nuin-Tara to let all the fires except one small upright little flame die down and took up his spear. Telling them to rest as well as they could, he hurried off into the night without explanation. Since Nuin-Tara had not organized any sleeping places like the night before, Nonnie assumed that Xhabbo would not be gone long and that their rest would be an unusually short one. She therefore made no move to leave a fire in which her spirit even more than body found comfort. She made herself as comfortable as she could, doubled up, her head on her haversack near the haversack on which François was resting on one elbow, his head in his one hand and the other stroking Hintza, lying by his side. Nuin-Tara soon took up a similar attitude on the other side. And in this manner, tired out as she was, Nonnie fell uneasily asleep.

How long she slept Nonnie could not precisely tell, but it

could not have been more than a few hours. She was immediately aware of Nuin-Tara and François getting to their feet and saw Hintza already standing on three legs, his tail stretched taut and straight behind him and his nose sniffing and sniffing at the dark beyond. Within a few seconds Xhabbo emerged at a run on the bed of the stream and slowed down to walk purposefully up to the fire. Without any effort at conventional greetings he began a report which Nonnie knew at once was urgent and ominous.

He told François, she soon gathered, how in the dark he had been up to the fringe of the enemy's camp. He arrived there just in time to see the two Hottentots brought into the camp by two black soldiers. He had watched them present a white paper to another white chief. He had watched the white chief talk to them at great length. He had seen the white chief send for other white chiefs and these white chiefs vanish again into the far side of their camp where immediately they started blowing whistles as they had done during the attack and their escape from Hunter's Drift.

He was utterly certain that the Hottentots had seen into the true nature of their spoor and hurried on there in the dark to prevent them crossing the road as well as to organize a successful search for them as soon as daylight came. They had therefore to get up and go at once. Because those Hottentots were not to be deceived again. From now on only speed and the fact that Xhabbo knew the land and they did not, could save them.

It was typical of Xhabbo's thoroughness in these matters that although he had declared himself convinced that their trackers could no longer be deceived, he made Nuin-Tara help him to scatter sand over their fires and eliminate all traces of their brief camp there before he declared himself ready to go. How their fortune had changed since the morning was evident now from the new order of their march. Whereas Xhabbo had preoccupied himself from Lamb-snatcher's Hill onward with the danger from behind and remained in the rear, he now led the little procession out of the bed of the stream and up the track back into the bush. Hintza went immediately behind him, then François, Nonnie and last of all Nuin-Tara. But this was the only innovation in the manner of their going. Xhabbo's injunction as before was for everyone to keep as much as possible in the footprints of the one in front; above all over the three pawprints of Hintza.

It looked at first as if they would rejoin the track of the morning but half-way there Xhabbo branched away along a narrow game track, so narrow and deep in the bush that François caught only an occasional glimpse of starry sheets of sky blotted with leaves of ink. The bush still maintained that determined, aloof silence which had so dismayed Nonnie earlier on, until after a bare half an hour's march it was broken by the sound of trucks labouring in heavy sand in the far distance ahead of them.

Xhabbo immediately stopped and let the others join him. Wordlessly, they stood there listening to the trucks coming nearer, as it sounded, directly at them. Had they not been certain that they were in a narrow game track deep in the bush and judged their situation by the harsh, grating sound alone, they could have believed themselves to be standing exposed in the middle of the road along which the trucks were travelling. Soon the power of this illusion was increased by flashes of headlights brushing the leaves and tops of the tall trees. After a while, the flashes of light were so strong and continuous that they could see one another by them. When that happened Xhabbo, far from being dismayed, had turned to look at François, a wide smile of satisfaction on his face, followed it by a movement of his right hand, to point his spear in front of him to the right, and in a nearly inaudible whisper said, 'Foot of the Day, it is just there!'

The 'it' apparently was the great Hunter's Road and, that demonstrated, Xhabbo went down quietly on his stomach, flat on the ground. Without a word, Hintza, so wise in the ways of hunters, went down on his stomach, and their example sent François, Nonnie and Nuin-Tara over like a collapsing pack of cards, to lie flat on the ground as well. They lay there then, the sound growing so loud, the light no longer flashing but steady and swelling over the trees, and the shadows cast by branches and trunks so clear and dark round them that it was almost impossible to believe the trucks were not going to crash through what could surely now be only the thinnest of screens of brush and branches between them and the road, and run them over. But suddenly the angles of light of the first of what sounded like five trucks, curved away, to be followed by the others, and gradually the sounds receded.

Still Xhabbo did not move but went on lying there until both light and sound had died away. Soon, far away on their right, so still was it in the bush, they heard men singing, singing again in the most beautiful natural bass voices, the sloganized music of so-called liberation that they had sung first on the night after the massacre at Hunter's Drift.

Nonnie was aware only of the sound of music. But François lying there in the dark, with his hand on Hintza's back, knew at once there was more than music to it and the sound of singing itself was suspect. For the hair on Hintza's spine was erect and electric, his nose turned in François's direction, his mouth hissing his own special warning of great, unseen danger. Almost at once François knew what it was. The sound of music was not one but divided in two. One part, with the greater volume, appeared stationary. The other, smaller and more compact, was coming nearer to them, he feared from a patrol marching along the road in the dark, probably to be in a position for the great search which Xhabbo anticipated at daybreak.

François, had he been in command, would there and then have led the party straight across the road and quickly put as wide a distance as possible on the other side between the road and themselves because the singing told him the men were still half a mile or more away. So convinced was he of the necessity of this that he crawled forward and suggested that they should do precisely that. But Xhabbo firmly said no, and told him to lie still where he was and to see that Hin and Nonnie remained still beside him. Indeed, so great was Xhabbo's sense of the need for silence that he made no attempt to explain his refusal to François but resumed lying in the track as flat as he could, his hand on his spear.

François complied immediately, but having noticed Xhabbo's state of readiness and realizing it was not merely a perfunctory or routine readiness, silently cocked his own rifle, undid the safety catch and loosened the knife in his belt. Although Nonnie could not see precisely what was happening, the unusual movement was enough to forewarn and alarm her. She longed to crawl up to François and ask him what was happening but as Nuin-Tara hard by her did not move, some new instinct stopped her. All she allowed herself was to grasp François's ankle just in front and to hold on to it tightly. It was enough to make François turn very slowly without a rustle towards her and just for a moment, to put his hand reassuringly on hers. And so they lay there listening to the singing coming nearer just as the sound of the trucks had done, but, unlike the trucks, when the singing was suddenly almost upon them, it abruptly stopped.

A loud voice of command suddenly called out: 'Platoon, halt!' followed by a: 'Stand at ease!' – 'Stand easy!' and a final: 'Fall-out!'

Immediately the sound of men talking and relaxing took over. It was all happening far too close for comfort and safety and yet there was nothing they could now do but wait – a wait which made François think again, as he so often did nowadays, of that francolin mother he had once pointed out to Nonnie, as an example of true courage. They both had watched the place where it was brooding, still and silent, with only a tremor of grass to show the pulse of fear racing in her heart and eating in vain at her courage. It felt to Nonnie that the men at their ease, so close that she could have deciphered their conversation had she had a clue to their words, would be there for ever or if they moved, would deploy to beat the bush around them. She never had any idea how long the conversation, the joking, laughter, back-chat and the occasional authoritative pronouncements, all so deceptively and plausibly normal and harmless in their tone, continued. François himself was afraid that they might be there until dawn, and be deprived of any advantage of time and dark they had in their flight. But after what he calculated to have been almost the longest half hour of his life, the voice of command again rang out with a peremptory, 'Platoon!'

Immediately there was a great scurrying and shuffling of feet and soon the command, 'Platoon, attention!' followed by 'In threes, by the left, quick march!'

At once the night was loud with the measured tramp of feet. Another of those natural bass voices started up a marching song.

The others joined in and the men began to vanish purposefully to music away into the night.

When it was clear what was happening, Xhabbo turned about as swiftly as one of the turning foxes of the desert to face François and whisper that he wanted them to lie there while he inspected the road alone. He vanished and was back in a few minutes, beckoning to François and the others to come quickly. The road on which they had heard all that fearful traffic was not an arm's length away as it had sounded, but a good hundred paces.

Once on the edge of the road, Xhabbo made François take Hintza in his arms and step across the road, Nonnie and Nuin-Tara following. He stayed behind only long enough to erase all signs of their spoor some distance back along the game tracks, in the road as well as the track on the far side. He accounted for the obvious disturbance of the surface by making with the nails of his fingers the hoof marks of a tsessebe father, mother and their young; the buck which most favoured that part of the world. That done, he hastened to join the others, once more took over the lead and, their eyes being fully readjusted to the dark, made them press on at a pace which the wounded Hintza, and Nonnie, found hard to maintain.

They must have travelled like this for some three hours with only the briefest of pauses, when suddenly the bush came to an end. At one moment their feet were firm in the track that was a deep scar of earth in the bush, scarlet by day but now a dark crayon line of its own. The trees and brush pressed tight and domineering upon them, so full of their own urgent business that it was almost as if François could hear the sound of new life started up in them by the heavy dew gathering in the air, and listen to it mounting to a kind of strumming and humming at his ears. At times it became almost a drumming from the oldest of trees, pumping sap from its deep well of being in the fecund earth of Africa and sending it sizzling up to the tips of the highest crowns of black Indian green. And then the next moment, their feet were sinking into sand. Suddenly all was space before them and everywhere they looked it was as if the gates of some ancient fortress of light had been flung open and they had passed through them and found all round them high secure battlements, lofty turrets and dark towers manned with belted constellations and sworded stars to welcome the return of authentic members of their garrison from a long and dangerous reconnaissance of the forces of darkness in the furthest recesses of the night. So dense indeed were the walls of space with armament of light that there was hardly any black left at all in the sky. Only star upon star joined to one another by a common phosphorescent incandescence until the night was a shining lacquer wherein the stars were not only presented individually but collectively reflected; not silent and still, as in the humid hemisphere to the north but loud and lively and some of them quite ostentatiously tapping, as Xhabbo would have had it. Indeed, all was so clear, wide and open in front of them that on the far horizon François observed star after star setting, and could follow them until only the last of their five spikes showed a platinum tip above the ripple of shadow that was the limit of a brave and frank new world.

But strangest and perhaps most exciting of all was an Isabella-white glow which emanated from the earth all round them and made Nonnie, despite a fatigue greater than any she had yet experienced, feel elated as if she had suddenly burst out of bondage. All the reflexes of her spirit were miraculously restored to her and breaking all her resolutions not to take any initiative of her own while on the march, she moved up quickly to join François so as to ask him what it all could mean. Xhabbo's voice, speaking in a normal, uninhibited manner, stopped her. So bright was the starlight that she could see his hand holding a spear, clear-cut against the sky and note that for all its normality the voice underneath was taut with profound emotion.

'Foot of the Day, Nonnie,' he exhorted them, 'look and feel as I, Xhabbo and Nuin-Tara feel, that we have utterly come to our home.'

Neither François nor Nonnie could think of any words adequate to reply but went up silently to stand beside him and Nuin-Tara and Hintza and almost as in an act of silent worship to allow the night, which had appeared irrevocably locked against them only a brief minute before, to complete its welcome, and so let the sea-murmur of music from the distant smoking beaches of the universe speak for them.

It was significant that Nuin-Tara herself did not speak either. She stood there close beside Xhabbo as silent as they themselves. After what seemed no time at all but actually had been some ten minutes, Xhabbo himself broke the silence.

They had better sit down there together, drink a little water and eat, he told them, for their journey was not over yet. He wanted them to go on as fast as they could until sunrise because in this place where they now were, there was no concealment of their spoor possible and their only safety would be the distance they could put between them and the men who might be coming after them in daylight. Provided they could get deep into the land in front of them, he doubted whether their enemies, least of all their Hottentot trackers, would follow them for long, knowing as they must know, that only Bushmen knew the secret of the rare water concealed underneath the sands of so immense a thirst land. A day, perhaps two days of pursuit at the most, he thought, was all they would have to expect. That would mean four days in all without water except what their enemies carried on them, and he doubted whether even the Hottentots would be capable of more.

They sat there in a circle, therefore, having a few carefully rationed gulps of water, some biltong and a handful of dried apple and apricot which François handed to each of them except Hintza, who had half of François's share of water as well as his own, and a whole piece of biltong as well as some dried peaches. François knew that of all forms of conserved fruit these peaches were Hintza's favourites, and considering the long way he had come without complaint, wounded and on only three of his four legs, François thought that even his favourite food was not good enough for him. At first Nonnie thought that she could not eat at all. She felt sick with fatigue and longed only for water, and more water. She would probably not have succeeded in eating at all, had not François produced his flask of old Hunter's Drift brandy and made first her, then Nuin-Tara, Xhabbo and finally himself take a great gulp of the spirit.

Hintza too would have had his share had not François known it would be dangerous after all his sedatives. Yet although he knew it was for Hintza's good he felt oddly mean when a great sigh like a sob fell from Hintza and the head that had been raised expectant, nose sniffing ardently at the bouquet of Huguenot Cognac, sank back to rest despondently against François. Nonnie, on the other hand, was convinced that the brandy would make her condition worse. But after a few minutes her resilient body quickened to it, the smell of apple and apricot suddenly became appetizing and she ate her ration with relish.

That done, she felt almost ready to go on, though when the moment came to start after an hour and she came to her feet, she doubted whether in fact she could walk for long.

Happily Xhabbo led off to the north-west at a deliberate pace, as if he realized that walking in the sand, easy as it was for himself and Nuin-Tara, would be difficult for François and Hintza. Yet, even that measured, long-distance pace of his became more than Nonnie felt she could manage. Her tiredness made her desperate, her desperation rebellious and unreasonable, and she began to project her unreason on to Xhabbo and above all on François.

She persuaded herself that they had long since come far enough and only typical, insensitive, masculine stubbornness was urging them on. When the Dawn's Heart came up swiftly over the broad line of the black bush behind them, she felt that surely they had gone far enough and had not only earned the right but were more than safe and could now find a place to rest. When the Dawn's Heart was followed by a fast colourless dawn which filled François and Xhabbo with foreboding, she almost cried out to them to stop. But still she managed to hold her peace, until an impetuous sun threw itself high into the sky with what seemed to be the speed and fire of a great passion denied far beyond its due, and a strange noise sounded in the blood in her ears almost like a shrill shriek of heat and light, mad with excess.

She was convinced she could not go on. She called out in despair to François who whisked round and looked at her with alarm.

'I'm so sorry, François,' she managed to plead for herself through a parched mouth. 'I just can't go on. If you and that Xhabbo of yours want to go on walking all day long you can leave me here. This is the end as far as I'm concerned.'

It looked as if she would collapse and fall to the ground, but once more there was that familiar rush of feet from behind. She found herself gripped by Nuin-Tara, firmly held up, being shaken and she thought in danger of being slapped, unfairly, for hysteria. Then she realized somehow that the shaking was intended to bring her out of herself and to look up at Nuin-Tara. As she did so, she saw a face inclined towards her full of understanding and a pair of deep, dark eyes glowing with experience of the first things of life, and before her own eyes, a long hand, holding out a bulb selected from the supply of tubers they had dug on the previous day's march. From a great distance, unblurred by the singing of light and heat and fatigue in her ears, she heard François's slow, measured voice, pleading, 'Please take and eat what Nuin-Tara is offering you, Nonnie, it's terribly good for thirst.'

She took the bulb almost incapable of any show of gratitude and obediently bit into it. Immediately she was amazed by the fresh, clean taste, astringent on her palate and the instant retreat of the parched feeling and re-emergence of moisture in her mouth and throat. And yet that was not the end of the matter. Her tired, rebellious self automatically informed François, stammering with the rush of unpremeditated words, that one miserable tuber might help her thirst but that her legs, muscles, indeed her whole body had definitely, finally and irrevocably come to the end of their day.

'No, Nonnie, no, they have not.' François spoke in what was to her a patronizing, deliberate, and totally non-understanding tone. 'I promise you, I've often felt as you feel now. I know how desperate it is for you. Please, please believe me but if you can't believe me, believe Mopani and 'Bamuthi who taught me that when you say it's the end, it only means that you've come to the end of what your experience of tiredness believes to be the end of your strength. Just forget all you've ever known about tiredness. Just try and go on. You'll find as Mopani and 'Bamuthi showed me, that there's no such end inside yourself. They taught me that the only end is an end forced on you from without. There's no such thing within. You've been marvellous, and I know you can go on for as long as necessary.'

Somehow François's words made her struggle on but they did not deprive her of resentment and incomprehension, and she began reciting to herself with increasingly fierce reiteration, what became, had she but known it, the marching song for another Nonnie as old as life itself, whose existence she had never suspected and who seemed to have taken over her consciously surrendered self. She would mutter to herself, remembering even the character she had hated most in her school *Hamlet:*

'Damn Mopani, damn!' – the recurrent refrain beat in her head.

> 'Damn 'Bamuthi, damn!
> Damn François Polonius damn!
> Damn Polonius François damn!
> Damn that son of a schoolmaster, damn!
> Damn him for trying to schoolmaster me, damn!'

And so they went on deeper into what is not only the greatest pan François had ever seen, but is perhaps the greatest pan in Africa if not on earth. Far behind them the bush receded into a thick, dark line, and gradually, as the sky became hotter and the air between them and the bush was turned into a trembling, quicksilver smear, the line wavered, was broken, lifted in enlarged bits of itself to be suspended above what looked like a sea of flaming water. On the far rim of the pan ahead of them the line of a vast tumult of dunes, covered with bush and strange thorn trees looked deceptively near, as if they were only a few hours' marching, instead of nearly two days away. And for all his confident words to Nonnie, François, looking into his own exhausted self and to Hintza labouring in front, became profoundly and acutely afraid.

For he realized at once where they were. This was the great desert plain which 'Bamuthi and all his Matabele teachers had warned him all men should fear, because it was so far away and wide, desolate and uninhabited, that when men came to it their hearts cried out loud, 'Kwa'mamengalahlwa – Oh mother, I am lost!'

He sought and found comfort as he always did in the presence of Xhabbo and Nuin-Tara, knowing that this immense

259

wasteland was merely the doorstep of home to them. And his comfort was sustained by the unwavering, confident way Xhabbo was leading them. So suddenly he was forced to realize that perhaps it was not this plain that was troubling him, however fearful his Matabele teachers had tried to make it for him, but some undefinable other thing.

Impulsively he turned about to look apprehensively behind them. He was amazed to see Xhabbo turning about simultaneously and was moved, more than he could put into articulate thought, at how their two spirits seemed always in communication and accord at levels beyond need of words. The little line came to a stop. Hintza, Nuin-Tara and Nonnie turned about too and likewise looked fearfully behind them as if afraid of being followed. Their spoor stretched out in an alarmingly clear, deeply etched and, of course, easily discernible line to where half a mile away it was lost in the glare. They all stood looking deeply into the glare as into a great crystal, and though they could see nothing, François was certain that they were all as uneasy as he was, particularly since Hintza had lifted his head and was giving him a look which only François knew was Hintza's way of intimating he had a hunch that even this new world was about to turn against them.

They remained there on watch like that for some ten minutes. Then Xhabbo, with a shrug of his shoulders, not reassured but clearly determined not to allow the lack of perfection in their awareness to be an enemy of what good he could accomplish at the moment, announced that there was no point just then in going on, and that he would lead them to a place nearby for rest.

He turned sideways into what seemed to François just another empty blaze of light where the sturdy nimble body, close as it was to him, was reflected on the shining air as in a distorting mirror. Soon they came to a shallow hollow in the pan, surrounded by a wide fringe of tall, brown, almost burned-out reeds which came alive there when the rains fell. They threw a kind of shadow that was more a paler form of sunlight, but, nonetheless, was shelter of a sort and sifted the heat and glare into a finer grain. Xhabbo threw down his pack almost in anger, and told the rest to follow his example.

260

CHAPTER TEN

Pillar of Fire

It was late afternoon when François was woken by Hintza, amazed how he could have slept so soundly in so hot a place. Hintza appeared to have woken François for no specific reason, except that Xhabbo was awake and on his feet and that his eyes showed him to be as full of unspecified apprehension as ever.

François sat up and looked around him. Nonnie and Nuin-Tara were fast asleep side by side, so he stood up without a sound and carefully went over to join Xhabbo. The glare and distortion had gone from the day. It was cooler; the scene again spread out clear and precise. Xhabbo was pointing without speaking in the direction from which they had come. There, where the dark line of the distant bush had once more been restored to the earth, just at the point where François reckoned they had emerged from the bush in the early hours of the morning, a blue column of smoke stood tall and straight.

His eyes had barely located it when the still, early evening air over the pan began to tremble with a strange kind of intensive vibration. The vibration became a definite sound. The sound increased and made Xhabbo look questioningly at François, as if it were the sort of noise which François ought to recognize and not he, Xhabbo, be expected to name. Indeed, within moments the noise was substantiated. High in the sky there appeared an aeroplane, translucent, blue and silver against that long, level light, and heading straight for the smoke.

François had no doubt, as Hintza and even Xhabbo, who knew nothing about aeroplanes, appeared to have none either, that smoke in such a place could only have been sent up and was being maintained by their pursuers for the benefit of the plane. He was certain at once that the Hottentots and other searchers must have found their spoor in the course of the day and tracked it to where it emerged in the open, where they could not fail to watch it running out straight across the pan as they themselves had seen it in their moment of desperation in the morning. They stood there, appalled to see their fears confirmed, for when the plane arrived above the pillar of smoke it circled it several times and then came streaking towards them.

Their situation seemed to François nearer his sphere of knowledge than Xhabbo's. After all, Ouwa and Mopani had been through a world war together and told him a great deal about it, and he did not hesitate to resume command and tell Xhabbo that they had better join the women and take cover in that ring of reeds as quickly as possible. Once in cover it was vital, he explained, that none of them should look up at the sky, because he remembered both Ouwa and Mopani stressing that it was unbelievable how faces and eyes not only of human beings but of animals shone almost like mirrors from the ground to anyone watching from a plane above. He assured Xhabbo that he himself would do whatever watching was necessary by lying on his back, shading his face with his wide-brimmed bush hat and keeping his hands carefully concealed inside its brim. Xhabbo accepted all this without question, and almost at once was beside Nuin-Tara who was already stirring.

Nonnie, her face still flushed from the heat of the day, was still deep in her sleep and looked so at home and at peace in it now that the fire had gone from the atmosphere round her that it hurt François to wake her. He was more than hurt when she came out of her sleep too startled to be really aware of what was happening and still joined to the rebellious, overwrought self with which she had gone to sleep.

'Oh go away!' she exclaimed. 'Leave me alone. I hate you all and I just won't go on.'

Muttering wildly she became fully awake to see a surprised and wounded look on François's face, thin, drawn with all he had endured plainly inscribed on it and despite the rest, eyes great and bright with underlying weariness. Her resentment vanished and it was all that she could do not to burst into tears.

'Oh François, forgive me please, dear François,' she pleaded, contrite, 'I was only talking in my sleep. What is it, please? Do forgive me and take that stricken deer look off your face, at once, please! And tell me what it's about. I didn't mean one word of what I said.'

François immediately was his unwounded self and explained that all he wanted was for her to creep right into the reeds, turn over and lie on her tummy with her face on her arms until he told her not to.

'Oh what bliss!' Nonnie exclaimed, apparently too tired to be alarmed, 'As long as we're not to go on walking again, I can lie here until the end of time. What bliss . . .'

Immediately she crawled forward, turned over and snuggled down to earth, her head in her arms, leaving François, whose foreboding was so full and acute that heartened as he was by her show of spirit, he feared she might have been provocatively flippant. But he left the thought there because already the aeroplane seemed to have arrived over the spot where Xhabbo had branched off from the main line of their spoor in the morning to lead them to their shelter among the reeds.

François, who had been as conscious as any of the long hours they had marched across the pan, and had been convinced that they had come extremely far, was dismayed how the distance was demolished by the realization that it had only been a few minutes since they had first heard the aeroplane come out of the sky over the bush and its arrival almost overhead. He lay there on his back, sombre with the thought that this was something quite outside his and Xhabbo's calculations. With aeroplanes and trucks at their enemy's command, no matter how fast and hard they themselves marched, their pursuers could easily out-speed and out-distance them. Once again their only safety would be in finding cover as soon as possible. But cover, where, and how? And, above all, would they be allowed the time to make it?

He completed this desperate conclusion just in time to see out of the corner of his shaded eyes, the aeroplane appearing from the right and speeding towards the bed of reeds. It moved across his direct vision, disappeared out of the corner of his eyes to the left and, presumably having found that their spoor did not emerge on the far side of the reeds, returned and circled their hiding place, gradually coming down closer and closer in a spiral until it could not have been more than a hundred feet above them. Then it started re-ascending in tight circles until François judged it had achieved the height of Lamb-snatcher's Hill above them. There a bright light shot out from its nose, soared straight up to explode high in the blue and release a dark cloud of smoke. That done, the aeroplane vanished again to the right, François hoped for good, but in a moment he heard it coming back and low towards them. When the searing noise was almost above them, the pan all around them suddenly came alive, shaking and spurting upwards. There followed immediately a rattle-tattle, quick, sharp, and the earth beneath shook as with the thud of hail, audible above the screaming engines. The air was filled with dust and a mist of the finest fragments of shattered and pounded reeds. The violent process ceased as abruptly as it had begun. The engines receded away to the left. Dust and a fog of pulverized reeds and dust descended on them; so thick that a loud sneeze of protest burst out of Hintza. It was greeted by a muffled, 'Bless you, Hin!' from Nonnie – a reaction which struck François as one of the bravest of many brave incidents of the day.

Then he heard the plane streaking back again. Once more the machine-gunning, as François had recognized it to be, began. He heard himself shouting the obvious platitudes that serve disaster, while his hand firmly held down Hintza, who was stirring full of desire for action beside him.

'For God's sake, Nonnie, don't move, this is no joke ... they're machine-gunning us. Xhabbo, Nuin-Tara, please don't move or look up!'

The machine-gunning was repeated six times right and left of them before the aeroplane zoomed upwards sharply. The noise of its engines faded the way it had come. François felt it safe to sit up. He looked about him amazed. The others sat up too, apparently untouched. It had all happened so fast that, like them, he had had no time to be truly frightened. But now that it was over, he realized how shocked he must have been, for he was drunk with exhilaration that they had all come through safely.

'You know, Hin,' he said to Hintza in Bushman, 'I don't think that aeroplane ever saw us, or we would have been hit. He was just shooting wildly for luck. Our real trouble, I fear, is still to come.'

Getting up he went over to join the others, who appeared far more excited with curiosity over what had happened than concerned with the danger they had survived, except Xhabbo. He was not only on his feet but pointing with his spear to the far side of the ring of reeds, a complex half-smile not just of amusement but of rare compassion subtle on his face.

A desert fox and his vixen were standing by the hole in the sand that was their home nearby. Their coats were lit and gleaming and their keen shapes, enclosed in a ring of fire drawn from the setting sun. Their expressions betrayed indignation at so brutal an interruption of a siesta essential to all who dined so late at night.

François had to smile as well and, more than smiling, was touched in his tenderest feelings when the foxes, after a time, turned to look at them without fear but for evident support of their feeling that they were justified in resenting so vulgar an intrusion. So neighbourly was the long, frank regard from their intelligent faces that it was almost as if François could hear them thinking, 'What have we done to deserve all this? The natural order must be crumbling if this sort of thing can be allowed.'

'Look, Foot of the Day,' he heard Xhabbo saying beside him. 'Feeling yourself to be looking, feel also how here, where on their heels upright walking Xhabbo's people have always come and gone without fear, even the foxes who hide by day feel as we do and that we are not alone.'

It was as if the Ishmael in Xhabbo were honouring the Ishmael that these foxes were in the animal world. François was more moved than ever. He remembered the voice of his father far back, re-telling him at his request the story of Ishmael, and the words of Hagar, his mother, which for a reason he had not yet discovered had held his imagination. 'Even here in the desert have I seen God and lived after my vision.'

And his father had spoken the words somehow as Xhabbo had done now, as the exile in himself speaking for all that is exiled in life. He stood there thus until the foxes turned back to their hole not to enter it but to lie down at the entrance, as if to watch the skies at their ease in case the intruders returned. Only then did he reluctantly move away. He moved because what he had thought was a great distance between them and the enemy with aeroplanes at its command, was no distance at all, and the attack had impressed him deeply with the need for immediate action.

He and Xhabbo were at once in consultation. François's fear of pursuit by trucks across the pan was dismissed out of hand by Xhabbo. He assured François that there was no road or way at all from the Punda-Ma-Tenka to the pan; only the thickest of bush pierced by a few narrow game tracks like the one they had followed the night before.

Xhabbo was certain that the greatest danger now was that the men who had just been shooting at them would tell the Hottentots where the spoor ended and that the Hottentots would soon be sent out across the pan after them. They themselves must hasten towards the great dunes ahead of them. Once in those dunes, Xhabbo assured François, they could hide and make themselves invisible from above or below and hard to trace, and after no more than another day they would be safe, because no one except he would know where there was water.

'But how long will it take us to reach the dunes, Xhabbo?' François asked anxiously. 'I think I can just go on as long as necessary but I'm not sure that Hin and Nonnie can go much further without more rest.'

François's tone was as apologetic as it was anxious. He knew from old Koba what a strict code of ethics ruled Bushman conduct in moments of grave crisis such as this. He knew, for instance, that when the old people, no matter how beloved and honoured, were not strong enough to keep up the pace of movement necessary for the survival of their clan, they offered without prompting to stay behind, and the clan, however reluctant and sad, would be compelled to abandon them to certain death, so that not only the clan but life itself could move on and survive. The urge to be knightly was natural and instinctive in all men and not the monopoly of civilization. He felt compelled to tell Xhabbo that perhaps the moment had come when Xhabbo and Nuin-Tara should move on and leave himself and Nonnie and Hintza behind.

An exclamation of profound emotion broke from Xhabbo. He took François's little finger in his hand and said, 'Foot of the Day, you speak the words Xhabbo felt you would be feeling. You speak utterly as if your mother and Xhabbo's mother were utterly one. Xhabbo utterly feels that we are brothers. As brothers we stay or go as one.'

And then quickly, before François, warmed through and through by his answer, could respond, he went on to explain that the dunes were little more than a long night and half a day's march away. If they started at once, they could be there when the sun was in the middle of the sky the next day.

François, with the melancholy of desperation, just shook his head hopelessly. 'You know, Xhabbo, neither Nonnie, nor Hintza and I doubt even I could march that far in that time.'

Xhabbo's vehement reaction was accompanied by a smile of understanding. He knew, Bushman that he was, that it was too much all at once. All he wanted to say was that if they started out marching now, some time about half-way between the middle of the night and the coming of the Dawn's Heart, they would reach a shallow cleft of a dry river-bed emerging into the pan. There was bush and cover enough there to hide. After resting there they could follow the cleft almost into the midst of the dunes. Only they would have to start at once after quickly doing one more little thing. Between them and the dunes there was no water. They would have to refill their almost empty flasks now. Once in the dunes, they would find first melons enough and later water for their needs. But here and now was their last chance of the water they needed badly.

François could hardly believe him. There was no sign of any water in their vicinity. It had been one of the first things he had instinctively looked for. Yet he accepted implicitly what Xhabbo told him. He fetched his own ration of water and gave it to Nonnie, insisting that she drink it and, as she was still thirsty afterwards, finish her own supply as well, despite her protests. He then made her collect all their dixies and follow him to join Nuin-Tara, who appeared busy with something at the far side of the ring of reeds. They arrived there to find she had uncovered from a lonely place in the sand, a pointed Bushman digging stick of ironwood, as well as a long, narrow tube which she cleared of sand by blowing delicately into it like a flute player clearing his instrument of dust.

267

She then led them some fifty yards over the sand to where Xhabbo was pointing with his finger at a place for her to start digging. Xhabbo meanwhile collected some of the finest reed tips, and bound them tightly round the tapered end of the tube. When Nuin-Tara had dug as far as her arm, fully stretched, could reach into the sand, he took over, inserted the end of the tube, filled the hole round it with freshly dug sand, stamped it carefully in with his heels until a bare foot of the tube showed above the sand. He placed an empty dixie close beside the tube, put his mouth to the opening and started sucking at it. His shoulder heaved with the effort he put into it. For two minutes he drew with all the power of his lungs at the tube until the sweat ran from him and made an orange satin of his back in the setting sun.

And then, suddenly – Nonnie could not believe her eyes – a spurt of bright water shot from the corner of his mouth to fall quickly into the dixie at his side. She watched, amazed how like an automatic pump, pumping water, he became, the water pouring almost in a continuous pulsing stream out of the side of his mouth, so fast and automatic were his actions. He went on until all their dixies and flasks were full. When he and Nuin-Tara and Hintza had all drunk as much as they could, he started again until all their dixies were refilled.

'You'd better have your fill of water as well, Nonnie,' François said. 'But I'd better . . .'

He got no further because such a look of distaste came on Nonnie's face that he nearly laughed. But, afraid of hurting her, he managed to restrain himself, as well as taking it as a sign that she could no longer be so exhausted if her palate could be so discriminating again. He quickly added, 'I was going on to say that I don't think you ought to drink this water until it's been boiled. You haven't yet had the immunities that we've got against it. What about getting some tea out of my pack and having some tea instead? I'll just ask Xhabbo if he minds a fire in this place.'

Nonnie felt inclined to retort, 'Your precious immunities were not exactly what was worrying me,' but held her tongue and watched Xhabbo signal to François that he did not mind a fire, provided it was only a discreet one.

As the sun went down they drank their tea and ate some rusks and biltong. So fresh was the evening air that with the re-emergence of the stars Nonnie's rebellious self vanished. She was still aching all over with tiredness and was beginning to realize how shaken and perturbed she was by that attack from the air and its implications, that she could not talk to François about it or even attempt to analyse it for herself. But there was no doubt that basically her spirits were restored in great measure and that the sheer necessity of having to move on again, was attracting her as a means of escape from the backlash of the shock of their attack, and the horror of that long march through the night and the morning before.

She stood up willingly enough, therefore, when the moment came to go and somehow managed to keep going until some time towards morning when they found the cleft in the pan as Xhabbo had promised. Just for a moment they all stood on its edge, while Xhabbo and François tried to judge the time from the position of the stars. Their pursuers, they both agreed, would have been unable to follow them far in the dark, and would have had to wait for morning before coming properly after them. That in François's reckoning meant that they had between ten and twelve hours' start on the enemy and that now they could have at least a rest under cover for the whole of the coming day, before they moved on.

This quick sum, tired as François was, made him smart all over with hope. He could not resist turning to Nonnie, who was now sick with fatigue and trembling in every muscle, and whispering, 'I believe we've made it, Nonnie, we've made it!'

And with that, they followed Xhabbo and Nuin-Tara down into the cleft, worked their way southwards to their left along its sandy bed, until they found a sharp bend where the water apparently formed a pool in the rainy season. There, dense wide thorn bushes grew in abundance and gave them the certain promise of real shade against the sun in the coming day. Quickly they made themselves another brew of tea, breakfasted and fell asleep like sheep in a close huddle.

François felt he had hardly slept at all when Hintza woke him. Xhabbo was already awake, sitting up beside Nuin-Tara and listening. The sun had just risen. The air was cool, clear and still, and there could be no mistaking what had woken them. Their old friend the aeroplane was coming back after them. François looked around him to make certain they were indeed as well hidden as he had imagined the night before, and was reassured. Carefully, so as not to wake Nonnie and Nuin-Tara, he and Xhabbo and Hintza crawled over into the shelter and dark shadow of the bank of the cleft opposite them. They rose carefully, not raising any dust, until they could just peer over the rim across the pan.

The aeroplane, droning like an angry bee loud in their ears, was hardly bigger than one, so far away was it still, but clearly visible in the yellow light, circling over their resting place of the day before. Soon it found their spoor and followed it fast, straight towards them. François immediately signed to Xhabbo that it was time to get back, under cover from where they watched the plane appear above the place where they had gone down into the cleft. It circled it for about a quarter of an hour and then reconnoitred the cleft up and down repeatedly to the right and left of them. François feared that the cleft too was in for some more machine-gunning, but the aeroplane on this occasion seemed interested only in exploring the nature of the place where their spoor had vanished so abruptly, because after about half an hour it turned around in a wide circle and returned the way it had come.

They were all immensely relieved except Hintza. Sitting beside François while he and Xhabbo discussed their situation, Hintza began suddenly nudging François repeatedly with his head, and when François looked down at him at last Hintza returned his look with a steady but portentous expression like a shadow over his eyes, as if to say he wanted to swear to François by the nose he valued more than any organ in his body, that they had all better beware, for it was not over yet.

How right Hintza had been was proved in the early afternoon. François came out of a light, after-luncheon sleep, woken by another noise loud on the air, but this time it was not the noise of an aeroplane. It was some other kind of machine which did not drone, vibrate or scream so much as produce a jarring, cast-iron clatter. Alarmed, he and Xhabbo immediately manned the far edge of the cleft again.

A large helicopter, looking like a fully mechanized kind of pterodactyl, was coming towards them with graceless deliberation. It too was obviously making for the place where their spoor disappeared into the cleft. There was something infinitely purposeful and sinister about it as if it knew exactly what it was going to do and was not just scouting as the aeroplane had been. So much so that François felt bound not to take cover as before but to stay on in the shelter and shadow of the cleft, and watch every movement of the weird new machine.

When the helicopter arrived above the cleft, it hovered there like an immense spider, dangling on an invisible thread, and then slowly and methodically turned to pass over their heads and follow the cleft for some miles. Just as slowly and deliberately it came back and followed the cleft to their right for a similar distance. That done, it came back to where their spoor disappeared into the cleft, hovered there for some five minutes and then, slowly, to François's dismay, moved somewhat sideways and away from it all and started to come down with the obvious intention of settling on the surface of the pan – settling, François had no doubt, to discharge a cargo of soldiers complete with Hottentot trackers.

The noise from the helicopter was so close and loud that François had almost to shout in Xhabbo's ear, 'Xhabbo, I've no time to explain . . . the danger is too great. You must go at once with Hin, Nuin-Tara and Nonnie and hasten away down the cleft as fast as you can! No, Xhabbo no. There's nothing you can do to help me here – Nonnie and Hin are the two who will hold us back. We'll need all the start possible and more. You must lead them therefore utterly from this place. Any minute now our enemy and those two Hottentots are going to come out of that screaming thing there. They are fresh and strong. We are tired and only two. I'll stay here to hold them up as long as I can. When I can no longer hold them, I'll come after you. But in the name of Mantis now, go!'

At that Xhabbo, Hintza and François rushed to join Nonnie and Nuin-Tara who were sitting by their haversacks which of course had been packed and ready for instant travel after their last snack as Xhabbo had insisted before they rested. Nuin-Tara had an expression not so much of alarm as of intense curiosity and an air that Xhabbo would know exactly what was best to do, believing that the less she said or thought about it the better. Nonnie, characteristically, was trying to make light of it all, pretending to stop her ears with her fingers against the terrible noise, putting out her tongue and making a face in the direction of the now invisible helicopter. François told her as briefly as possible what he had told Xhabbo. When it looked as if she would protest, he told her in words as uncertain as they were rough with the need for speed that he would not listen to another word and expected her as Hintza's nurse to take him off immediately.

Somehow this one solid fact, that she would have some being to look after other than herself, more than anything else François had said, persuaded and silenced her. Hintza was another matter. He did not complain or whimper but looked at François with a deep, still reproach that nearly unmanned him. Quickly François turned away, just raising his hand slightly in farewell, snatched up his own haversack, field flask and pouches of ammunition, hurried over to the bank at the far end and moved further along it sideways towards the left where there was a deep indentation in the dry river-bed closer to where the helicopter was settling. Just before disappearing into it, he noticed that Xhabbo, Nonnie and Hintza had already vanished around the curve in the cleft to his right and that Nuin-Tara, following last, was on the point of doing so.

Quickly he emptied the magazine of his rifle which had been loaded ever since they had marched across the pan with lead bullets, in case he had a chance of shooting game for food. François reloaded it with steel pointed bullets and then came slowly up to his full height, pressing hard into the bank in front of him. Thank God, there were some bushes on both sides of the cleft and he found that he could work himself into a position where both his face and rifle were in the shade and yet where he had a clear field of fire in the direction of the helicopter.

The helicopter was now almost touching the surface of the pan some fifty to sixty paces away, its whirling blades drawing up grains of sand and spreading them outwards on the air all around before they came down like sleet again. But the moment

272

it touched down, the blades above it ceased whirling. The noise of its engines spluttered and stopped and the silence and illusion of calm, by contrast, was so sudden and great that it was deafening.

Yet it was real enough for almost at once François heard distinctly the iron squeak of metal and a door in the side of the helicopter began to open. The sun behind him was low enough to shine as much into the interior of the helicopter as on its outside and François, looking over the sights of his rifle, watched the door open wide and a black man, an automatic rifle on his arm, appear in it and slowly begin gathering himself together, as if preparing to jump down on to the pan.

François knew he could not allow this to happen. But unlike that last fatal encounter with the enemy on the foot of the hill above Hunter's Drift, he had just enough time to observe and to reflect. He found himself reluctant to kill. His rifle long since at the ready was made at once to bear on the shoulder of the enemy soldier. With a slow deliberation that was better and more accurate than speed, François did not squeeze the trigger so much as let the need for stopping the soldier without doubt, do it for him. The sharp, quick snap of the shot, characteristic of his remarkable little rifle, broke the crystal silence. A spurt of dust darted out of the soldier's uniform, between his heart and his shoulder. The automatic rifle at once fell from his hand and crashed on the pan. The soldier stumbled backwards into the helicopter and immediately the sounds, first of astonishment and then great confusion broke out inside.

François knew that somehow he must not allow order to come out of that confusion. The door of the helicopter was still wide open. He saw through it to what he thought was the outline of the body of the pilot still at the controls and the sunlight gleaming in points of silver and gold and crystal on the instrument panel. With a speed that never lost its deliberation and with no distortion of aim, he shot once at the pilot and when the pilot's shape seemed to vanish, he methodically emptied the magazine at whatever shone or glistened on the instrument panel. Reloading his magazine, he was encouraged to hear that the confusion was not being sorted out and that a kind of panic was compelling somebody inside to try and shut the door again and in the process preventing what François feared most, a rush that would bring the men inside tumbling out faster than he could shoot. His magazine full, he immediately resumed shooting into the helicopter before the door could shut. At once the movement of the door stopped, and François more deliberate than ever, continued his destruction of the instrument panel.

Having done that, he reloaded and started to shoot systematically at the helicopter from nose to tail and wing-tip to wing-tip, spacing his shots some three feet apart, until he realized he was using perhaps more ammunition than he could afford and that when he had emptied his magazine this time, he would shoot no more, but wait until there was a specific human target for his rifle. Accordingly he fired three more shots with greater care than ever at what he hoped were the fuel tanks. He was about to fire a fourth, when a sheet of flame suddenly shot out from the helicopter and hard on the sheet of flame there was a great explosion. Fragments of metal whisked by François and spattered down so close that he ducked low. When he raised himself to look, what was left of the helicopter was fuel for a fire racing upwards, until it stood in a pillar of flame and black smoke high above the pan.

François somehow was certain, great as the distance was between the fire and the edge of the bush, that as the flame and smoke were so high and dark they would be visible to the many watchers the enemy must have deployed on the other side of the pan. He glanced in haste at the sun and realized that there was at the most an hour of daylight left. Considering how long it had taken the aeroplane in the morning to mount the helicopter operation, he knew that at the very least they were safe from pursuers for what was left of the day. Only too glad that there was no need to watch the cremation of the helicopter and its cargo of soldiers to the end, he prepared to leave, helped along because all that had just passed so quickly and terribly somehow seemed remote and impersonal, except for that brief moment of specific humanity imposed on it all by his fleeting glimpse of pilot and black soldier. But even that glimpse now was made singularly matter-of-fact since the soldier and his friends had so obviously come to kill, had he allowed them to do so.

Amazed as he was by how sheer necessity and a summons to defend all that there was left for him to love in life, could make him so easily calculating a person, something else utterly beyond his powers of definition and expression, must have stirred deep down in François. He was looking his last on that pillar of fire soaring into the sky, so unlikely in that spare desert setting that it might have been something conjured up not by man in a modern context but some supernatural manifestation prophetically evoked to point an Old Testament moral.

Suddenly François found himself shutting his eyes on a command from within and murmuring, as he had so often done from his earliest days at Hunter's Drift, the psalm, 'The Lord is my shepherd,' right through to the verse 'Though I walk through the valley of the shadow of death . . .' Knowing how much in the shadow of death they had all walked for days, his seared, vulnerable and bereaved heart was suddenly full and brimming over with an immense thank-you. Hard on this he was close to tears, because a hope so great that it nearly persuaded him it was a certainty, cried for recognition, newly born out of the total wreck of all that had hitherto passed for hope in his experience. The pillar of fire and smoke at once became a sign for him to hasten.

Shouldering his haversack, ammunition pouches, and buckling his field flask into position, his rifle at the trail, he started at his long-distance run down the bed of the stream after his vanished friends. And for the first time since the massacre, he did not pause once to look back.

CHAPTER ELEVEN

The Voice of the Lion

The sun had just set when François caught up with Hintza, Nonnie, Xhabbo and Nuin-Tara. Although they must have been warned long since by Hintza of his coming and could not have failed to hear him hurrying up behind, he was impressed by the fact that they were also travelling as fast as they could without looking back. They did not stop until he caught up with them. If he had needed any proof of how at one they had all become, this solitary fact would have been conclusive. Also they could not have failed to hear the explosion of the helicopter. Despite the cleft, and distance in between, they must have turned then to see that pillar of fire in the sky. They could not have known except through Xhabbo's tapping, that the fire and smoke and the violence to which they had testified had not brought about François's own end as well. Yet they had kept faith and pressed on as he had begged Xhabbo to do. He was delighted therefore, that in explaining his conduct he could prove how justified was their faith in one another. As a result they spent their most carefree night yet and experienced briefly a state as near to real happiness as people so afflicted could possibly achieve.

For once they could choose a site and make camp together at their leisure and rest without immediate anxieties of any kind, only a few yards from where François had caught up with them. They slept soundly in their beds of sand. François, with greater natural ease and relaxation, was helped in this because both Hintza on one side of him and Nonnie on the other seemed to find a level of sleep without pain, foreboding or retrospective sorrow and so established a rhythm of communication between them as precious as it was deep.

Happiest of all, early in the morning when he and Xhabbo told Nuin-Tara and Nonnie to stay where they were and cook another casserole while they hurried up towards the top of the dunes not far away, Hintza himself, with eyes clear of pain, a nose shining and active as ever, obviously taking it for granted that he was to be the vital part of the exercise, reported to François as usual for duty.

But François held up a finger and shook it gently at him, before telling him in Bushman with great tact that it was his duty to stay behind and protect the women. Hintza saw through François's white lie at once, put up a paw to scratch a protest with his claws against François's leg. It was something that he had not done for days, and indeed could not have done because of his wounded leg. But now that he was scratching away until his protest got through, François was compelled to look down. He was amazed to see that however tentative and still somewhat trembling from the stiffness and ache of it, Hintza's wounded leg was propped on the sand and making his attitude of protest possible.

For François this was so speedy and miraculous a cure, and so powerful had been his fears for Hintza, that his joy was irrepressible. He shouted out aloud, 'Oh look Nonnie, look, his leg ... look, his leg! Xhabbo, Nuin-Tara ... look at his leg ... look!'

Nonnie did not say, 'Why, what about his leg, it's still there,' as she might have done out of her incorrigible and even to her at times incomprehensible love of teasing François, because for her too it was miraculous. Had she not herself looked with blurred eyes into the raw, red wound? She clasped her hands with delight in front of her, before doing a graceful curtsey to Hintza saying, while Hintza dribbled at the mouth with satisfaction, 'Oh Hin! Of all the dogs in the world you are king, and I, Luciana Monckton, the least of your subjects.'

Hintza was encouraged in this and other ways to stay behind with relative composure while François and Xhabbo hastened by themselves to the dunes. They reached the summit of one of the highest, well before the air over the pan was too hot to distort the view. From that height they looked to where the bush some forty miles away lapped like the shadow of a great water at the edge of the orange pan. No matter how minutely they searched the scene, they detected no sign of pursuit. Only once as they lay there had they cause for apprehension. They heard the familiar noise of an aeroplane coming up fast across the pan on a line some miles away to the north. They watched it circle over the ashes of the cremated helicopter. After circling low over the place for some fifteen minutes it turned about and vanished the way it had come.

And *that*, Xhabbo decided, once more in command, was their *that*. He declared himself now, with a firmness which surprised François, for the first time utterly without fear of pursuit. For safety's sake, however, one of them would have to stay on watch on the dune all day, but there was no need for them to move from that well-shaded, well-found camp of theirs. Unless the day provided anything untoward, they could get the rest there which they all needed so badly, before they travelled on.

They stood watch on the dune in turns until close on sunset. No aeroplane or aircraft appeared to trouble the desert calm, no dust rose out of the pan to suggest pursuit on foot, and they ended the day with the conclusion that the enemy had finally called off pursuit as vain; abandoned it perhaps all the more readily because they felt that what they had failed to do, the great thirst-land would accomplish instead.

Early the next morning, after another night of untroubled sleep, they prepared to go on in the way of the wind from which the events of the last two days had forced them to deviate. Although Xhabbo had no fear that they were still being followed by the enemy, it was typical of a thoroughness that explains the survival of his people against millenniums of persecution by nature and man, that he insisted on one last reconnaissance of the land behind him from the top of the dune.

François volunteered immediately and Nonnie, who knew enough already from the general trend of Bushman sounds if not actual words, to guess what he intended, clamoured to go with him. Hintza neither clamoured nor volunteered but just calmly took it for granted that he was to be the spearhead of the excursion and had already moved off in the direction of the dune to the edge of the river-bed which had been their camp, and there turned round to look expectantly to see why Nonnie and François were so slow in following. Impressed as

François had been by the progress of Hintza's wound, he was not impressed enough to allow Hintza to test it on a steep climb in deep sand through grass, thorn and other forms of resistant bush for some three hundred feet up into the blue. Hintza's instant reproach for which he had a special genius as always had the effect of shaking François's faith in his own decisions and made him uneasy with guilt, and yet he managed to insist. Injured in his male pride, as if unfairly condemned to a prison sentence, Hintza attached himself to Xhabbo, like someone who had changed allegiance for good.

It was Nonnie's first excursion for excursion's sake with François since her return from Europe, and François's unusually relaxed manner, free as he was of any immediate danger, gave an immense lift to her spirits. Now that she was physically rested, she was perhaps more eager than she knew to move on and away from a vast area of injury.

The view from the top of the dune over the pan left her speechless, which was all the more remarkable in one so articulate. The sun had only just risen and François could point out to her precisely the way they had come across the pan to where, far away, the bush cancelled the shining, vacant space in between with a determined slash of ink, and there, beyond and above the bush, away to the south-east and to the right, just on the horizon, was the purple shadow of the gorge and the hills leading up to the mound of blue with its crown of yellow sunlight that was Lamb-snatcher's Hill. More, even further to the right, the range of hills continued, in spite of repeated interruptions by minor clefts and gorges to the hill above Hunter's Drift and below it, a silver streak of the broad Amanzim-tetse river.

'Have we really come all that distance, François?' she asked, not believing her own eyes, 'Could I really have walked and run all that way? I don't believe it! It all just feels part of a nightmare of sleep.'

She stared at him with the questions so ardent that they made her dark, wide eyes brighter than ever and gave her a look so young, innocent and vulnerable that François felt as old and experienced as Mopani and as protective as he was moved.

He put his left hand on her shoulder, to say, 'No Nonnie, no. It's neither a nightmare nor illusion. You've done it all and it's one of the most remarkable things anybody has ever done. Nuin-Tara and Xhabbo only last night told me how much they admire you for the way you've kept up and how testing they found the journey themselves. I'm sorry I had to be so rough with you, but I always knew, I promise you, that you could do it. I can't tell you what I feel about the way you did it. Had you panicked or fallen out, it would have been disastrous for us all. But you were just wonderful.'

Nonnie indeed had never experienced anything so sweet as the effect produced in her by such praise. She was immediately convinced that she could do a dozen journeys like that, one after the other, if they ended in a welcome so warm into the select company of François, Xhabbo, Nuin-Tara and all those who had run races with death in the long story of man and for whom François and his two friends were for her such shining plenipotentiaries in the present. She resolved there and then that she would keep the memory of this moment alive not merely as a constant reminder of what she could do but also in order that whenever she had to go through other trials, as no doubt they would have to, it would spur her on with some foretaste of the reward that awaits those who endure to the true end of chance and circumstance.

Not daring to look at him she felt as a result that her response was totally inadequate: 'You made me do it, Coiske! It was all you and your beloved Hintza, of course. He had not just that ghastly wound but himself to carry on only three legs. I can't tell you how the sight of him struggling on in front, hour after hour, frothing at the mouth and never a whimper, made me ashamed of my weakness and gave me new determination.'

Fortunately for her self-possession, François changed the subject, because even emotions as good and healing as those alive between them just then tended to set off a train of other dark, hurt, deprived and powerful feelings still waiting at his and Nonnie's door for admission.

With disconcerting abruptness he became the matter-of-fact scout Xhabbo expected him to be, declaring, 'I wonder, Nonnie, if you agree, but I cannot see a single sign of anything moving across the pan or even smoke at the far edge. I think they've given up, don't you?'

Nonnie, also relieved, perhaps for similar reasons, after another dutiful examination of the pan, remarked with an upward turn of voice, 'Thou hast the reason of it, François Joubert, as your ancestors would have said.'

And still François, with no rational cause for going on examining the land taut and just beginning to tremble beneath the blue, found himself reluctant to take his eyes off it. Having pin-pointed the whole scene, he just could not bear to turn away from that glimpse of his much loved Amanzim-tetse, the familiar flash of a rushing, forever either murmuring, roaring or singing but always, whatever the mood, the Lady Precious Stream of his first memories. The beauty invested in all, even the most trivial of things, when one believes oneself to be looking on them for the last time, overwhelmed him.

He knew that Xhabbo would be waiting and that the purpose for which they had mounted the dune was achieved and that they should now return. Yet he was plunged into a conflict that made his heart beat faster and his eyes in danger of smarting with tears. So violent was the rupture in his feelings caused by the imperative need to turn away, that it resounded in his spirit not like the firm turning over of a page that it should ideally have been, but as the sound of one torn from the story of his life and thrown crumpled, away. He found himself, in the process, transferring to Nonnie words that were really intended for himself.

'Promise me Nonnie, promise me!' His voice startled her with its vehemence. 'You'll never look back again! We must promise each other here and now that we'll never look back and that all we see now spread out before us is once and for all to be put behind. All that matters now is what Xhabbo calls the way of the wind, in front of us.'

Saying this he turned swiftly about, taking Nonnie's compliance for granted. A shadow was in her dark eyes. The lively, lovely young face was suddenly sombre as if she had been asked too much to accept at once. She gulped and asked, almost inaudibly, 'Isn't it perhaps a bit too soon, François, for us to promise that?'

'No! It's never too soon,' François went on, still in a rough process of admonishing himself by heaping admonishment on Nonnie. 'If you could have asked 'Bamuthi and Mopani, they would have told you at once that it's a bad, bad thing – perhaps the worst thing in life, to go on looking back on misery and destruction in the past. You should hear Mopani on the subject, expanding on what happened to Lot's wife as an example. And I wish you could have heard 'Bamuthi tell you his endless stories of beautiful young Matabele girls and splendid warriors who were overpowered by supernatural forces because they didn't heed the warning not to look back.'

Nonnie thought that she knew what he meant. Yet it sounded all too wilful and heartless at such a moment to be true. She knew that François was far from a heartless person. So perhaps all this was just a sign of the hurt and tragedy speaking in him, to impress him with the need to move on into a part of himself where they did not exist.

Accordingly she touched him for a moment with her hand, to say in a low voice, without daring to look into his eyes, 'Whatever I may feel, I can promise you one thing. I may not be able to forget all at once but I can promise you my eyes will never, never look back again. There!'

Her tone was forced out of her lighter self and she whisked about as if to start obediently down the dune in order to move away and on, but François stopped her.

Filled with gratitude he pleaded, 'Not so fast, Nonnie, just hold on a moment! It may help to look at what's in front of us.'

Nonnie obediently looked and had her first close and comprehensive view of the desert. Despite her first liberating sunset intimation of it from Lamb-snatcher's Hill, she was totally unprepared for such a view and her eyes, though full, clear and steady, were strangely unbelieving. She of course had never seen anything comparable and neither indeed had François, until the morning before when he had come to that place with Xhabbo, and neither of them had any words ready for what it did to them. Silent, they surveyed the immense wasteland unfolding to the south, to the west and to the north of them in one great heaving expanse of land, like a sea caught in some equinoctial tidal pull.

It was more open and wide than any country François had ever seen. But most exciting of all was the fact that it did not look like a desert at all, because the fertile sand was covered with grass, bush, brush and enormous spreading thorn and acacia trees. The wide troughs in between the swell of great dunes were vast level stretches that Nonnie could only think of as natural parkland with great trees, so high, wide, handsome and well-spaced were they. And what was more, in that light, since the rains over the desert showed no 'sign of breaking the grass was bleached, and the bushes and trees shone and the sand in between looked so satiny and of so pale a yellow that basically it was platinum blond. By contrast it made the shrill green of the broom bushes, the dark witch-holly of the ipi-hamba thorn, the tall, spreading giraffe acacia and storm trees sparkle and shine like the olives and ilexes of some privileged classical scene. Never before had either Nonnie or François believed that the sky could accomplish so high, wide and flawless a dome with the proportion of earth so reduced and that of the blue so increased, as the one imposed on the firm horizon in front of them.

Yet it was not just desert, however fertile, nourishing grass, bush and trees to express some unique green thought of their own in their own green shade. It was also dedicated to other equally revered forms of life, for a great choir of birds was singing close by them and other birds taking up the song below their dune to be joined by greater and rarer voices far away. Not even in the earliest days at Hunter's Drift before the birds had changed their tune, had François heard such singing just for singing's sake, nor seen trees and grass and bushes so single with purpose just for being's sake. And wherever he looked great birds rose effortlessly on the wing and the flashes of feathers of many colours made fire out of the shadows between one bush, one tree and one spread of grass and another. At the heart of the glittering bird song he distinctly heard the impassioned outpouring of giant bustards to their mates while scarlet bee-eaters, peacock blue Abyssinian rollers, golden aurioles and lacquered starlings, drew a swift Tartar pattern of the music in their flights. Every now and then some male ostrich from the base of his long throat boomed a patriarchal note of blessing and in the rare intervals of silence in the overall community singing came the call of the dove especial to the desert: small, neat, precise in figure, and immaculate in a dress of mauve and purple with a buff cravat held in a jade-black ring to a delicate throat, a throat always on fire with a phrase that Xhabbo and his people called 'po-por-ri'. Indeed it had made them name the bird itself the 'Po-por-ri' bird and they valued it precisely because this phrase, round as a magic circle, was believed to be the call that their beloved mystical eland (of whom François had no doubt there were vast herds concealed in the dunes beyond), once had followed to a store of honey without end. So the Bushmen who came after in the clicking electric footsteps of the great antelope, were enabled to commune with bird and beast in the transubstantiation of the honey into the sweetness of wisdom itself. But above all the view was unpolluted; not just free of the unnatural smog human beings inflict on the earth they inhabit, but in the more subtle and profound sense that it had never even suffered the intrusion of sophisticated minds and civilized eyes, acute and slanted with calculation of how to exploit it for their own uses. Indeed, it was so uncontaminated by anything that was unnatural, was so much an expression of creation for creation's sake, that spread out as it was in the elegiac early morning with a light that fell upon it like the tongues of fire wherein the authentic spirit of creation had first come to comfort a small group of bereaved and frightened people in a moment of great darkness in Palestine. There was something sacred about it. Both François and Nonnie became so full of awe that they shrank from troubling it with the sound of their own voices.

François perhaps was more fortunate than Nonnie because he had an example to help him contain the impact the view made on him. He remembered Mopani repeatedly telling him that perhaps the greatest experience of his life had been the privilege of setting eyes on country which no other European or African had ever seen, and for which he himself had not been prepared mentally in any way whatsoever by his upbringing. The new land, therefore, could present itself purely as itself to him. When that happens, Mopani stressed, one is amazed how one's inner self responds, as if it too until that moment had been some unknown and undiscovered country, and for the first time had a mirror in which it can both see its reflection and recognize the love and infinite care of detail with which both oneself and one's mirror have been made. It was, Mopani would say, almost as if coming to country uncontaminated by the mind and will of other men, one is not just exhilarated by seeing something new, but feels for the first time what it could mean to be oneself, how much of a child of life in one's own right one is; how much a ward in a great all-embracing chancery with a rich and lawful inheritance of one's own spread out before one.

Nonnie had no such guide and was made to feel singularly small and powerless in the face of it all, as one does alone on the wide veld with a great thunderstorm bearing down on one. More, she had an added complication that was more devastating because although her eyes could take in the beauty, the delicacy and the sanctity of the scene, it was almost as if her reaction stopped short there and refused to let these things enter her heart and there become transformed into feelings. For the first time in her life she could see and register beauty with her mind and yet not feel it. And since it was the first time she was without any standards of comparison, she could not suspect that her feelings, still too wounded and withdrawn to turn to the world without, might be the cause. All she had of creative feeling, was needed to nurse the stricken aspects within. This suspended dislocation of heart and mind became almost more than she could bear, and somehow she had to put a limit to it all as best she could. She asked François urgently, 'Surely all this comes to an end somewhere and can't go on for as long as it looks from here?'

She was amazed to hear François answer her frankly in terms of fear.

'I'm afraid, Nonnie—' he was suddenly his solemn self again – 'it goes on like this from here for some fifteen hundred to two thousand miles where it ends in the sea.'

Resenting an ignorance which made her feel reprehensibly naïve with astonishment, she exclaimed, 'Dear God, how do we ever get out of it then? And if we do, how long will it take?'

François, whose fear had not been the fear of distance or the hazards that might lie ahead, so much as fear of how Nonnie would react when she realized how far they were then from the outside world and help, hastened to say: 'Xhabbo and Nuin-Tara will get us out of here all right!'

He said this confidently enough, though he withheld the one reservation that all depended on their not running into the enemy where the desert impinged on a vast green swamp, the rivers that made it and the fertile African settlements of the Portuguese colony to their north and the newly emancipated British African states to the south-west. He added as casually as he could, 'It all depends on how we get on for food and water, and how fast we go, but I dare say a year or fourteen months ought to see us out of it.'

Seeing the look of profound agitation on Nonnie's face he tried to make light of it all, quickly adding, 'Just long enough for you to learn Bushman and become a good honorary Bushman woman yourself.'

What would François have turned to say had he known the real cause of Nonnie's agitation? He might have been inclined to think her flippant and not adequately prepared in her mind for so strenuous a journey. Luckily she was determined that he should have no inkling of the cause of her dismay. But had he been more experienced, he would have had a suspicion from the quick, searching, panicky way in which she looked herself up and down and took in every detail of how stained with sweat, dust and even mud her own slacks and matching bush-shirt had become. The clothes she had so carefully chosen for what was to be her first joyful excursion with François into the bush on her return, had been tailor-made for the occasion and, road-worthy as they were, had been a tribute to the Paris fashion-house that had designed them.

Having taken in all this detail and signs of early wear and tear, the terrible thought which came to her can be summed up in an inward exclamation, 'A year or fourteen months – heavens, what am I to wear?'

Flippant as this may have sounded aloud, it is perhaps regrettable that Nonnie did not give François the chance of seeing that this remark would not have been possible were it not for her trust in him, Xhabbo and Nuin-Tara. It could have proved to him how neither the distance before them nor time was bothering Nonnie, but that it was a consequence of having come through their ordeal with her fastidious self intact, and concerned to be at her best in the days to come.

Nonnie came out of this concern as fast as she had gone into it. François was still standing before her, his dismay over her moment of agitation plain on his face. Determined as ever not to let him know the cause of it but nonetheless somewhat remorseful for having perturbed him, she felt compelled to take the initiative.

'You know, François, there was a Chinese Mopani once,' she said, her eyes sparkling with mischief, 'who says that the journey of a thousand miles begins with a single step. Now, who's going to take the first step of this monstrous journey, you or I?'

François, less sure than ever what to make of it, was still thinking up an appropriate answer when Nonnie said, 'I see, ladies first as usual,' and without waiting for him started fast down the hill and so was the first to be welcomed by Hintza.

From there they started at once on the firm bed of what must once have been one of the greatest rivers of Africa – a river which no doubt had made a great lake of the immense pan behind them. On either side of them dunes rose some two to three hundred feet in height and yet the bed of the stream was so wide that they had no sense of being shut in so much as following a broad corridor leading to the freedom of that frank and full confession of space and earth they had seen from above. This feeling of being guided by the earth itself was heightened by the behaviour of Xhabbo and Nuin-Tara. The farther they travelled along the dry river-bed, the more cheerful the two of them became, as if this were not the forbidding lost world, the extention of the Kwa'mamengalahlwa that European and Bantu senses had warned François to expect, but a well-beloved drive of some stately home in the country and they a pair of dispossessed proprietors returning for good from exile to reclaim their unfairly sequestrated possessions.

More and more they would stop and point out familiar bushes and trees and landmarks to each other and at one place threw themselves on an outcrop of smooth stone, patted it with their hands, pressed their cheeks against it, fondled it as if it were some beloved living thing and flesh and blood and stone joined in an act of reconciliation. Nonnie was amazed to see for the first time tears bright as beads on Nuin-Tara's apricot cheeks and finally abolished all her reservations about the capacity for composure of Xhabbo's 'utterly woman' which had seemed so great at times as to make her suspect it of being inhuman. Clearly all these things were honoured in their imagination not only because they had been experienced before but were also dignified in stories, legends and myths that coloured any event of their unobserved desert lives.

At one point, Xhabbo stopped and showed them what was clearly a partially filled-in hole. There he told them when he was a little boy they had dug up the greatest tuber recorded in Bushman history – a tuber so great that it had kept them in food and water for four whole days; a tuber so magical that all the Bushmen of his own age who had witnessed it were known throughout the Bushman land as the men of the tuber. His eyes shone and his whole manner was lively and excited and he seemed as if he could not stretch his arms wide enough to indicate the size of the miraculous plant and even his quick and adroit tongue not nimble enough to convey the sharp click of the lash of wonder the event still inflicted on his eager imagination. Though neither Nonnie nor François could have made a concept out of their reactions, there was a profound reappraisal of values implicit for them both in this, considering that the discovery of a new plant was chosen from all other candidates to set its seal upon a whole generation of Xhabbo's people. Whereas in Nonnie's Europe, and even the African world of François's childhood, some man-made melodrama or horrific event would have been preferred as milestones on their road through time.

This was the first of many examples that made Nonnie realize how the vast wasteland she had allowed into her mind from the top of the dune that morning, was home to them, and however much one plant, dune and bush tended to look like all the others to her, they were all different and individual and that each difference was acknowledged and honoured, even sanctified, in the spirit of Xhabbo and Nuin-Tara, so that an extraordinary atmosphere of all-belonging enfolded them. François himself, better prepared than Nonnie in this regard, nonetheless was more impressed than he could have imagined possible by the feeling Xhabbo gave him that not only had he and Nuin-Tara this specific relationship with the country into which they were moving but also that in some very strange way, the country down to the smallest of its multitudinous detail appeared to reciprocate it.

The excitement of this feeling rose rapidly. He was being evoked in the completely new way Mopani had so often described to him. That he was not being fanciful or in any way deluding himself seemed confirmed by Hintza's behaviour. Hintza looked more like Hintza than he had ever done, growing in stature by the mile until he was, incredible as it might appear, more of a natural dog than he had ever been before. At times François smiled to himself at the proprietory airs Hintza gave himself and the proud, assertive way he scouted around them as if he had known and experienced it all before.

As for Nonnie, everything in the world of François's bush had in any case started out by being so different and remote from her sophisticated upbringing that this part of the journey at first tended to be only an extension of the newness of Africa for her. But as the tiredness and the memory of tragedy, danger and fear were suspended, she too became increasingly aware of differences within the difference. Somehow something hitherto unsuspected within herself was beginning to emerge and become drawn into harmony with the new world about her.

This other dimension was enlarged and enriched by the fact that she was fast learning a new language as well. François had already been amazed by the ease with which she had picked up Bushman words and how accurately her tongue managed the difficult clicking consonants – an achievement that would have been remarkable at any time, but was all the more so when one considers the terrible circumstances in which she had had her first lessons. Almost from the start of their new march towards the interior along the way of Xhabbo's wind, nothing new was allowed to pass without her insisting on being told the Bushman words for it and then marching on, muttering to herself again and again the new words and phrases like an aspiring actress learning her lines for her first main role in a great new play.

But all these and many other more subtle, and almost inexpressible nuances of meaning associated with these changes found a natural voice to speak for them at their camp that night. Although it had not been a hurried march, it was a long march and they travelled far. Xhabbo's thoroughness insisted that they take the precaution of increasing the distance between themselves and their enemies as much as possible, however unnecessary he himself believed it to be. Because the wind of the evening was cooler than any they had yet encountered, Xhabbo and Nuin-Tara allowed them a bigger fire than usual and after eating, they gathered beside it relaxed, leaning on their haversacks and talking quietly over the day between them, urging Nonnie, who was drowsy with healthy fatigue and warmth, to take part in her newly acquired Bushman. Nuin-Tara and Xhabbo at times clapped their hands and laughed loudly with delight over her efforts and in such a way that even her mistakes in pronunciation and at times kindergarten phrases were elevated into great achievements.

Hintza, free from pain and for once unsedated, had managed to stretch himself out flat on his tummy in his favourite conversational attitude between François and Nonnie. At one minute he was shutting his eyes ecstatically over the warmth and comfort that was flowing over him from the fire and the company. The next he would be looking out of his left eye at Nonnie but with the right as firmly shut because he had a great sense of economy of effort on these occasions, and never believed in using two eyes when one was enough. Then suddenly he would be shutting the left eye and looking up out of the right at François before closing both. He did not look at Nuin-Tara and Xhabbo across the flames opposite him. It was not necessary. His nose kept him close enough in touch with their being and was wrinkling finely and re-wrinkling delicately with his own select enjoyment of their savour, as if his nose were a vessel of sheer joy, full and overflowing. And he would then lick his lips with satisfaction, as if to say, 'Now only a fool of a mongrel could think a dog could be better situated . . .'

This would be followed by a sigh of the deepest philosophic

satisfaction. Hearing it, Nonnie could not resist stroking him fondly behind the head, though lightly so that it should not irritate, while saying to François, 'You know, it's most extraordinary. But I do honestly believe Hin is perfectly aware of the fact that Nuin-Tara and I are women and you and Xhabbo just men.'

François was almost insulted that anything so elementary could for the most fleeting of moments have even been thought of as something beyond Hintza's capacity for discrimination.

Nonnie in her quick way, however, anticipated what the response was about to be and was at once tempted into a provocative vein, 'You see, I don't think it's just a fantasy on my part, but he treats me and Nuin-Tara quite differently. He shows us, if I may say so without being thought vain, more respect than he shows you and Xhabbo. There's really something quite courtly, almost knightly, in his attitude to us – an example which I think you and your beloved Xhabbo might well study to your advantage.'

It is uncertain whether François would have realized that Nonnie was deliberately baiting him into a response that would enable her to confuse him all the more, so that she could have the ultimate joy of delivering him from discomforture at its highest. He himself had no time to think of a reply. Nonnie had hardly finished and the light of new mischief barely arrived on her face and in the upward sideways glance she gave him, when the lion roared.

François had heard countless lions roar at Hunter's Drift and in the deepest bush on his journeys with Mopani, but he had never heard a roar like this. It was not that the lion was unusually near that made the sound unique. It was the quality of the roar and François, who thought that he was rather an expert on the voices of lions, recognized at once that it was the most immediate of all roars he had ever heard. Between the impulse to roar and the roar itself there was no interval at all; impulse and achievement were one as they were one with indifference to its consequences. As a result it came out of the silence like lightning sheer, uncompromising and uninhibited. Even the flames of their own precise camp fire, trembled with the reverberation of the sound and as it finally cut the silence in two, curtsied low to the ground before so royal a sound.

For the first time François experienced the truth of something Mopani had always stressed to him. Even at Hunter's Drift the lions no longer roared as they roared in Mopani's youth. It was as if they were becoming dispirited by the propinquity of unnatural men and the threat they were to their surroundings and their security. Almost as if the ruthless destruction of their kind accelerated by the arrival of white and black in Africa had entered their electric apprehensions and dimmed the great fire life had originally lit in them. Neither 'Chaliapin' nor 'Caruso', nor even Boris Cristoff, the greatest of a new generation of roarers or any other member of the choir of the hereditary order of heraldic lions appointed to his home, equalled the fullness, the purity, the power and the speed of this desert voice. It sounded as the voice of the first lion must have sounded as it walked still warm from the magnetic fingers that had just fashioned it through the first night in the garden at the beginning.

François responded in every nerve, cell and tissue of himself as if to a charge of electricity, and the hair on his head felt as if it were standing on end. Again and again the lion roared, and so gave him just time enough to adjust to his dazzled senses and look at his companions.

Nonnie of course came first, not just because he was concerned that she might have been frightened. She thrilled him by showing no sign of fear. She was sitting with her hands clasped tightly in her lap, her lips apart and her eyes bigger and wider than normal, so it seemed to him, full of wonder and amazement over the lightning and thunder of the sound. Hintza, characteristically, the moment the first lightning flash of sound struck the camp, was at once on his feet, his tail stretched out taut behind him, his nose aligned on the sound, every hair on his back erect and sparkling in the firelight. His lips were drawn back not entirely, as Nonnie thought out of eagerness to protect them from any menace.

But most remarkable of all was the reaction of Nuin-Tara and Xhabbo. The two jumped to their feet, laughing and almost crying with delight. They joined hands and did a gay little dance on their side of the fire, crying, 'It is he, oh yes, yes, yes! It is he feeling himself to be utterly a lion again, calling to us in the voice of a lion! It is he, it is he!'

'And who is he?' François could not help demanding. But they were far too involved doing their dance of delight either to hear or bother with questions. But when the lion's last roar died away they waited breathless, wondering whether such beauty could ever again be restored to the darkness of night. The silence, from which all the other small, multitudinous, delicate and sensitive voices that can only venture to raise their tribute to their own small share of creation under cover of darkness, had vanished. Nonnie found her tongue and exclaimed, 'Oh François, do look at Hin! Don't you think you'd better hold him back because he might go after that lion at any minute. He looks beside himself with rage and typical male aggression.'

She was amazed to hear François say, 'Oh, he's not angry, he's just full of envy.'

François would have left it at that, but his reply was so unexpected and sounded so strong that Nonnie's curiosity was at once in full cry for more. He had there and then to describe in minute detail Hintza's complex about lions. Only when he had done did she take Hintza into her arms, fondling him and saying, 'There, beloved Hin, there. I wouldn't like you any different, not in one hair, tooth, dribble, nail or even snore of yourself. You're perfect as you are!'

Only then was François free to question Nuin-Tara and Xhabbo, who had resumed their places on the ground by the fire still laughing and exchanging delighted thoughts between them.

For Nonnie, educated in the belief that lions were the most dangerous animals in Africa, François's attitude, Hintza's behaviour and now Nuin-Tara and Xhabbo celebrating the lion's roar as the happiest of events, was so revolutionary a manifestation that she waited impatiently for the explanation François extracted from Xhabbo.

'They know him well,' François was able to tell her, after much too long a time for her liking. 'They call him "Old Black Lightning" because he's not only lightning in voice but also in temperament and behaviour. Black because they say he has a long thick mane of midnight hair, hanging low over a coat of sunlight. And he's not really a lion at all, they say, but a great magician who likes to hunt in the shape of a lion, and he is very friendly to all Bushmen. They say he raises his voice in this way so that far and wide Bushmen can know precisely where there's game in plenty for them to hunt and eat. Tomorrow, they say, we'll see how true the voice is, and find masses of game to give us the food we badly need now, because as you know our supplies are nearly all used up.'

Nonnie could accept all that, except believe that the lion was really a magician. However, she still was not satisfied that she knew enough about François's reaction, insisting, 'But you, François, you have a something of your own about that lion. You should have seen the look on your face! It frightened me far more than the lion, because you looked, I promise you, almost as if you'd just heard the voice of the good God in Heaven Himself.'

François, although he ignored the deliberate exaggeration, took her question seriously and answered it with complete spontaneity, so deeply resolved was his deliberate self after the sound, and the almost unbelievable nostalgia for the unblurred and abundant beginning of life to which the voice of the lion had just testified and from which the dim and blurred present excluded them.

'You see, Nonnie, it's just that for me the roar of the lion is one of the most beautiful things on earth. It is the most miraculous of sounds and I promise you that the lion we've just heard has the greatest and most beautiful voice of any I have ever heard. I don't know ...' he paused as his imagination fumbled after a meaning almost too swift and adroit to grasp, and added as if aware of the innate feebleness of his words, 'I don't know, but it was rather as if Old Black Lightning was speaking for all the lions that have ever been and reminding us of something we've lost. But it's not only I who have this thing about lions. 'Bamuthi would have told you the same; and so would Mopani. Mopani says that the four most beautiful things in life are thunder, lightning, a falling star and the roar of a lion.'

'But poor old Hin,' Nonnie exclaimed, seeing Hintza beside her no longer angry with envy but looking singularly abject and deprived, as if he were profoundly dissatisfied with himself, 'Look at him. What can we do to rid him of that horrid complex for good?'

'If I had been at Hunter's Drift,' François told her, 'I would have played him some of his favourite music. It's the only thing that helps him somehow on these occasions.'

'D'you think it would help if perhaps I sang to him?' Nonnie asked.

'What a marvellous idea!' François exclaimed joyfully.

Almost at once Nonnie began singing to Hintza in a soft, round and surprisingly clear and confident voice. François had never heard her sing before or even knew that she could. He was as entranced as Hintza was, by the natural uncontrived quality of her singing. He realized at once that she was singing in Portuguese and felt disappointed that he could not follow the words as he followed the music. But the effect on Hintza was magical. He sighed his great sigh of contentment; shut his eyes, and only his beautiful pointed ears erect in the firelight showed how carefully he was listening.

The tune that Nonnie sang, beautiful as it was, was perhaps also too charged with its own form of nostalgia for such a moment. It certainly became evident after a while that even Nonnie was being drawn by it into a remembrance of things past that were dangerous for her self-possession. The moment Hintza appeared thoroughly soothed, she stopped singing. Her hand on Hintza's head, she sat there looking into the fire as if she were seeing and hearing things far beyond it.

She started when François, whose instinct urged an immediate return to their here and now, asked, 'What was that you sang? And you do sing beautifully, Nonnie. You must please do it more often for us. Just look how happy you've made old Hin!'

'Oh, it was just a fado.'

'A fado? What on earth is that?' he asked, instantly in love with the sound of the word.

'It's Portuguese for a song of fate.' Her tone was final as the answer was brief.

'But what were the words, Nonnie? Could you translate them for us, please?' François begged.

'If you don't mind, François,' Nonnie pleaded, obviously hating to refuse so obvious and simple a request for reasons of her own, that she was anxious not to disclose, 'I'll gladly do it some other time. But I'm very tired tonight. I wonder if you'd mind if we went to bed now. Look, Nuin-Tara and Xhabbo are already settling down. I don't think they thought much of my singing.'

But how wrong Nonnie's last remark had been was proved first thing the next morning. As they prepared for the journey just before sunrise, and Xhabbo and Nuin-Tara scattered the ashes of their fire and obliterated the marks of their camp so that it was almost impossible to tell that any human being had ever rested there, Xhabbo passed his left hand over the place and pronounced something in the tone of a priest uttering a blessing. In the midst of all the other sounds Nonnie heard her own name, and so promptly asked François what Xhabbo had been saying.

To her amazement he answered, 'He is giving a name to our camp and he is calling it, "The place where Nonnie sang to the Lion".'

Nonnie blushed with embarrassed pleasure, and asked quickly, 'Do they always give names to the places where they camp?'

François nodded. 'Yes, always,' and seeing the 'Why?' already forming on her lips, explained, quoting Xhabbo, that they did it 'so that the place should know that they were feeling how the place had given itself to them and how they in turn were giving something of themselves to the place, on account of it,' so that, quoting Xhabbo again, 'the place can always feel that although they themselves have gone, they have left feeling that something utterly of themselves would always be there feeling itself part of it.'

CHAPTER TWELVE

Below the Horizon

The march that followed turned out to be the shortest ever.
Soon after sunrise, before the heat could distort the view and
deprive an unstained morning of its freshness, they rounded one
of those slow curves in the dry river-bed to see Xhabbo halted
and Hintza elongated and stretched immediately behind him,
trembling with excitement. François, Nonnie and Nuin-Tara
joined Xhabbo who, with one finger to his lips and his other
hand pointing to show how truly Old Black Lightning had
spoken the night before, out of his sense of abundance that was
life at the undimmed beginning, but also of abundance in the
desert here and now. The wide river-bed, the heavy swell of the
dunes at the sides and the whole scene on to another far bend
smoking with morning blue, all was aflicker and aflame with the
greatest congregation of springbok François had ever seen.
The nearest of the elegant smouldering geodetic shapes was
barely forty strides away, and they had all stopped grazing and
lifted their fine drawn heads to look at the newcomers.

The light was so clear, their pose so near that Nonnie could
see their long, dark lashes shading great dark brown eyes, full of
the pooled reflection of the morning. And those eyes, far from
being alarmed, were looking them up and down out of natural
curiosity as if wondering, 'What are these shapes and these
smells we have not met before?' And after staring at them,
innocent and totally unafraid, they gave an almost perceptible
shrug of their aristocratic shoulders, indicating that they accepted the enigma of the newcomers as a natural part of the
mystery that life was in a desert out of which something new
was forever coming, and so impossible for antelope senses to
define or to be allowed to interfere with the enjoyment of the
lovely pasture spread out before them with its dressing of dew.
One by one they lowered their heads and went on breaking their

297

fast so ardently that the sound of munching was loud on the air and made Hintza lick his lips.

But occasionally some of the males would suddenly bound straight up into the air without warning from where they stood, high above the massed assembly. And as they bounded, thousands of heads would be raised to watch how high they could arch in the blue and justify the presumption of interrupting their meal. Some of the performers achieved greater heights than others but there was none among them who was not distinguished and did not circumscribe movements more beautiful than any in the several ballets Nonnie had seen. Most impressive of all, not a male arrived at the summit of his bound without arching his back like a bow strung for an arrow aimed at the sun, and there unfolded the gleaming gold of hair along the curve of his spine and let it fall down along its flanks like Brussels lace, exposing the white underneath flashing in the sun.

In the process of unfolding the lace, he would do a quick double *entrechat* with his legs so that the black pointed patent-leather hooves glanced like mirrors before he regained the earth with sprung ankles and quick elastic hooves and at once would rebound forward and up again, repeating its performance, so rapidly and so often that the pattern of movement was a ricochet of arches skimming a still water-surface of grass. Each time this happened all the teenagers among the gypsy women, and some of the mothers, grandmothers and even great-grandmothers were so provoked by the bold eurhythmic virtuosity of their men, that admiration resounded from far down in their throats and sent their breath whistling through wide dilated nostrils in a manner Nonnie thought more uplifting than any *olé* or *bravo* she had ever heard.

It was extraordinary how much more shy, almost apprehensively feminine, the vast herd of ewes appeared after each such performance, and how demurely mothers and virgin daughters resumed their grazing, with their tails more firmly drawn than ever into their foam-white thighs.

It was all that Nonnie could do not to cry out, 'Oh no, no! You can't! You just can't possibly do it to them!' when she saw that Xhabbo was making signs at François, that now was his moment to shoot. Unbelieving, she watched François unsling

298

his rifle and kneel down to take aim. She looked at Nuin-Tara for support in the protest clamouring for demonstration. But Nuin-Tara, like Xhabbo, was looking steadily, with an expression that seemed to Nonnie inhumanly detached at François, as if only interested in divining what he was aiming at.

Suddenly she felt deeply and unreasonably resentful of François. There was no room for thought in her feelings. And she had no idea how reluctantly he was accepting this charge of killing which their need to keep alive had put upon him. She could not tell that although he had done shooting of this kind for so many years, he had never become reconciled to it and always felt as if his past experience were not of the slightest use to him, and he was doing his killing for the first time again. Yet as always, he made the only concession possible to his reluctance to shoot by selecting the oldest buck in view. When he had him firmly lined in the sights of his gun, a prayer at heart that his aim would be true and his target feel no pain, he shot it as it stood, an Etruscan image of flame beside an outcrop of salt some two hundred yards away. His shot took it just behind the glowing shoulder, and François was full of relief to see it fall to the ground without a struggle.

Even so, Nonnie remained standing where she was, her eyes blurred with tears of hurt and anger, her whole being crying out, 'Oh, how *could* you, François? How could you of all people? As if we have not all had enough wounding and killing and death already!'

Even the whole fresh feeling of a newly born desert morning, trembling with the uprush of life and light out of the shadow of night, rushed in to aid and abet her darkening spirit of reproach. She stood there irresolute watching, and might have remained there until François and Nuin-Tara had finished skinning and cutting up the buck had it not been for a slight incident.

Nuin-Tara turned about and, amazed to see Nonnie still and inert, without apparent intention of joining in their work, raised her hand to beckon her imperiously forward. At once François, his hands red with blood, caught Nuin-Tara's arm and said something to her. Nuin-Tara obediently turned about and knelt down to help the two men. Nonnie somehow knew then that François was aware of what she was experiencing and anxious to spare her feelings. That knowledge instantly relieved her of resentment though it did not deprive her of her reluctance to be a witness of what still felt like murder to her, and death to the beauty and innocence of a morning full of faith and hope of life. But divided as she became thereby, she was able to will herself forward and resolve not to be out-done by Nuin-Tara. Happily, by the time she joined them, the buck was no longer recognizable as one but skinned and half cut up. Yet she just could not speak to any of the three of them.

For once she even spurned the attentions of Hintza, who was trying to make her appreciate what a great deed François had just accomplished on their behalf. Finally, one long look in Nuin-Tara's eyes shamed her into a different self. Nuin-Tara had never regarded her so sternly, and without speaking, just beckoned Nonnie with impatience to join and help them piling the warm pieces of cut-up flesh on to the skin. That done, each of the four took a corner of the skin and so together carried it with its load for half a mile into the shade of a wild fig tree where Xhabbo announced they would camp for the day. If Nonnie thought she would have had any respite there from the distasteful task of handling the raw meat she was soon proved wrong. For immediately François began cutting up the meat into long, slender strips while Xhabbo went running back to the place where the buck had been shot. Soon he returned with a satchel full of yellowish brown grains gathered from a natural outcrop of salt Nonnie was to be told the Bushmen called a salt-lick.

Muttering the Bushman sound aloud to herself, she forced herself to help Nuin-Tara rub rough salt into the strips of meat and then hang them up, slung over the lower branches of the trees, to dry out in their shade. And slowly in the course of working with the others, her sense of the necessities of their situation re-emerged to reconcile her gradually to the killing. The process of reconciliation was made easier when she observed how after the first reaction not of alarm so much as of astonishment at the unusual sound of a gun-shot, the immense congregation of buck without exception calmly resumed their grazing as before. If they could accept and overlook the death of one of the greatest of their number, Nonnie felt she had no right or cause to set herself apart and sit as a prim judge in a court of law of her own, condemning the occasion.

One mentions this incident in some detail not only because of its unique impact on Nonnie but also because it has to serve as an example of a great long series of other similar occasions when Xhabbo and François had to kill all sorts and conditions of animals and birds for their food. Moreover, with this introduction behind her, Nonnie managed with Nuin-Tara first as a stern and then encouraging teacher beside her, fully to adapt herself to a new role and become an ungrudging and fully committed working partner of their dedicated little company.

A sign that this had not passed unobserved came that very evening. They were resting in the camp, waiting for their new supply of food to dry out, so as to become emergency rations for the next stage of their journey. At sundown Xhabbo came to her and presented her with a digging stick of ironwood which he had been making in secret all afternoon. When François announced that it was the Bushman equivalent of a diploma that she had graduated from the university of Bushman womanhood, Nonnie's eyes shone with tears of release. From then on she carried the stick with her always, with a pride no soldier risen from the ranks carrying a Field-Marshal's baton could have equalled. This camp, the next day, was blessed accordingly with the name, 'The Place of Nonnie's Digging Stick'.

From that morning on she would follow Nuin-Tara every day, armed with her own digging-stick, for lessons in collecting edible bulbs and tubers from the earth. Nonnie was amazed by the vast varieties of the desert potatoes, turnips, artichokes, parsnips, onions and truffles that came out of the ground. Also, at the foot of dunes and sheltered levels, there were the melons and cucumbers protected by sharp spikes, looking like vegetable hedgehogs; wild little triangular figs, raisin berries, dried plums and nuts. The melons and cucumbers François and Xhabbo greeted joyfully, explaining that they were one of the desert's greatest delicacies, the rare eland cucumber. When she looked unbelieving at François he took his knife, skinned one of the fruit carefully and held it up to her nose and she found it

301

smelt more like a cucumber than any she had ever savoured anywhere else. The result was that they would often dine by their fire at night on fresh liver, kidneys and whole ribs of venison grilled on wooden coals with fragrant desert herbs heaped over them, accompanied by a desert *macédoine* of vegetables and fresh cucumber salad as well.

Sooner than she would have thought possible this role of helping in the cutting up of the meat François and Xhabbo brought home for them, curing and drying it for the journey onwards, the search for tubers and bulbs to supplement their diet, became a routine of Nonnie's life to which she looked forward eagerly every day. She found that somehow she was busier than she had ever been in her life before. One of the things that had appalled her in her first view of the desert from the top of the dune was its apparent emptiness and a threat implicit that the hours and the days and nights ahead would be as empty and to be consumed only in a relentless physical effort and recovery from effort, so that she could travel on into something more and more vacant. But now her days were full and overflowing with work, new and made meaningful in a way women understood better than men, by the fact that it was devoted to finding food for survival. It was as if she were acquiring a new art of reading by letting Nuin-Tara teach her how a mere twist and curl of a tiny leaf above the sand was a sign that there was a great bulb concealed in the earth underneath. She learned from Nuin-Tara to read the sounds birds make when game was near and when not; what insect glitter or spatter of song betrayed the presence of water hidden in the sand, and how there was not an animal, bird, insect, tree or plant that was not part of a vocabulary of a meaningful prose, inscribed, as on a great and ancient hieroglyphic parchment, recording the essential story of life in the desert.

Even when the day appeared to her done and she was ready to camp down, help with cooking their dinner and then hasten to bed, she found that her duties were far from ended. For instance, François insisted that while the light of the day was good they would not relax until they had repaired the damage done by the day to their clothes. He produced from one of his haversacks a couple of military 'housewives' and he and Nonnie would sit side by side mending the tears in their clothing. This of course in itself was no great labour. But before her physical self adjusted itself to being on the march and at work from dawn to sunset every day, it was almost more than she could manage. But once she was adjusted, she began to look forward to this domestic end to their constantly recurring nomadic days, as a moment of total and blessed reunion of their full company, perfect for recreation and conversation. But before long even this hour was threatened with fatigue from a new cause.

François all along had been far more concerned about their clothes than even Nonnie had been, though a different way. First of all he was convinced that not only his own ankle boots but Nonnie's would not last much longer on so long and harsh a march. So on the first day the river-bed suddenly curved away towards the south, where Xhabbo announced it wriggled on to a part of the desert where there was a route used by men who could be their enemies, they climbed out of it on to the dunes. As they felt the wind on their faces, showing the direction on which they had to go through grass, brush, parkland and the deep, though now almost scarlet sand of the desert itself, François made Nonnie take off her shoes and socks as he did his own.

He explained that the sooner they got used to walking barefoot in the smooth desert sand the better, because they had to preserve boots and socks for the rougher country which they would encounter in a few months' time. He made them do this at first only for a couple of hours in the cool of the morning and the cool of the evening because the desert sands in between were too hot and rough for their comfort. But gradually they were able to increase the hours until finally there came a day when sewing by the camp fire Nonnie had an extraordinary feeling of accomplishment which she could not explain to herself. She became unusually silent with the effort of tracing its cause. Suddenly it came to her. She dropped a stitch, threw down her mending, jumped up and did a little step or two, imitating Nuin-Tara's trip of joy and gratitude.

Coming to stand in front of François, who was gaping at her in astonishment, she exclaimed, 'But don't you realize it, François? Look at you sitting there with your obsequious Hin

303

by your side as if nothing had happened! Don't you realize that for the first time in my life, perhaps even in yours, you blasé old Huguenot, we've gone barefoot all day long?'

François felt rebuked and despondent because he had been insensitive enough to overlook it, and not realize truly what an accomplishment it was for Nonnie. Significantly enough, Xhabbo had known at once what Nonnie's dance portended and spoke to her in simple Bushman words that she could now well understand. Soon, he hoped to give her not only Bushman shoes for herself but also for François and Nuin-Tara and himself as well, because already he had a tapping that hartebeest were near; the antelope that was Mantis's second favourite and whose skin he wore as a cloak and used to make shoes not only for his children to walk on through life but out of which he created the greatest love of his life – the eland. And indeed, the very next morning, almost as if in command to Xhabbo's tapping, a great magenta hartebeest presented itself alone, being obviously rejected by the young bulls from its little family group. Though still vivid with life, it stood before them condemned to exile by an inexorable law of natural succession.

So François, at Xhabbo's bidding, had less compunction in shooting it and making camp hard by the place of the killing, although the day had barely begun.

That very afternoon Xhabbo pegged out the skin and cleaned it meticulously of all wet tissue and blood so that it could dry slowly in the warm of evening. Early the next morning, since Xhabbo declared that where a hartebeest was killed they would have to live for at least three days if they were not to waste the meat and cure all of it, he borrowed Nuin-Tara's digging stick, went off into the desert and returned with an enormous white bulb which he could only just carry. The bulb was cut up into chunks like cakes of soap and Xhabbo set all four of them from then on to take turns in soaping and scrubbing the dried-out skin with their portions. In the rubbing, the acid juices that came out of the bulb made the skin change its character until by evening it was clean as a skin newly delivered to a cobbler's from a sophisticated tanner's yard. In the morning Xhabbo made them stand barefoot in turn on the skin and traced the outlines of all their feet with the point of his knife on its surface. That done, he sent Nuin-Tara off into the desert from which she soon returned with the leaves of the wild sansevera, from which they then extracted thread for sewing by the yard.

Borrowing François's needles, which Xhabbo admitted were better than the ones he could make out of the thorn he used as a rule, he set to cobbling. By the evening he had made four pairs of sandals, each sandal with a long leather thong which they passed between their big toes and tied back finely round their ankles, like the finest of sandals to be seen on the earliest Greek urns. And that was the end of their barefoot marching.

It was so suddenly and delightfully brought to an end that Nonnie could not help making fun of it, remarking, 'I really cannot see, François, how you could have inflicted all this misery of learning how to walk barefoot in these awful sands when you must have known all the time that we could have had sandals from Xhabbo for the asking. Or was this something not thought of in your philosophy, you old Bushman Horatio?'

François was far too happy over such a display of exuberance from Nonnie to bother defending himself. He just told her that sand or no sand she would never regret the hardening the soles of her feet that walking barefoot had brought to them. Besides, hadn't it been fun in such lovely sand? Hadn't it been wonderful to recover the freedom of one's own feet after years of imprisonment in boots and shoes.

François had good reason for responding so light-heartedly. Although Nonnie had maintained a plausible show of high spirits with a courage and constancy that François admired more than he could say, and although no one could have been more conscientious in doing her share of the work on so strenuous a march, he knew that she did it all not with relish but with great effort of will and out of natural sense of duty. He knew this because after all, he himself was moving through a similar valley of shadow. They were in that sense identical twins of fate and needed neither words nor thought even to know what each other was feeling. There was clearly no real and spontaneous joy in her as yet. Her moments of happiness, bright and vivid as they inevitably were in a temperament naturally so

305

urgent as hers, were isolated and not joined in a chain of continuous experience as they had been before the massacre. For many weeks now as one crowded day after the other took them deeper into the desert, he looked in her as he looked in himself in vain for signs of permanent change. By day they had too much to do to give a thought to themselves and were absorbed utterly in the necessities of the moment. But in the evenings, when there were lulls in their conversation, and they had nothing special to do, he would find her staring into the camp fire as if into a place of shadows where fire was unknown.

However, recently he thought that her breakthroughs into enjoyment had come near to enjoyment for its own sake and were more frequent and prolonged. This one, sparked off by so light a cause, seemed to him the best of all.

As a result, he hastened on in a happier tone, 'We've not only thought of sandals, Nonnie, we've other plans for you. Guess what?'

Nonnie, taken aback, stared acutely at him. 'Now come off it, François,' she exclaimed, excited, 'don't pretend that you can be at all mysterious and unpredictable to me. You're just bluffing because you feel ashamed of the way I've caught you out over the sandals.'

'Oh well, if that's the way you feel about it,' remarked François, determined to repay her in kind, 'We'll say no more about it, shall we, Hin?'

He looked down at Hintza beside him, to find Hintza did not know who to turn to next for intuition of what was to happen; Nonnie or François. Utterly bewildered, he was flashing his great purple eyes from one face to the other for suggestions like a spectator following the passage of a tennis ball flying from one champion racket to another at Wimbledon. It was not Nonnie's happy protest that made François speak, so much as this look of perplexity and frantic search for enlightenment on Hintza's features, a Hintza who he knew was terrified at times that there might be even the shadow of real differences in the pretences exchanged between François and Nonnie and he would be called upon to take sides.

'Perhaps you can't guess what it is because you don't think it's much,' he declared. 'And perhaps it would not be to a civilized person like you. But it's just that we're going to make you a dress.'

'Oh you're not François. How can you be so cruel to tease me like that?' Nonnie exclaimed, as dumbfounded as afraid to put too much hope in so intoxicating a prospect.

'Indeed we are,' François assured her. Convinced at last, she felt her face go warm all over with delight. 'Xhabbo, Nuin-Tara and I have only been waiting for a duiker to turn up. It's only because we haven't seen one yet that we haven't made your new dress before.'

And he explained himself fully to Nonnie, her eyes shining with a light that would have told anyone more experienced than François, how much more than joyful anticipation was alive in them then. They needed a duiker, he enlarged, because it had the lightest, softest and most flexible of all buck skins available in the desert, except that of the steenbuck who was too small for the purpose and even more rare in that part of the desert. It was a skin softer than that of the finest chamois. It was to other skins what silk was to man-made materials.

A long nine days later François and Xhabbo, out alone, came across a family of duikers, unusual in their grouping because they tended as a rule to go their way by day singly, a fact that convinced Xhabbo it was another sign of how they were being protected by Old Black Lightning who announced his presence to them nightly by his roaring. He was so punctual that had they had a watch, they could have set it by his calling. François was able to shoot two of the largest of the buck and in the evening came home not only with meat enough for the next fortnight but two skins of a quality that made Nuin-Tara react like a sophisticated woman who had just come across a completely new weave of wild silk in some leading fashion house in Europe.

The curing and tanning of the skins took four whole days. It was only on the fourth evening that they were able to sit by the fire, passing skins from one to the other for approval, before Xhabbo finally placed them in Nonnie's lap and told her to look and see how ready they were for her at last. She felt the skins all over, fingers trembling with excitement and unbelieving that the softness was real. She had to hold them up to her face and test the feel of them on her cheeks again and again before she accepted that such supple material could grow in so harsh an environment.

There and then she was made to stand unusually shy and tender within, by a fire heightened for the occasion, while François tried the largest skin round her waist, folded it almost double round her and saw that it reached just to her knees. He made her hold it to herself so that he could fold the other over her shoulders. It reached down to her waist. Nonnie, a little fearful that François would let Xhabbo make the skins into a replica of Nuin-Tara's clothes was astonished to hear him say, 'If you don't mind Nonnie, I'm going to make the dress myself. I had to learn to make my own boots, leather trousers and jackets and to work in leather years ago. It was part of a man's education at Hunter's Drift. I think I know exactly what to do with these skins, if you would let me.'

Nonnie for once did not know if her trust, great as it was, went quite so far as to accept François as both dress-designer and tailor. But when she looked down at him, on his knees like some *haut couturier* beside her, holding the skins against her slender body, seeing the warm, enthusiastic look in his eyes, love seemed more important than trust. She did not have it in her either to protest or tease any more.

Moved almost beyond words, she managed to say, 'Oh, would you, François, would you please, quick! How dear and wonderful of the three of you.'

At once François produced the pencil which he kept with his dispatch book. Keeping Nonnie standing there by the fire as a model, with a shapely silhouette the most select of models would have envied, he tried and retried the skins in many ways upon her, until satisfied that he could mark out the simple design he had in his mind in dark firm lines on the cream-white skins. Though she was still not without fear and anxiety, something compounded of gratitude and love too great in their sum for subtraction made her watch him closely as he spent the next two hours carefully cutting out the skins.

François longed for some magic whereby he could present all complete to Nonnie there and then, but it took him another fortnight of slow, constant stitching by firelight before he had the skin provisionally sewn to his design. Even then he had to be as patient as the patience demanded of Nonnie, who found it maddening that when the sewing appeared almost complete and she was burning to try his work on, in order to have some idea of the shape to come, François stubbornly refused. He just packed the skins neatly into his rucksack, saying that she would only get the wrong impressions before it was complete.

For another week she had to watch him carving round objects out of blood-red wood which he had cut from a branch of a dead tree and only towards the end of the week did she understand when she saw the first smooth dark red glowing wood transformed before her eyes into a perfect oval wherein two holes were burned with the fine tip of Xhabbo's spear, heated in fire.

'Francois, you old fox, or should I say jackal,' she remarked impressed. 'You're making buttons! And if I'm for once allowed to speak uninterrupted, very original and beautiful buttons indeed.'

The next day François disappeared mysteriously from camp. This pretence of going hunting was not convincing and was fully exposed as fraudulent when in the evening he returned to hand Nonnie a skirt of suede with six buttons down the side, fitting firmly into her waist and reaching just below her knees. To match it there was a cape tied with one single great round button of the same wood round her throat, enfolding her shoulders like the cloak English nurses wear.

When she walked into the firelight from behind the great storm-tree where she had changed, Nuin-Tara and Xhabbo greeted her with a clear cry of admiration and delight. Nuin-Tara even paid the dress the compliment of upbraiding Xhabbo in fun for the first time on the march by demanding why he had not thought of making something like it for her. And yet even that was not the end of this addition to Nonnie's wardrobe.

Nuin-Tara and Xhabbo now took a direct hand. They had just come to an area of the desert where they found great nests of ivory ostrich eggs. Almost daily they were eating vast ostrich egg omelettes at dawn before starting on their march and Nuin-Tara would select the finest of the egg-shells. In the evening, while they sat talking and sewing round their fire she would fashion hundreds of round beads out of the shells, until she could line the hems of Nonnie's skirt and the dividing line from waist to hem with the beads of the softest cream. What is more, she made a broad band of the beads of the same shells, like the one she wore round her head, for Nonnie to wear, and it glowed in the firelight like a tiara of pearls, against her fine and abundant hair, always shining as with a reflection of her own vivid allotment of life.

It was a gift more decorative than practical because Nonnie still had her specially designed bush-hat with her, bleached into a faded khaki without by the sun but its lining of pillar-box red silk was still surprisingly bright. However, Nuin-Tara from the start had been fascinated by the abundance and quality of Nonnie's hair and seemed almost overwhelmed with impatience towards the end of the day for the moment when Nonnie, arriving at camp, would remove her hat, throw it casually aside and let her beautiful hair fall down to her waist. At times Nuin-Tara would come over to her, take a thick shining strand between her fingers and stroke it with a deep unbelieving wonder. She would watch Nonnie use her own hands as best she could as a substitute comb and when they had water enough, soak her handkerchief in it, and sponge the dust and sweat from it, until it looked like a darker weave of the camp fire itself.

Once indeed Nuin-Tara had moved Nonnie almost to tears by saying, as she fondled a strand of hair between her fingers, 'We who feel that the clouds in the sky are feeling themselves to be the hair of the people who have gone before us, gathered by the wind that breathes also in our bodies, know thus all the more now for seeing hair like yours, that clouds and hair feel themselves to be forming and forming always together from one into the other by the same wind on account of it.'

For the first time, head-dress in place, she could not resist putting her arms round Nuin-Tara and kissing her on the cheek, resolving to wear the new head-dress every night, the moment they arrived in camp.

Also, from then on, Nonnie's carefully chosen suit which had served her well was neatly folded and stored safely in the bottom of her rucksack; the fear that it would not last out on the journey laid to rest for good. She wore only the dress that François, Xhabbo and Nuin-Tara between them had fashioned for her, until weeks later, it was augmented and, in her imagination, made perfect by a bolero tailored out of the even finer steenbuck skin. The day she discarded her European suit for this dress, Bushman in inspiration and European in design and execution, it was as if she had stepped out of an outworn shell of herself and become a new person.

How new a person was revealed at the end of the first day of walking in procession under the witch-blue glass of the sky of the desert, like one of those figures to be seen in a Poussin painting of some myth and legend of her pagan European beginnings.

It all happened at perhaps the most beautiful of their camps yet. Xhabbo chose a site just underneath the rim of one of the highest of the dunes where they would be sheltered against the wind of the night which, however slight, was becoming increasingly cool and also because deep within the dune itself was a vast reservoir of water which, whenever the rare rains fell, sank instantly into the deep sand and was preserved there from evaporation by a sub-tropical sun. As a result it was covered with melons and cucumbers. The melons particularly were vital because for many weeks now they had had to take the place of water in their lives; sipwells were far behind and even farther in front of them.

Every evening it had become a routine duty before they ate for Nuin-Tara and Nonnie to slice up the melons, pile them high in their dixies and slowly reduce them to a pulp which could be squeezed out to fill their flasks with liquid for their march. By night they ate the melons themselves and both liquid and melon tasted oddly sharp, almost too bitter, and not at all to Nonnie's or even Hintza's liking at the beginning. However, after weeks of experience they came to love the juice and found it even more satisfying than water. Nonnie was continually amazed at how that bitter taste had an afterlash of sweetness hidden in it, which not only drove the thirst of the day utterly out of her throat and blood but soothed her spirit.

There then, high as they were, on a dune that was higher than the one which had given them their first glimpse of the desert, the view stretched so wide and far that it made them silent and particularly solemn. It was almost as if taking in the view was a whole-time occupation, demanding all their senses and powers of definition to contain it. Moreover the day, dying peacefully, was summoning all that there was of colour and delicacy of tone in nature to accompany its going, and render the end as gentle and loving as possible. The night itself, coming up in the wake of a bright blue half-moon, seemed unusually compassionate and maternal. François thought at first that it was the natural drama, inherent always for him in the great transitions of the universe, that was making Nonnie as silent as himself. He gave no special thought to her behaviour, all the less so because of an interruption from the darkening world around them. Just as the night snuffed out the last sacramental candle of light on the horizon, there came from far away the voice of the lion which had accompanied them nightly on their long march. François had come to know and love it well and did not doubt the premonition that it was a voice of farewell and that already it was speaking from below the horizon away to the south.

If he had doubted it, his doubts would have been stilled by the reaction of Nuin-Tara and Xhabbo. The roar had hardly reached them when both jumped to their feet. They turned their backs to the fire, raised and held their hands out before them in the ancient Bushman gesture of farewell and stood there until the lion had spoken three times. Then the voice vanished for good. Only then did they lower their hands and turn about, sit down, sad and forlorn, until Xhabbo spoke up in what François imagined must have been the tone of an Old Testament prophet who had seen the last of the privileged manifestations of his god.

'Oh Foot of the Day,' Xhabbo explained, 'Foot of the Day ... he is gone and in his going was telling us that he has brought us far enough and that we are now on our own, left only with our tapping and the tapping of the stars and the wind to help us on our way.'

'But why, Xhabbo? Why has he gone now so suddenly?' François asked.

'Look, Foot of the Day,' he answered sombrely, 'Look at the

way he has gone and feeling yourself looking utterly, you will feel the answer.'

François looked. From below the horizon, he saw one after the other, great flashes of fire of lightning, fed by invisible thunder-clouds, flame and flare and flicker in the dark. It was the first lightning he had seen for months, and a sign that somewhere the universe was still in business, renewing the earth and reprieving even sand so parched and apparently condemned to death as desert sand. Utterly absorbed, he hardly heard Xhabbo explain that even so great a magician as Old Black Lightning, like all the animals and birds of which he was chief, would have to say, when such a call came, 'Yes, oh Lightning, look! I come!'

'But why good-bye, Xhabbo? Why do we not follow him then?'

'Oh, have you not heard then Foot of the Day, that he was not asking us to come with him, but feeling himself parting from us, saying farewell, knowing we have to stay and go on our own way. And this is the way Xhabbo's tapping said from the beginning we must go. But if the animals do not hasten to show that they are obedient to the lightning and have hearts utterly ready to listen to what the thunder has to say and be there to rejoice in what the rain brings, showing how they care for the rain and the thunder and the lightning, they will all three go utterly away and never return again. Even now, all Xhabbo's people seeing the lightning wherever they are in the desert will hasten towards it too on account of their feeling utterly thus. Yet the way of the lion now, towards the lightning, is the way of death for you and Nonnie, because it is where your enemies are.'

And Xhabbo went on to explain how they were approaching the great swamps and rivers in the western desert, how there was only the narrowest of desert strips along the edges of the swamps to give them a chance of getting through a broad ring of African tribes, all sympathetic or actively involved in the cause of their enemies. Only by following their present course would they have any real hope of reaching the great water where the people constantly coming up out of the sea could take care of them.

With that their dinner was ready. As always in people immediate with instinct as Xhabbo and Nuin-Tara were, they tried to relieve François, Nonnie and themselves from the pain of that final sense of separation that the voice of the lion had inflicted on them, by distracting themselves afterwards with some of their many fireside games. The first games were almost too esoteric even for François's comprehension but suddenly he realized they were being treated to one of the greatest of Bushman games: a riddle presented through movements of the body.

Xhabbo had suddenly gone down on his hands and knees and circled the fire in tiny movements, unbelievably quick and precise. At the end of the circle, he would make his arm give way under him and hit the sand with his shoulder, look behind him, examine his body with a look of stupefaction and then resume his crawling rapidly round again on all fours. At the end of the circle he would collapse as before and so on and on, until he had done it a score of times and the sweat was running down his body. Then stopping in front of Nuin-Tara, he looked at her as if to say, 'Now have you got it yet?'

Nuin-Tara, exasperated, shook her head and François was convinced that if one so experienced as she did not know the answer, he had little chance himself. When Nonnie asked him for an explanation, and even Hintza roused himself from his bed of comfort by the fire, to stand on all fours looking at Xhabbo scornfully as if he had gone off his head, all he could say was, 'He's acting out a riddle. If we don't get the answer by the third time of asking – they never ask more than three times, it's an article of faith with them – he will humiliate us all by telling us triumphantly and count himself the winner. Just look at Nuin-Tara, how infuriated she is with herself that Xhabbo can go one better than her in so old and familiar a game.'

They watched Xhabbo until he was near the end of his third repeat and hence triumphant finale when François breathed heavily into Nonnie's ear, 'Good Heavens, I think I've got it.'

'Oh do tell me,' Nonnie begged.

'That wouldn't be fair,' he answered. 'But's its incredible, he's become the thing itself.'

He had hardly finished when Xhabbo halted for the last time

in front of Nuin-Tara, looked at her long and steadily as if he pitied her for being such an idiot and waited for her to ask for illumination. Still sullen as the game demanded in order to enhance Xhabbo's ultimate triumph, she refused to speak and he was free to deliver the killing answer of his own accord.

A long crackle of electricity sparked on his lips as he uttered a phrase which Nonnie had never heard and of which the explanation had to be delayed, because at once both Xhabbo and Nuin-Tara were flat in the sand wriggling with merriment, laughing and re-laughing their laughter with such a glittering, happy, helpless intensity that even Hintza was affected. Suddenly, without warning, he started running all out round the fire, in wide circles, maddeningly trying to catch hold of his own tail. Hintza's performance, the laughter and the fact that François began laughing as Nonnie, not even in the happiest of their days in the past had heard in one who specialized after all in laughing inwardly, and the whole frenzied drunken eruption of merriment affected her so that, although she herself did not know the answer, she joined in, almost as hysterical and helpless as Xhabbo.

'Surely you know now what it was,' François exclaimed when at last they came gasping out of their laughter. But Nonnie still shook her head, and, in despair at her dumbness, intercepted Hintza, who was still chasing his own tail, as if the meaning of it all depended on his grasping it, and gathered him to her saying, 'Enough, Hin, enough. I'm certain it's not worth your or my effort!'

François looked at her and quietly said, suppressing another eruption of laughter with difficulty, 'The answer is a centipede with a sprained ankle.'

Nonnie let out a loud yelp of laughter and set a delighted Xhabbo and Nuin-Tara laughing all over again, which made François far happier than the immediate cause justified.

When at last she had finished her laughing she suddenly sat up and with her face unusually solemn, took François's hand in hers.

In one of her swift, bewildering changes of mood her eyes filled with tears, and she exclaimed, 'Oh, Coiske, do you know, until this moment I thought we could never laugh like that again. I feel almost guilty that we could, with Fa and Your Lammie, 'Bamuthi, Amelia and Ousie-Johanna and all those dear people and many more than we know of killed. Is it right that we can laugh so happily and soon after they've gone?'

It was the first time that Nonnie had spoken of the killing at Hunter's Drift direct to François, and he realized that he had been an accomplice to the suppression of the subject. He had not been ready to talk about it either, even to himself. He confessed himself accordingly to Nonnie and was about to say more when Xhabbo joined them, took their hands in each of his and remarked, 'Foot of the Day, Nonnie. Nuin-Tara and I know that the sadness in you is no longer without a name and has found its voice. When sorrow finds a name and a voice, it is like the lightning you see calling and the thunder speaking after it to say that soon the rain will fall on you again.'

Xhabbo's words filled Nonnie's eyes with tears. As a result, she and François talked far into the night that followed, because this great suppressed area of hurt within them was suddenly something out and about in the open, acknowledged and honoured both in thought and speech. It was almost as if the hurt parts of themselves had become personified as two close bereaved friends, brought back into a present where they could be comforted and promised that they would have articulate company to speak for them always, no matter how far they travelled from the place where they had been bereaved and nearly extinguished. At the end of their talk, they fell into a kind of sleep so deep and still and apparently dreamless that for the first time on the march not just Nonnie but François had to be roughly woken by Xhabbo and told that no one called 'Foot of the Day' could be so late in welcoming his great begetter, striding up so fast in front of a red explosive dawn.

From then on for the first time too Nonnie and François found themselves talking openly about the future, thereby confirming a law of whose existence Xhabbo's remark the night before had been as implicit as midnight is with noon of day. It is simply that until one acknowledges one's whole past, however painful and humiliating the process might be, and dignifies it with an honest, frank and full admission of its nature into one's daylight self, one is not free for a future of one's own.

316

CHAPTER THIRTEEN

The Singing Tree

For the first time now François was not afraid that he might frighten Nonnie with the facts of what lay ahead. He could tell her frankly of the hazards, the necessity and danger of breaking through a ring of enemies all over again, and then having once more to work their way for months through a desert, increasingly inhospitable, towards the sea and safety.

Far from being alarmed, Nonnie asked in her most matter-of-fact and companionable voice, as if all that was irrelevant now, 'But François, have you any idea how long it is since we started out? I promise you I haven't the faintest.'

François took out his dispatch book, looked at two closely marked pages in it before giving the amazed Nonnie not only the number of days but the month, date and year.

'We've been on the march for exactly one hundred and ninety-seven days,' he announced evenly. Then he paused, looking up to the sky and measuring the angle of the sun, thinking that this was a chance to give her a taste of her own teasing, and added, 'And seven hours, six minutes and forty-three and a half seconds.'

One need not dwell on Nonnie's reaction, and the banter that followed this open acknowledgement of the time it had taken to come so far. It was the time and distance travelled which made it impossible to record all the names conferred daily by Xhabbo on the camps they had made in the desert. A list of these names would have read partly like a roll of honour of all the beautiful and bright birds and animals of promise that had given their lives so that the five of them could live, and the rest like a catalogue of all the food available in this self-service department store of nature, which was the great desert.

Some names, however, outside this norm, deserve mention in their own right, like the camp from which they were about to move. It had just been baptized, 'The Place where Laughter came back'. Also there was, for instance, the camp far back that was named, 'The Place where Nuin-Tara sat on a Thorn'. This was no laughing matter to Nuin-Tara although it was to the others, particularly Xhabbo, who was inclined to think that if he suffered at all, it was from the fact that Nuin-Tara was too house – or should one say camp-proud. He was therefore, not undelighted to discover this slight flaw in her domestic perfections, because it was elementary that thorns had a high priority and were scrupulously looked for and ruthlessly ejected by women from the places where they slept with their men.

There were names that spoke both for themselves and of their slow, harsh progress and long, long days; names that made François tell Nonnie how both 'Bamuthi and Mopani had always declared that no matter how bare and awful the place where human beings camped, they always left something of themselves behind. These became a cord of gold in the labyrinth of their memories which neither moth nor rust of time and space could ever corrupt. There was 'The Place the Mamba paid a visit', where François was nearly bitten by the most poisonous snake in Africa. There was 'The Place the Stars fell over', where shooting stars plunged and burned out in the dark at such a rate and in such profusion that their eyes were blinded by the flare and the night was like a great display of fireworks. They were all overawed by the strange beauty and solemnity of the spectacle, all the more so when Xhabbo, orchestrating the pronouncement first made on the evening after the massacre, said, 'The stars go falling in this manner only when falling, they feel themselves travelling in order to inform all others at distant places that many men and women and children, who have been walking on their heels upright, have utterly fallen over, and that the killing by the men of blackness we have left behind us is now greater than ever.'

There was the camp of 'The Hyena's Disappointment', because it was where Hintza intercepted a hyena scrambling up a tree at midnight to get at their biltong, and bit it so smartly in the heel that it went off roaring like a lion with pain. There was 'Foot of the Day's Stupidity', where François failed to resolve a simple Bushman riddle, usually tried out on only the smallest boy. And there was a place with a name of the gravest impact called, 'Xhabbo's Reprieve', because they had waited there for seven days in despair for Xhabbo, who had gone out on a journey of reconnaissance. For once he had been unable to find either melons or cucumbers or tubers for his return journey and had arrived back almost dead in their midst.

There was 'The Giant Bustard's Delight', where on one shocking pink dawn they were woken by the impassioned, volcanic outpouring of a male bustard's love and, just as the sun rose, seen him tumble his woman for his delight. There was another camp called 'Our Grandfather the Elephant'. There, an enormous old bull elephant had mysteriously appeared without a swish of footfall or vibration of sand to announce his coming, and, having come, stood all night long just on the far rim of the spread-out cloth of their firelight, quietly watching them out of half-closed eyes.

François had wanted to move away, thinking the great elephant too close for comfort. But Xhabbo had been almost angry with him, saying that the elephant was there to see if the desert were treating them well and would not go until he was certain that this was so. On no account must he be given offence, but welcomed with joy and courtesy.

And as one final example from the journey behind there was the camp on a moonless night when the sky was not black so much as a bright midnight blue and the stars were clear and not glittering but steadily bright like drops of newly fallen dew, so that Xhabbo remarked, 'Those are stars feeling themselves to be the eyes of the herds of springbok the Dawn's Heart hunts for food for his utterly beloved lynx on earth.' He had gone on to beg that when they next could look close into the eyes of the springbok to notice how at the back of the night shadow cast by their long, dark lashes, François and Nonnie would see how the eyes were feeling themselves to be part of the star glow above. This camp was called, 'The Night of Springbok Eyes'. And so on to 'The Place where Laughter came back'.

From there their march became more exacting than it had ever been. It was immediately clear that most animals had followed Old Black Lightning. Only a few birds and desert hares were left and more and more they had to live on what the earth of the desert could produce. So long had those fertile sands been without rain that food from them became increasingly scarce and even melons hard to get. And yet, despite the harsher conditions of their life, their camps had never been livelier or happier; places of lively conversation, endless Bushman story-telling, and singing. There was perhaps only one grave and solemn evening, and that was at the camp where Nonnie out of her new self, insisted on François telling her every detail of what had happened to him in those desperate periods when he left her in the cave, ending with that day when Hintza had been wounded.

He told her everything and it was only at the end that she could confess to him how grateful and proud she had felt, despite the fact that her mind told her it was a sin to feel as she was feeling, when he told her that he was glad he could kill the soldier before Hintza and he himself could be killed. She wanted to know if he was absolutely certain now that all that killing, the blowing up of his home and the cremation of a helicopter and its crew, did not haunt him with a feeling of having done wrong, because she wanted him to know that however awful these deeds might appear, she in her heart had nothing but gratitude that she had a person like him to take on the cruel burden of protecting them in just such a way.

He thought for a long time before answering, 'I know, Nonnie, it must sound awful but I really don't regret that first killing at all. I didn't feel so relieved over the helicopter business because the danger was not quite so visible and it was awful to think of those men being burned alive. I wish it could have been different, but what else could I do? I've no doubt they would have killed us all and as a result I have made my peace with it. My home had to go because I told you how they wanted to make a death-trap of it and it hurt me more than it hurt them, I'm sure. But there's another killing in my life I've never told you for which I've never been able to forgive myself. It's strange . . .'

'Oh, you mean Uprooter of Great Trees?' Nonnie interrupted, 'You've told me about him already, and I do understand, I promise.'

'No, it's not even that, though I was very sorry for old

Uprooter of Great Trees. No, it's something you might find quite ridiculous. It all happened when I was very small and something, I've forgotten what, had put me in a bad temper. I walked out into the garden at home and came to the edge of one of our water furrows. A worm was crawling along it. Suddenly, I don't know to this day exactly why, I pushed it with my foot into the water and watched it lying at the bottom of the furrow, wriggling; tiny bubbles of air coming from its nose. Then it stopped wriggling and the bubbles ceased. D'you know, at once the singing of the birds, always shattering in the garden, became a terrible kind of song of accusation, and I've never, never been able to get rid of the memory of it.

'I think I know why now, because it was a killing that was utterly unnecessary. I think unnecessary killing is the only real killing there is, because we kill others then out of something in us we hate and don't understand – at least that's what Mopani says. He insists that killing which is forced on one as killing on behalf of life, is not really a thing for which one can be blamed at all. And do you know, the strangest thing about that poor little worm I murdered is the fact that on that very night after doing it, I went to sit with 'Bamuthi in his kraal and I heard him tell his children, in one of his wonderful fireside chats, that "the knowledge of the unspoken evil a man has done is a worm eating his heart away". That worm has been my conscience ever since and I only wish I could let it know that even as a worm it has not lived in vain, because it changed the whole of my attitude to life. I have never, never once since then, killed anything that I didn't have to.'

'Oh François,' Nonnie said, taking his hand and pressing it to her cheek, 'you must really stop being such an old Huguenot with such a fanatical conscience! You must really go in more for the confession you Protestants denounce. I'm sorry there's not some saintly Father here to tell you now that with this first confession of the killing of your worm, the worm is forever out of your life. As a good Catholic, I'll just have to be your Father-confessor and pronounce absolution, total and complete, from your crime. For our good Mother in Heaven knows that you have more than earned it and done penance enough for my sins as well. But oh, I do understand because even here in the desert, whenever I've watched you shooting, though I know it's necessary, I've wished there was a way of life without death.'

'If there were such a way,' François declared confidently, for here he was on well-travelled ground, 'it would miss the point of life.'

'But how?' Nonnie asked.

'Because Mopani says,' François went on, 'that birth and death are the only way to something greater. They are only a part, he says, of something greater even than their own full sum. He says death is as much life, as life is birth, and will even tell you, with one of his wriest smiles, that life is a deadly business.'

'You love Mopani very much, don't you?' Nonnie broke in with apparent irrelevance.

'Love' was a big word for François. Considering the cool upbringing behind one who was always 'another person' in his home, he was half afraid of the vision of fire and warmth it evoked, and said, taken aback and shy, 'I expect I do. But why?'

'Because you're always quoting him. He seems as full of quotations as Shakespeare and I tell you, master Joubert, that if you piled together all the quotations from Mopani I've heard from you, they would sink a ship.'

And she wanted to go on and ask if he did not think he overdid it, and should not consider seriously whether Mopani did not stand in the way of his being himself and should he not try to speak more for himself?

But such a rare, exposed, far-away look had appeared on François's face, that she instantly rebuked herself, just in time to hear him say, as if to himself, 'All the time, from the moment I first left the cave, I have felt Mopani near me, almost as if he were just behind me, whispering in my ear what to do, helping and protecting me. I know I couldn't have done all this without him. So clear, so sure has this feeling been that I've often looked over my shoulder, expecting to find him there. But . . .'

His thought faltered to an end as it was translated into a searing vision of Mopani as he first remembered him; a horse called Noble, two great ridge-back hounds racing ahead, Mopani's neat, tall and dapper figure upon it, his shadow becoming a Daumier imprint in sunset crayons on the scarlet dust of the silhouette of the elongated knight of La Mancha starting out on his quest.

Seeing the look, all the quotations immediately became quixotic flesh and blood for Nonnie too. With a rush of inspiration she announced with certainty, 'He must be alive then. Don't you see François, it can't be any other way.'

To her amazement François only remarked, solemnly, 'Perhaps', because, though he would not tell her, 'Bamuthi and Ouwa, who were both dead, at times also felt reassuringly and disconcertingly near. How could one so young, however resourceful, deal with so great a paradox?

'There's no perhaps about it.' Nonnie, who had all the confidence of one who after all had never known what it could be like to have been 'another person', even before one was born, hid her feeling of absolute anti-climax in a show of vehemence. 'Just you wait, François Joubert, just you blooming-well wait!' And there, all that there was of solemnity between them for the moment, ended.

Many days later there was a camp where one of Xhabbo's finest stories was interrupted by the loud sound of jet engines in the night. They all jumped up in alarm to see, unusually low, a great passenger aeroplane flashing its lights stacked in two neat rows upon each other, and flying almost straight above them. It was their first intimation since they had left their enemies behind that somewhere beyond the desert there was another world still going its impersonal, twentieth-century way. Nonnie was almost overpowered by the comparison it evoked in her imagination between her own plight now and that of the Nonnie who had often travelled in planes just like that.

She could not help talking to François about it, and he became so interested that he begged her to tell Nuin-Tara and Xhabbo about it. She started obediently but diffidently to give her account, but in the telling soon became so involved, that she could not leave out a single detail of what the inside of an aeroplane looked like; how scores of people sat comfortably in it; how tables were opened in front of each of them; linen, knives, forks and plates laid out glittering, and so on right down to the courses of a first-class dinner menu, complete with a description of the films and music that followed. At moments she was afraid that she might be boring Xhabbo and Nuin-Tara, but their eyes were so great with wonder, like children in a nursery hearing their first fairy-tale that she was encouraged into giving more detail. François himself, who had never been in an aeroplane, was utterly absorbed in her account and she had to finish to a disconcertingly long silence.

Nuin-Tara and Xhabbo went on looking at her until at last the fact that the story was really ended penetrated. Xhabbo took up a knife and cut the air between him and Nonnie as if he had been tied to her eyes by an invisible chain. He gasped like a diver coming up for air, shook his head from side to side and said, 'Nonnie, you are a wonderful liar.'

Nonnie, getting over her astonishment that for the first time in her life her honesty had been in question, protested and declared that she was grossly insulted, and would never tell them anything again. At that both Nuin-Tara and Xhabbo rushed to her and took her hands. Dismayed, they begged her never to threaten them like that again, saying it was the most wonderful story they had ever heard and would she please tell them more like it.

'But what's the use if you don't believe me?' Nonnie exclaimed, half-laughing with perplexity.

'Well, can't you see, Nonnie?' Xhabbo told her, 'the stories like the story I have just told you of how Mantis made an eland out of a shoe discarded by his son, are just true stories. Everyone knows that they are just ordinary stories of ordinary things that happened, but your story is a great story because it is a story that no one could possibly ever believe. Only the greatest stories are stories men cannot believe.'

And Nonnie, defeated, was compelled to leave it at that, though they could not. And thereafter she found herself compelled to tell them night after night, about the outside world, things like underground trains and smoke and fog in cities so great that they made the sky like night in the middle of the day, all things that a European child knows are everyday facts of life in the great technological world beyond the desert. On each occasion she found herself rewarded with the dubious compliment of being 'the most wonderful liar there had ever been'.

Of this part of their march only two more camps deserve

special attention. There was the camp at which François, Nonnie and Hintza were woken by the unusual behaviour of Xhabbo. Nonnie had become so attuned to her new life that it had become impossible for François and Hintza to sit up straight out of their sleep at intervals as they had always done, and listen to the noises of the night in case anything abnormal was coming their way, without Nonnie doing so too. On this occasion all three came out of their sleep upright side by side, to see Xhabbo take a burning piece of wood from their fire, walk some ten paces into the night and build a new fire there. He sat there by this fire until it was completely burned out before coming back to his place by Nuin-Tara's side, apparently without noticing that the three of them were watching. Twice more they woke up for the same reason, and saw Xhabbo follow exactly the same procedure. It was too much for Nonnie. She had to ask François in a whisper, 'What d'you think he's doing? Is there anything wrong?'

'I don't know,' François answered gravely, 'it depends on the dream.'

'The dream?' Nonnie exclaimed, 'What have dreams got to do with what's going on?'

'Everything,' François replied. 'They only do this when they've had a great dream.'

And he went on to explain how old Koba had told him that always when a great dream came to speak to a Bushman at night he would take a burning stick from their fire as Xhabbo had done, in order to show the dream that came out of the darkness within, the way through the darkness without, to where it could be warmed and brought alive by a fire of its own, and so become clear to the eyes of whoever dreamt it.

At their dawn breakfast, Xhabbo was unusually sombre. It looked for a while as if he was not going to speak to any of them that day. This was something so unusual that François was increasingly perturbed. But just before they shouldered their haversacks to set out on another long march, Xhabbo shook his head, begged them to wait, saying he ought to tell them all of a dream he had had three times in the night. Although he had done all that he could do to bring the dream out of the dark and the cold and make it warm and alive by a fire of its own, the dream was still cold and dark within. He could not understand it all, as he should have been able to do by now. The dream had come first when he had hardly fallen asleep. It began with his hearing a voice of a woman singing, as Nonnie had sung to the lion, but singing as if she felt herself, unlike Nonnie, in a place without friends. He had gone towards the voice, recognizing it to be the voice of a woman of the people who had come out of the sea. He had come to see her bound with ox-hide thongs to a tree whose top was high in the sky and branches spread far and wide. He had tried to go and cut her free but could suddenly not move nearer because there was water full of crocodiles and hippopotamuses in between. Full of horror over his helplessness he woke, to perform the prescribed ritual without effect.

This had happened not just once, but three times. When a dream came to one three times and was still not understood, he declared, distressed, the time for all was bad indeed.

Nuin-Tara, François and Nonnie all tried to comfort Xhabbo but he was not so much in need of comfort as enlightenment. He told them this with a flash of his upright spirit, and added that all that was necessary now was for all three of them, and Hintza too, to use their eyes for him because he was afraid that his own eyes would be full of the dream and would not have room to be as full of the way they were going as they ought to be.

Accordingly, François, Hintza and Nonnie took the lead, and while marching along Nonnie questioned François closely about Bushman dreams and their meaning. All he could tell her was that for a person like Xhabbo, whose name was the Bushman word for dream, dreaming would have been more important than for most. That was saying a great deal because Old Koba had told him all Bushmen believed that there was a dream dreaming them. Often as a child when he had woken up with a dream that troubled him she had taken him out into the garden at Hunter's Drift and made him a little fire just as Xhabbo had done in order to bring light out of the darkness of his dream or, as Nonnie he thought might have put it, interpreting it. It was extraordinary how that had helped him as a child and demolished all the unpleasantness left behind by the dream.

Indeed, very early on, Koba exhorted him to remember that a dream which had become part of the light of a fire, lived on to help one along. She wanted him to know that it was the same with wood. The wood itself burned out in the making of a fire, but the fire itself went on. A particular dream may be burned out in the fire, but the dreaming would go on as well as the dream dreaming it. Dreamers, like wood in the fire, were burned out, they came and went, but the dream dreaming them from the beginning always went on.

One is compelled to orchestrate this phase in the theme of François's story because of the light it throws on the essential nature of his companions. Instinctively they moved in a Shakespearean view of themselves as 'such stuff as dreams are made on'. It explains why the place they were leaving behind with an increasing sense of impending end to an important phase of their march, was quite naturally called, 'The Place where Xhabbo Dreamt a Dream'.

And they had not moved far from it before François suddenly stopped short, angry with himself for having been so dense, telling Nonnie rather peremptorily, 'Look, join Hin. Wait, and keep your eyes skinned on the desert ahead. I've something important to talk over with Xhabbo.'

'Xhabbo!' he began to ask his friend, who came up from behind with singularly uncurious eyes. 'Have you ever heard of the singing tree of the Makoba?'

At the word 'Makoba' (people who had been the Bushmen's enemies for close on two centuries), Xhabbo was immediately roused out of his preoccupied state to say that of course he had heard of the great tree of the Makoba, as everybody had. He had even seen it, countless times as it rose high and wide from a ring of twanging and singing papyrus in the swamp ahead. Indeed their own way would pass close by it and, were it not for the fact that they would have to go by it at night, François would have seen for himself what a great tree it was. But as for it being a singing tree, he had never heard it called that.

François hastened to tell him all he himself knew about the tree, the belief surrounding it, about Kghometsu and the report of Kghometsu's wife that the tree was singing again. The news made Xhabbo take his dream even more seriously than ever, if

327

that were possible. He affirmed that the tree in his dream, now that he had listened to François, could have been the tree of life of the Makoba. Though he still could not see the plain meaning of it, he was now more certain than ever, that there was an important message for them in it and that this message concerned their enemies. They would just have to be on their guard again, as they had not been since Lamb-snatcher's Hill. Meanwhile, he would go on letting the dream grow in him and begged François to lead on.

The growth towards clarity must have been considerable because by evening Xhabbo seemed certain that the dream within was now on a true course of its own and could be left to take care of itself. While the others prepared camp, he went up a great dune alone and came down in the twilight with the news that the swamp was only two days' marching away, and that after one more night they would have to hide Nonnie and Nuin-Tara somewhere while he and François scouted ahead, because they would be close then to a country once more full of enemies.

'How strange,' Nonnie remarked when François, in keeping with their new relationship, told her the grim, uncensored facts. 'How strange, that we should have to come back to a world of men to find ourselves in danger of our lives again.'

It was ominous that they all, including Hintza, slept uneasily that night and sat down to breakfast to hear Xhabbo tell them how he had not so much dreamt his dream as clearly heard, far away on the edge of his sleep, the sound of the singing so like Nonnie's in his first dream. So loud and clear did it sound on the wind of the night that he had sat up and listened very carefully as if by turning his ears to the wind he would hear it, but alas, it was a singing to be heard only in the stillness of sleep. Then all night between sleeping and waking he had seen more clearly the face of the singer, a woman clearly of Nonnie's people. But not like Nonnie's, smooth, happy and healthy. It was thin as if she had not eaten for months and was near death. In between her singing she was crying, as if feeling her heart had utterly fallen over.

Nonnie, her curiosity awakened, over this repeated comparison of the dream woman to her and her mother's people, had a queue of urgent questions forming in her mind for

Xhabbo. She was prevented by the appearance immediately above their heads of the most imperious of honey-guides.

It sat on a delicate, intricate ornate bow like a piece of third-Empire gilt in the morning sun, beating its wings and singing with a crystal clarity. More importunate even than the honey-guide which had so sorely tempted Xhabbo on Lamb-snatcher's Hill two hundred and seventeen days before, they heard its ancient refrain, 'Quick! Quick! Honey . . . quick!'

Xhabbo, as if still full of remorse over that breach of his on the hill of the terms of the Bushman's alliance with the bird, dropped his empty dixie, seized his spear and said, 'Person of wings and a heart of honey; look how hearing you, quickly I come!'

François immediately picked up his own rifle, haversack, water-flask and ammunition pouches, calling on Nonnie, as Xhabbo called upon Nuin-Tara, to come after them with all their dixies as soon as they had scoured them out with sand.

The honey-guide, seeing that it was being followed, was in no hurry. It fluttered from tree to tree to perch where it was most visible in the full sun before it flew on to the next. As a result Xhabbo and François were joined by Nonnie and Nuin-Tara before they had gone very far, just in time to hear in the distance another strange, urgent whistling call followed by an almost chuckling sound, from far down the throat of some eager hurrying animal.

Xhabbo stopped, turned about and whispered that they must all be silent please; a most wonderful thing was about to happen, a thing that could be happily set as a sign against this dream which he did not fully yet understand.

Significantly, the honey-guide, perched on a branch a bare twenty feet away, was looking first to them and then in the direction of the new sound coming steadily nearer and sounding as if it were coming out of the earth a hundred or more yards away to their right. Suddenly the new sound ceased. At once the honey-guide became alarmed and resumed its call with a glittering, desperate intensity, beating its wings hysterically against its side, so that it could utter the maximum volume of command of which it was capable. Xhabbo's face was transfigured and transformed with wonder into an ancient Pan-like beauty as there came bursting into view a robust, grey-dark animal, trotting fast on sturdy, somewhat curved legs, with a distinct, business-like air that would not have been inappropriate on the face of someone who was something in a great city, determined to catch a bus.

'Good God, a ratel ... a honey-badger,' François began in a whisper to Nonnie. But got no further because the moment the badger arrived under the tree to exchange passwords with the honey-guide, the honey-guide, paying no more attention to their little group, took off at full speed and they had to hasten after the ratel with his strange, flute-like whistle and odd Dionysian chuckle. This duet between ratel and honey-guide was transformed into a trio by Xhabbo who now kept on informing their two guides ahead, in a crooning, soothing song: 'Oh person of wings, and a heart of honey; oh bravest of the brave persons! Do not look behind but feel yourselves hastening and feeling it, know how hastening too, we come!'

François, in explaining all this to Nonnie, elaborated how there was no animal in, on or above the earth that was as brave as this animal and that even a lion, or the maddest of rogue elephants would leave it alone. Even for Mopani, who knew animals so well, it was the one animal who proved, as he put it, that in the world of nature as in the world of men, only courage made life free from fear. It was because of its utter freedom from fear, the Bushmen believed, that the ratel was given the ultimate reward of valour, that was honey.

Nonnie, watching the strange animal shape hurrying after the light, ethereal singing bird, entranced and excited by it, characteristically had an association uniquely her own which no sooner found than was revealed in the remark to François, 'How like Caliban he is, and how like Ariel the bird; and when you come to think of it, how like a magician, a sort of desert Prospero, your beloved Xhabbo looks just now!'

Before long they arrived at a vast termite hill, which in itself was a sign of how near to the end of desert sand they had come, since the hill was a temple of clay. The termites had long since gone, driven out by an ant-bear who had clawed a hole in its base and so made it a fitting home, full of vacant cells and cunning corridors for an immense concourse of bees, that were coming and going in long amber processions between the entrance and the distant waters and flowers of the swamps, which Xhabbo had declared were so near.

They watched the Ariel bird perch itself, silent upon the tip of the termite summit, still quivering like an electric bell just after the summons rung on it had ceased and began to look highly pleased over the faultless way it had just performed a delicate duty, before it began sharpening and cleaning its beak between its wings and claws for the delight to come. But strangest of all was the behaviour of Caliban. No sooner had he arrived at the mound than he whisked about, went smartly backwards and thrust his sturdy behind firmly into the opening of the vast hive.

'He must be mad!' exclaimed Nonnie, mystified and aghast, 'to do a thing like that to bees.'

'Oh, Nonnie, this is the most wonderful part of all!' François announced, 'You see, he's gassing all the bees inside so that they can't sting anyone getting at the honey.'

Told this in a different setting at third-hand, Nonnie might have been inclined to laugh. But as a close witness, indeed a committed accessory before the fact, the wonder of the resourcefulness implicit in the whole arrangement into which she had been drawn, seemed miraculous and so beautiful that she watched it all with shining eyes. It was amazing. Almost at once there died away the steady reverberating murmur of bees chanting their devotions in that Gothic cathedral built by insect-priests. Soon the honey-badger could step aside, and for the first time turn his attention to them. He looked steadily and fearlessly into their eyes as if to say, 'Now look, it's time you did something as well.'

Immediately Xhabbo, still crooning, went eurhythmically forward, knelt smoothly by the entrance and pushed his hands slowly and evenly through the dark cathedral door. After feeling what appeared to be delicately around within, he pulled out a long, broad comb of purple-black honey, and broke off a large segment. Held out towards the honey-guide it went translucent with morning sun and looked more like a dream of honey than any honey found on earth.

'Oh person of wings with the heart of honey,' he begged, 'take and eat.'

The honey-guide's precise shape vanished in a flutter of feathers and wings and emerged in a swift glide towards Xhabbo, who was carefully laying out honey in the shade of a bush like a feast. As he stepped back, the bird flew in and at once pecked away at the wax that encombed it.

Xhabbo went back at that same smooth ritualistic pace to the entrance, once more felt inside and pulled out another great comb, shedding large tears of glistening honey.

'Oh bravest of brave persons, who knows how to put the bees to sleep,' he called out, holding it like some magical substance towards the watchful badger. 'Take, oh please take, and eat!'

Moving smoothly forward, he laid the comb at his sturdy partner's feet, who strikingly enough made no move to eat but went on watching him keenly. And again Xhabbo went back, brought another comb and laid that too at the feet of the honey-badger and begged it to eat. This time the badger ate, and Xhabbo was free to extract two more great combs, bring them to Nuin-Tara so that she could break them up and store them in their dixies. François knew that in so great a hive he could have extracted many more combs but it was as if Xhabbo knew instinctively that never had it been more important to observe the proportions implicit in the claims of bee as well as man, bird and beast. With a movement of profound gratitude and his most respectful gesture of farewell at the honey-bird, the honey-badger and the hive, he turned about and in the same devout tone commanded, 'Now let us too take our honey before the bees wake from their sleep, and eat, my children, eat!'

It was the first time Xhabbo had ever used a paternalistic expression. It was totally unlike him even now, and it sounded as if he were speaking on behalf of someone else. It could only have come, not because he was feeling fatherly, but out of a conviction that they all had been uniquely fathered just then.

It was one of the most beautiful events in which François and Nonnie had ever participated. Neither of them was capable of expressing what they felt. It was as if they had witnessed a manifestation of the sweetness that life could achieve if only man, bird, animal, insect and flower were allowed to enact fully the terms of the alliance to which they are in their deeps contracted by the act of their being. For this final taste of honey on their tongues which had long forgotten what sweetness is, seemed to erase all that had been bitter in their experience, to such an extent that even if this were to be their only reward, the travail to which they had been subjected would still have been worth it.

The camp they had just left, therefore, became the first camp to have its original name cancelled and to be renamed with a phrase which meant, 'The Annunciation of Honey'.

In their next camp the night air became strangely dank and towards morning a mist came swirling over the land hiding the stars, making them for the first time so cold that they increased their fire. In the night Xhabbo had heard again, louder than ever, the singing and the crying of the woman by the tree, and at dawn he commanded Nuin-Tara and Nonnie to stay quietly and watchfully at home, because their enemies once more were near. He was certain they were closer to whatever the vision portended than ever he had realized. He and François would have to go looking out carefully the way ahead before they could all move safely on.

Accordingly the two of them, accompanied by Hintza, were out of the camp before sunrise. Within a very short time they found what François took to be a game track until it was joined by other tracks. When the mist gave way before the sun and showed up the ground clearly, he realized with instant apprehension that they were cattle tracks. Just as there was no smoke without fire, he concluded sombrely that you had no cattle without men. He noticed too how fast the dunes had declined and the earth was levelling out ahead.

They had gone only a few miles farther when the cattle tracks became bolder and too frequent for Xhabbo's liking. He swerved aside and led the way up a large mound of sand covered with bushes of thorn. From there they looked out on a new world of trees and long green savannahs sinking slowly into a vast depression where the advance of earth was arrested against dense dykes of papyrus and bulrushes and in between the sun glancing upwards sharply from copper and bronze water. Behind and beyond the water, the theme of trees was resumed in great island clusters. The trees on those were denser, taller and greater than any François had ever seen. Even where the horizon drew a dark blue circle in the west, the reiteration of islands of trees and barricades and bulrushes and slashes of metal-coloured water went on without interruption.

One great island of trees to the far south held François's eyes particularly, because it looked more massive, darker and higher than the rest and was almost cut off from the others by a broad stretch of water. Just beyond the water it appeared to touch on ripples of sand and grass and brush, where the desert reasserted itself and quickly mounted to the east into the great swell and oceans of dunes they had left behind. He had an odd feeling that he had seen it before. And that made no sense to him.

Yet just then, pointing at that very island, Xhabbo told him, 'Look, there is the place of the tree of life of the Makoba. Tonight before anyone can discover or know that we are here, we must pass close by it and into the swamp at the back because look, Foot of the Day, how everywhere else we have enemies.'

François saw what he had missed in his general survey of the scene. All round and in between them and the lip of the depression, were round, beehive huts surrounded by kraals of thorn and over every kraal and hut rose a tall straight plume of light blue smoke. More ominous than smoke and much nearer, he heard the sound of cattle calling to one another, goats bleating, and however faint and far away, the bright sing-song prattle of little black herd boys. Worse still, out of the north-west all along the edge of the swamp and trees, long sleeves of scarlet dust hung on the windless air and the familiar and fearful sound of trucks came to their ears.

Xhabbo let out a series of Bushman clicks incapable of alphabetical transmission, which François knew was a compound of protest and irritation to the effect that fate might well have spared them this last refinement. The discharge of electricity complete, he explained the traffic was worse even than when he and Nuin-Tara had passed on their way to warn François. It could only mean that their enemies were still at work and could only be at work so openly and on such a scale because the people of those kraals and fires were their friends.

François would have liked to stay longer and study the scene more thoroughly but Xhabbo said no. He told François that he knew the way they had to go well enough for both of them, and in case anything happened to him, Nuin-Tara knew it just as well. They must get back to their camp to eat and rest, for as soon as it was dark they would set out to pass by the place of the tree of life well before morning.

François had one quick last look at the scene. Judging by the dust, some of the military trucks had broken station and were moving out of convoy straight for the great tree itself. He pointed it out to Xhabbo, who dismissed it with a casual shrug. At nightfall, he said, judging by past experience, the men of the trucks, like the people of the kraals, would keep away from the swamp because of the mosquitoes that came out of the swamp dense as thunder clouds, trembling with a song of anger.

Xhabbo said all this confidently but for the first time François had a doubt of his own, not of Xhabbo's accuracy so much as a doubt caused by something that had to be outside Xhabbo's experience. From all he had seen of the enemy, he had been impressed by its organization and attention to detail. He could not imagine that an enemy so efficient and contemporary, would have left mosquito nets out of its reckoning. So that there would be no reason why it should avoid that low-lying mosquito land at night when the shortest and best route demanded they should take it. He realized how for months now he had been more than content to leave everything to Xhabbo. Had it not been for Xhabbo, his imagination would not have been free to help himself and Nonnie to deal with the inner consequences of the disaster which had overtaken them. His debt to Xhabbo seemed immeasurable, and this sense of obligation transformed his doubting into a positive resolution, that in returning to an area of life outside Xhabbo's experience, he would take a greater share of responsibility.

This and the evidence of a world thickly populated with allies of their enemies as well as their enemies themselves, made him more thoughtful than usual on the way back to the camp. His news made Nonnie thoughtful too and at times so despondent that she became angry with herself. Her anger found tongue in the afternoon, when François told her that the moment had come when she must change her desert dress and sandals for the clothes in her haversack. She looked as if she were about to

335

refuse and François hastened to explain how the rough country ahead and, particularly, the mosquitoes by night, flies and other insects by day made it necessary that she should have as much of her body covered, adding, 'You've no idea yet how clean and healthy a place the desert is, no flies, no mosquitoes –'

'And, above all, no people,' Nonnie interrupted, 'and how like people, that where you have them, you also have pests and sudden death. Oh, how I hate them!'

Nonetheless she went obediently to change and returned to stand in front of François. Her suit, compared to his bleached, much mended and frayed clothes, looked surprisingly fresh. Her face was vivid with self-indignation as she exclaimed, 'It's fantastic, François. I feel just as I used to after a long summer holiday, having to go back to school. I really ought to grow up and be my age by now.'

Nuin-Tara and Xhabbo refused as always to look beyond what was immediately at hand, and like all instinctive people, put their trust in instinctive reaction to the unknown ahead, however disconcerting and perilous it might look, rather than meeting it with some preconceived plan. They napped on and off through the long afternoon. François and Nonnie, with Hintza beside them, rested with their arms on their haversacks, talking until just before sunset, when they all had their evening meal. The moment it was totally dark, they scattered sand over their last desert fire and set off at a fast, steady pace towards the swamp.

The night was even danker than the previous one but as yet without mist, and the starlight clear enough for Xhabbo to carry on without faltering for some two hours before he suddenly stopped. The reason was plain to all. They could hear the barking of dogs from a dozen or more points in the night ahead and once or twice, in between the barking, human voices, presumably calling out to the dogs, with the only result that the dogs barked back louder.

Hintza, dog of action and, when out of action, of profound contemplation, did not think much of such exhibitionist barking, and he clearly dismissed it as being of the ill-bred mongrel kind. Like his master, he was more interested in the fact that the barking indicated the presence of human beings. So he sniffed the air carefully ahead for a sign of what sort of men they might be, before he turned about and put up a paw against François's side, to scratch a warning. Then he went up to Nonnie, rubbed his head affectionately against her knee and was rubbed behind his ears for his own comfort as well, before he took up his position again, more alert than he had been for days.

Xhabbo stood there until he had the measure of the barking to his satisfaction, and looked up at the stars before he whispered to them to follow as quietly as they could. He led off at a steady pace, though not as fast as before. The barking drew rapidly nearer and the first voices seemed to be joined by others. Soon all round them they heard the bright, sustained, animated and inspired conversation that delights Bantu Africa in the early hours of the night.

Presently they drew level with the first line of barking dogs and passed between them and the first clusters of bright conversation, until they were surrounded by the noise. Xhabbo paused just to whisper to François that they would have to run now because the rising night air would carry their scent to the dogs. They had not gone far at the run when behind them the volume of barking became so great and sustained that François had no doubt the dogs had their scent. Indeed, the unfamiliar scents in their noses of Europeans and Bushmen and a strange dog, seemed to drive them so frantic that their masters, talking in their kraals, could no longer ignore them.

The din became even greater when only a hundred or so yards away one chief came out of his hut to reprimand his own dogs. He managed to silence them but apparently, noticing how far and wide the barking had spread and that it was still going on unabated all round him, he started calling to his neighbours for enlightenment.

Soon, neighbours were calling to one another everywhere with an intensity which convinced François that they suspected something foreign, if not menacing, had entered their remote world. Suddenly the dogs in front started barking as well, but luckily, it seemed, just in sympathy with the rest of their kind, not because of any strange scent. Yet this state of alarm proclaimed such a great community of dogs and men that he wondered whether they would ever break through.

Xhabbo, however, seemed undeterred by any misgivings; he knew that the only thing was to go on as fast as they could. He did not look back once to see if they were being followed, not even when, close on their right, there appeared on the dark a sudden glow of firelight, as if some alerted husbandman more cautious than the rest had lit the fire always kept ready by his kraal for the protection of his cattle. But before the flames could rise high enough to light up the earth where they were running, they were hidden in a new area of darkness ahead. More fortunate still, the noise of the dogs and men was now so loud that there was no danger of them being heard as they rushed forward faster than ever over the ground.

Soon, although to Nonnie it had seemed hours, the noise behind them began to recede and Xhabbo was able to fall back into a fast walking pace. Even after all the noise had completely died away, he did not pause. François knew why, and thought it would help the new Nonnie to know as well. He explained that they had to get as far away as they could from this settlement because by the light of day their spoor would be plain enough for all to read.

To his amazement however, Nonnie, who was as little out of breath as he or Xhabbo was, remarked bravely, 'For once, François, it may interest you to know that I had already worked that one out for myself.'

Reassured, François said no more and concentrated on the special form of vigil which his doubt of that morning demanded from him.

An hour or so before midnight, Xhabbo stopped for the first time. The bush of trees and thorn and its clearings of grass through which they had been travelling had come to an abrupt end. The smell of impounded water was on their noses and before them a vast stretch of papyrus and in between the papyrus, the glitter of stars deep in water. Beyond the glitter, like a great castle of shadow, was the outline of an immense grove of trees. Between them and the trees the stillness was broken every now and then by the snorting of hippopotamuses, the nostalgic piping of water-birds and an ecstatic chorus of frogs, which seemed to provoke the hyenas on the desert edge into hysterical laughter, and draw from the jackals, somewhere in the direction of the Southern Cross, a sharp, cynical reply. Close as he was to Xhabbo, François felt at once that he was deeply perturbed, and that his reason for stopping was not because the bush had ended and that their dim track was now leading out into a new world of water-grasses, bulrushes, papyrus and stagnant water channels.

'Can you not feel yourself hearing it?' he asked. François listened but heard nothing, except those African collaterals of the 'musical frogs of the marshes and bogs' which according to poets serenaded the entrance to the underworld of the Greeks.

He might have thought that Xhabbo, perhaps out of sheer fatigue, was re-crossing the frontier of a dream that had plagued him hard and perhaps too long, had it not been for Hintza. Hintza appeared to be listening to what Xhabbo had heard. For once he was not smelling the dark unknown ahead but had his musical ears cocked at the castle of shadow in front. Suddenly he turned abruptly away, and looked up straight at Nonnie. He let out the faintest of whimpers as if pleading that she now ought to come forward and explain it all.

'I'm afraid I do not hear it yet, Xhabbo,' François replied. 'But look at Hin, he hears it and is as curious as you.'

Xhabbo looked immensely relieved, as if he had been on the verge of doubting himself, and was encouraged into leading forward again, only much more slowly, picking his way with great care. The fortress of shadow imposed on the night by the trees loomed high in front of them, spangled like Christmas pines with stars. He stopped again and at once not only François but Nonnie heard the sound as well. She grasped François's arm. Her grip tightened until it hurt.

'Dear Mother in Heaven,' she exclaimed, inexplicably near to tears. 'Dear God, what is it? Can't you hear it too? Tell me quick, can you hear it too?'

'I can hear what sounds like singing,' François replied, more perplexed than upset, 'but I don't know what kind of singing, or why.'

'But François, you idiot,' Nonnie exclaimed. 'Can't you hear, it's my fado! It's the song I sang to you that night of the lion. I haven't heard it since I was in Lisbon with Mummy. Everyone was singing it in Lisbon then. But here, dear God,

339

how can it be possible? Oh Coiske, what does it mean?'

'I can't tell you what it means literally,' François answered portentously, as his perplexity was invaded by a sense of the ominous. 'All I know is what it is believed to be. It's the great "tree of life" of the Makoba and it is singing, as they put it, "in the voice of a woman of the people who come out of the sea". This singing is foretold in an ancient prophecy, which says it is a sure sign that the time has come when all the black races of Africa must unite and drive the people who came out of the sea, back into the sea. I'm afraid that between that singing and our enemies, there's some vital connection.'

The grasp on François's arm tightened even more and he thought that in that small, dark space between them, satin with starlight, he could just see her eyes widen. But he could not know that at that moment, she felt almost as great a despair as anything on the journey had yet made her feel. She found a voice crying out within her that if something so innocent as this little song could be appropriated by their enemies, there were no bounds to either their power or their evil. This, added to the evocation first of a mother who had died in a massacre and followed by that of the father in another, dominated the more subtle, sensitive, nostalgic associations she had with the song. All at once, she felt herself, as indeed all of them, powerless to overcome an evil, so ubiquitous and great.

She let go of François's arm. She had no intention of making a scene; she was determined not to be weak and expose her despair. Yet at last she was forced to sit down on the ground, put her head between her arms and begin crying quietly to herself. But she had hardly sat down when Hintza was at her side and pushed his head under her arm and chin, trying to lift her face and lick away her tears.

This concern from an animal, in so many ways more helpless than herself, somehow checked her despair, and once checked, she realized that there was something more even than concern for her in Hintza's behaviour, because having licked her tears and made certain she had stopped crying, Hintza started to nudge her in the most suggestive way. After each nudge he turned his head sideways and with his ears cocked, pointed his nose in the direction of the singing as if to say, in his best scout manner, 'Now do your stuff Nonnie. There's something there that only you know, and you must help us now.'

So clear was the message, or so clear was the intuition Hintza brought alive in the intuitive person she had always been, that she found herself listening again to the singing, but more objectively. This time she could no longer doubt. There was a woman singing with the faultless diction of an aristocratic Portuguese voice. She jumped to her feet and rejoined François, who, more and more anxious at what was happening below him, was about to come to her.

'François,' she begged, 'please can we go on and get a bit nearer? I'm sure that's a Portuguese woman singing over there.'

CHAPTER FOURTEEN

The Great Thirstland

Meanwhile, the singing had had its own impact on Xhabbo. Certain that everyone in their little company had now heard it as he had first heard it in his dream, he became the full, confident self he had not been since his dream. Not only was he himself proved right but the validity of the dreaming process within him was reaffirmed. This process had brought him and his people out of the dark, unrecorded past, through centuries of persecution and, though still cruelly persecuted in the present, it gave life no matter how awful and grim a meaning that they always accepted gratefully as some undeserved gift worth far more than the price living demanded. A clear appreciation of what the situation required flared in him again and, of his own unprompted accord, he softly told the others to follow him. Their only way now was past that place of singing with the trees looming so high and dark about it. They would have to hasten by it, because he wanted them deep into the swamp and under cover by daylight. He led forward, doubled over and keeping in the shadows of the bush and at the base of the tall papyrus, flared and crackling with the impact of the starlight over the track.

A bare hundred yards on, the track widened. The singing was clear and near and just beyond it was the after-glow of many fires thrown up from the far side of the fortress. Xhabbo halted at once. Never in all the experience of Bushmen, who in their constant coming and going between the eastern and western halves of their vast wasteland had constantly rounded this strategic cape of swamp, jutting into their ocean of a land, had the fires of men been seen at that place.

He waited until François joined him and was about to point all out to him but it was not necessary, because François was already commenting, 'I was afraid of this, Xhabbo. I was afraid the enemy would have medicines against mosquitoes. When I saw those trucks coming this way in the morning, I expected to find something like this. But do you feel we can get by the fires without being seen?'

Xhabbo muttered out of a self newly restored again by the proof that the dream vision had been true, that never yet there had been a fire of man which a Bushman had not somehow managed to get by in the dark. All they had to do was to follow him.

And follow him they would have done, if it had not been for an unexpected complication. This came from Nonnie. She had stood silently by, while Xhabbo and François had been discussing their situation, listening to the singing. She knew without doubt that only a Portuguese woman could be singing that song as it was being sung. She could tell from the tone that it was too tragic even for so nostalgic a song of fate, and believed the unknown woman was in terrible trouble, singing against her will. A feeling of utter helplessness communicated itself to Nonnie out of the manner of her singing, as she heard the flow of words that can be translated only roughly as:

> 'This song of fate was born on a day
> When the wind hardly stirred
> And the sky prolonged the sea
>
> At the home of a boat of sail
> And in the heart of a sailor
> Who being sad, sang:
> Oh how great the beauty
> Of my earth, my hill, my valley
> Of leaves, flowers and yellow fruit!
> Look, if you see lands of Spain,
> Sands of Portugal,
> Look, blind with tears!
>
> In the mouth of a sailor
> On a fragile boat of sail,
> The hurt song dying . . .'

Here the singing stopped, and Nonnie thought she heard the singer crying, but soon the unknown woman took up the song again.

> 'Pray that although another day,
> When the wind shall hardly stir
> And the sky prolong the sea
> At the prow of another boat of sail
> Shall sail another sailor,
> Who being sad, will sing:
> Oh how great the beauty . . .'

Nonnie did not wait for the chorus to be repeated for she knew at last what she had to do. She went up to François and Xhabbo to announce, with a vehemence that surprised them, 'I don't know what the two of you are planning, but I want you please, please not to go on until we've spoken to that woman singing. I know she's Portuguese and, from the way she's singing, she's in trouble. I'll never forgive myself, or you, if we go by without trying to help her.'

François had never seen Nonnie quite so sure of herself. He would have liked, after his highly trained nature, to give the matter deliberate thought but he was not allowed to, because to his amazement Xhabbo declared that he was feeling utterly that Nonnie was right. Had not he, Xhabbo, been asked in his dream to cut that woman from the ox-hide thongs that bound her to the tree? He too must be obedient to his dream if the dream dreaming him was not to abandon him and the evil ever to end, and they to go safe to the sea.

He did not wait for the approval of the others. He just went down into his favourite stalking position on hands and knees, and began crawling forward as rapidly as he had done that happy evening, when he had pretended to be a centipede with a sprained ankle, and laughter had returned to them. Ah, where was that evening now?

Within moments, the others following him, they reached the outer edge of the papyrus wall to find a moat of star-filled water between them and the castle of shadow. But fifty yards to their right a broad causeway of earth had been artificially flung across the diamond water to connect the forest of trees with the mainland. Some hundred yards behind the causeway, just slightly over and behind the raised brow of the island, flickered the tips of many fires and, outlined against their glow the hoods of many military trucks. By the edge of the water there was a dark shape, obviously that of the lone singer, now singing almost as if to herself.

Xhabbo beckoned Nonnie forward and immediately she was whispering loudly in Portuguese across the water, 'I say, I say . . . can you hear me? I say!'

The singing, now almost a kind of crooning, went on. Nonnie repeated herself twice, each time slightly louder, before the singing stopped. They heard a gasp as of shock from the singer. Nonnie was certain the singer had heard and waited, her heart thumping loud in her ears, for an answer but, as none came, she whispered in a more urgent tone, 'Please answer! Don't be afraid. I am Portuguese myself and am with friends, and we want to help.'

There was no doubt that the singer had heard Nonnie again but apparently did not believe what she was hearing, for Nonnie heard her crying to herself, 'Oh no! Dear Mother in Heaven, no! This is too cruel . . . this is the final depravity!'

'No, no, it's not cruel at all, it's true. I *am* Portuguese and I want to help. Who are you? Please don't be afraid, and speak to me!'

The singer, if not entirely convinced this time, was moved enough to test the reality of that voice in her own tongue, coming out of the dark, and called, somewhat less loudly than Nonnie, in a tentative, trembling voice, 'If you are not the voice of madness and are truly not deceiving me, then I am Maria Henrietta d'Alveira, a captured Portuguese woman and a prisoner here. Do you hear me?'

'Oh yes, I hear you clearly,' Nonnie, thrilled at the response, answered almost too loud for safety. 'You are Maria Henrietta d'Alveira and please go on, but hurry, so that we can help.'

Quickly and this time more confidently the woman warned, 'For God's sake be careful. There are a hundred soldiers and two thousand tribesmen who have come to hear me sing on the other side of the island. If I stop for long, some of them will be here to see why, and see that I go on doing my duty. But who are you?'

'It doesn't matter who we are,' Nonnie retorted, 'all that can come later. The point is, do you want to come with us? You must! Don't speak any more . . . just come and join us, I beg you, in the name of God! We'll get you away. I am with friends, we're armed and we'll protect you.'

'Are you certain? Dear God, if only that were possible. How could you get me away from this terrible place? Oh, if only I could believe you – I'd throw myself into this water and join you at once, before those men can get hold of me again. I've been here nearly a year, a closely-guarded prisoner, and nearly every night I am brought out to sing by this tree. I've long since given up hope of getting away. I think I'm near dying, I'm not sure that I have the strength to go far, and that it would be right for me to join you. If you are prepared to help me, you must be their enemies and in as great a danger as I am, and I don't think I can walk a mile in my state . . .'

'Oh forget your state and your scruples!' Nonnie's voice suddenly spoke for all the Portuguese Amelia-governesses there had ever been, out of a practical, realistic self that so often confounded François, and which the desperate situation now demanded. 'And don't bother to throw yourself in the water,' she continued. 'It's quite unnecessary. Just hurry to that causeway, cross it as fast as you can and we'll be on the other side to meet you. But you must come at once! We've no time to lose. Leave the rest to us. We know all there is to know about your captors!'

Nonnie's tone now was so confident, and the matter-of-fact administrative ring of it was obviously the sweetest and most comforting thing the singer had heard for months.

'Oh dear God, how wonderful,' she called back, the flood of life flowing back into her spirit, quickening the husky tone of a born fado singer.

At once she stood up, gathering something long about her. Breaking into a new kind of song with a quickened rhythm, almost too revealing for Nonnie's discerning ear, though probably not, she hoped, to their enemy's, Maria Henrietta d'Alveira began to walk towards the causeway as casually as if setting out on another perfunctory round of her singing duties, while Xhabbo led the others on a course parallel to meet her. She reached the causeway with no sign of alarm from their captors. Maria Henrietta's voice faltered, as if she were losing her nerve, and then stopped altogether, before she turned sharply in their direction and started on tiptoe across the causeway.

She had only taken three steps forward when a suspicious sentry challenged, in Bantu English, 'Who goes there? Stop, or I fire!'

Nonnie was about to call out, 'Don't listen – run, run as you've never run before' – when Nuin-Tara's hand clamped down on her mouth and prevented her speaking. It was just as well for her call would have been unnecessary. The woman broke into a run of her own accord.

'Stop or we fire!' the sentry's challenge rang out louder, shorter and more imperious than before. As she did not, he repeated it once more, and as she ran on he screamed rather than shouted the command: 'Fire!'

Instantly the darkness from seven different points flowered seven vivid red flashes and a rattle-tattle of automatic rifle-fire drowned any sound the woman might have uttered. Xhabbo and François, by now on the edge of the causeway, threw themselves forward to the ground, dragging down Nuin-Tara, Nonnie and Hintza in the process. Bullets whistled and droned and a storm of lead and steel beat over their heads and sent shattered papyrus tops showering down on them. When they could look again, they saw a shapeless bundle, darker than the darkness, lying still on the causeway. The automatic fire stopped and another voice, presumably that of a superior African officer, rang out.

'Oh you fools! Oh, you bloody, bloody fools! You've killed her! Now the singing tree will stop singing, and a thousand and more tribesmen here to witness it. Oh you bloody fools, you bloody, bloody fools!'

Nonnie was struggling fiercely with Nuin-Tara on the ground. Xhabbo and François had to rush and help her persuade Nonnie that the woman was truly dead and that they must get back to the shelter of the papyrus as fast as they could. The sentries, François reasoned, would not have shot if something had not made them more than usually suspicious, so much so that they might mount a search on their side of the mainland at any moment. Nonnie, however, had no heart or ear for reason, although the will of her companions contained her for the moment. Even so, they might not have succeeded in con-

347

vincing her, had not some ominous new order come out of the clamour which broke out among the soldiers as a result of their reprimand.

The voice of the man who had given the order to fire, was protesting; 'But, sah! I promise you, there was something strange going on. I would not have shot, if I did not think I heard that person talking to someone across the water.'

'Well, why didn't you say so before, you fool?' came the impassioned retort. 'Enough! I repeat, for the last time, enough of excuses, and your stupidity in shooting that woman. You've just spoilt years and years of careful planning. There's going to be the most God-almighty row about this. But if you did hear people across the water, we can perhaps still stop the matter from being a worse mess than it already is.'

Immediately the blast of a whistle, loud and long, went out over the island in the piercing way that François, Xhabbo and even Nonnie and Hintza had first heard it one dawn at Hunter's Drift. At once, from behind the brow of that great fortress of shadow, somewhere around those fires, came the sound of a great military camp breaking into immediate action.

Xhabbo hesitated no longer and ordered François to follow without delay, for happily the old Bushman track he had originally taken passed over a secret ford on the far side of the island, and with all that noise, their chances of getting by the fire and the island garrison were at their best.

Nonnie still protested and clamoured at François, 'Oh François, we can't leave her like that. We're not even sure she's dead. Oh please . . .'

François was more rough with her than he had ever been, because the killing had shaken him almost as much as her, and also because their danger was great. He was embroiled in an argument of his own almost as violent as Nonnie's, upbraiding the necessity of a flight that their safety imposed on them. Accordingly he said nothing to her that he was not saying in greater measure to himself. Taking her by the shoulders, gripping them so that it hurt, and shaking her, he muttered, 'Of course she's dead, or I would not be leaving her. And will you shut up and do what you're told or we'll all be dead as well. Come on Hin.'

With that, not even looking to see if she was following and so unaware that the tears were streaming from her eyes, he went as fast after the vanishing Xhabbo as possible, certain that if Nonnie faltered, Nuin-Tara would deal with her.

The noise of the enemy organizing itself for action was almost deafening, before it declined into the sound of armed and heavily booted men running over the causeway and up and along the road that led to and from the island, and in a direction which took them further away from the papyrus fringes of the swamp.

Soon Xhabbo was back on the old Bushman track and they were on their way to the heart of the swamp, on towards the sanctuary and the prospect of freedom in the other half of the desert beyond. They could tell the contentment with which the soles of Xhabbo's feet re-established their communion with the imprints of soles of countless vanished Bushmen feet that had made and maintained the track almost since the beginning of African time, because at once his pace became rhythmical and accelerated. The noise of the enemy, loud as it had been, quickly faded, the glow of the camp itself disappeared and the swamp and its own manifestations of being took command of the silence and the night.

By dawn, never once having paused, they halted at last on an island fortress of trees where Nuin-Tara, raking the sandy marshland earth, disclosed to them the ashes of other Bushman fires, which gave them a wonderfully healing feeling of company.

They were now in a world, Xhabbo said, where he had left no spoor that even a Bushman could follow and they could light a fire, prepare some food, eat and then go happily to sleep. But before they sat down François interrupted Nonnie who was going about her share of preparing camp as Nuin-Tara was. He took her hand and pleaded, 'Believe me, Nonnie, I was as sad as you were to leave that Portuguese lady. But I promise you I knew she was dead and I knew that if we did not go, we'd be dead too. All the time we've been walking, I've been thinking of something else that might help you, as it's helped me. I'm certain from what she said that she did not have long to live anyway. The swamp is full of terrible diseases. But more, I

349

know you were right to take us to her and I am sure that she did not die for nothing. You heard how angry that officer was afterwards. He had every reason to be angry, because from what I've heard about the African tribes and a lot of their recruits who give the enemy so much support, they believe in the prophecy of the singing tree as you believe in the Virgin Mary and her son. With this tree suddenly silenced, they'll take it as a sign from the great tribal spirits that the time of the fulfilment of the prophecy has not come. It might even make them realize how they have been tricked and used and turn on our enemies themselves. At the least, I wouldn't be at all surprised if, from now on, support for our enemies dwindles, on such a scale that they might be forced to withdraw.'

Nonnie was too tender within to speak or look at him but she pressed his hand in a way that meant more than words.

Their journey through the swamp, well-nourished on all the teeming game and bird life seemed long. They were travelling through another world, new not only to Nonnie but also to François; a world that merited acknowledgement in its own unique and rich right. Moreover, something happened on their second day after arriving in the swamp which, because of its potentially devastating impact on the future, changed the shape and character of their journey.

They slept all day and all through the night that followed at their first camp. They did not name it because it already had an honoured name which, according to Xhabbo, it would be unlucky to change. In a rough, idiomatic translation of the complex Bushman original, it was called, 'Big toe in the swamp', being the merest of thresholds to the great world of the swamp beyond.

On the second day they set out at a steady pace. At noon they came across an old buffalo bull asleep in the shade of a great thorn tree. Seen from amid the tall grass crackling with sunlight, and through an air white and undulating like liquid glass, the shade was black and the bull itself so dark that only Xhabbo, trained as even François was not, in the different shades of swamp shadow, knew it was the compact shape of a volcanic buffalo. For once François wished that he had a heavier rifle with him, as buffalo are notoriously hard to shoot, and so he had to try and compensate for the light calibre of his rifle by stalking the iron-clad bull, at great risk, until he was only fifteen feet away and could hear how it rumbled in its sleep. He could see plainly how tightly the eyes were shut, how deep the wrinkles made at their corners both by age and the burning impact of the fiery swamp and double-edged steel of sunlight. He noticed how the tail, even in so deep a sleep, constantly lashed the air all around his behind in order to keep off the flies and insects trying to draw blood from the sleeper. He marvelled at its massive marble horns, and the wide delicately carved nostrils glistening with health and breathing in and out as regularly as any automatic valve designed for a diver into great deeps.

He hated to try and kill it in its sleep. Sleep, he had been taught by Mopani and 'Bamuthi, was an act of trust without reservation by man, beast, bird and plant in their contract of life with nature, and to kill any sleeping thing was like killing someone in the midst of an act of holy communion, and gained one no good will in the life to follow. One carefully woke one's target no matter how small, and allowed the waking life which is part of death, as sleep is not, to join in the issue between one and it. But François felt he had no option. With the greatest care he aimed at the softest place just behind the shoulder blade, shot it precisely there, three times, before the bull could even be fully awake. The impact made it fall thrashing on to its side, and François had time to run in and shoot it three times more through the ear. Only then was it dead.

Xhabbo and Nuin-Tara were exultant, because they declared that they could now settle in the place for many days, feasting and making enough biltong out of almost a ton of buffalo meat to last them for months to come. And he and François at once set about the heavy task of skinning the vast animal. After some time, pausing for breath, François suddenly noticed that Hintza was lashing the air round himself with his tail and bounding up in fits and starts to bite himself all over. Worse, he found that both Nonnie and Nuin-Tara, watching them from nearby waiting for their call to help, were constantly slapping themselves and he heard Nonnie utter an unwilling cry of pain. He soon became aware that he too was being bitten, then glanced at Xhabbo and to his horror saw that

351

Xhabbo's neck and shoulders were covered with a score of flies, perched there in their dress of drab, Calvinist missionary calico.

He went dark all over as the name of the fly presented itself to his tongue with an ominous hiss, tsetse! He remembered Mopani and all his ardent reading of books on Africa, stressing how the game and people in and around the unexplored swamp were infected with 'ngana', the deadly sleeping-sickness, or *trypanosomiasis*, and that tsetse fly was the unflagging carrier of the disease to both humans and their cattle. There was every chance therefore that some of the flies stinging them were capable of transmitting both the animal and human varieties of the infection.

So unforeseen had this been, even in François's measured reckoning, that immediately he ordered Nuin-Tara and Nonnie, in a voice near to panic, to leave the shade of the tree and sit out in the grass where the sunlight was brightest and hottest.

They looked at him as if he were insane.

'Look, Nonnie, this is no joke,' he told her. 'These insects biting us all are tsetse flies and though they may well be as harmless as they look, there's a chance that they may be carriers of sleeping-sickness. I'm not going to let any of us take any chances. You are both to sit out there in the sun, hot as it is, because these flies hate the sunlight, and it's the only way I can protect you. So for Heaven's sake be a dear and do at once as you're told, and take Hin with you.'

He and Xhabbo, of course, had no option but to stay where they were until they had skinned and cut up the monumental buffalo and hung the meat in strips over the branches of the thorn tree, to be dried and cured. Only then could they hasten to join the others.

Xhabbo and Nuin-Tara were willing enough to believe him, since they both knew that the Bushmen themselves did not live in the swamp, and only used it as a safe way of travelling between the two halves of the desert, because it was known as 'a land of the plenty that is death'. And as Xhabbo emphasized, they never used it at this time of year. He would not have brought them here now if there had been any other way.

Nonnie took longer to convince because she had to have a

rational explanation of why François was so perturbed, although he did all he could to lessen the impact of his original dismay by making light of it.

'Perhaps only one in a thousand is infected,' François told Nonnie, 'and with the human strain of the sickness, and at this distance from human settlements, the proportions might be even greater. But we can't afford to take even a thousand to one chance.'

But Nonnie in her intuitive heart was not fooled. She suspected that nothing had worried François more than this intrusion of that horribly stinging, hideously drab and fantastically persistent fly. She marked, noted and inwardly speculated all the more widely, therefore, when François suddenly changed the subject of conversation and asked Xhabbo exactly how long it would take, from where they were, to get to the sea. For once, her suspicions made her an impatient listener to the long, round-about description of what might come; how all depended on what food they could find in the desert; on the game, water and effect on the country should the rains not come, as they had not come now for twenty moons; and how all important was the fact that at every perennial waterhole ahead there were human settlements which might be occupied by friends of their common enemies and if not, certainly by enemies of Xhabbo and Nuin-Tara. All in all, that meant they could not follow the way of the wind direct as a bee would to the water or flower of its choice, but would have to travel a round-about way, weaving in and out of their main direction as best they could, so that the journey could take anything from four to eight moons.

François absorbed Xhabbo's information meticulously and listened without word until this final summing-up, before breaking in, 'We've got to do it in four moons,' he declared fiercely. 'We've got to do it at the most in five, and the very utterly most, six moons, Xhabbo. We've *got* to do it. From today you must please not spare any of us but lead on as if feeling the enemy is coming fast on our heels.'

Nonnie, thinking, 'you protest too much, François,' was convinced that there was more in all this than François wanted to meet their eyes, particularly hers.

'And why suddenly in such a hurry?' she asked aloud. 'Are you not happy in your work any more?'

'I think you've been here longer than is good for you, Nonnie,' he tried to reply, as if there were no truth in her jesting, 'And the sooner you get back to your finishing school the better.'

Nonnie was not deceived, but out of the wisdom of the new 'Nuin-Tara' self she had so painfully laboured to acquire, she held her peace, hoping from day to day that François would say more to her of his own account. Yet he did not, to her increasing dismay. His knowledge seemed to him too dreadful to disclose before it could serve any useful purpose. And this knowledge which he kept so closely to himself was simply that if someone was bitten by a tsetse fly and infected with sleeping-sickness, and was not given proper treatment within six months, he would be beyond any cure that would not leave terrible after-effects. If it went untreated for more than six months, the disease would progressively establish itself in the central nervous system and within a year the person would be beyond any cure at all. He could rule out death from the disease, but he could not bear the thought that any of his companions, whether Nonnie, Hintza or Nuin-Tara, if cured, should be cured so late that their bright, physical selves would be dulled or maimed in any way. In his fear, one of Mopani's sayings became a kind of motto to him on the march that followed: 'Preparing for the worst is the only way of giving the best a chance to happen.'

In a manner that perturbed them all, he was suddenly a strangely clouded companion from then on, particularly when they had just come through another tsetse fly attack, as for some weeks almost daily they had to. It was no good him saying, when they emerged at last into the western desert, that it was all great fun, and that he was laughing inwardly all the time as never before. No one was deceived, Hintza least of all. He showed his anxiety by hardly ever taking his eyes off François. Whenever they were at rest or asleep, Hintza pressed against him harder than ever, as if to say, 'Look, I am here, and when I am here, how can anything possibly ever go wrong?'

Every day François was the first to wake, urging them to

354

hurry over their eating, urging them out of the camp, and then wanting them to march longer than ever during the day. Even so, at the end of even the longest marches, he would complain that they could have gone on further. This tendency in François became all the more pronounced when, twenty-seven days after the first tsetse fly attack, Nonnie was unusually difficult to wake up.

When she was thoroughly awake at last, she remarked to François, 'I'm mad with myself. I've suddenly begun to wake up with the most awful headaches, and it's not because you or Hin has kept snoring. If I may say so, you've been unusually quiet sleepers of late. Haven't you, darling Hin?'

She uttered her complaint lightly but François had already noticed that she had not been eating so much as usual. He had noticed too that Xhabbo had gone off his food and on several occasions was reprimanded by Nuin-Tara for not eating as a man ought to eat. So when Nonnie finished speaking, François looked across their fire and saw Xhabbo rubbing the temples of his head with both hands. François asked if it was true then that his head was troubling him, and that he had not been eating as well as usual. Xhabbo smiled dutifully and admitted that for a fortnight or so now 'I, Xhabbo, have not been I,' but he was sure it would pass. And he smiled all the more when François went to his medicine store and gave both Nonnie and Xhabbo a pill for their headaches.

François, never inclined to jump to conclusions, was more reluctant than ever to do so now, because the only conclusion could be sleeping-sickness. The only optimistic factor in their situation was that however closely he observed Nuin-Tara, Hintza or himself, none showed signs either of headaches or loss of appetite. Indeed, Hintza was eating enough for four. But he watched Nonnie and Xhabbo even more carefully, and within days he was certain that their headaches were worse, the loss of appetite greater. He was sure they were both showing the early signs of sleeping-sickness.

There and then he determined that while Nonnie and Xhabbo still had some of their former strength, and still could eat sufficient to keep up this strength, they would march even faster and that, in order to reach the sea under six months he would take short cuts which he knew were a calculated risk and which before they would not have contemplated.

François never went back on this last decision. After due consultation with Xhabbo and Nuin-Tara he cut out what Xhabbo had estimated as nearly the month's hard marching which absolute safety demanded, and risked going through the middle of a long, straggling line of African settlements stretched between a series of permanent water-holes. They went between one water-hole after the other, very much as they had gone through the far more densely populated area at the entrance to the swamps: dogs barking at them at night; men shouting to one another and lighting great fires, but never alarmed enough to come after them. Yet his plan to march Nonnie and Xhabbo to the limits of their strength was another matter, for it seemed to him that from the time he began taxing their infected bodies in a way hard for even his un-infected body to take, the illness accelerated. He remembered just in time the Matabele saying that the longest way round a hill was often the shortest way to the summit. He recalled how he had been taught that man, thrown on his own resources in the world of nature, could survive only by strict observance of the law of proportion.

It came to him all the more vividly at the end of the last of his desperate marches. They were assembled round the camp fire. Nonnie refused to look at him and appeared close to tears. François had no inkling that, feeling increasingly ill and exhausted, and knowing that Xhabbo was hardly any better, she was perceiving first with unbelief then utter incomprehension how François, knowing it all too, could drive them as hard as he was. She ended up not only by feeling more ill, but that night for the first time she was full of resentment against him for what she thought was such obvious and senseless lack of understanding and common humanity. She tried in vain to convince herself that he must have a reason. But if so, why did he keep it secret, and a secret, above all, from her? In that past at Hunter's Drift and Silverton Hill on which they had promised never to look back, where she had been the first to become aware of a secret self that François had endured alone far too long, had they not pledged themselves not to have any secrets from each other again?

So when François asked her in a voice full of concern what the matter was, she looked at him with eyes as bright with resentment as they were with the first touch of the fever of her sickness, 'You, only you, François,' she blurted out, 'I could never have believed you to be such an unfeeling brute!'

And with that she burst into tears.

François looked at Xhabbo and Nuin-Tara for comfort. They avoided his eyes and looked instead at Nonnie, and he knew where their sympathies were. Only Hintza, glancing first to Nonnie and then to him, so puzzled was he, stayed shivering with apprehension by his side.

All at once he was full of remorse and the doubts which had been forming within him became a single thought. He took Nonnie's hand and started to speak.

'Please forgive me! Oh please forgive me Nonnie,' he begged her. 'Please listen before you condemn me – there is a reason for it. Xhabbo, Nuin-Tara, please come and listen and I'll tell you why I've been forcing us all to march so hard.'

Quickly he confessed his fears to them. He explained in detail why he was convinced that both Nonnie and Xhabbo had been infected and why it was so important to get to the sea as soon as possible. He was not half-way through his explanation before three pairs of eyes were turned to him, not just full of understanding but of a gratitude anchored in total reassurance and certainty that he had been hurting himself much more in hurting them, and done it all unselfishly and solely out of concern for them. Indeed, Nonnie let out a whimper almost like Hintza, moved towards him and put one arm round Hintza and came to rest with her head on François's knees and kept close to him as if nothing had ever divided them at all.

François did not spare himself, but having come to the end asked them all to judge and in judging please to tell him what else he could have done? He did not wait for a verbal answer because the pressure of Nonnie's head on his knees and the eyes of the others told him enough. But he hastened to say how recently he had had a growing feeling that they should go each day only as far as Nonnie and Xhabbo felt they could go. Anything more, he feared now, would only help the disease. There was only one thing; he would have to ask Nonnie and Xhabbo to promise to tell him each day when they had gone far enough, unless of course Nonnie would allow him to decide for her. Knowing her, now that he had told her everything, he was afraid that she might press herself even harder than he had done. And perhaps Xhabbo would let Nuin-Tara decide for him when he had had enough for he was not certain that Xhabbo would not behave exactly like Nonnie in the circumstances.

'Oh yes, please, Coiske,' Nonnie mumbled without lifting her head from the place of comfort where she had found such reassurance and re-communion. 'Yes, you will decide for me, and I promise to obey.'

Xhabbo's reaction was even more marked. He looked at François with great relief. He exlaimed that a disease or two would make no difference between such friends as they were, and no amount of marching, however hard, could ever have made him doubt a brother his heart loved so much as Foot of the Day. What had really troubled him all that time was feeling himself weaken, feeling his liver leaving his body empty and without strength to move with the sun in the sky, as he put it. He was afraid that he had been wrong about the dream and was being punished for bringing about the killing of that singing woman. But now that he had been told the real cause of his weakness, he was full of the feeling that Foot of the Day would make him right as he had done when he had been hurt in the lion trap. He was full of this feeling because his tapping was back now to tell him all would be well.

Xhabbo had not mentioned his tapping for so long and considering that he was ill with a deadly disease as well, this re-emergence of long-distance signalling in his spirit impressed Nuin-Tara even more than Nonnie and François. She jumped up gracefully to her feet and did a little dance of gratitude to the fire, finishing with a backwards dip to a vanishing new moon.

Nonnie and Xhabbo kept to the letter and the spirit of the pact concluded in that camp, which was inevitably named by Xhabbo, 'The Place where Four became One'.

From then on, every day François left the three of them to march in the direction Xhabbo decided. He refused to allow Xhabbo to take part in hunting for food, for obvious reasons. He set out alone with Hintza at sunrise and searched far and wide for food in the harsh new western desert, where by day it became more difficult to find game to shoot. It meant that often he walked twelve times farther in the day than the plodding, dogged little line of three in which Nuin-Tara coaxed Xhabbo and Nonnie along like a hen the last two of a brood of chickens.

Somehow, always when their supplies of meat and tubers were about exhausted, he managed to find something to shoot and to enable Nuin-Tara to make the stews and meat-broths their sick companions needed more and more. It became rare for him to rejoin them before twilight and not find Nonnie and Xhabbo already half asleep and having to record the alarming fact that the day's march, even in a direct line, had been less than the previous one. The strain, the anxiety over Nonnie and Xhabbo, the greatly increased physical exertion made him fear that he might fail to carry the burden for them all, and not bring them safely to the sea.

What would have been minor practical difficulties earlier on became intolerable additions to a weight already almost unbearable as, for instance, coming home at sunset exhausted, only to have to set out again to find the melons for their thirst which Nuin-Tara had failed to get. This thirst in Xhabbo and Nonnie became all the greater as the sickness progressed and their embattled constitutions needed more and more liquid for fighting the disease. So far he had never failed, even on moonless nights, thanks to Hintza's nose for these things, to find either melons or water, but he feared it was only a matter of time before he would fail in a world of which he had no experience.

Also his supply of ammunition was running low, since Xhabbo's bow was no longer there to help him shoot lesser game. Often he was forced to use valuable rifle ammunition on shooting desert pigeons, sand grouse and, on one terrible foodless day even button quail which Xhabbo would normally have shot by arrow. Also there was the problem of medicine. None of the medicines he carried were of the slightest use against sleeping-sickness. He had foreseen all other possible infections of the blood. He had medicines for malaria, dysentery and any of the infections that the bite or claws of a wild animal or scratches from any thorn could inflict. But he had never thought of this. The only drugs of any use were the pain-killers and sleeping draughts, and these he had to ration, administering them only after their last meal at night, so that Nonnie and Xhabbo at least could sleep relatively well. But it meant that they had to endure walking like sleep-walkers in a nightmare of pain in the heat of the day, un-sedated and with only their will and courage to drive on their aching and weakening bodies. And of these medicines, counting them like a miser his coins, on the night they had made their pact he had only enough for another seventy-three days.

Nonnie, though she never complained and would never have told François, had a fear of her own which made her oddly immune, by sheer disproportion, to what she was suffering physically. Often she would look at François and her heart, as Nuin-Tara would have put it, turned to water. She saw how much taller he had grown, how his shoulders had widened but also how gaunt he had become. He had never had any fat on him but here in this unforgiving desert light she was frightened to see how fine-drawn, how distinct the aristocratic line of bone beneath the skin had become, and how deep and great the purple-blue eyes were now behind the absurdly long eyelashes, so wasted on a young man, since they were overlong even for shade against the sun. His face and arms were almost burnt black; his hair was beginning to lengthen like a girl's, and, always unusually fine, was now bleached into a strange, platinum colour. Even the ridiculous eyelashes – and the sight nearly made her cry – had their tips dipped in the platinum of the inexorable sun. Looking at a face that to her was the most beautiful and beloved in the world, she would cross herself and pray, 'Dear Mother in Heaven, I don't mind dying for myself, I feel so ill, but don't let me die, because what will become of François if I do?'

And in this she was as truly objective as any human being could possibly ever be. By being utterly the subject of her emotions, by going down into herself to the point where she was the last strained link between the world without and the world within her, by being in this process utterly the subject of the life to which her flesh and blood had been so urgently contracted, she attained a startling, crystal, objective clarity she had never before experienced, and knew that her concern in this was not for her own self but totally for François. She realized how from the moment her father had first taken her away from Silverton Hill and kept her for a year at a finishing school in Europe, she had had a crystal vision of the day when she would be François's guide in her world as he had been hers in the world of nature. This vision had gained in detail and magnitude and authority with every day of the march behind them, because of her knowledge that Hunter's Drift and the world of François's childhood had gone for ever, and that as he had pledged her there would be no looking back. She could not see François and his Hintza on their own coping with the world as she knew it. She could not bear to see all that was to her something so pure, innocent, upright and true go unarmed and vulnerable into what she now feared despite her youth, was a twisted, devious, calculating and selfish world, armed to the teeth for its own slanted purposes. She had accordingly seen herself as a kind of heroic Amazon, fighting off the world to give François the time to grow into the man who would deliver her from any need of playing the unfeminine role to herself. She had an eloquent picture of François, uncorrupted, confirmed and wise in the ways of her world, taking his place by her side, to defend them both there as he defended them now. She never doubted for a moment that chance and circumstance, which so mysteriously and with such a complex, infinite and resourceful precision had combined to bring them together, from such totally different backgrounds and from such unlikely and remote points of departure, could have done so without some grand design of its own.

She was too young for names or definitions of this relationship. She did not even give much thought to it in terms of the much-debased coinage of the word 'love', which despite the devastating current abuse, one is compelled to use, because it has no substitute or alternative. Love was so taken for granted that it had not even been uttered, because the relationship, in her own intuition, felt like something quite new in the chronicles of life and time. Young as she was she had no doubt that never in real life, never even in literature, and she had read far more than most young women of her age, never in the ultimate of legend and myth, could there ever have been anything to match what fate had given her and François to share between them. She had no urge or desire to define it or make conceptualized thought or philosophy out of it, only the deepest and clearest of feelings derived from an unshakeable conviction that their relationship, their total coincidence of being, was utterly unique and that it just would have to be lived. If it were not lived, life and the world would be the poorer for it. So always at the end of the day as at the beginning, indeed often in the middle of the night amid some terrible dream, the final thought always was for François, and, if at all for herself, only in so far as it prompted François's well-being and his relationship to life. And she could truly feel within the emerging woman in herself, that in so far as love had to be brought into an argument that was settled in her heart before it started, if she acknowledged a love for François, she loved him not for herself but on behalf of life.

This, somehow, even in her darkest moments, when it seemed that her body and mind had become a new invincible despotism of pain, the flame and fire of the feeling arrested the power of, if it did not abolish, the ice-age of sickness and darkness creeping into her physical well-being. At once she would know that, however much her body might want to fall out of the march of life, the sense of a great universal necessity working through her and François would bear her up so that she could pursue to a true and full end what life had originally intended by bringing them with such a mysterious symmetry together, and that one day yet it would be fulfilled, sheer like lightning, without reservation or compromise. She would snuggle up closer to him and Hintza, feeling that in life summed up thus, the three of them were at one, and like the desert stars bright and resounding above their fire, they were set in a lawful course of their own that nothing could arrest and deny.

After such a night François would know that he was even closer to Nonnie. Just the merest touch of her skin startled him with its message, as if one skin enclosed them both. And his being closer to her, to Nuin-Tara and to Xhabbo, sustained him when away alone hunting. He would remember the physical nearness of Nonnie and the look of trust with which Xhabbo would always watch him go in the morning. It was the same look Xhabbo had given him the day he rescued him from the lion-trap. It was a look François had seen elsewhere only in Hintza and the animals who had never before looked into the eyes of other men. He remembered Mopani telling him about this very look that one sees, as he put it, 'only in the virgin eyes of the children of nature. It is a look one must never betray, little cousin.'

He could almost hear the beloved voice itself there in the desert where he walked alone: 'One can perhaps betray oneself if one must, and hope some time for pardon from life, and one can betray the men of the twentieth century because they have all betrayed one another for so long that they have some kind of terrible immunity to betrayal. But for people of nature and animals and birds still capable of such a look, there is no such immunity, and betrayal is death to them as it is ultimately to the betrayer.'

Intangible as all these feelings and intimations and recollections were, they did François more good than any amount of medicine, ammunition or the help of others could have done. Once they were recognized, welcomed and made at home in his daily reckoning, he would be reassured, composed and more resolute. And he would come back, tired as he was, night after night, with whatever little of food he had gathered from the desert, eagerly looking forward to seeing those dear, trusting faces, dismayed though he would be by noticing again how ill and thin they looked, asking only that they should open their eyes and show him that the ancient, first look of trust was still there.

The detail of every evening was stored up accordingly in his memory as a new source of wealth and daily he would hasten back, spurred on by a feeling of going 'home', however strange it may sound in a desert where no one had a fixed home, where home was not in any given place but in the feeling of being at home anywhere in the universe, by instant right of the fact that one is a child of it and the life it lit on earth.

He was helped in this by a new kind of sunset. He had never seen sunsets with such a range of colour. It was amazing how so stark and uncompromising a wasteland produced such tender colours and such delicacy of tone to accompany the dying sun, as if nature were entering through them a plea for forgiveness to the parched and wounded earth that had suffered under it all day long. And François was deeply moved, for the earth seemed instantly to respond and become alive with compassion, gracing the last aftermath of colour with the first fall of its own special benediction of dew.

There was one sunset when he saw his first hills on the horizon, and his heart soared like a bird; not only because a heart that has been nourished for so long only on desert levels flew by reflex of the spirit after the swift, god-like flight of physical vision to the hill-tops, but also because Xhabbo had told him, 'When you feel your eyes feeling themselves full of hills, feel yourself utterly to be near the sea.'

Those first hills were of a startling, precise and yet midnight blue, announcing in their almost melodramatic outlines that the thrusting desert wave of earth in search of form had come to an end, and that an ordered pattern of land and stone would now contain, fashion, and give it the definition it lacked before. And when the sun went down behind them, it left the landscape in between filled with the scarlet light that was the blessed light of the great Heitse-Eibib himself, and François walked on a yellow beach as it were of sand, under a Hottentot copper sky with a sea of light like blood breaking over it to send foam and spume of itself to drift a mist of gold before his smarting eyes. Nothing could have been a better omen on the threshold of the night.

The next day the desert, soft with sand and lush by comparison with bush, scrub and plant, fell away behind them and the earth stretched far and wide on all sides of them, lean and with nowhere any fat to be seen on it. They passed slowly between the hills and Nuin-Tara helped Xhabbo up that night to show him the sun, first a bright yellow and then red on the greatest of the hills. Xhabbo somehow managed to greet it firmly with his most reverent salute before he told François that it was good. That was the hill where the Bushman God had first discovered fire, to give it to the people of the early race. If

François looked at it, at that moment as he, Xhabbo, was looking, he would see how the hill and even the ring of iron-stone around its crown was burning with everlasting fire.

They struggled on and on, the next day and the next, until the hills all vanished, and they were suddenly back in a desert of dunes, but dunes that dwarfed the dunes behind them. They were dunes of pure sand with no plant of any kind upon them. The sand was so deep at their base that it was only with the greatest difficulty that he and Nuin-Tara could manage to get Nonnie and Xhabbo to stagger on through the day. François feared that if they had to go on much longer in this world of sand their water would give out and since the strength of his partners was declining so fast and they were moving so slowly, they might be unable to reach a source of replenishment. Yet significantly neither Nuin-Tara nor Xhabbo was dismayed. On the contrary they smiled at him and for the first time announced, 'We feel ourselves to be near to where we are going.'

Towards evening they found a pass between two mountain dunes, the equivalent of Everest and Annapurna in desert terms. On their towering crests, curved and curling like two waves raised by a great typhoon, they saw from the narrow trough in between, the wind of evening driving a spume like smoke from their tips and heard a strange singing rise up on the still, tender and darkening air. Xhabbo and Nuin-Tara clapped their hands and exclaimed, 'Listen, oh listen, and feel how they are singing to the singing and dancing sea!'

After a struggle too long and too painful to be capable of comprehension in some soft-chaired moment safe in a room of amber, where it might be declared beyond human possibility, they passed out of this winding valley of sand. They emerged suddenly on the banks of a broad fragment of a dry river-bed, like a kind of valley-meadow, though their horizon was still a ring of more great dunes. François suddenly saw with unbelieving eyes, a flash of shining kingfisher blue beyond a river bank and a wide pool of water lined with bulrushes. He was startled by the song of birds singing one of the sweetest songs ever heard by deprived ears. He and Nuin-Tara hastened to prepare their camp before the sun finally set, because Nonnie and even Xhabbo were speechless, and so grey and thin that

François feared that they might die there and then, if they were not instantly rested and fed.

At that precise moment Nuin-Tara told François with a lift of even her stoical voice that they had 'arrived' and that in the morning, he would have to cross the dune in front, see the sea and then follow the shore away to the north-west to where the way of the wind ended on the great water wherein it was born. By noon he ought to reach the place of people who come out of the sea. It was known to the Bushmen as 'The Place of Chains', because so many Bushmen for a century or more had been taken away bound to that place, never to return. But as François too was a child of the people who come out of the sea, the place would be good to him and he would find the help he wanted.

The feelings roused in François by this pronouncement were so violent and the prospect so dazzling that his own exhausted senses were at once a mixture of intoxication and unbelief. He had counted and added up carefully every day from their first encounter with the tsetse fly. He took out his dispatch book and stood there with the twilight wrapped round him, opening it slowly and studying it like some apprentice alchemist his ultimate formula. Yes, he was not drunk with hope. It was exactly one hundred, thirty-seven and a half days since the first tsetse fly attack.

Immediately he bounded like an impala to where Nonnie and Xhabbo had already been made comfortable side by side in front of a newly lit fire. Stabbing at the pages in front of him with trembling fingers, he exclaimed, savage with exaltation, 'Nonnie! Xhabbo! Do you know, it's taken only a hundred and thirty-seven and a half days to get here! Only one hundred, thirty-seven and a half days!'

Nonnie opened eyes that hurt. After that terrible struggle through the thick sand and heat, aching and weak, she might have been forgiven for not taking in the import of his message as quickly as she would normally have done. Indeed she managed to give a plausible appearance of having failed to do so. Yet she reacted as she did ultimately because any sign that the deliberate François of their journey could be so impulsive with light and joy as he now was, made her so happy that she just had to balance her feelings with a pretence of detached and affectionate mockery, for she exclaimed, 'is that all? Only one hundred, thirty-seven and a half days? Dear God, I thought it had been much, much longer . . .'

'But, Nonnie . . .' François, disconcerted, was his most vehement self and about to protest at length, but the warm look in her hurt eyes corrected him. A tremendous feeling of quite undeserved gratitude rose up like a fountain in him. Humbled and overawed by all they had been allowed to come through, as he was convinced now that they had done, he remarked in a voice low and reverent for him, 'You see, Nonnie, it's just over four months. It's well within the limit of six that the illness sets us. You see, by tomorrow night, if all goes well, I shall have help. There's no reason on earth now why in a few weeks you and Xhabbo shouldn't be well and not a bit the worse for the infection.'

Nonnie quickly turned over to hide her head in her arm, so that François should not see how the tears prompted by such a complex of emotions, smarted in her eyes. She was glad that Xhabbo's electric voice broke the silence to distract François. Gravely, and in the most appropriate of Bushman metaphors he was saying that he had never doubted that his Foot of the Day would bring them to this place; this place in particular which as every Bushman child knew, was the place where their father Mantis had always come in times of trouble. Foot of the Day would remember the many stories of how their father Mantis when in peril, when life seemed to have come to the end even for a god like him, as for instance when he was set upon and nearly killed by the 'persons who sit on their heels', and on many, many other occasions of anguish and near extinction of which Xhabbo had no time now to speak, he had always gone to a place of water and reeds and rushes where birds sang in the desert and in the water there, had made himself whole again. This, Xhabbo announced, was that very place.

François's feeling of having come through swelled into a transcendent emotion of resolution, exalted by this proclamation of the magical associations Nuin-Tara and Xhabbo had with the place. In consequence they all slept more calmly and deeply than they had done for many, many weeks.

CHAPTER FIFTEEN

Hunter's Testament

François and Hintza were the first to wake because of the birds by the pool announcing the day. He got up quietly and sat on the edge of the bank, and watched the dawn break over the yellow dunes, singing a high soprano to the invisible and at that hour remotely audible and constant bass of the singing and surging sea. The yellow dunes had a presence, almost a personality, so powerful that even the shadows where he sat were somehow made golden by them. The sky above was a piercing blue with a shining lacquer of black in the west. The light in the east was scarlet, the tops of the dunes themselves smoking white in the morning wind and the air in between soon had a magic-lantern glow. He watched weaver birds coming out of the nests they had woven so beautifully round the tips of the tallest bulrushes that their weight made them bow their heads to the sacred pool. The birds themselves looked so normal and busy that he could not help smiling à 'good morning' to them as if they were good middle-class citizens opening up house for the day. Then, looking into the water which had become a delicate Chinese painting on silk with reflections of tall reeds, their tassels, nests and birds and colours of dawn, he remembered how fevered and parched Nonnie had been the night before.

He went quietly back to their camp to fetch all their dixies, rinsed them out thoroughly by the water where his own reflection and Hintza's lay as if in a mirror. So long was it since he had seen himself in a cool, objective frame that he was amazed to recognize himself in the water, and had an odd sense of a return to reality, almost as if until then he had doubted whether all that had happened, had really happened to the person called François.

He filled the dixies and went back to Nonnie, who had just woken up. He took his kerchief and made her sit up and delicately sponged her face, neck, shoulders, arms, hands and feet again and again, until she declared that she had experienced nothing more wonderful on the whole of their journey, and was already completely cured.

Something of her old, bright, spirited manner flashed in her. She looked out of fever blurred eyes at him to say, 'I think after this, François, you can consider yourself to have entered an order that poor old Fa always longed to get into, but never succeeded. Regard yourself fully invested as a Knight Commander of the Bath.'

François helped Nuin-Tara to do the same for Xhabbo. Then, once he had eaten, took his rifle and haversack. He left his ammunition pouches because his last seven bullets were in the magazine. He told them he would not be long, that is, long by their reckoning of time. He would be back by evening or early the next morning, without fail. He was rewarded with such a look, not of hope or anticipation but absolute certainty that he would be as good as his word, that he almost feared it might be too provocative of fate.

He quickly embraced Nonnie and gave Xhabbo and Nuin-Tara their own salute of farewell. Then, without waiting, eager to be better than his word, went fast on the way Nuin-Tara had told him he had to go. Just below the crest of the first dune, he looked back. The smoke of their fire was growing tall and straight like a royal palm tree in the still air. Nuin-Tara was installed beside it and within touch of her hand were two still shadows in the shadow of the bank where they sheltered, no doubt those of Nonnie and Xhabbo, lying near each other.

Reassured, François, with Hintza beside him, then climbed up to the crest of the dune. It forked out below him, one arm curving away to the south; the other and higher one hid his view to the north. He felt a breeze colder than any he had ever felt on his face and heard a vast, urgent murmur, swelling to a sound like the noise of a rushing river. There below him was the blue and heaving sea; a water almost as blue as the sky, so that it was difficult to tell sky and ocean apart. Below him was a wide, long yellow beach and the swell of the sea drawn towards the land by white horses, like the horses of the god of which Homer wrote in François's beloved *Odyssey*, pounding over the hollow sands with flashing hooves. All along to the south where the sands were out of reach of the sea and the shining silk of the wet beach was roughly translated into the roughness of land and black rock, the beach was thickly populated with seals, walruses and masses of strange, upright and oddly clerical and dogmatic looking penguins. Over their heads, his eyes were drawn to and unbelievably uplifted by a white bird which gave him an immediate feeling of kinship, almost of inborn familiarity, although he had never seen it except in books. It was a vast bird, and did not use its enormous spread of long wings at all but just kept them fully spanned against the thrust of the breeze, to soar and re-soar apparently for the delight of it, through the resounding blue air, and at times dipping so low that the spune blown from the white manes of the horses of the sea smoked over its wings. He knew he was seeing for the first time an albatross, the lone white hunter and great slayer of big ocean distances. He wanted to stay to enjoy the exhilarating sight and the new taste of life raised by the scene in his senses but the one desperate pre-occupation of months' standing, made him turn abruptly and go back over the northern shoulder of the dune.

He straddled the summit and stopped short suddenly on the skyline; a thing he would never have done even a day before. He stopped, because there, in the comparative calm of the open bay, formed by a long spit of sand, he saw a fleet of warships.

He stared hard and long at shapes exactly like illustrations in his books and counted seventeen warships in white tropical paint, swinging at anchor, all washed down, scrubbed, neat and polished so that they flashed like jewels in the morning sun. For a moment he was not at all certain that the ships were not a vision of his own starved self. Could they be part of his urgent reality? Then the feeling of conviction, from the fact that his doubt did not make them vanish, became a new kind of music, and as music made his hair and Hintza's stand on end.

He would have gone on staring at them, had he not suddenly noticed that between the ships and the shore, scores of very strange dark green boats, smaller and square and flat, were hurrying towards the beaches. Some of them had indeed already stuck their noses fast into the sands. Armed men with rifles, machine guns and heavy packs on their shoulders were already running fast down their broad ramps and spreading out in military formation along the beach in front of him, and beginning to advance in the most ominous and deadly fashion towards the dune on which he was standing.

His joy in the scene went and the fear which clutched at him, after such hope, was the darkest he had yet known. For a moment he was convinced that it could only mean that their enemies were there in command as well, and about to discover him. He did not give himself time to argue that powerful as their enemies had proved to be in the past, they were hardly powerful enough to mount so great an exercise with a fleet of seventeen warships on the open sea. He forgot that he thought he had seen a white ensign flying from the greatest of the ships and the stars and stripes from another. He only remembered 'Bamuthi's 'the buck has got out of the pot', and immediately fell flat on the sand, his own rifle in the firing position. Hintza, without prompting, lay flat on his stomach in the shadow beside him.

But he did not go down fast enough. He had, in fact, stood there longer than he realized, enjoying the spectacle of a modern fleet of war complete with aircraft carriers, cruisers and attendant ships. The officer supervising the landing of the brigade of marines had seen him, trained his glasses on him and remarked to the man at his side with an ominous calm, 'I wonder what the hell that ruddy comedian thinks he's doing up there complete, of all things, with a dog? After all, we've circulated everybody in this god-forsaken place, and the magistrate has had his police out for weeks to tell everyone to keep away from this beach for a fortnight. But look, there's that idiot walking straight into our field of fire. We'd better get him out of there, before he gets hurt.'

He immediately detached two marines from the platoon deployed nearest him and the three of them came, at the smartest naval double to the place where François was lying invisible.

François was without field glasses and not at all certain what it could all mean. But he was prepared to find in them another enemy, considering how many white faces had already proved to be his foes in the past. He had them lined securely in the sights of his rifle, and waited, planning what to do after he had shot them. He was determined above all not to make a break over the crest which could only result in bringing the inevitable pursuit down on his friends. But suddenly the three men stopped and began calling and waving their caps at him.

Still he lay flat where he was and they had to come closer. It was not until they were within fifty yards of him, that he was certain that they were British, for he heard himself being addressed in English, 'You sir, you over there! Will you be good enough to show yourself, and explain what you are doing?'

Only then did François begin to believe he might have no cause to fear. He jumped to his feet, his rifle on his arm and the safety catch still released, just in case, and slowly stepped forward with Hintza no less prepared.

The officer was already on the point of upbraiding him for his slowness in responding to the challenge, when somehow he realized that there was something in the vision before him that was most unusual. He held his peace, observant and too curious now to be angry. When finally François stood in front of him, looking in that morning light just as Nonnie had seen him, with more than a year of suffering of mind and body, hunger and fatigue, written large all over him, a face almost black with sun, as well as a strange, alert, long and burnished dog beside him, the officer was moved to wonderment. He hardly noticed that François was holding out his hand, saying politely, 'Good day, sir, I am François Joubert.' In François's upbringing, this was the polite way of introducing himself to a stranger, giving the stranger the right opening for introducing himself too. The officer had the strange English distaste of shaking hands with other men, and he took François's with some embarrassment, responding, 'Michael Featherstone, Commander, Her Majesty's Royal Navy sir. But pray, what are you doing here and – '

He stopped as he nearly winced under François's grip. François had been taught that if one shook hands at all one shook them always as if one really meant it, and he was amazed at the officer's limp response.

'I've just come across the desert with my friends, and we need help desperately,' François answered in a steady, considered voice. 'Can you help me please, sir?'

And then in a few minutes the quintessence of his story was

out and the marines were sent running back to the beaches to return with a yeoman of signals. Commander Featherstone at once took over the yeoman's walkie-talkie. Characteristic of a service wherein one is given one's first taste of command and lesson in accepting responsibility at the age of thirteen even if it is only responsibility for taking a liberty boat alongside, he had no hesitation. Despite his bland and casual exterior, he was in a hurry. While the yeoman of signals was flashing his aldis lamp to the aircraft carrier which was the flagship of the fleet, he called over his radio phone, 'Featherstone calling C-in-C himself with urgent repeat urgent request for exercise to be suspended and permission to come on board.'

The signalling on the lamp direct to the officer of the watch was an additional precaution to ensure that he could speak direct to the admiral himself. For in exactly seven minutes now the force of marines were due to advance on an imaginary enemy, esconced among the dunes, behind a barrage of live shells and rockets, to give them as realistic a feel of war as is possible in peace. As a result the exercise was suspended for the moment and within half an hour François and Hintza were being helped on to a ramp, into a landing craft full of staring marines, and out at the far end of the landing craft into the admiral's barge itself. With the Commander by his side he was taken straight to the flagship at full speed.

They followed Commander Featherstone up the great ship's ladder. The ship itself was dressed with sailors, and all the sailors looked down full of curiosity at them. As they went up the ladder both François and Hintza heard what is perhaps one of the most exciting and moving of man-made sounds, the high fountain-wise pitch of a bosun's whistle, piping an officer on board a great ship at sea. François found it inexplicably hard not to cry when he heard it. But Hintza seemed to be uplifted by it. When he saw the officer step from the gangway on deck and jump to attention to salute the quarter-deck and without the least prompting by François, he did his greatest 'grandfather curtsey' as if dropping it to the greatest of baboons.

François had more feelings than thoughts about what was happening so fast to them, and could only just hold on to the clearest thought available; he was being brought to someone who would get help quickly and so save Nonnie and Xhabbo from what for months had seemed certain death.

The salute and curtsey over, they were rushed down a companionway, along a narrow ship's corridor and up to the iron doorway of the admiral's cuddy. His guide knocked and opened the door. Michaél Featherstone was about to walk in when he recollected that never in naval history would an Admiral of the Fleet have had to receive so odd a deputation, in particular one so well armed. He knew his Admiral well and was certain that it would only be a matter of time for the Celt he inherited from a Highland mother to respond with imagination to François's story. All that worried him was the effect of the first impressions of such an unorthodox entry in such unlikely company. For once he was uncertain.

'I say,' he remarked in an undertone to François. 'I think it might be a good idea if you parked your gun there by the door. It's not . . . you see that of course, don't you.'

The single-minded François saw only enough in his embarrassed sensitivity to respond, 'How kind of you.' But still, not out of obstinacy or bad manners, only years of habit, he gripped his rifle all the more firmly, determined not to be parted from it.

The Commander-in-Chief was sitting at the head of his table. He had a map open in front of him and all round him a team of senior staff-officers. He saw a highly uncomfortable Commander step in, followed by a dog of legendary appearance and François, as one has described him, his rifle in his right hand. The Commander-in-Chief's face was a mixture of red and tan, after forty-seven years of service at sea. He had the nose and features of an ancient Roman, with large and unusually bright, clear and acute blue eyes. Yet, trained as he was to shocks of war, sudden emergencies and nuances of crisis of all kinds, he could not help a flicker of astonishment and a reddening of even his weathered face, while wondering, 'What the blazes does Featherstone think he's up to? I hope he knows what he's about, and has some better reason than this scarecrow for making me hold off manoeuvres.'

The reaction was understandable, not only because of François's unlikely appearance but because Featherstone had been unable to say much more in their curt radio exchange than that he had intelligence of an urgent and most unusual kind to justify suspension of the exercises, and was bringing the intelligence itself on board. Was it this rag-and-tatter and hollow-eyed apparition with long, blond hair like a wasteland hippie? All this and more passed through the computer of his long experience of life and men. Had it not been for a traditional concept of discipline at sea, where firmness and grace of command are regarded not only as highly compatible but essential to one another, he might have been angered by this outrageous appearance of such an intrusion. But all he did was to speak in a tightly controlled and forthright manner and tone, that could not be denied. 'Now come on in, young fellow, m'lad, come in at once and explain if you can, what reason you have for holding up the South Atlantic exercises?'

François, immune in the conviction of the all-importance of his mission, as well as in his innocence of a service world, explained at once that he did not have the time to explain. Since the massacre – and at this word all the officers looked to one another for enlightenment and sat up straighter with interest – he and his companions had travelled for more than a year across the desert and now two of them were just on the other side of that dune dying. Could the Admiral please help them by sending a message to the magistrate at that nearby place to which he had been walking in order to get help, when he had run into the marines that morning? Could he please instruct the magistrate there to send a doctor to them without delay?

'But who are you, young man, and who are these companions?' the admiral asked, as if playing for time to test the authenticity of a messenger bearing so incredible a tale.

'I am François Joubert from Hunter's Drift, on the other side of the desert,' he answered, speaking faster but still clearly and firmly. 'My companions are Luciana Monckton, the daughter of Sir James Archibald Sinclair Monckton, who was massacred by terrorists with my mother and all our people. She will die if you do not help us quickly, and with me too are Xhabbo . . .'

He got no further. His audience were completely held by the unexpectedness and enormity of his statement, as well as startled when the Bushman click implicit in 'Xhabbo' fell on their ears. But it was the mention of Nonnie's father that really produced the breakthrough from incredulity into belief. The Admiral himself was the first to exclaim, 'James Archibald Sinclair Monckton? Good God, you don't mean young Jamie Monckton? He served with me in the war, and I know he's been reported missing believed killed in Africa, for more than a year. So that was the manner of it. You must tell us more – come and sit here next to me and will someone see to it that they have something to drink and eat immediately. They both look as if they can do with it.'

And then the whole background of what he had been referring to was plain in under fifteen minutes of quick and highly condensed telling. From then on all the readiness to help from a service that is always prepared and rejoices in helping even more in peace than in war, was there in over-abundance for François's asking. The guard on duty at the cuddy went off at the double to fetch the Surgeon-Rear-Admiral and François was subjected to a clinical examination of Nonnie's and Xhabbo's condition which, thanks to his reading on sleeping-sickness was so convincing that the medical Admiral turned to the Admiral and remarked, 'He would make a good doctor this young man, sir, but I fear I've not got the right drugs with me here. With your permission I suggest we send a signal to base, and that you give the signal and compliance with the signal the highest priority. The young man is right, it's a matter of life and death.'

The Admiral immediately ordered his flag-lieutenant to draft the appropriate signal, specifying the drugs needed and in his own hand inscribed the form 'Personal from Commander-in-Chief, to Supreme "O", Most Immediate', which is the highest priority of all in service signalling. The Most Immediate was boldly underlined.

That done, he turned to François, with a smile on his weather-beaten features, to say, 'That ought to satisfy you my lad. I don't think this degree of priority has been used or requested since the dropping of the atom bomb on Hiroshima. But is there anything else we can do?'

François hesitated, feeling he had already asked too much,

but there was such a look in the experienced blue eyes of willingness, even anxiety, to do more, that he ventured to ask tentatively, 'I wonder, sir, could you possibly let me have a little more ammunition?'

'Is that all?' the Admiral sounded surprised as well as disappointed in the smallness of the request, yet stirred to admiration by what it told him of François. 'What sort of ammunition?'

'Please, sir,' François answered more firmly, on his own ground, 'twenty-five steel pointed .22 high velocity and twenty-five lead pointed of the same kind.'

'Have you got that, S.C.O.?' the Admiral asked the Captain of Operations, who had been following François's story on a map.

He looked back steadily at the Admiral, obviously a man of action rather than words. 'Have heard, sir. Can do. Will do.' And then, without turning his head, he said over his shoulder to a naval Commander sitting behind him. 'You've heard, number one? See to it.'

'Aye, aye sir,' came the reply. Before leaving François had his ammunition.

Meanwhile Hintza, who as of right had made straight for the head of the table and at one moment had his chin on the admiral's map as if reassuring himself that his location had been pinpointed correctly there, was being fondled, stroked and admired, and now treated to endless helpings of the hottest, sweetest and milkiest chocolate he had ever drunk. But François, to everyone's amazement, refused refreshment and food of any kind. He refused, moved though he was by the urgent offers of men stirred by the marks of suffering and deprivation beyond even their varied experience, as much as by the record of endurance and heroism of epic proportions of the four young people.

François just went on thanking them warmly and said they were much too good and kind, but reiterated that he never drank or ate on the march between sunrise and sunset. He did not disclose that it was a Bushman point of honour, first learned from Koba and then Xhabbo, that the one who went to fetch food and help for stricken companions only ate and drank and benefited by the help obtained when all could eat and drink together again. He was not even tempted by Hintza's obvious relish over his chocolate and he gave his mind over entirely to answering more and more thorough questions as to what other things they needed most. Even so, his own feeling of desperation was so successfully conveyed that within an hour of arriving on the ship, the Admiral, Michael Featherstone and the Surgeon-Rear-Admiral in his battle dress, were summoned to the flight deck on the flagship.

François did not hear, as the door closed behind them, the captain in charge of operations throwing down his pencil on the cuddy table and bursting out, 'I don't know what you all think. But there ought to be a special kind of medal struck for people like that young man. I've never heard anything like it. If you fellows followed his story as well as I on this map you must realize what a staggering thing he and his friends have done. I hardly believe it yet myself, dammit. And damn the men who drove them to it.'

'I'm afraid, Tug, these things are never as simple as our desires.' (Tug was the inevitable nickname of a Captain called Wilson, in a service where all Wilsons automatically became 'Tug'.) The naval D.N.I. now spoke directly to him in that kind of reflective, contemplative voice that good D.N.I.s often have. 'I've been through two world wars now and from what they've taught me there's no medal or order yet designed to reward that kind of person and that sort of thing, even when it is recognized. I fear the reward for them has to be left to what the doing of it gives them.'

'Oh hell, there you go again,' the Captain exclaimed, 'you'd make metaphysics out of old rope. I still say that that boy ought to have some sort of award and the C-in-C ought to see about getting it for him. If he won't, I shall.' He glared fiercely at them.

Meanwhile, as is the way in ships, rumours of François's mission and what he had gone through had flashed through all quarters of the great ship. When François and Hintza appeared on the flight deck, some thousand members of the crew assembled there spontaneously gave them the most rousing of naval cheers. It made François tremble at the knees, but sent Hintza, hardly knowing how to hold his head for pride, high-stepping out towards them, not aware that it was all that François could do to get himself to the helicopter, already warmed up and waiting. Those hurrahs and the feeling of return, welcome and goodwill and all else given to him, made it difficult to say good-bye and thank you adequately to the Admiral, who saluted him and Hintza as if they were his superiors. He barely managed to become sufficiently composed in the helicopter afterwards to beg Michael Featherstone not to fly over or too near the camp he had left behind, explaining what unfortunate associations they all had with helicopters. As a result they landed on the far side of the dune nearest to the camp, to let François and Hintza out first.

Hintza, knowing what they were about, was ready to dash at full speed towards their camp, assuming that François himself would want to do it at the run, but François stopped him, knowing how Hintza would outrun even himself. He took a leaf from his dispatch book and quickly wrote, 'Nonnie, all is well. I'm coming fast with all the help we need. Please prepare Xhabbo and Nuin-Tara for visitors and tell them not to be alarmed.'

He folded up the note, tucked it underneath Hintza's collar which Nonnie had bought him, and told him, 'There, Hin, run as you've never run before and take this to Nonnie. Quick Hin, quick!'

The rear-admiral, Michael Featherstone, the medical orderly and nine sailors unloading blankets, food, thermos flasks of meat broth, not omitting chocolate, milk and other foods and comforts, found themselves held by the sudden crackle of electricity of the Bushman command on François's lips, and even more by the amazement of seeing Hintza vanish; an elongated streak of burning gold over the summit of the dune. One Cockney sailor could not restrain himself from telling his companions that Cor, and tickle him pink, but that wild and likely-looking lad seemed to speak the language of dogs as well as humans, let along old ironside admirals, for if they had not noticed it, he certainly had. That 'old dreadnought' of theirs was just about ready to eat out of that young cock sparrer's hand.

François did not hear him, because he was already following

379

in his long hunting stride after Hintza, so naturally and easily that the Commander remarked to the Rear-Admiral, 'He's not only got the eyes of an antelope, that young fellow, but he runs like one as well.'

As a result, François arrived in the camp in time to amplify the news in his note and to help Nonnie and Xhabbo to sit up to watch the procession of eleven; the Rear-Admiral in the lead followed by Commander Featherstone and nine marines almost up to their knees in the sand under the load of blankets and other provisions they were carrying.

François had never seen, even in Mopani, so great a delicacy and gentleness as that of the naval doctor examining Nonnie and Xhabbo. After their examination he gave them injections against their pain, took some blood samples and then drew François aside. He explained that he was as convinced as François that Miss Monckton and the chap with the unpronounceable name had sleeping-sickness and that he would not wait on the result of the analysis of the blood samples but treat them the next day when, he was absolutely certain, the right drugs would arrive by aeroplane.

'But of course the quickest way to get these people well,' he added dutifully, his hand on the anxious François's shoulder, 'would be to take them to hospital. I can easily arrange that and they would be bedded down in the capital almost as soon as the drugs could get here. It would be the right thing to do, you know.'

'Oh no!' exclaimed François, going quite pale at the thought. 'It would be the death of them, at least the death of him,' indicating Xhabbo.

However, he realized that perhaps he had sounded ungracious, and he explained about Xhabbo, and the Bushman horror of being shut in, ending, 'You see, sir, it'll have to be here with us all together, as we've been since the beginning.'

'How stupid of me,' the surgeon hastened to reply. 'Of course you're right, it's just got to be here.'

Two hours after sunrise the next day, François, for whom life had suddenly become all light again and the darkness behind already little more than the shadow of a dream, was just happy to be sitting near Nonnie and his friends who thanks to their injections had passed a night almost free of pain. They were well enough to be raised to sit up and watch a big military transport plane pass overhead. Barely another hour later a helicopter, not hesitating on this occasion to appear right over the camp, hovered there for a moment and then came down at the far end of their meadow of sand. The naval doctor reappeared and came hurrying to give Nonnie and Xhabbo the first of the right injections. The very next morning François thought he could already see signs of improvement, and knew that any fears he had left, were now laid for good.

Meanwhile, the helicopter which brought the doctor also brought an urgent request for François to return to the flagship, which he could not refuse. This time he left Hintza behind, full of reproach because his newly developed taste for the sea and stirrings of an ambition to qualify as an ocean-going dog, a master-mariner of his kind, were being denied as soon as born.

François spent the morning and the whole afternoon going over his journey, answering the most searching questions from the Admiral and his D.N.I. That very night, as a result, on radio in Britain, America and in Europe, on television screens and from printing presses, the first factual account of the massacre and what had followed, the long pursuit and their hazardous journey, indeed a summary of all the main facts were presented to millions of people in that complex of the spirit which is the western world. Brief and official as this account was, it could not help out of its very nature to savour so much of the unusual and to be so evocative that it fired the imaginations of newspaper editors and purveyors of contemporary affairs as nothing had done for years. At once instructions were going out for strategically placed special correspondents of newspapers and magazines from Britain, America, Germany, France, Sweden, Italy and Japan to name only a few countries, to hasten to the scene so that their readers could have more.

François, completely innocent of how interest in their fate and their story would sweep like a grass fire through the imagination of the great outside world, at the end of his interview with the admiral and the D.N.I. asked for one last favour. He asked it very diffidently of men who he felt had already done more than he in his wildest dreams would have thought men could do for one another in so hard a world. He asked if they could please transmit a telegram for him too. This was addressed to Colonel H. H. Théron, c/o Parks and Reservations Board in the capital. How strange François felt, writing out the formal address of Mopani – who he was not even sure was still alive. The message merely read, 'Hope you too are safe and well. Nonnie and I have arrived safely at the sea. Please come to us as soon as possible. We need you. François and Hintza.'

It was on the tip of the D.N.I.'s tongue to say, 'You must be a bit more precise, my lad. The sea's a big place, and unless you are more explicit, this Colonel Théron, whoever he is, will hardly know which end of it to go to.'

But one look at François's trusting face, made keen and desperately young by the thought of Mopani, implying so clearly that for the moment the only point on the sea that could possibly matter in the universe and be described as such, just had to be the place at which he and his friends had arrived, made the D.N.I. rebuke himself. After all, he could easily deal with this deficiency in the signal himself.

When François had gone, the Admiral remarked, 'You know, D.N.I., I can't get over it. You must have noticed it too. That boy told his story as if he were quite unaware of how remarkable it is. He's full of praise for his friends but he doesn't seem to be aware that he himself has done anything worth mentioning; no indication at all that he knows how he was challenged by fate in a way I would not like to be, and asked to do something that no young fellow really ought to be asked to do. He just talked about it as if it were all a fact of life that one in his position had to expect. I do believe he won't know how incredible it is until somebody else tells him, and I doubt even then if he'll agree. That to me is perhaps the really extraordinary aspect of the most extraordinary affair I've ever encountered.'

And it is a pity perhaps that the Admiral did not talk to François about it, for he would have discovered that there was no conscious suppression of egotistical self-esteem in François. After all, it was only natural in one brought up as he was and

382

who for instance at his most impressionable age had to witness young Matabele boys, barely in their teens, naked and armed only with their wits, take on the challenge of crocodile and lion as on the day of the 'washing of the horns'. Life constantly exposed to the threat of death was a platitude of his upbringing, and he had no thought ever of its making exceptions for him. Besides, in so far as François felt he might have achieved anything at all, he was convinced that he owed it not to himself but to what he described as the prompting over his shoulder of others; above all Ouwa, 'Bamuthi and Mopani, and so could claim little credit for himself.

The great and dazzling hero for him was Xhabbo; the real courage and unselfish endeavour, his and Nuin-Tara's. As for Nonnie, there were no words to express what he felt about her part in the journey. She was the least prepared for such an ordeal. She could even have been expected to fail. Indeed she could have been pardoned for failing and fatally imperilling them all. Hers was courage of the highest quality of all, because her fear must have been the greatest; her endurance of the highest, since her physical preparation at the outset was lowest.

Three days later, just after midday, François was talking to Nonnie and Xhabbo in camp, a Nonnie and Xhabbo who were already restored to something of their lively and habitually bright, conversational selves, when he heard the familiar noise of the helicopter approaching. They saw it come like a great yellow spider over the top of the smoking, singing dune and land in its usual place on the far side of the dry river-bed. He got up and, followed by Hintza, went over towards it at leisure. Yet, even now that he knew the sound, still as always with his rifle at the ready on his arm. Nonnie could not help smiling affectionately and saying to herself, 'When we get back to civilization, I'll have to see he doesn't take that damned gun of his to bed.'

And watching him, she suddenly saw François start and then break into his fastest run. A very tall and oddly familiar figure had jumped, as if still young, from the helicopter and was striding with the long-distance stride of a born hunter towards François. Above the dying splutter of the engines, the pitch and quality of the glittering shout, 'Mopani!' made her turn quickly away from her companions, to hide the eruption of tears in her eyes.

When she could look again, she saw what she had always thought one of the nicest things about life in the bush at Hunter's Drift, the boy only just a man unashamedly embracing a child-like man.

She could easily imagine what they were feeling and saying to one another but could hardly see them because Hintza was running round the two, jumping and bounding with such fantastic energy that they were hidden in a cloud of dust. Then out of the dust the two of them appeared arm in arm, Mopani with one hand trying to calm Hintza, saying again and again, 'There now, Hin, there boy, I've told you and I tell you again for the last time, Nandi's all right. 'Swayo's all right, and so is Noble.'

At last the message got through to Hintza. He streaked across the space in between to bring the good news to Nonnie, Xhabbo and Nuin-Tara. He whimpered it in the ears of each of them and then in a mad dash threw himself in fast circles round the camp. Then he was off again to François and Mopani.

Mopani's greeting of Nonnie was as gentle as it was delicate and comforting to her. It made her feel she was at once taken to the centre of that tight circle that enclosed François and the hunter. But for Mopani it was a greeting made difficult by the shock of seeing what he remembered as one of the most beautiful, healthy young girl faces he had ever seen, now so thin and ill and at the same time poignant, with a new loveliness as of something imperishable burnt in it by the fire of a suffering few are called upon to endure, and fewer still at so early an age. But his introductions to Nuin-Tara and Xhabbo completed, Mopani allowed himself to be seated by the fire and was persuaded to have some hot chocolate with them all. Because of Hintza's and Xhabbo's preference for these things it had become the equivalent of champagne in their camp.

He sat there upright, circumspect and fastidious, as if he had not just flown some two thousand miles to come to them but just emerged from his own room, bathed and dressed in newly pressed clothes. His pointed Quixotic beard was as trim as ever; the skin of ivory on his forehead where his hat normally protected it was by contrast with the tanned features below, as startlingly young and smooth as ever; a visual paradox of innocence and experience that had always moved Nonnie as it did François, and in the process abolished all imposition of years between them. His wide hunter's hat with glowing leopard skin band was perched on his knee as he spoke, and one would have thought his appearance as timeless as it had always been in the past, were it not for the look in his eyes, which showed how wounded even his staunch spirit had been by all that had happened at Hunter's Drift and after, above all from the conviction that the future which had always been specially implicit for him in François, was apparently extinguished for ever.

Sitting there then, restored to his dearest role in life, he told them something which lifted the curtain of unknowing on their past and so conveyed the first intimation of how they had not gone through all in vain. He told them that as a result of François's desperate dash for his camp, one of the messengers dispatched by 'the major' he had left in charge, had got through the ring of invaders and intercepted him and Noble as they were travelling home in the company of Hintza's distinguished parents, Nandi and 'Swayo. Some miles farther on he would have run into the ambush prepared for him and no doubt would have been killed. He described how for more than a year now a desperate, highly organized guerilla war had been fought in the region of Hunter's Drift, how both François and Nonnie had been thought dead, because the day after he had been forewarned, a reconnaissance aeroplane had brought back a devastating description of François's gutted home and everybody was convinced that they must all have been killed, since the messenger who intercepted Mopani had known nothing about the origin of the message itself.

So when Mopani returned with the advanced forces brought up against the invaders, he found his old headquarters too burned out and everyone killed. He owed his life therefore to François, Xhabbo and indeed Nuin-Tara and Nonnie too, as well as Hintza. But almost more significant still, in the last few months a marked change had come over the situation. The enemy which had been gathering in strength, had suddenly appeared to weaken and begun to withdraw. He thought that could only have happened because the 'singing tree' had suddenly ceased to sing.

He gave François and Nonnie just time enough to translate the impact of this for Xhabbo and Nuin-Tara and to witness the transfiguration of meaning caused by the news, reflected in their eyes, before declaring that for the moment, their exchanges would have to be left to that brief factual level. He apologized profoundly that he had been forced by events just to greet them and see that they had all that they needed. Now, if Nonnie would allow it, and Nonnie was thrilled by the way he asked her permission, as if he already completely accepted the claims of a very special relationship between François and herself, the same events compelled him to take François away on urgent business in the flagship.

This urgent business was that in the plane which had brought Mopani, he had travelled with several newspaper men dispatched from all over the world to get the full story. Mopani knew enough about François and enough about the world to realize how exacting an ordeal it would be for him. The last thing he could allow was the descent without warning of many sophisticated gatherers of news into the midst of François's camp. So he had persuaded the Admiral that the press conference on which the Admiralty in London had insisted, should take place in the flagship and that it should be limited to an hour only and with him present to assist François. The Admiral had readily seen the point and agreed.

So François, this time accompanied by Hintza, for he felt it would be too cruel to separate Hintza from Mopani who was like father and mother to Hintza's parents, and who after all had brought Hintza into his life, walked into the ward-room of the flagship where the talk was as loud as the sound of the bees he had heard at their devotions in the cathedral of ants on the day of 'The Annunciation of Honey'. Oh, how far away and full of light suddenly that morning seemed! As they went in, with Hintza confidently in the lead, alive and glowing, looking like a dog modelled on one of those great hunting archetypes carved on Scythian coins of gold, the assembly, who were just on their third pink gin, stopped talking with a suddenness that was almost comic, and stared at them with unbelief.

François, Mopani and Hintza went in total silence to stand in front of them, so that François, on Mopani's advice, as well as out of his own instinct, could tell his story in the deliberate, even, factual and contracted manner natural to him, and leave out for the moment the facts that his guides and companions across the desert were Bushmen. He did this because he feared the additional sort of reprisals that might be be carried out against defenceless Bushmen in the desert, should this fact become known by their enemies and friends of their enemies. But all the same he felt a Judas for referring to people who in his estimation were the real heroes of the story as 'a friendly indigenous hunter and his wife'.

Afterwards he had to survive the ordeal of keen but happily sympathetic questioning, which would have gone on far into the evening and possibly the night, had not Mopani had the wisdom to specify the flagship as the place of meeting. For it was soon interrupted by the impressive Captain of Operations himself who, after precisely one hour, appeared and announced in a manner that ruled out protest, 'I'm afraid gentlemen, for reasons that you will well understand, that this young man has really had a packet. This for the moment must be it. Besides, dinner is served.'

That night, the various communication rooms in the ships of the fleet had all to be called into service. Long dispatches of what had happened went out in morse-code, tapped on the keyboards of some dozen ships, as if they were an exteriorized version of Xhabbo's inward tapping. All over the world the story became immediately one of the great human sensations of the year. Its impact was profound. The human aspect of it dominated people's imagination, but for a few exceptions. Consciously or unconsciously we are part of our time and whether we like it or not live not just our own lives but also the life of our time. Our own enigmatic ration of days is limited with a negation peculiar to our time. There is implicit in all a strange envy for what is true and noble, an element of what François's ancestors so aptly called a *nostalgie de la boue*, so that despite the story's obvious humanity, there were men who refused to see it for what it was, and out of their own one-sided and slanted selves, tried to prove that it was something less.

For instance, questions were asked almost immediately in the British House of Commons. There was a member from a constituency in the Midlands who wanted to know from the Secretary of State how he could possibly justify the immense expenditure of an over-taxed country's money, which was implied in all they had heard of the melodramatic rescue of what after all were little more than two children. Could not the whole thing have been done in a more simple and less expensive manner?

The Secretary of State thought not and from the volume of cheering, the negative reply in this regard complied with what is known as the wishes of the House. But another member from a constituency in Scotland immediately jumped up to ask whether it would not be true to assume that if the young lady of whom they had heard so much had not been the daughter of a titled governor who had served an imperialist establishment well, but the daughter of a simple working-class family, the help given would not have been so eager and lavish, and the publicity not so great?

The Secretary of State thought that this kind of question was unworthy of the dignity of the House, and deserved no answer, and the applause indicated once more that he had the House with him.

Another member wanted a Royal Commission appointed to investigate such extravagance and such departure from the norms of the Admiralty. This too, clearly, was against the will of the House, who thought, to quote the Secretary, that the admiral had behaved in accordance with traditions of a service that was always as ready to answer a call of common humanity in peace as it was to respond to the needs of the nation in war.

Yet another metropolitan member put a question which implied the certainty of that member, though obviously not that of the House, that the whole story had been grossly exaggerated. He suggested that it was part of a neo-Imperialist plot to bring the whole movement for the emancipation of the sorely oppressed black masses of Africa into disrepute and to disguise the fact that the real villains of the piece who deserved the censure of every right thinking human being in the world, were the European establishments which oppressed the black workers of Africa and by their intolerance had provoked them into a reaction which should surprise no one. He would always be the first to deplore any unnecessary loss of human life, but the behaviour of the European establishment in Africa made the taking of human life essential so that a vicious racial despotism could be overthrown, and the common man there could be made free. Besides, young people were notoriously inaccurate and given to fantasy these days, so what objective proof did the Secretary of State have that what was perhaps only a molehill of truth had not been made into a mountain of fiction by an over-excited and dubiously encouraged imagination of the young son of a white settler?

The Secretary of State was happy to relieve the questioner of his anxieties and help his search for the truth. Only that morning his department had received remarkable evidence that the story as presented to the House was if anything an understatement. A great Scottish newspaper had telephoned the permanent head of his department to say that they had been approached by a gentleman in Glasgow who wanted for obvious reasons to remain anonymous but had volunteered to testify that the real story was even more sinister than apparent from the facts correctly revealed by the Admiralty. For instance, there was the episode of the 'Singing Tree' which had puzzled the House to such an extent that the Leader of the Opposition had dismissed it as pure Rider Haggard and not something that should be paraded as fact before an overworked House. According to this evidence, the Maria Henrietta d'Alveira mentioned, had been captured on the borders of Angola and Zambia in the company of her mother and father, a distinguished public servant from Portugal, on an urgent mission of inquiry of high international import. She was promised, according to this testimony, that her parents would be well-treated, and after two years of benevolent custody set free, provided she accompanied her captors and did whole-heartedly what was asked of her. This was to sing every night at this mysterious place of the tree mentioned in the Joubert account. There were reasons for harbouring the gravest fears about the fate of the d'Alveira couple but details had to wait on proper examination of the informant, who claimed to be the Scottish officer mentioned in the Joubert account. This officer had refused to go on serving with the invading forces, had narrowly missed being executed himself by the invaders and had escaped and made his way to safety after a long journey, the after-effects of which were still confining him to hospital. The Secretary of State had already dispatched an experienced law officer to interview him and would, if so desired, lay his testimony before the House.

The reaction in America, if more emotional and vociferous, was simpler and unashamedly human. No dissenting voices were heard in Congress or anywhere else. There was a unanimous voice to the effect that Vice-Admiral Digery G. Winflow Jun., Second-in-command to the combined South Atlantic Fleet, had in his support of the British Commander-in-Chief done all that the great American public expected of an officer of the United States Navy. Moreover he had been informed that if he should think it expedient and desirable to invite the four gallant young people, irrespective of their race, creed or colour, to come to America at the expense of the United States Government, he should not hesitate to do so, so that the American people could have a chance of showing that it still honoured the qualities of courage, self-sacrifice and unselfishness, above all others, no matter from which quarter they came. This statement made the sour voices heard in Westminster more sour and more convinced that they were right in suspecting all along that sooner or later the C.I.A. would be shown to be involved in so flagrant a conspiracy to discredit the 'freedom fighters' of Africa.

That meeting in the ward-room of the flagship, however, was the end of what Mopani regarded as François's duty towards the press in general. There was just one section of the press however with which Mopani wanted him to deal a few days later. Mopani brought five famous newspaper men to see them on the dune behind the camp. One was from a distinguished American magazine, one from the most authoritative newspaper in Britain, one each from their German, French and Italian counterparts. He asked François to tell these men the whole story as he, Mopani, had come to know it. François, and for a while Nonnie, spent a whole day talking to these men. He told them most of what happened, though obviously still without intimate personal matters and shades of thought and feeling too delicate for public discussion. Late in the afternoon, one photographer representing all five was allowed to come into the camp and photograph Nonnie, Hintza and François, but again not Xhabbo and Nuin-Tara, for the reasons already stated.

When François returned to the top of the dune with the photographer to say good-bye, he was puzzled when the American, shaking him by the hand said, 'Great! Just great sir, perhaps the greatest human story ever, certainly the greatest one that's come the way of your humble servant here, and I'm not at all surprised that my magazine has agreed to pay more for such a story than they did even for the memoirs of Winston S. Churchill. You deserve every cent of it and more.'

It had been so long since François had thought of or heard mention of money that the exclamation broke from him, 'And so you people still use money then?'

When asked why he had arranged this special meeting, Mopani explained that it was all due to a friend of his in the newspaper world who had done a great deal over the years to help him in preserving the wild life and natural environment of Africa. This friend had warned him from the start that such a story was extremely valuable in terms of money. At Mopani's request he had taken care of the financial aspects of the newspaper, magazine and in particular film interests of the affair, which were immense. As a result, François and Nonnie would be well provided for in the future and have money to spare for any cause dear to them. But more of that later, when Mopani could discuss the future in detail with them.

And so there came a moment when the Admiral himself asked for permission to call on them. Nonnie had recovered so much that she insisted on changing out of her European clothes and putting on the dress which François and Nuin-Tara had made for her nearly a year ago in the desert. She did this because she felt that Nuin-Tara's profoundly feminine self might feel uncomfortable if she did not. As a result, when the Admiral in his dazzling white uniform and shining gold epaulettes which made Xhabbo and Nuin-Tara clap their hands at such a glitter of sheer beauty, appeared in their midst, he had difficulty just for a moment in telling Nonnie and Nuin-Tara apart. Only when he came near enough to see Nonnie's features, dusky with sun as well as shade of their camp, and observed the long, shining, fine hair falling out from underneath a dazzling ivory tiara of ostrich beads, which had been washed and scrubbed in the sacred water that morning, was he certain.

He immediately went over, took her hand in both of his and said in his most chivalrous manner, 'There you are at last, young lady. So you are Jamie Monckton's daughter. I knew your father well, and when this is all over you must both come and stay with us in Devon.'

In saying this, he made it all sound so normal and casual that soon they were all at their ease. All four were genuinely sad when he announced that he had come to say good-bye and that in the morning his fleet would up-anchor and in the way of ships vanish over the rim of the ocean. But if it were at all possible, and he begged François and Jamie Monckton's daughter to try to make it so, would they all please be in a place at dawn when they could see his ships put out to sea, because he promised that it would be a fine and, although he said it himself, a sight worth seeing.

The following morning then, Nonnie, François and Hintza, with Xhabbo and Nuin-Tara and Mopani, somehow managed to be on the top of the dune. On their left, a large pompous penguin pontiff, robed in the black and white of the uniform of the ultimate in dogma, assisted by two penguin *evêques*, three archdeacons, four canons and innumerable priests, as well as oecumenical delegations of monks and nuns from all the far-flung Antarctic island retreats of this devout species, performed matins for the seals and walruses, unaware that one old walrus, grey at the temples and with a long white moustache, snored loudly throughout the service, and one immense white albatross on archangelic wings, hovered overhead at the centre of a Pentecostal flame of resurrected sun.

On the right, in the wide open bay, the fleet, as the Admiral had put it, was upping anchor. They watched that great assembly of ships, flashing so circumspect in the early morning light, form up in warlike formation; the escort vessels moving into station ahead, abeam and abaft, the two aircraft carriers in between, followed by the heavy communications cruiser, the marine-commando ship, the submarine tender and finally again the rear escort ships, all in one glittering, swinging procession. But to their amazement, the line did not immediately make for the open sea. It swung round on a new course almost as if the ships were determined to beach themselves, but at the last moment they came smartly about towards the south, until they were close and parallel to the shore. They saw then that all the ships were 'dressed over-all' with flags and pennants from bow to stern, all streaming in the wind of morning; the wind that had been their way.

Underneath the flags and pennants straining in flame of sun and wind of day, the sides were lined with sailors all as if for a royal occasion and as each ship passed the dune on which they stood, it dipped its ensign, and the watchers heard, across the blue water and over the yellow sands in between, three long and loud hurrahs. But the greatest surprise of all came when the flagship sailed by them, the sea unfolding on either side of the razor bows like a fleece of gold, so fast and deep did it cut through its swell. It not only added its quota of cheers to the others but followed them up with a salute of twenty-one guns; a salute which made the admiral turn to the Operations Captain by his side and say, 'That's one thing you will not enter in the log book. We've had enough questions to answer in Parliament already. But I trust this is something towards the award you've been pestering me to get for those young people.'

François and Nonnie were so absorbed that they did not notice how, long before this moment came, Mopani had quietly retreated. Installed on a flat piece of sand behind the dune, he took out his pipe, filled and lit it, as he thought, 'It's purely their occasion and theirs alone, no one has the right to intrude.'

That night by their fire in camp, Xhabbo shook his head and for the last time the male equivalent of a Mona-Lisa smile appeared on his antique features. He looked provocatively at Nonnie to declare that he was not feeling at all certain that he, Xhabbo, that day had really been seeing the things which brought Nonnie's people out of the sea taking them gliding back into the sea, but just things that were part of another of Nonnie's many great stories.

Nonnie fell into the trap, and asked, 'But why, Xhabbo?'

'Because you are such a wonderful liar,' he replied, and fell over backwards on the sand with merriment.

And then a morning came when Nonnie and Xhabbo were pronounced completely cured. In spite of an experience and love that bound them to one another, they all knew the moment to go their different ways had come. The time was upon them when, as Ouwa had so often said, if a page had to be turned, it was best to turn it firmly. François, Nonnie and even Hintza, who knew as always when great changes were imminent, though he might not know their precise nature, were heart-broken; Nuin-Tara and Xhabbo not any the less. They would not have been capable of breaking such bonds even then, had they not known instinctively that in its apparent breaking, they would create another living bond, binding them more securely to one another, and that if they tried merely to preserve that particular end of their journey, something would go rotten on them and the continuation presupposed in the journey they had just accomplished, rendered impossible.

So one morning at dawn they had to say good-bye. The words of farewell were extremely simple, and the looks in their eyes and the few gestures exchanged had to convey more than words or gestures had perhaps ever had to convey. Xhabbo could just repeat three times, which was his idea of a magical way of pre-serving the truth of a statement, that even when his 'Foot of the Day' became the 'Heel of the Night' and the wind of the desert that had shown them their way had blowing removed from the sands all the signs of the footprints of the four of them, who on their heels upright walking had travelled together for so long, the heart of him and the heart of that utterly woman of his, Nuin-Tara, would be full of Foot of the Day and Nonnie, and that somewhere, some time, the wind which had removed all signs of their feet from the sand would join the wind from their bodies and form clouds out of the hair of all four of them, making them one high up in the blue as they had walked over the desert as one so that new rain would fall on account of it.

François and Nonnie could only respond in kind and thank him again and again, and say that if it had not been for them they would not have had any life to live at all, and that Xhabbo and Nuin-Tara were not only brother and sister to them but father and mother of what they might become.

And then Xhabbo declared simply, with a voice like the deepest note on a violin, that if he and Nuin-Tara, in going, did not look back, they must please not think that their eyes were not full of Foot of the Day and Nonnie. It would only be because if they looked back, it would be as if they did not trust what their own eyes were full of, and that in looking back they might not be able to go forward with what their eyes felt themselves full of on account of it. Yes, they would have to go on looking forward, never glancing backwards, so that the look in the eyes of Nonnie and Foot of the Day going forward with them, would detach itself from the bodies standing there and free itself to lead them like starlight into the unknown beyond. So please would Foot of the Day and Nonnie stand there by the fire, watching until they had gone over the dune in the East, never taking their eyes from them but always letting their eyes be full of Xhabbo and Nuin-Tara so that they themselves would not lose heart but go forward, looking ahead with them all the way.

François could only bow his head in agreement and stammer that Xhabbo must please know that he and Nonnie would come back to see them again and again. Then Nonnie cried out, 'Oh yes, we shall, but Xhabbo, Nuin-Tara, how shall we ever know how to find you?'

Xhabbo answered for them both: 'Just come, and, feeling that you know us utterly just ask for us because in this desert through which we have walking come, there is nothing that does not know Xhabbo and Nuin-Tara as Xhabbo and Nuin-Tara know them and all know one another as they feel themselves to be known and all you have to do is to feel yourselves asking, and Xhabbo and Nuin-Tara will know, and feeling it, running will come!'

François then took out of his pocket the only presents that he and Nonnie had been able to devise for Xhabbo and Nuin-Tara and which was the first thing commissioned and bought for them by Mopani in the capital out of money paid for their story. For suddenly there had been nothing in that great civilization of theirs that seemed to them of the slightest use to

Xhabbo and Nuin-Tara, nothing that would not just clutter up their lives and make them more difficult. Never before had they realized so completely the worthlessness of the European world of things. The presents then were two large, round gold medallions on which the names of Xhabbo and Nuin-Tara were inscribed. Underneath each name, minutely and deeply engraved, was the injunction, 'You are commanded by Her Britannic Majesty to aid and protect these two persons wherever you shall find them and to admit and allow no impediment, let or hindrance, into their lives. In case of doubt, sickness or trouble, you are to contact Her Majesty's nearest representative.'

Below the injunction was the seal of Her Britannic Majesty and the motto, 'I shall maintain'. Both medallions were complete with chains of gold and so were in every detail immune to rust and corruption.

Nonnie hung the medals round the necks of Xhabbo and Nuin-Tara and embraced them both. But François in the way of the ancient Bushmen he had learned from Koba, just held out his hands to them and they put the tips of the fingers of their outstretched hands, one after the other, to his. They held them so there for a moment, the tips trembling as their pulses met and beat together, and then, quickly, they removed their hands, turned about, and walked out of the camp.

François and Nonnie stood there and watched them go as they had promised. They kept them in view for close on an hour as they went steadily up towards the dunes in the east, until Nonnie was crying in her heart and praying that they would relent and look back, so that she could have one more glimpse of those beloved faces. But they did not. In tears, she gripped François's arm and only with difficulty prevented herself from crying out the anguish of the separation opening up wide in her, so fast and so deep.

Even Hintza, who was sitting bolt upright beside François, could not restrain himself and whimpered. François had to soothe him with a hand. In him the feeling of separation was burning high like a new kind of fire that dispersed any tears as soon as they formed. And so they waited and looked until Xhabbo and Nuin-Tara appeared at last, clear-cut on the dune against the blue in the east out of which the day comes infinitely new and renewable again. They did not, as Nonnie's heart was imploring them now, stand still even then but went steadily on and over the other side. It was as if she and François were standing on a yellow beach and the sky there so blue that it looked like the blue of the sea which had swallowed up all those brave and jewelled ships of war. Yes, Xhabbo and Nuin-Tara went down into the inexorable blue as if they were going down into the sea itself. At one moment their heads were still there bobbing bravely up and down on the immense blue surface and then suddenly the blue closed over them and all around them the burning desert seemed to go dark and empty.

That same evening on the dune, Mopani and François sat side by side for the last time there, looking out over the desert and the sea, and talked quietly and long about their future. François, with all that heightening of perception which separation from what one loves most dearly brings, talked as if his whole awareness were made innocent, true and virgin again, so that whatever life henceforth might bring could be written as new upon it again. He told Mopani not only about the debt he owed to Xhabbo but how he knew now that all had started with Ouwa. None of this would have been possible if it had not been for Ouwa, invaded as he was at the time by knowledge of his own impending death, realizing how Lammie's 'other little person' needed companionship of his own, and so had gone to Mopani to bring back the little puppy who had become the great and glorious Hintza at his side.

François and Nonnie would most certainly have been killed like all the rest in the massacre because, if it had not been for Hintza, he would never have known that Xhabbo, caught in a lion trap set by the men of Hunter's Drift, was even there to be saved. It was strange that in saving Xhabbo he was really saving himself and a Nonnie he did not even know existed. Yes, it was in Ouwa's concern for what might have been thought of as mere sentimentality in a lonely young boy that all this saving really began.

Mopani took him up on that and said, yes-no, he was so glad that François could see it like that. It proved what he, Mopani, was feeling more and more on the rounding curve of his own brief life, long as his life might seem to François. Nothing that was ever done was ever wasted or without effect on life. Nothing was ever so insignificant as to be unimportant. Everything in life mattered and ultimately had a place, an impact and a meaning. Centuries could go by before the meaning revealed itself just as years had to go by before the effect, and more, the meaning of Ouwa's recognition of François's need, could show itself in the light of François's day. Perhaps it would be even longer still before the impact of Lammie's concept of François as that 'other little person' would be elucidated.

François started violently at the mention of Lammie. A strange, familiar feeling of secret guilt, personified almost like a dream figure, stared with an ancient mariner's eye, and pointed a finger at him from around a corner of his mind. He realized that of the voices which had helped him so loud and clear on the journey behind, that of Lammie, the beautiful, the steady and the clear, had been conspicuously absent. It was not because her going had left him indifferent. His heart was like a ship awash at the thought of the cool, precise, reassuring presence it had lost with her death. But what was this strange resistance within that had silenced a voice like hers with such a clear right of its own to be heard?

The clue perhaps was in what Mopani was saying. Yes-no, he, who had loved Lammie dearly, had himself been taken aback when he was informed like all others of François's coming as that of 'another little person' to join her and Ouwa. It had often, he must confess, tended to make him critical of Lammie, as if there were a shade too much head and not enough heart in her attitude to François. Now, he was not at all so sure – and here for the first time François saw Mopani in grave difficulties with an emotion that made him hoarse and pause before he continued – yes-no, he was not certain now that it was not one of the bravest things; something of an especially feminine courage, he had ever encountered. For he realized that this concept of Lammie's was intended to wean François in the most profound manner even before he was born. One could criticize the timing, one could say that the concept was premature, but when one contemplated the havoc caused by mothers

398

and daughters in the lives of sons and lovers by never weaning them in their spirit as they weaned them from the breast, one could only marvel at Lammie for having the courage of such unique, improbable foresight.

Mopani realized more and more how a major source of corruption in men was their excessive love of the power of ideas – a love so excessive that they did not hesitate to kill and murder one another for them. In women, however, the source tended to be possessive love, a compulsion to command permanently the object of their love, most especially the love of the person from their own bodies. Yet out of her own supreme love of Ouwa, Lammie he was certain, had come to know in full the temptation and dangers of the all-possessive love of her sex and so determined that François should never be a victim of it; that he should never be a mere extension of her and Ouwa's love, bent to express some unlived aspect of themselves. She seemed to know how that would be the death of him, as if she recognized it already as the explanation of the gap which had opened up so disastrously between parents and their children, between old and young – a young who insisted on being themselves, however unarmed for the task, and not just another pale version of their parents' pattern. If he were wrong in this, Mopani asked, what other explanation could there be of the ease, the absolute coincidence of the coming of Nonnie into François's life? Had he ever felt a shimmer of shade even of Lammie come between him and Nonnie or did he not see, as Mopani thought he saw now, how François's imagination had been opened up and furnished, complete with guest-room ready for the coming of someone like Nonnie. François, he was convinced, owed such readiness in a great measure to Lammie.

Hearing it like that, François's heart wept for Lammie as it had not wept before. He found himself stringing the beads of his 'Bamuthi's beloved metaphor, as stars are strung along the rope of the Milky Way. More, he found himself proving to himself again the truth of old Koba's admonition in his childhood, 'Little Feather, always look for the word, as Mantis did in the beginning, when he gave things their names and their colours, because there is nothing in life too terrible or too sad

that will not be your friend when you find the right name to call
it by, and calling it by its own name, hastening it will come
upright to your side.'

Yes, Lammie was at last in the blessed company at his side.
They were only technically dead. Koba, Ousie-Johanna, 'Bamuthi, Lammie, Ouwa and many more, had almost acquired a
living definition and dynamic clarity in death which they had
not possessed in life and their voices would be with him always.
It was as if suddenly like a flicker of the lightning they had seen
below the horizon on the night the voice of the lion had said
hail and farewell to them, he had a glimpse of the meaning of
immortality to mortal man and how it communicated itself to
the living through the intensity of their feelings for the dead,
and how a sense of permanence of purpose on earth depended
on just that. For a moment he saw through the dark night of the
singular lack of grief, the ominous incapacity of contemporary
men for experiencing sorrow, that impoverishes the life of our
time. And then, with what blessed relief he was free of it, for in
remembering the names of praise, as 'Bamuthi used to put it, of
all the dead he had loved, he knew he would be remembered by
them and spoken to, as Lammie evoked by her name of praise
on Mopani's lips, spoke to him now and begged him to hold his
peace and listen on.

It was always like that with what one did, Mopani was
saying. It was always like that with meaning. All had always to
begin as something infinitesimally small, something even ridiculous in the light of reason and terms of immediate human
need; something only some accepting and listening heart could
hear in the kind of stillness of inner isolation such as Ouwa had
known and had to answer alone.

Mopani had been told that there were stars in the sky whose
light even now had not yet reached the earth and whose existence one could tell only because of their effect on the movement
of other stars. It was precisely so with the life of men on earth.
Their deeds were like a kind of starlight that came into being at
the moment they were enacted but whose meaning, the light
that was in the purpose, the accomplishment and the doing,
would take years still to reach life itself, let alone become clear
in the human spirit. One could not, therefore, live one's life

400

with a great enough reverence for what was small, not only in oneself, but in others. The significance of the great could only be real in so far as it was significant in the small, even when so small that at the moment of beginning it was more like the point defined by Euclid as being of no size or magnitude, but only position. Yes-no, it was position in the spirit and the sense of direction that followed logically from the sense of position that was all important, and yet increasingly overlooked because of its lack of discernible substance.

And it was this sense of direction now that he had to discuss with François. Both of them came from a people who had left Europe centuries before and come to Africa. They came originally not out of any petty or selfish motives because had they conformed to the life of their time in their native context of Europe, they would have been rich and comfortable in the homes they were about to abandon. No, they came not in order to make life more safe and the material rewards of life more abundant but to find a new and better way of being. It was wrong to judge things out of the context of the time which gave them birth. He did not wish to imply that their ancestors had not been right and probably justified in following the truth as they saw it most clearly in their own day. But the truth of yesterday could be the lie of today. They had come to Africa on the assumption that by moving to a new world they would leave their problems behind and find a place where there were no such problems and no such hindrances. They seemed to have had no inkling that human beings, whether they liked it or not, carried their problems about with them wherever they went.

So in their three hundred and twenty years of a new life, even in the Africa of their promise, when this craving for a better way of being seemed thwarted, they had again and again renounced homes and possessions just as readily as any in Europe and moved deeper into the interior, looking once more for a place where their problems would not exist, where life would be innocent like a slate wiped clean, and they could write all over it perfect phrases and sentences of the perfect life on earth. They had of course found no such thing. They had not only not found it but had gradually begun to create a greater form of tyranny than they had opposed and fled from in the beginning, so unaware were they of the new heresy of believing in places where evil did not exist. Not only were there no such places in Africa but there were none anywhere else in the world. Man had run out of places, had run out of geographical solutions for his problems and changes of scene as a 'cure' for his restlessness. The journey in the world without as an answer to our searching and resolution of our failings was dismally bankrupt.

There was only one thing which could lead to an answer and that was to let the sense of journey expressed for so long in travelling the world without become a journey within the spirit of man. Statesmen, scientists, philosophers, even priests and the whole intellectual trend of the day put up a plausible pretence that our troubles were due to imperfect political systems, badly drawn frontiers and other environmental and economic causes. The whole history of man as he, Mopani, knew it, had tried all those approaches over and over again and at last, as far as he was concerned, they were proved utterly bankrupt. The real, the only crisis out of which all evil came was a crisis of meaning. It was the terrible invasion of meaninglessness and a feeling of not belonging invading the awareness of man, that was the unique sickness of our day. And this sickness, he was convinced, was the result of the so-called civilized man, parting company with the natural and instinctive man in himself. Never had the power of the civilized over the natural been so great and never had power corrupted man within himself so dangerously. For that reason the journey within could not be resumed soon enough, the journey of what he called the exiled Jacob back to the Esau, the hunter, whom he had betrayed and with whom he had to be reconciled before he could come home again to inherit his full self.

This journey to total reconciliation within depended on man standing fast at last in his surroundings and there refusing to give in to any assault on his integrity. He had been horrified by the extent to which people were leaving Africa, saying that they were leaving it for the sake of their children and going back to other amply discredited geographical points of departure and patterns of behaviour as a way out of their problems. Yes-no, we had to stand fast and in standing fast bring out into the world around us what was revealed to ourselves on a new

402

journey within and make it part of our here and now; make what was first and oldest in us, new and immediate. Man had to give all his imagination, all his devotion, before it was too late, to whatever was nearest at hand, refusing nothing, however humble or insignificant or even distasteful that came out of him and at him from his immediate surroundings, but accepting all as the raw and only material, however base, on which he could work, just as those old alchemists of whom he had heard so much from Ouwa, took the basest of all metals – lead – and tried to transform it into gold. By accepting what was nearest at hand and working through it out of love in the most imaginative, precise and intimate cooperation with nature around and within him, man could make himself ready for what would become in time the greatest journey in the world without and that was the journey to the stars.

He stressed this because it was precisely in this area of cooperation with nature without as with the nature within which seemed to him nearest to his and François's hand. They both had been born into a true partnership with animals, birds, insects, plants, flowers and instinctive men, and knew what wonders it could bring about. That knowledge of theirs somehow had to be made immediate. On this journey which had preceded the massacre at Hunter's Drift, he had been profoundly depressed by what he had seen abroad. He remembered first going to Europe as a young man to fight in the First World War and from the deck of his troopship, seeing the woods and green fields of England across the Solent stretching towards William the Conqueror's great New Forest. Oh, that green after Africa had seemed to him a miracle, and he found himself saying to himself, 'What a beautiful, truly beautiful country – how it puts my eyes to bed!' It was a world with a sheen upon it as that on a newly born eland calf. But on this last occasion not only in England but all over Europe he had seen signs of a terrible change. The green was not so green. Everywhere grass and trees looked tired and dispirited as if they knew themselves to be there purely for the selfish use of man. They looked as if not all the rain in England could clean them of the smoke, the chemicals, and the indifference to their own especial being with which men were polluting them. He had been even more dismayed by what he had seen in the eyes of the animals; in the dogs, dragged on leads through streets, and the domestic animals by which men lived, like the horse and the cow. The horses looked as if they knew they were doomed and about to be ejected from life for ever, or to use a terrible expression he had encountered on his last visit to England, to be declared 'redundant'.

He found unbearable what he saw in the eyes of cows, bred into an unnatural state by men, so that instead of yielding half a gallon of milk a day that was necessary for rearing their calves, they were bred to develop udders bursting with milk so that they could hardly endure the anguish of it. And all so that they could yield twelve to fourteen gallons a day, not for calves but for men. They were treated not as warm-blooded mammals who had rendered men single service so much as soulless factories. And the milk was often not even drunk but made into synthetic materials, turned into vests, cardigans, underwear and even buttons. They were not even allowed the natural solace of keeping their calves to suckle, because the calves were removed at birth and fed by the hand of some indifferent herdsmen who had just come from fitting a milking machine to the bursting udders of the mother.

It might not sound much but this look of accusation in the cow and other animals in Europe was a look he found everywhere to some degree in the world of nature. There was no need to expand on this to François and enlarge on how this exploitation which produced that look, extended even to the earth and its contents, like oil and coal, gold, platinum, iron; the same great exploitation was everywhere there as well. And in their own Africa already the signs of the same great heartlessness to the claims of nature were multiplying as fast among black as among white. The European threat was spreading fast into an Africa which their ancestors had sought out, convinced that they could make it a model for all mankind.

François would remember how at Hunter's Drift, even the bravest signs of nature as they issued, so certain of their right to exist in the universe, as for example in the call of the lion, had become dulled. Even the lions had begun to roar in almost a perfunctory way as if the joy of it had left them for ever. Even

404

in his own great game reserve, he had seen the animals sprayed with dust from the crammed buses of curious tourists, so that they got up and turned away, disgusted with an intrusion that would not let them be and respect their privacy.

All this to François, remembering how the voice of Old Black Lightning had come up out of the desert at 'The Place where Nonnie sang to the Lion', remembering also with infinite nostalgia its last, valedictory roar as it left them to return to the world of lightning, thunder and rain, was like a pain in his heart.

He had to put his hand in Mopani's for comfort and hear him declare that he nonetheless was certain that, whatever the world said or did, as long as there were people like Ouwa and, he hoped he was not immodest, himself and, above all, François who still cared and grieved, and who would hold on to the meaning of the inner voice that had called them first to Africa and live openly by it among their people, giving it its contemporary idiom, there would be hope that the meaning would not only be preserved but increased. For that was how all real change began; a change of position in some lone, inexperienced and suffering heart like Ouwa's, not in great collective resolutions and movements and consensus of established opinion. Only one heart had to find its own true position and travel on from there and all the rest would follow, for no matter how isolated the *one* felt itself to be, in the deeps of life all were united and no one could move accurately without all ultimately moving with it; just as no star could make a lawful change of course without all the others keeping station with it.

He hoped therefore that François would not try to re-establish Hunter's Drift in the image of what Ouwa had made it, nor abandon it and go out into the world to look elsewhere for his answers as he now could because he and Nonnie had more money than they had ever had before. Rather, he hoped François would equip himself first with the necessary knowledge and contemporary skills, the mastery of facts to match his feelings, go to college and university, and then return to stand fast in his own context of Africa, resolved never to let anything drive him away, but work to bring it back into harmony with the voice of their original calling, and of that great natural surround of Africa which still made it almost the only continent in the world with a soul of its own.

At the moment there was not a plant, bird or animal in Africa that would not breathe a profound sigh of relief if the last men should suddenly vanish from the earth. They would have to change. If life on earth were to survive, not a single man, plant bird or animal must be allowed to lose its life except through some great necessity of life itself. And in the losing all men should join in with every plant and animal and bird to praise it and mourn its passing as that of something infinitely precious that had given life the service for which it had been conceived and rendered itself well. He was an old man now, but he was going to stand fast. He would ask François and Nonnie to stand fast in this spirit beside him.

He asked this without qualification because of a strange kind of confirmation he had experienced just before he heard the news that François and Nonnie were miraculously alive. It was a kind of confirmation the thin-lipped, rational, materialistic men of our time would scorn, but somehow he knew that it would be as decisive for François as it had been to him. It was simply this. On the way out of his own great Reserve a complete reversal of his sense of reality seemed to take place. François would remember the two imposing gates at the main entrance which were always opened at dawn and shut at sunset. Visitors passing through the gates at dawn, he was told, always felt they were entering a fortress of wildlife, a besieged place where a desperate battle was being fought to preserve nature. When they left the Reserve again they would speak as if they were going back into the real and greater world. But on this particular occasion with all these things he had discussed with François on his mind, the oddest of sensations overwhelmed him. He felt acutely that he was not going out into the real world at all, but entering not even a fortress so much as a new kind of menagerie, a prison in which partial forms of life were being preserved in a condition of unreality against some macrocosmic reality of which his reserve appeared a microcosm. Of course he was strangely restless, dissatisfied and despondent at the moment. Yes-no, he had the most contradictory sort of feelings assailing him, as for instance that the older he grew, the closer he was drawing to the past; the nearer his physical end, the closer his beginning, as if end and beginning were one in something greater than either. In a way which would have no meaning for a mere logician, the past stretched endlessly before him, the future long behind, and only this world of natural beauty, vivid and immediate with instinctive life that he was leaving, possessing intimation of ultimate reality. Yes-no, it was larger and more urgent than real, and charged with a kind of exhortation and a calling, through all sorts of odd flashes of remembered beauty that emerged with a rainbow vividness out of the darkness of his mind.

Suddenly he was full of memories of the beauty of all the sunsets and daybreaks he had ever seen in the bush; the rounded sound of the unimpeded song of the uninhibited bird, the lightning voice of the lion, the triumphal arch the impala imposed high on the columns of its flight, the look of morning in the eye of the kudu and the fall of night in those of the purple inyala; the victory roll of the peacock-blue winged and lilac breasted im-Veve, the spitfire bird that their people knew as the pledge of truth; the lamp of the lynx; the fire of leopard and flame of the lion; the glitter of the red and mauve tsessebe moving exultant with the song of the wind of its own speed in its ears; the star-glitter of the voice of the crickets performing their devotions at night; the measure of the elephant; the hymn to the sun of the Mopani beetles and the Halleluja of the massed choir of birds at nightfall and daybreak; the flake of snow of an ibis falling out of the high noon blue and the plover's sea-whistle farewell to the star of morning. All these and many more which François could imagine for himself were with him just then, not just as visions of things of beauty but like a reveille on a trumpet calling his senses to awake and fulfil the abundance of life reflected in the mirror of the garden at their beginning. Yes, he had said beginning deliberately because as he had implied, he now believed it was posed there not as a record of what had already been but as a kind of miraculous mirror to reflect the invisible in what is to come.

Then in the midst of searing regret at leaving his own natural world and the dissatisfaction caused by these glimpses of a total beauty that was not yet, he came out of himself to see one of the greatest thunderstorms he had ever seen in Africa bearing down on him with divine solemnity. He just had a glimpse of the sun vanishing behind a cathedral of Gothic cloud, two arch-angelic wings of light stretching far, wide and high on either side of the tumultuous spire, illuminated with lightning and shaking with reverberations of thunder, when the smell of rain falling on the parched earth many miles away reached him. It came to him on a cool wind travelling from the storm, like breath of sacred spirit, and rose like incense in the cathedral of the storm piled above him. The lightning at once was divine revelation and the thunder the voice of its meaning. He had never known a more naturally religious moment.

Suddenly the restlessness left him and an urge to take part in the renewal of life which that smell of the rain on earth evoked possessed him. And then he was riding down an aisle of cloud into the presence of the storm itself and the long lightning of Africa, the longest lightning on earth, striking deep into the parched ground and after each flash, a long roll of thunder like the voice of creation itself, followed by a greater downpouring of rain than ever. Normally he might have got off his horse, because such storms were notoriously dangerous to man on horseback, but there was no apprehension of danger in him, only the most intense feeling that this was how life should be; first the heart of man filled with an unutterable longing to ac-complish in the manner those evocations of beauty he had just mentioned commanded him and then the rain of the doing of it. Yes, this longing of his, he was certain, was part of the longing for rain which the drought-stricken earth of Africa around him had sustained for millenniums over and over again against all odds of hopelessness of fulfilment and rejection by the sun.

Yes-no, he knew then that all began in an improbable longing and in the sustaining of the longing against all odds of man and nature, and in the end the lightning would flash, the thunder sound and the rain fall and the brave earth be made full of increase. So it was with the human heart. The storm for him was intensely allegorical. The longing of man, the longing of the earth for rain, the same call of love to serve the increase of meaning with the greatest immediacy of which nature was capable, first in lightning, then in thunder and rain. Indeed, so great was the immediacy of the storm that those three were not different and distinct time processes but only one and indivisible moment. More, the storm was so violent and so great that nothing that was false could withstand it. All round him, for instance, ant-eroded and worm-rotted trees crashed down and only what was true, upright and growing remained, so that he recognized storm, suffering and disaster, however terrible, as instruments of truth and love and fear at one.

All these things of which he had spoken, far from being reduced before the power and majesty of the storm, seemed at home in it and invested with new authority by it to such an extent that he, Mopani, felt they had brought him to the place where meaning was made, where the paint of dawn, the colour of sunsets, the lightning, the thunder, the rain and the wind of morning were born.

He felt this so keenly that he just had to dismount and stand beside the head of Noble, put his arm round his neck and say for both of them a new kind of Lord's Prayer that came unbidden to him there. He no longer remembered the whole of the prayer and recollected mainly the feelings associated with it, above all the feeling that he, Noble and the storm and earth were all counterpointed in the same abiding rhythm. Only he was certain that his words were not addressed to the Lord in Heaven alone. François must forgive him if it sounded arrogant because he had not felt less arrogant and more humble than at that moment at the altar, as it were, in the great temple of the storm, but he was convinced that there was something lacking in a unique approach through the Father, wonderful as that was. It was just this. His prayer began, 'Our Father, which art in Heaven, Thy will be done. Our mother, which art in earth, thy love be fulfilled, and love and will made one.'

All that followed was implicit in that approach; the will to do and the love to fulfil made sheer and immediate and abundant in man as the lightning, the thunder and the rain of the storm. He, Mopani, like François, had known to the full nostalgia for the bush into which they had been born. He knew only too well the hurt of it but great as that nostalgia was, it was nothing to this home-sickness for the future that presided over his prayer.

For him this confirmation was absolute and final, and that was why he had spoken to François as confidently as he had done.

And that, he remarked with his wriest of smiles, was the over-long testament of all he would like to leave François, far more than all the worldly possessions he had long since willed to him.

François was unable to reply to Mopani at once, so moved was he, and Mopani wisely did not ask for an answer. The answer was in the feeling François gave out that a child at last had found the man, as he, Mopani had found the child in François. Indeed there was neither the need, nor any such thing as an immediate answer beyond that, but only the challenge to live life from then on so that it could be a process of growth into some sort of an answer. There were no short cuts to creation, Mopani knew, as Ouwa had known it. All creation was slow, patient and loving growth until suddenly one day it issued from the heart of man like lightning, sheer and immediate into new being. Yet he knew, by the last fire in camp later, that the living towards the answer had already begun when he heard François say to Hintza, 'Now you would grin less, Hin, if you knew where I am taking you. You're to be the first dog in Africa to go to college. What shall we do with you there? What is it to be – Economics, Political Philosophy, or the humanities?'

Hintza looked back so tragically puzzled, that François stroked him immediately and declared confidingly, certain that it would relieve Hintza of his bewilderment, 'Don't worry, my beloved little old insect, my little old *goggatjie*! The humanities and a touch of classical music it shall be for you. But what about you, Nonnie?'

Nonnie, smiling, happy and infinitely relaxed, was thinking, 'Anything, anything as long as we three are never separated for a split second again,' answered with a mischievous pretence of a condescension she was far from feeling, 'I might consider medicine if you begged me, François. I think I'd like the idea of healing the sick, particularly animals and people suffering from sleeping-sickness. And you?'

François did not answer her directly. He thought long and hard and then said obliquely, as if far away, 'The first thing we'll do when we finish with our new schooling is to come back to find Xhabbo and Nuin-Tara and save them and their people from extinction.'

Mopani, in the silence that followed, took out of his pocket a long telegram, to say, almost apologetically, 'Little cousin, I have something here I haven't shown you before. It asks something of you both I hope you will agree to do. I think it is perhaps the most positive and hopeful thing that has come out of all this. It's an invitation to go north to the oldest kingdom in Africa and there receive on behalf of the new nations of Africa some form of compensation for the injury done to you and Nonnie. It is important because although there are some African nations who did not associate themselves with this request, the news of your and Nonnie's story caused as much dismay among millions of Africans as anywhere else. There is something, I don't quite know what, to be presented to you both, except that I believe it represents the feelings of many of your black countrymen, above all the young among them, and I hope you will say yes.'

One longs to linger over this last night by the fire near the renewing water of Mantis, the god of Xhabbo and Nuin-Tara, the god of the great in the small, where they slept for the last time in the desert with the sea sounding like a last post of nature over their last journey.

Some mornings later François, Hintza and Nonnie were driven in a large Rolls-Royce to a palace on the side of a mountain in the far north of Africa in a capital called 'The New Flower'. The same blue of Africa they had seen in the blue over the desert in the far south was there to proclaim the kinship of north and south and the basic community of the earth in between, so that they did not feel themselves to be in such a strange new country as they might have done, but almost as if another room of a home of many mansions.

As they stepped out of the car at the Palace entrance, Nonnie and François and Hintza were startled to see that they had to pass between two enormous live lions lying on pedestals, as watchdogs over the doorway itself. Involuntarily they both looked down at Hintza, knowing his complex about lions. They saw him draw back and stand almost contorted in a struggle

411

with himself. His hair from his toes to his spine, indeed every bit of hair on his burnished body was standing on parade and to attention. He fought hard and long with himself before a new look of resolution appeared on his face and he stepped, determinedly and ritualistically forward as if he too were obeying Mopani's injunction and accepting what was nearest at hand as his own special task in life. Slowly he came up to the pedestal of the nearest lion, lifted his leg and sprayed it, as if he were putting out a fire.

'Gosh François,' Nonnie exclaimed, scarlet with embarrassment, not of the deed but the thought that it was not something that could be done to the lions of so great a king, 'd'you see what that incredible hound of yours is up to? Shouldn't you try and stop him? He can't do that to lions of Judah and get away with it!'

'No Nonnie, certainly not,' François, the happy light of a smile in his eyes, answered back. 'No, he's just getting rid of that old complex of his for good.'

And so they went into a thickly carpeted room, hung with satins and ancient Byzantine-looking tapestries. A footman in satin opened an inner doorway and they were summoned in. An old gentleman, small in stature but looking almost tall because of the height of his spirit, came forward to meet them. Nonnie immediately dropped a graceful curtsey and Hintza, his reflexes of the quickest, now that he had finally put the lion in its place, went down so fast beside her that his chin hit the floor and was flat on the ground, from where, shaken but unabashed, he looked up searchingly out of his large purple eyes, to see what manner of a person it was that could make him curtsey as not even the greatest of baboons had ever done.

He saw the imposing, grave, great little figure, holding out his hands to them. At once Hintza was up on his haunches and condescending to hold out a burnished paw. He found it gently accepted and himself addressed in French, which to his annoyance he had not yet acquired: '*Et enfin, le voilà! Hintza, le redoutable, lui-même. Sois bienvenu, notre cher grand chien, qui mérite tant de nous tous!*'

Then the paw was released and two sensitive hands went out to Nonnie and François. Speaking in slow, deliberate French which Nonnie translated for François, he said in the low, soft voice, that the dignity of the oldest dynasty in Africa, if not the world, demanded: 'Welcome, my children, welcome. We are profoundly happy to see you here, because we now can ask you ourselves on behalf of Africa to forgive us for what was done to you. We are permitted to ask you this because it is not something that we have not asked of ourselves. We too have seen our own country brutally invaded. Our own people too were slaughtered and killed in thousands by Europeans and we ourselves like you lost many beloved ones as a result of it. Moreover – we were driven into exile before you were born. We endured years of a life that was existence more than living, in a foreign country where we were ignored and neglected, and only after a bitter and long struggle were we allowed to come back to our home.

'But on the day we returned to our capital we kept our people and a delegation of generals waiting so that we could first pray in a chapel in the pass that leads to this city. We had to pray there alone with ourselves lying prostrate on the ground and – you will both understand, I am sure of it – crying with gratitude at such goodness of life after such suffering. We prayed so that all bitterness could be taken from us and we could start the life for our people again without hatred. We knew out of our own suffering that life cannot begin for the better except by us all forgiving one another. For if one does not forgive, one does not understand; and if one does not understand, one is afraid; and if one is afraid, one hates; and if one hates, one cannot love. And no new beginning on earth is possible without love, particularly in a world where men increasingly not only do not know how to love but cannot even recognize it when it comes searching for them. The first step towards this love then must be forgiveness. Will you, can you, therefore, forgive us all?'

Listening to him there, looking into their own hearts, they were amazed to see that there was no need even to forgive, that in having pursued to its true end the journey so harshly thrust on them, there was nothing of hatred or resentment left, but only a desire like flame to live on, so that no such journeys should ever be necessary again, a flame so great that in a sense it hardly needed urging on from this descendant of the Lion of

413

Judah, the Solomon that was wise and the Sheba that was beautiful, but an urging which nonetheless was profoundly evocative, since it came from the only authentic royal voice of Africa, so that Nonnie and François could truly say together in voices low with emotion, 'Majesty, there is no need to forgive and we can only thank you.'

And there we must leave them for the moment, leave them looking out of the great palace windows into the blue of Africa, blue as if the blue swell of the Atlantic itself were breaking over the blue of the mountain beyond, because at that moment the light of which Mopani had spoken, the meaning of all that had happened, came to them like the story of a wind from a far-off place, and at last they felt it.

FOR THE BEST IN PAPERBACKS, LOOK FOR THE 🐧

In every corner of the world, on every subject under the sun, Penguin represents quality and variety – the very best in publishing today.

For complete information about books available from Penguin – including Pelicans, Puffins, Peregrines and Penguin Classics – and how to order them, write to us at the appropriate address below. Please note that for copyright reasons the selection of books varies from country to country.

In the United Kingdom: Please write to *Dept E.P., Penguin Books Ltd, Harmondsworth, Middlesex, UB7 0DA*

In the United States: Please write to *Dept BA, Penguin, 299 Murray Hill Parkway, East Rutherford, New Jersey 07073*

In Canada: Please write to *Penguin Books Canada Ltd, 2801 John Street, Markham, Ontario L3R 1B4*

In Australia: Please write to the *Marketing Department, Penguin Books Australia Ltd, P.O. Box 257, Ringwood, Victoria 3134*

In New Zealand: Please write to the *Marketing Department, Penguin Books (NZ) Ltd, Private Bag, Takapuna, Auckland 9*

In India: Please write to *Penguin Overseas Ltd, 706 Eros Apartments, 56 Nehru Place, New Delhi, 110019*

In Holland: Please write to *Penguin Books Nederland B.V., Postbus 195, NL–1380AD Weesp, Netherlands*

In Germany: Please write to *Penguin Books Ltd, Friedrichstrasse 10–12, D–6000 Frankfurt Main 1, Federal Republic of Germany*

In Spain: Please write to *Longman Penguin España, Calle San Nicolas 15, E–28013 Madrid, Spain*

In France: Please write to *Penguin Books Ltd, 39 Rue de Montmorency, F-75003, Paris, France*

In Japan: Please write to *Longman Penguin Japan Co Ltd, Yamaguchi Building, 2–12–9 Kanda Jimbocho, Chiyoda-Ku, Tokyo 101, Japan*